D0505918

# Valentine Grey

Also by Sandi Toksvig

FICTION

Whistling for the Elephants

Flying under Bridges

The Travels of Lady 'Bulldog' Burton
(with Sandy Nightingale)

Melted into Air

NON-FICTION

Gladys Reunited: A Personal American Journey

The Chain of Curiosity

# Valentine Grey

SANDI
TOKSVIG

virago

VIRAGO

First published in Great Britain in 2012 by Virago Press



A CIP catalogue record for this book is available from the British Library.

Hardback ISBN 978-1-84408-831-7
C-format ISBN 978-1-84408-832-4

Typeset in Sabon by M Rules
Printed and bound in Great Britain by
Clays Ltd, St Ives plc

Papers used by Virago are from well-managed forests and other responsible sources.

MIX
Paper from responsible sources
FSC® C104740

Virago Press
An imprint of
Little, Brown Book Group
100 Victoria Embankment
London EC4Y 0DY

An Hachette UK Company
www.hachette.co.uk

www.virago.co.uk

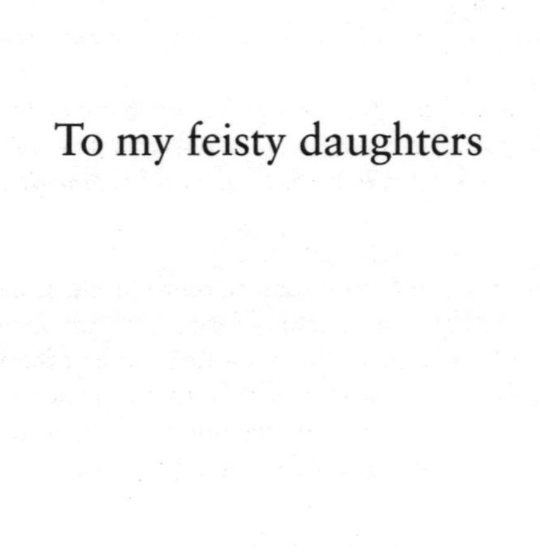

To my feisty daughters

# Valentine Grey

# One

Although Uncle Charles's home lay in the heart of London, once the jubilee was over and Queen Victoria had returned to her silence, so too did the house. The hush was unbearable. At times I could hear the sound of horses' hooves passing by, the newspaper seller calling out on the corner and occasionally a bell on a bicycle, but I missed the familiar barking of the wild dogs in the night. It even smelt quiet. And it was cold. The house was five storeys high, painted white with a thick, shiny black-panelled front door and a fanlight above that on bright days cast the shadowy reflection of the words *Inkerman House* on the tiled floor of the front hall.

Aunt Caroline, who loved a mourning garment better than any other, undertook to drown me further by sheathing me in black. My petticoats had a black ribbon sewn on the hem and even the handkerchiefs into which I was supposed to weep had black borders. It was as if we mourned the passing of all colour as well. Yet I did not cry in front of my aunt. I would not have her believe that Papa was dead.

Papa used to say that the world is full of untold stories. Wherever we went, whoever we met, he would seek out tales like a man searching through tea bush after tea bush for the sweetest, most tender of leaves.

I was born in Assam in the year the British ban on the Assamese using their own language in their schools and in the courtroom was lifted, thanks, in part, to Papa, who loved them and fought for them. Stories should be told in their native tongue, he said. 'Tales that need to be told find a moment when the time is right, Valentine,' he would declare, 'and how marvellous if we happen to be there.'

I used to think of these things as I sat in Aunt Caroline's drawing room, behind the sash windows, each with its twelve panes of fine plate glass. There were no stories here. I sometimes looked out for my cousin Reggie but mostly I sat, counting the panes over and over as I tried to quell a kind of hysteria that often rose in my throat. We needn't have been trapped, Aunt Caroline and I, for there was also a set of French windows that led out to a first-floor balcony with iron railings, but the windows were never opened. Someone had once made the mistake of telling my aunt that she had a delicate constitution and ever since she had lived in as enthusiastic a state of delicacy as good manners would permit. Instead of fresh air, the drawing room had pot plants and mirrors carefully positioned to reflect any outside greenery. It almost made me laugh. To me, who had grown up running through tall elephant grasses, it did not feel green at all. It felt like death.

Perhaps because Papa had so distressed my grandfather, Lord Grey, with his marriage, his brother Charles had been more circumspect in his choice of wife. He wed Caroline Birkbeck of the Birkbeck banking family in a match arranged by both families. It was a society event, a union approved by everyone. Then, when my grandfather died, Uncle Charles assumed the title. Perhaps that rather went to Aunt Caroline's head, for it was in her capacity as Lady Grey that she came into my life.

I can see Papa standing in the dappled light on the veranda, sipping tea from our own plantation and reading her letters. Not knowing that they would one day change my life, I enjoyed them. They spoke of an existence I could not imagine, a life that was nothing to do with us. In my aunt's world, people were 'at home' or 'dined out' and Reggie was always up to no good. I liked the stories. I would run to stand beside Papa as soon as a letter arrived.

'Tell me about Reggie!' I would beg. 'Has he been expelled again?'

Papa loved the Assamese, their food and their language, but he could never be anything other than an English gentleman. His name was Albert Grey. He was the most important person in the world to me and thus the handsomest of men.

He was tall and fit with a great wave of dark hair and a fine bushy moustache – but no picture could capture what made him good-looking. Anything in nature that bursts with life attracts the eye and I never once saw Papa without energy and enthusiasm; he was always desperate to escape the confines of the drawing room. It was no wonder that he left Inkerman House. How he would have railed against my imprisonment in that place.

Papa was still in his early twenties when he met my mother, Elizabeth Perreau. Everyone said that I inherited her features. She was tall and angular with auburn hair. Papa would often tell me how he fell in love with her across the footlights. Night after night he sat in the dark of the theatre, looking up at this shining creature. At last he went backstage and introduced himself.

'She fell for me in an instant,' he'd boast. 'Couldn't resist my charm. I used to be charming, you know, Valentine.' He'd smile at me and wink his eye. These were stories I couldn't get enough of and he played to his gallery: me.

They were soon engaged to be married. It was not, however, an arrangement that pleased everybody; my grandfather would not hear of it, nor indeed would he allow my mother into the house.

'"If the Greys do not have theatricals to dine then they most certainly do not marry them."' Papa would quote his father, pretending it hadn't cut him deeply.

But he was a stubborn man. Once he made up his mind to do something there was no persuading him otherwise – a trait, I suppose, he passed to me.

'Passion, Valentine! It is the beginning and end of everything. You must feel deeply or not bother with things at all.'

Papa had a small trust fund, not much by his family's standards but enough to give him the courage and the wherewithal to marry his Elizabeth in secret. Almost immediately they set sail for India to live on a tea plantation that he'd bought through a small advertisement on the front page of *The Times*.

Our plantation lay in the lush green valley where the Barak river flows down from the Manipur Hills. He built a *chang* bungalow, a single-storey wooden building raised up on stout wooden stilts, a design common to the area to keep wildlife at bay. There was a deep, shady veranda with a sloping roof that looked out across wide acres of tea bushes that spread over the valley like a comforting green blanket. Here my mother would sit sheltered from the burning sun while Papa, with a happy mix of laughter and bravado, accommodated himself to his new life.

'Look, Lizzie, I can get straight on the back of the elephant from up here!' and he would ride off, pleased with himself, trumpeting more than the vast creature he rode upon. Then on

14 February 1882 I arrived in the world. I was not, however, to grow up in my mother's care, for she died, as mothers of the British Raj so often did, a few hours after my arrival.

Papa never told me that story. That was left to Bahadur. Dear Bahadur, it's hard to know how to describe him. I suppose others might have called him Papa's manservant, but he was so much more than that. Bahadur, the dark-skinned man of Assam who taught Papa how to live in India and whom Papa trusted like a brother. He was there when I was born. He said Papa wept the tears of a *bordoichila*, the thunderstorms that came in the afternoons and washed down the dust.

Of course I only knew the joy of growing up at my dear papa's side, striding with him across the plantation as he called out to the workers. I can see the women sitting on their haunches to gather the first crop of leaves, the coolies spreading them out to dry on low tables in a sheltered courtyard. The men wore turbans and only a *suriya*, a length of cloth wrapped around the waist and the legs and knotted at the waist, and took orders from Papa as he stood, with a bamboo *jaapi* hat on his head edged in brilliant red.

I didn't go to school because there wasn't one for miles, and really because Papa did not want to let me go.

'I lost one great love, Valentine,' he would say. 'I haven't the heart to lose another.'

We fished the Barak and sat on the banks of the river drying our *koroti* catch, which we would eat with great dollops of sweet chutney. Oh, what I would give for a taste of that now. At night the men would make food so spicy it warmed the air. I tried every morsel and refused to be undone by the way it cut the back of my throat.

We would go jackal hunting with our motley pack of dogs, always led by Little Jock. Although he was a terrier and thus the smallest in the pack, he had no fear. Papa led the way on his stallion, whip in hand and baying for us all to follow on through the long grasses. What would Aunt Caroline have thought if she knew that Papa had taught me to bring down anything I aimed at with my rifle?

'That's it. Steady, Valentine. Mind over matter. You can do it.'

It was a wonderful life and I was entirely content.

We were as far from the concerns of London as it is possible to imagine. If London held any interest for me, it was only for news of Reggie. He was two years older than me and forever in some scrape or other. Sometimes Reggie wrote to me himself and then I almost longed to go to boarding school so that I too might have such fun. But Papa was my only teacher – until one of Aunt Caroline's letters arrived.

'She is most insistent, Valentine.' He read her words aloud: '*No one expects a child past the age of seven to remain in India. I'm sorry to have to be so indelicate as to mention it but, regrettably, Valentine is motherless and needs the guidance of a woman's hand if there is ever to be any hope of introducing her into society.*'

'But I don't want to be introduced to society,' I declared firmly.

'No, indeed,' agreed Papa. 'Most disagreeable.'

Nevertheless, the letters continued to come over the next few years until just after my fifteenth birthday, when I became ill with high fever and delirium. Bahadur said Papa was frantic and sat by my bed day and night. By the time I had recovered he had booked my passage to London.

'It's just for the summer,' he insisted. 'Just one summer. I want you to get strong again. Have an adventure.'

'I have adventures with you,' I wailed.

Perhaps Papa was afraid that I might be developing my

mother's intolerance for the climate. Bahadur said later that he must have had a premonition.

'It's just a few months. Bahadur will go with you. He will protect you and bring you safely back to my arms.' Papa held me tight, his jacket so familiar against my cheek, the smell of him so safe.

'Come with me, Papa, please!' I implored.

My nursemaid, my *bai*, had done her best to adapt a few of Mother's old dresses for me, but nothing truly fitted and in any case I had no idea how to wear a dress. She hugged me as she had done all my life and her skin was soft as she wrapped her arms around me. Bahadur dispensed with his usual loincloth and wore one of Papa's old suits but he still sported his turban and, disliking shoes intensely, often forgot to put them on. No one on the long passage to Southampton spoke to the dark-skinned barefoot man and the strange child. We arrived at Inkerman House on 3 May 1897 in a great London fog. From the moment I set foot in the place all I wanted to do was to escape.

I was due to stay for three months but just a few weeks later news came of a devastating earthquake that had hit my beloved Assam. When Uncle Charles received the telegram, he called me into his study and told me kindly and gently, while Bahadur held my hand. I did not understand and looked up at the tall man from Assam who had been beside me since I was a baby. Everything had changed.

I sat on the stairs waiting, waiting for a telegram from Papa to say he was alive. To say he was coming for me. Bahadur left ten days later to catch the first boat available. I tried to hold on to him and force him to not leave me behind.

'Little *konya*,' he said soothingly, 'I will see you again but for now you must stay here with your family.'

'But you are my family,' I sobbed. 'I don't want anyone else.'

I made a terrible scene, I'm sure, all the worse for my aunt because it was conducted both in the street and with a black man. London did not know that the world had stopped. Everywhere you could hear the noisy celebrations of Queen Victoria's Diamond Jubilee.

*So join with me, all of you, while I sing Britannia's praise,*
*The Empire on whose shores the sun has cast no setting rays . . .*

Bahadur's hansom cab pulled away and his hand was wrenched from mine as he called out, 'I will be back, *konya*, I promise.'

I sat alone in the dark hall, listening for the doorbell. People came and went. Harris, the butler, opened and closed the door to visitors, the footmen and maids delivered items to the rooms where they were required and still I sat. I did not belong in England, in this confining and foreign place. I should not be here. Nothing would have happened to Papa if I had been with him.

Eventually Uncle Charles came to sit by my side. He was an intensely formal man and I don't suppose he had ever sat on the stairs before. We sat in silence for some while before he awkwardly slipped his arm around me and said softly, 'My poor child, I cannot bear it but we must face this terrible news. We must be resolute and brave. I have had another telegram. I am afraid it is true. My brother . . . your dear father . . . is dead.'

He was being kind but I could not, would not, hear what he had said. His hand rested near my cheek and as he spoke I turned and bit his thumb with all my might.

# Two

Death rustled in every corner of Inkerman House. It was not even Papa's passing that had introduced the darkness. When I arrived, Aunt Caroline was already drenched in black. Although her father-in-law had died more than two years before, she had not yet given up mourning him. As soon as the news was delivered from his bedroom, she had ordered black silk bombazine dresses from Jay's of Regent Street. Jay's was a veritable mourning warehouse, where I was to learn that the staff knew such important things as the correct width of a grieving daughter-in-law's hatband. The loss of my papa, whom Aunt Caroline had never even met, meant that, with a sigh, she was able to continue her outward displays of grief.

The truth is I think she liked black. She was the thinnest, palest woman I had ever met, a woman who appeared too thin to allow anything as vulgar as blood to flow through her system. The colour red was not for her. Her dark dresses were trimmed with a hard, scratchy crape that had a strange crimped appearance and made a crackling sound as she walked.

Maisie shook her head over it all.

'It's bad luck, you know,' she whispered to me as Aunt Caroline rustled past.

'What is?' I answered boldly, although I knew by now that chats with Maisie were sternly forbidden.

'Mourning past time. It brings more death to the house, you mark my words.'

Maisie was the 'between maid'. I had never heard of such a thing. In general, it seemed to mean that she did the work no one else in the household was inclined to. She helped in the kitchen, served in the servants' hall and was assigned to me because everyone else was already busy. Maisie and I arrived at Inkerman House at about the same time and were the same age, yet Maisie, born and brought up in London, seemed worldly-wise to me. She knew how to get stains out of white satin slippers; how to stop chimneys from smoking and that the time was right for Aunt Caroline to pack away her grief. Meeting Maisie showed me how little I understood; how little I belonged.

'I'm Valentine,' I had declared, sticking out my hand. She had ignored my proffered greeting and furrowed her brow silently. 'What's the matter?' I'd gabbled. 'Don't you know your name?'

'Can't remember,' she had replied. 'I just got here and her ladyship said it so quickly.'

'Maisie,' announced an uninterested Aunt Caroline when I asked her.

'But she didn't seem to know,' I persisted. 'How could she not know her own name?'

Aunt Caroline dismissed my question with a wave of her hand. 'I believe she has just arrived.'

'What's that got to do with her name?'

Colour rose in Aunt Caroline's cheek. It looked out of place against her high-necked black collar. 'Valentine, the staff are not your concern. Kindly do not engage with them.'

'But I don't understand how anyone could not know their own name.'

Aunt Caroline frowned at me. 'The between maids at Inkerman House have always been called Maisie. It makes it easier for everyone to remember.'

I was a cuckoo in the house and for a while everyone despaired. It was clear that my odd ideas, overheated emotions and grief needed to be confined and checked. Part of Maisie's job was to help me get dressed each morning. Aunt Caroline was not available to assist for she was busy with her own maid, Bess, who pinched and pulled her into suitable shape to face the world. I certainly needed help, if not an instruction book, for here were clothes I had never encountered before – corsets and petticoats that nipped me in and weighed me down as if the still waters of the house were passing silently over my head. I railed against the pins that constrained my hair, like a young colt brought from wide pastures to suffer for the first time the bit and bridle. I had never worn the dresses of a young girl, just the loose trousers and tops of the coolies so I could sit astride a horse like a boy.

'There are a few simple rules,' Aunt Caroline explained as she and Maisie positioned a large mirror in my bedroom. She seemed astonished by my reflection. 'Heavens, you must be as tall as Reginald. Now, there are certain essentials which you must always bear in mind. Sham jewellery is always vulgar no matter what anyone says. You've a large head so we shall need a good-sized bonnet.' She began to measure me with a tape. 'A woman's neck should measure twice the circumference of her wrist and your waist,' she eyed the tape and sighed, 'remember, there is nothing more deplorable than a large and clumsy waist.'

She told me all this but she could not tell me why. Indeed the question 'why?' rarely arose about anything. Every detail about the running of Aunt Caroline's life followed a rule laid down by someone else, someone we didn't know, but nevertheless the rules had to be obeyed. Suddenly Aunt Caroline gave a great start and for a moment had to lean against the bedpost to catch her breath.

'What's the matter?' I asked, thinking she might be ill.

She pointed to my feet. 'Oh, my heavens, whatever shall we do with those?' she gasped.

I looked down. Years of running barefoot had left me with wide, strong feet.

'They're enormous,' whispered my aunt.

'Really?' I said, more fascinated than horrified.

I put my foot alongside Maisie's dainty one and saw that it was considerably longer.

My aunt took a deep breath and tried to pull herself together. 'Black,' she declared. 'You will only ever be able to wear black boots . . . with toecaps. We must do whatever we can to diminish them.'

By the time we had finished with my transformation and the seamstresses had been and gone, I stood once more in front of the mirror and did not know myself. The warm glow of my skin from the Indian sun was fading. Dressed totally in black, I looked pale and gawky as if I now came from a different race of people. Constrained by corsets and camisoles, petticoats and stays, and wearing tightly laced, uncomfortable boots with heels, it was clear that I could not even run away. I had turned into an alien being. Tears slid down my face. Maisie slipped her hand into mine. Aunt Caroline turned away to select a hat.

Bahadur had not been gone a week before my aunt began giving me daily lessons. It was clear that I needed instruction.

While other women spent their time dispensing pleasant philanthropy to the poor, Aunt Caroline now decided to devote herself solely to my improvement. Perhaps she thought it would distract me from thinking about Papa.

She would tap her fan on the back of the fire screen as we stood in the drawing room.

'Concentrate, concentrate. Now then, where were we?'

'Crossing the road,' I mumbled, still staring out at the seemingly uncrossable street. I thought I saw a woman on a bicycle and pressed my face against the glass for a better look.

'Don't steam the glass, child,' admonished my aunt. 'Did we conclude "conversation"?' she asked.

'Yes, yes.' I was not listening but instead willed myself outside.

'Quietly, Valentine, subdued tones, please,' insisted my aunt. 'We are not among your ... collies now.'

'Coolies,' I corrected her and then realised my mistake. 'Sorry, sorry ...' I was perpetually sorry. '... "When conversing with people who know less than you ... do not ... do not ... do not do something ..."'

My aunt finished the sentence for me. '"Do not lead the conversation where they cannot follow." Although that is unlikely to come up in your case,' she sniffed.

Aunt Caroline discussed everything that might possibly happen to a lady and what a lady might do when it did, but as we mostly sat at home it seemed entirely pointless.

I quickly learned that life at Inkerman House passed in much the same way each day. After breakfast Uncle Charles would retire to the library. During the day he dealt with 'business', which seemed to involve dark-suited men arriving and being shown to the library for much murmuring. At these times only Harris, the butler, was permitted to go in and out, bearing silver trays of refreshments from Cook's domain in the kitchen. After supper Uncle would move to the study, which housed his butterfly collection. Uncle Charles was an Aurelian, a keen butterfly collector, and he spent hours mounting the offerings of friends who returned from foreign climes with the delicate dead creatures carefully sealed in envelopes.

I think he liked the fact that the butterflies were dead, for he liked quiet. Quiet was the order of the day. Slops were emptied quietly, dusters shaken with care for fear of disturbance and stairs were swept in long, silent strokes. Throughout the day the stillness of the house was broken only by the doorbell when, three or four times at least, the post was delivered. Uncle Charles disapproved of letters being thrown through the letterbox and insisted on hand delivery. For a while the sound of the bell made me jump. I was convinced that a letter confirming Papa's survival and demanding my return would arrive any day, but no such message came.

Aunt Caroline was not unkind and I did not mean to disappoint her. I think we had literally come from opposite ends of the earth. She could have sent me away to school but instead she shouldered the task of educating me herself, beginning each lesson with as deep a sigh as her corset would allow.

'Oh, Valentine, there is so much to do. I cannot believe that your father, bless his soul, left you in this ignorant state.'

Everything about me was wrong. I was too tall to be considered delicate, my jaw too strong to ever play coy and my voice too deep to simper. When I did speak I had nothing suitable to say. I was doomed to be a hopeless member of polite society and would put my big feet in everything, including my mouth.

I did not sleep well. Most nights I had the same dream – that Bahadur was frantically pulling something from the rubble of our house. I thought it was Papa but when Bahadur turned to me, triumphant, it was an old doll he had pulled from the wreckage. Somehow she was crying. Her china face was smashed and blood ran from it. I would awake startled, often before the sun was up, and rush to the window to look out at the street to see if someone had come for me. The restlessness in me rose up as if my chest would burst with it. Whenever I awoke to find that I was not in my cool, wooden room in Papa's house but here in the still of London, I felt as though I were being punished for something I had not done.

Once I had calmed myself I liked those early hours. Dressed in my nightie and freed from my shoes, I would wander about like a silent ghost. One morning, as I padded miserably about the still slumbering house in my bare feet, I happened upon the nursery on the top floor. The door gave no indication of the excitement that lay beyond. Reggie was now too old for toys. They had not been touched for some time but still stood ready for play. These were not things I knew from childhood. There was the most wonderful clockwork train set all laid out on a great board with small trees and tunnels, a dapple-grey rocking horse with a leather saddle big enough for me to ride upon and a Noah's Ark with all the animals still waiting to board two by two. A strange object made up of a stand with two circular discs stood on a table. I spun the discs and together they produced a picture of a tiger leaping in a circus ring. It was the most magical room I had ever been in and I thought disloyally how much more fun Reggie's toys were than my poor playthings back home.

After that I would wake early each morning and go straight to the nursery, where I played with the alphabet blocks and did jigsaw puzzles. I found a marvellous penknife in a drawer and took to carrying it secretly with me at all times. One day I had stayed later than usual, sorting a large group of soldiers into ranks, when there was a sound at the door. I started up and knocked an entire regiment to the floor.

'I was just—' I began.

'It's all right, it's me, Maisie.'

Maisie grinned at me, somewhat aghast. 'They know you're in here? Not dressed and all?'

I shook my head.

'You better hop it,' she advised, bending down to pick up some of the fallen men. I reached down to help her and we began laying the ranks in formation once more.

'I reckon the blue ones look the fiercest.'

Maisie shook her head. 'Nah, got to be the reds.' Without further chat we took opposing sides, placing our men to advantage across a wooden table. After that we met most mornings in the nursery before the world was awake and we both had tasks to do. We put soldiers on the train and sent them off to fight, we cared for abandoned animals left ashore in error when the ark sailed and sometimes we rode off into the distance together on the back of the wooden horse. I had never had a friend of my own age. We might have carried on if we hadn't found the Diablo.

Maisie had seen one before and was quite the acrobat with the thing, holding the sticks in either hand, spinning the double-headed top and then tossing it high in the air before catching it again on the taut string. It made me laugh out loud with pleasure as the top occasionally flew high enough to hit the ceiling and bounce back down.

One morning, the nursery door opened and there stood Harris with a long and dark face.

'Maisie!' It was clear many rules had been broken.

Maisie put down the Diablo and scuttled out of the room. Slowly I followed her, padding past with my big feet. Harris looked down at me.

'Now, Miss Grey,' he intoned, 'we cannot have such loud laughter. Your aunt . . . ' He left the subject of what effect loud laughter might have on my aunt hanging in the air.

Harris shut the door behind us, locked it and put the key in his waistcoat pocket.

There was no more playing after that. Maisie, terrified that she might lose her position, stayed away from me. So now I kept to my room in the early hours, sitting on the window seat and looking out into the street. I still had Reggie's penknife and one morning was sitting gouging my name into the woodwork when a horse and cart stopped at the front door. It unloaded a large trunk and a young man dressed in a striped blazer topped with a straw boater.

I sat still and heard, 'Mama, I am home and I'm starving.'

It was Reggie.

I tugged on my clothes in the greatest hurry and rushed down to meet him. My newly arrived cousin was in the hall with his trunk open on the floor, pulling out all manner of things. I was so busy trying to see what he was like that I missed the final steps and fell in front of him.

Reggie laughed. 'If you are the new maid then Mama must remember not to let you carry crockery.'

I blushed, struggling to my feet. 'I'm Valentine. I'm your cousin.'

'Well, how splendid,' declared Reggie, as he helped me.

My silent, serious uncle and his parched wife had produced something unexpected. Where his father was sombre, Reggie was cheerful; where his mother was anxious, Reggie seemed to seize each moment with pleasure. Later I would try to imagine what might make Reggie serious, for he was hardly ever without a smile and a laugh. Papa would have loved him.

'Are you from the poor side of the family?' he asked.

'What makes you say that?' I demanded, anger instantly rising.

Reggie put his arm around me. 'You seem to have no shoes.'

I looked down at my bare feet. 'I forgot,' I said sheepishly. 'I don't really like shoes.'

Reggie squeezed my shoulder. We were roughly the same height and instantly I felt as though we fitted together. As if we were a match. He was slight for a boy and we both had the same sandy-coloured hair. He nodded and immediately sat down on the stairs, where he began taking off his boots and socks.

'Terribly confining, the old shoe,' he agreed. He wriggled his toes on the stair as I sat down beside him. We looked at our feet side by side. They were similar in size and shape, his perhaps a little narrow for a boy and mine a little wide for a girl.

'Funny things, feet,' he murmured. 'No one can do without them yet on the whole we pretend they're not there at all. The frayed edges of the body.'

'I have terrible feet. I shall need toecaps and everything to diminish them.'

'Reginald, Reginald.' My aunt entered the hall, her voluminous black dress like a galleon in full piratical sail. She came to an abrupt halt in front of us.

'Whatever are you doing?'

'Darling Mama, my beloved cousin and I were discussing feet.'

'Valentine . . . ' she began reprovingly.

Reggie leapt up. 'Valentine, nothing, Mama. It is entirely my doing. I have biology next term and I thought I might as well start at the bottom and work my way up. Before the thrill of further education is upon us, however, I have spent an entire and rather lengthy term learning the delights of the lathe.' He turned to me and in a theatrical aside whispered, 'Although how this piece of education will benefit anyone is a mystery.'

Reggie began rummaging once more in his trunk. 'After many hours and the odd regrettable encounter with splinters ... other than as a component part of a good fire, I fail, if I am frank, to see the attraction of wood ... I have created this!'

Triumphantly Reggie pulled out a delicate if somewhat uneven construction of tiny wooden shelves. 'It is for you, Mama, for your ... ' Reggie squinted and eyed his handiwork with a hint of doubt 'for your ... curios. It is a curio resting place.'

Aunt Caroline clapped her hands with delight.

'Oh Reggie, how thoughtful.'

Reggie led his mother off to find 'just the right spot' on her dressing table for her brilliant son's handicraft.

Now that Reggie was home, Aunt Caroline seemed more cheerful and even Uncle Charles did not spend all his time locked in the gloom of the study. I was allowed back into the nursery under Reggie's care, and we spent hours creating fantasy worlds where there was no rule that could not be broken. Reggie was everything I had ever imagined he might be. He became my brother, my other half. Occasionally we were allowed to walk to the park and I always took the deepest of breaths as we left the house.

'Do you like it here?' he asked one afternoon as we strolled under a great oak tree.

'I shan't stay,' I answered confidently. 'I shall go abroad soon.'

'I shall miss you,' he said.

'And I you, Reggie, but I don't belong. I wish it weren't so ... confining. Aunt Caroline has so many rules. Uncle Charles is nice but he's so ... dry.'

Reggie nodded. 'Yes, he is dry. Perhaps we ought to do something about that.'

It was a foolish idea but we were young and had, perhaps, a misguided notion of what might be entertaining. Maisie, who grew daring in Reggie's presence, fetched us a tin bucket from the scullery and we filled it with water. Reggie got a chair and between us we carefully balanced the heavy bucket on top of Uncle Charles's study door while he was out. It never occurred to us that anyone other than Uncle might choose to enter his study.

That night Aunt Caroline could be heard complaining in the fiercest of tones to Uncle Charles.

'I know she is your niece but, Charles, I cannot cope with her. I have tried, you know I have, but she is like a wild beast. Reggie had not been home two minutes when I found them practically naked in the hall. She could have killed me with that bucket and let's not forget that she also very nearly severed your thumb from your hand.'

I was listening outside the door when Reggie walked past me into the study. I could hear his voice, unusually quiet, as he spoke to his parents.

'It wasn't Valentine, Papa. It was me. I am so sorry. I had no thought of Mama entering the room. It was meant to be a joke. I am sorry. Valentine had nothing to do with it.'

I stood up and pushed the door open. Reggie was standing before his mother and father.

'Go away, Valentine, this is none of your business,' said Reggie sharply.

Reggie got a thrashing. I heard the sounds in my room where I lay on the bed weeping at his pain and my own cowardice. I had not cried since I had arrived but now I wept enough tears to wash Aunt Caroline's mourning clothes white. Maisie crept in and sat stroking my head. Then she lay down beside me on the bed and held me until I sobbed myself to sleep. No doubt there was some rule against it. I did not belong but Reggie, brave Reggie, was on my side and that helped.

# Three

It wasn't until Valentine arrived in his life that Reggie, for the first time in his teenage years, began to feel the simple pleasure of another's company. She was not some boy to whom he dared not get too close. This was his cousin, a female to boot, who was jolly and liked a dare. It was the Honourable Reginald Charles Albert Grey's destiny to become the eighth Lord Grey of Marchmont, with a fine house in London and a country estate in Northumbria. He was sent away to the same public boarding school that had confined his father and uncle, and he was expected to do well.

Like everyone else, Reggie spent the early boarding-school years as some older boy's fag, a menial servant to a more senior pupil. It involved the usual amount of minor bullying and thoughtless physical abuse, but no more than his forefathers had suffered in their time. Before, however, Reggie could rise up the ranks and bully someone else in turn, something happened and the only son of Lord Grey was asked to leave. No Grey had ever been expelled from this ancient school before their education was completed and everyone knew that it was hard on Reggie's father. How it was for Reggie was less clear.

A place was found for the banished boy at a minor public school where a new headmaster had recently been installed. The school was minor enough to be delighted to take in even the disgraced son of a man such as Lord Grey. The new headmaster had arrived on the tail winds of a scandal involving an affair between the head boy and a lad from the fifth form. Determined to prevent anything 'unnatural' occurring among his charges the new man instituted a regime that was less than successful. Indeed, if anything, it highlighted to anyone who had never thought of it before that affection between boys was a real possibility.

Trusted pupils were enlisted to spy on others, doors were removed from lavatories (turning them instantly into suggestive places), students of different age groups were forbidden to speak to each other and younger lads were not even allowed to smile in the presence of older boys. Supervised activities, in particular strenuous sports, were increased, based on the idea that a boy who had run his heart out on the playing field might be less inclined to play elsewhere. Even in the chapel, in the presence presumably of God, the seating arrangements were changed so that young and older boys did not face each other, and each night there were dormitory patrols which left many a sleepless lad feeling he might be under suspicion.

Reggie had not allowed his disgrace to dampen his enthusiasm for life. He joined the drama society and was a triumphant Rosalind in the all-male production of *As You Like It*. He spoke in the debating society and very nearly persuaded the school that women should be permitted to vote. He wrote poetry, did passable art and could parse sufficient Latin to follow the events of the Punic Wars. He did not triumph on the sports field, preferring to cheer on the first eleven rather than pad up himself, but he was, on the whole, deemed a success.

In the still of the night, however, Reggie suffered. As the dormitory patrols came round and shone lanterns in his face, he only pretended to sleep. Reggie felt guilty although he had committed no offence. He was awash with a sense of humiliation although nothing humiliating had occurred. Reggie felt certain that all the rules about contact between the boys were aimed at him. Just at him. He saw no one else who might break them. He was so full of self-loathing that he remained unaware of the many trysts between pupils of all ages going on around him. At this new school he kept to himself the shame of being expelled, which never left him. The irony was that he had not even liked the boy he'd been caught kissing. The carefree fellow of the daylight hours masked the boy racked with distress at night. He ran his hand over his body and wished his feelings away.

Reggie had felt utterly alone – until now. In the holidays he and Valentine became inseparable. They went on picnics together and occasionally persuaded Lord Grey to part with a little money for a rather grander outing. They both loved the zoological gardens, which were an easy walk away in Regent's Park. Reggie adored the monkeys, especially Mickie the Chimpanzee, who most days was dressed in human clothes as 'Captain Kettle'. And they were both mad about the bear.

The first time they had seen the bear was on a Tuesday morning. A few visitors were standing around the low railings gazing down into the pit where the brown bear lay, looking morose. A stout pole stood in the centre of the pit like an ursine maypole but the bear was not in the mood to climb.

'Is he sick?' asked Reggie of an attendant passing with a barrowload of hay.

The man looked down at the bear and shook his head. 'Nah, don't think so. Is it Tuesday?'

Reggie nodded.

'Yes. Takes Tuesdays off, the bear does. Monday, you see, is cheap tickets for the zoo so we gets a crowd. Everybody comes here with bits and bobs of food to make the bear climb up the pole. By Tuesday he's had enough.'

Reggie stood looking down at the bear who took the day off and Valentine could see he was quite saddened.

'Let's only ever come on Tuesdays,' said Valentine. 'Let's never make him do anything he doesn't want to do.'

There was a seat near the south entrance where they ate their sandwiches.

'Would you ever kill yourself, Valentine?' Reggie asked one day out of the blue, while munching on an apple.

'No,' she replied, 'most definitely not.'

'Why not?' asked Reggie.

'Because Aunt Caroline would be furious.'

Reggie roared with laughter. Nothing made Valentine happier than to see Reggie laugh.

The Carnivore Terrace, where the great cats, bears and hyenas were installed, featured a Bengal tiger and Valentine showed Reggie all the creatures she knew from Assam – the deer, the wild boar and the Indian rhinoceros, famous for his bad temper, who lived in a gabled house like some rough lord of the manor.

Then for a laugh they would run to the elephant enclosure where Jingo, an African elephant, liked to tease the hippo called Guy Fawkes who lived in the next pen. Jingo would reach through the railings and strike the hippo with his trunk. Enraged, the giant creature would rush at the bars, mouth wide with fury, only to have Jingo turn round and with his hind foot sweep a great pile of gravel into poor Guy Fawkes' open mouth.

Valentine made Reggie feel better. She made him feel that perhaps he might manage after all. He even toyed secretly with the idea that he and his cousin might marry when he left school so that he could please his father. He tried to imagine life with Valentine as his wife, but he could not see them sitting quietly together in some drawing room. The very thought of a restless Valentine pinned to a domestic chair was absurd.

In the final holidays before Reggie was to leave school he was spending his last days in London, gathering material for a history project. He had chosen the Acropolis of Athens as his subject and made his way to the British Museum to do some sketches to bolster his essay, having some sense that his drawings might be better than his lightweight words. Reggie had wanted to take Valentine out for tea that day but his father had insisted on the completion of his school project. He had walked to the museum with dragging feet and was bored before he got there. He wandered in under the grand front colonnade and headed towards the Elgin Room, stopping to read with idle amusement a plaque about Thomas Bruce, 7th Earl of Elgin, once 'Ambassador Extraordinary and Minister Plenipotentiary of His Britannic Majesty to the Sublime Porte of Selim III, Sultan of Turkey'. He strolled on to view the Minister Plenipotentiary's salvage from Greece.

The long narrow Elgin Room contained 247 feet of the frieze that once dominated the Parthenon. Reggie had never bothered to look at it before. He ambled over, trying to muster some interest, pulling out his sketchbook and pencil. On the frieze two men rode galloping horses. The man in front was beautiful, quite naked, his body turned to speak to his friend who galloped behind. What did they say to each other? What could they hear above the thundering hooves? Elsewhere more nude men sat so casually among lightly clad gods, all of them seemingly unmoved by the loss of limbs or even heads. Reggie began to walk along the frieze, mesmerised by the white marble lives played out before him. At the end of the long corridor there was a smaller space called the Phigaleian Room. Here a panel depicted a battle between a naked man and one whose lower half was that of a horse. The man had grabbed the centaur by the ear and pulled his knee up between the creature's front hooves. Meanwhile the bearded centaur had the clean-cut fellow by the throat.

'The Lapiths and the Centaurs,' said a voice behind him.

'Sorry?' Startled, Reggie turned to see a young man, immaculately dressed and carrying a smart walking stick topped with a silver bird's head, standing behind him.

'The man on the right is a Lapith,' said the newcomer, not looking at Reggie but pointing to the figure with the tip of his cane. 'Hard, of course, to know from legends whether they even existed,' the fellow continued. 'The Greeks believed in them. Thought they lived in Thessaly and on Mount Pelion. Anyway, curious thing, although they look nothing alike, the Lapiths were said to be related to the Centaurs as both were descended from the twin sons of Apollo.'

He turned to Reggie, who found himself silenced, not least by the young man's intense blue eyes and the chiselled look of his face. He was so perfectly carved as a person that he appeared to be made of marble; to have stepped straight from the ancient frieze and into Reggie's life. His voice was low but had a resonance that made every word carry like a whisper in Reggie's ear.

'According to the myths,' continued the stranger, 'one of the Centaurs' ancestors made the, I think, rather obvious mistake of mating with mares and producing half-men, half-horse descendants. They don't look it but those two who are fighting were probably cousins.'

The gentleman stopped speaking and tipped his hat to a woman who had overheard his little speech and was now retreating speedily from the room.

Reggie thought perhaps he would move on but the man turned back, pinning him with those eyes, and asked, 'What do you think of them being here?'

'Being here?' repeated Reggie, looking at his feet and feeling a little foolish.

'The marbles. Do you not think they should be in Greece where they belong?'

'I suppose,' he answered slowly, turning his head to find that the stranger was staring intently at a battle between a Greek and a feisty Amazon. Reggie noted that the woman seemed to have the upper hand.

Reggie thought he had never seen anyone more beautiful than this man. He was older than Reggie, perhaps in his mid-twenties, with the most luxuriant hair worn almost to his collar. The man's voice had the effect of wrapping Reggie in silk; it was the most mellifluous thing Reggie had ever heard.

Quietly, with a gentle smile, the man suddenly recited:

*'Dull is the eye that will not weep to see*
*Thy walls defaced, thy mouldering shrines removed*
*By British hands, which it had best behoved*
*To guard those relics ne'er to be restored.*
*Curst be the hour when from their isle they roved,*
*And once again thy hapless bosom gored,*
*And snatch'd thy shrinking gods to northern climes abhorred!'*

'Do you like that?'

'I don't know,' said Reggie, not knowing himself which he was referring to – the art, the poet or the poetry.

'Ah,' replied the man and paused, looking at Reggie with a slight smile. 'Let us start with something simpler then. Do you know if you have had your luncheon yet?'

Reggie had not and so he followed as the stranger led the way.

# Four

I turned sixteen still wearing black and still not quite the woman Aunt Caroline wished me to become. Despite being well past the age when it was permissible, I would often sit on the stairs. I don't know why. Perhaps I waited for some indefinable news. If anyone had asked, I suppose I would have said I was waiting for Reggie to return from an adventure but in truth I think I looked for my own chance to escape out of the front door. I sat there. The hall clock ticked and time passed.

Sometimes Uncle Charles would open the door to the library, see me sitting there and beckon me in. The heavy velvet curtains would be closed but the room was bright, for every gas burner in the place was alight. Cabinets lined the room, each containing narrow mahogany drawers. Uncle sat hunched at a large table, holding a pair of tweezers over an open glass jar, looking as excited as a small boy.

'Look at this,' he cried. 'Look at this. Magnificent. *Papilio nireus lyaeus*, the Green-banded Swallowtail.' Uncle Charles bent so low that his glasses practically touched the table. Then he gently unfolded the wing of a large butterfly. I had seen similar butterflies in Assam. I could almost see one now, resting on the wooden railing of our steps.

'Look, Valentine,' Papa would call gently, 'how beautiful.'

The delicate creature was more than three inches wide from wing to wing and brilliantly coloured – black with bright blue markings in a V shape and a lighter, dappled greeny-blue on the wingtips, as if someone had dripped a paintbrush across it.

'How your mother would have loved this fellow,' whispered Papa and pulled me into his embrace ...

Uncle Charles coughed and brought me back to his library. I looked again at the dead butterfly.

'Is it a boy or a girl?' I asked.

Uncle Charles chuckled. 'Definitely a boy. The females are much duller in colour.'

I wasn't at all surprised. Everything about being a female seemed duller than anything a man might be allowed to do.

Uncle Charles stood up and pulled out one of the narrow drawers behind him. It revealed rows of butterflies neatly mounted behind glass, their wings spread as if, were it not for the pin that held them in place, they would fly away.

'There,' Uncle Charles said, pointing at one of them. It was similar in size to the one on his desk but with much less vibrant markings. 'That's a female. Beautiful, aren't they?'

I looked at the creatures, their wings spread as if caught in mid-flight, and did not think so. Uncle Charles closed the drawer and went back to his table.

'How wonderful to fly,' I said.

He looked at me, perplexed. 'What do you mean?'

'I should like to fly,' I explained. 'I think it must be marvellous to soar in the sky and go wherever you want without anyone being able to tell you not to.'

'Indeed.' He nodded, smiling slightly, humouring me. 'Yes. I've never thought of it. Flying. What a thing.' Then he looked at me intently as if he was really thinking of it for the first time. 'You're right, Valentine, I suppose it would be wonderful.'

'What is the biggest butterfly in the world?' I asked.

Uncle smiled. 'They say there is an island in the Pacific that has a butterfly a foot wide. Imagine that.'

We sat for a moment and thought of such a thing.

'Why don't you go and find it?' I asked.

Uncle Charles looked startled. 'What?' he replied.

'Go and find it,' I repeated.

'Well, I . . . I couldn't. I couldn't . . . It's miles away.'

'So is Assam. Papa went there.'

Uncle Charles looked at me over the top of his glasses. I blushed.

'He was a good fellow, your father.' Uncle cleared his throat and looked back at the butterfly in the jar. 'Do you . . . like . . . mind . . . life here, Valentine? You've been with us some time now.'

I did mind it. I minded it terribly but I didn't want to hurt him. I was fond of Uncle Charles. He meant well.

'I should like to go out more,' I replied quietly. 'See things. Maybe, maybe . . . have a bicycle.'

'Heavens.' Again he looked at me, somewhat bemused. 'What thoughts you have in that pretty head of yours. Remarkable.'

I thought about outings a lot. One afternoon I was in the drawing room with Aunt Caroline and, as usual, I glanced out of the window. A soldier was striding across Upper Grosvenor Street towards Hyde Park. He was whistling and carrying a rucksack. I watched him walk away and as he did so he passed Reggie heading for the house. Dear, wonderful Reggie. Beside the khaki of the soldier he looked quite the dandy – his suit and frock coat were deepest blue and his waistcoat brilliant red, like the edge of my papa's hat. His top hat, worn to give himself height, was brushed to a silken sheen and his spats gleamed white against an ever-polished black shoe. He was not quite the man he might wish to be, for no moustache yet occupied his top lip.

With schooling now behind him, Reggie seemed liberated and determined to live every day to the full. Uncle Charles and Aunt Caroline had spent many hours trying to find Reggie a suitable profession but so far nothing had, in Reggie's words, 'stuck'. He had lasted but a day and a half 'in the City', declaring it 'dull beyond description'; he had dismissed the law as being 'awash with criminals' and laughed for an entire afternoon at the thought of the Church. Uncle had many friends in high places who offered entrées into all manner of occupations but Reggie was disinclined to settle. I watched him give the Tommy a mock salute with his cane, pick up the tune the lad was whistling and bounce up the flight of steps to the front door. At that moment, he had a look of my papa, with the same energy to enjoy the smallest pleasure. He couldn't help but make you smile.

Reggie disappeared from view and Aunt Caroline sighed with the weight of her responsibility.

'Now then, let us imagine that we are about to venture across Piccadilly Circus,' she said. A small shiver seemed to pass through her body as if it were impossible to conceive of anything more hideous. 'Gather the folds of your dress in your right hand and draw them to your right. Then raise your dress just above the ankle.'

Longing to be shot of the wretched garment, I grabbed it in both hands and began to lift the heavy fabric. Aunt Caroline let out a small scream and fell back into a well-placed chair. 'Valentine, Valentine, why must you be so vulgar?'

'Sorry. I was imagining it was muddy.'

Aunt Caroline did not have time to address the mud of Piccadilly before Reggie entered and took, as he always did, instant command of the room.

'Mama! Valentine! I have been to the most marvellous play! A melodrama – how perfect for a miserable afternoon! Well, that and oyster toast at the Blue Posts, which was divine. What a snug place. The wines are good and the gin-punch perfection.'

I could hardly bear that Reggie had done so many things. 'What was the play called?' I demanded.

'Valentine!' admonished Aunt Caroline but, for all her stiffness, she loved Reggie and Reggie was unstoppable.

Reggie leaned down and kissed his mother. 'Now, where have you two got to in the great stampede to education? No, don't tell me ... "Correct use of a fan at a dance"? No. "Gifts when courting"?'

Aunt Caroline began to speak but Reggie put up his hand. 'No, please, allow me, I just know I can be useful. Pay attention, Coz, for this is critical. A gentleman may bring flowers, chocolates or possibly a book ...' Reggie turned to my ear and whispered in a low voice, 'provided, of course, that it is terribly improving – I believe the sermons of the Archbishop of Canterbury are quite acceptable if a little low on humour.' He smiled and wagged his finger at me. 'A woman may not offer a gentleman a gift at all, no, not at all, until, of course – and this is bound to happen – he has extended a gift to her, after which she may present something artistic, handmade and inexpensive.' He turned and made a face at me. 'Handmade and inexpensive? Can you imagine anything more ghastly?'

Aunt Caroline shook her head. 'Oh Reginald, she's not ready for courting.'

'Ah.' Reggie eyed me carefully. 'No.' He clapped his hands. 'I know! Have you done "conversation on board ship"?'

I shook my head, giggling.

'Always a favourite, isn't it, Mama?'

Aunt Caroline was not smiling. 'You may joke, Reginald, but it is a serious business. Just think what happened to Miss Lockwood and Miss Preedy when they travelled to France unaccompanied!'

'It was shocking,' agreed Reggie solemnly. 'Miss Lockwood lost her purse and Miss Preedy her reputation – and neither was ever found again. So pay attention to shipboard etiquette.'

Aunt Caroline attempted to interrupt but Reggie ploughed on. 'If a lady and a gentleman have not been formally introduced, they should never engage in conversation, except, oh joy, on board ship, where the world, for reasons I cannot fathom, descends into a social abyss. There a "good morning" or "good evening" and a slight but graceful bow will suffice . . . ' Reggie grabbed my hand and inclined his head a little, 'or perhaps, "Miss Grey, I saw your name on the passenger list and I venture to introduce myself on the strength of my long acquaintance with, and great affection for, your dear cousin Reginald Grey. Does he remain as handsome as I recall? Of course he does. Who could doubt such a thing?" After such an introduction you may twitter away on deck, in the corridors and at table on such scintillating topics as the weather, the ship's run and whether the comforts of the vessel are quite what anyone expected. They never are.'

Reggie let go of my hand and for a brief moment sat down, throwing one leg over the arm of the chair as he did so.

'What was the play?' I persisted.

In an instant he was back on his feet.

'*Cheer, Boys, Cheer.* It was sensational.' He lowered his voice. 'It is set in deepest, darkest South Africa.'

I couldn't get enough. 'Who were the heroes?'

'Valentine!' Aunt Caroline sounded the bell of propriety.

'It was perfectly fine, Mama,' Reggie assured his mother, 'all titled ladies and gentlemen. No one lower than a sergeant. Anyway, some beastly Boer is leading Lady Hilyard, the heroine, and her party across the veldt when they stumble upon a Matabele uprising. Of course, the cowardly Boer slinks off, as you would expect from a Dutchman, at which point Lady Hilyard declares, "We are Englishwomen, sir, and do not fear any danger," and she boldly undertakes a night ride to warn the cavalry of the impending threat.'

Reggie moved to the centre of the room as if he were on the stage at Drury Lane. He held his hand up for effect and even Aunt Caroline ceased shaking her head as he continued.

'Our heroine rides off to fetch the cavalry, leaving behind a small group of soldiers including the hero, who has been battling with another fellow, played by the exceptionally talented Frank Rutherford, for Lady Hilyard's affection. For those awaiting rescue, it is not long before ... the Matabele attack once more and there is the moment of—' Reggie blew an imaginary trumpet, 'the Last Stand! This brave band is attacked ... Guns fire ... Many are wounded.' Reggie fell to the floor then rose again in mock pain. 'Those remaining try to fire again but ... oh no!'

'What?' cried Aunt Caroline, quite forgetting herself.

'The ammunition has run out. The end is near. Everyone,

including, rather splendidly, the wounded, stands and sings "God Save the Queen". Here, as you might hope, the Matabele respectfully cease firing during the singing.'

'But what about Lady Hilyard? Does the cavalry not come?' I asked, breathlessly.

Reggie nodded his head slowly. 'Oh yes, of course the cavalry arrive, led by the redoubtable woman, but sadly they discover that the only two survivors of this dreadful ordeal are the rivals for Lady Hilyard herself.'

'Who does she choose?' I almost squeaked the question.

Reggie looked appalled at the enquiry. 'Why, the hero, of course.'

'And his rival?'

'Naturally, because he is a gentleman, the rival, Mr Rutherford, who I thought was better looking, gallantly dies.' Reggie gave a great swoon and fell down dead on the drawing-room carpet. His frock coat fell open and his brilliant red waistcoat was displayed in all its glory just as the door opened and Uncle Charles appeared.

'I believe the dinner gong has already rung,' Uncle announced, seeming not to have noticed his son's demise. 'Lady Grey?' Stepping over Reggie, he put his arm out for his wife and they departed as if nothing untoward had occurred.

Reggie got to his feet and in turn offered his arm to me. 'Miss Grey?' As we headed to the door he confided, 'Fear not, dear cousin, I have a life-preserver about my person,' and showed me a half-pint bottle of brandy in his inside pocket.

Reggie was an original and I was to become his pale imitation.

Perhaps Uncle had noticed more than I thought, for after that the subject of my having 'outings' began to come up at the dinner table.

'I ran into Randolph Churchill the other day,' Uncle announced one evening. Aunt Caroline brightened. Any mention of the Churchills always made her cheerful, despite the fact that Lady Churchill was an American.

'He mentioned the Primrose League,' Uncle Charles continued, 'and wondered if you and Valentine might attend. His wife apparently, uhm . . . '

Aunt Caroline carefully wiped her mouth before speaking.

'The Primrose League, dear? Isn't that a bit . . . ' she lowered her voice to a hush as she glanced at the two footmen who stood impassively by the sideboard, 'political?'

'Nonsense,' replied Uncle, 'perfectly nice people. They take anyone, well, apart from atheists and enemies of the Empire, which is entirely understandable as they amount to much the same thing.'

It wasn't quite what I had hoped for but at least it was an outing beyond the confines of the drawing room, and so it was that my aunt and I joined the local branch of the league at St George's, Hanover Square. All the women present had paid their subscription in order to gain a small metal badge along with the chance to devote themselves to 'the imperial ascendancy of the British Empire'. Here we heard talks from members of the Ladies' Grand Council and were each given a small booklet entitled *The Primrose League – How Ladies Can Help It*, in which Lady Randolph Churchill explained how women might assist the Conservative cause at the next election.

'Wouldn't it be better if we could just vote?' I asked my aunt as we folded leaflets for the local man.

'Oh dear, Valentine, you are so young. The fact that women have no vote is positively beneficial,' she said firmly.

'How?'

'Lady Churchill says it helps to prove their disinterestedness when canvassing.'

We League Ladies tutted about atheists and took tea and vowed to maintain:

*The Constitution under which England has grown to be what she is – The Greatest Country in the World*
*The Unity of the British Empire*
*A Navy and Army able to protect the vast Commercial Interests of the British Empire.*

We admired the great map of the world and for the first time since I had set sail I saw my beloved Assam.

'It's so far,' I whispered, reaching out to touch my homeland, bright pink on the map.

Aunt Caroline nodded. 'That may be, yet it is the same colour as England, Valentine, and that is what we are here to protect.'

I hadn't thought of my childhood home as part of the Empire before. Papa never mentioned it and it was odd to hear a place so dear to my heart talked of as belonging to these women who had never been there.

On the way home Aunt Caroline got as close as she ever would to 'having a view'.

'Without the Empire there would be no Assam,' she explained, adjusting her league badge on her coat. 'Your father would be proud that you are taking such an interest. Without this work, all that your father achieved might have been for nothing.'

What Papa had achieved still seemed uncertain. We had received several letters from Bahadur about his estate but matters in Assam were proving difficult to settle. It seemed likely that I would have some money of my own but no one knew how much or when. While I waited back at Inkerman House, our Primrose League badges were put away in the jewellery box and the Empire managed without us just the same.

Once I had started going out to meetings, Reggie slowly gained permission to escort me to other things beyond the zoo and the parks. He began his campaign by cajoling my aunt into letting me accompany him to 'something improving'. Then, on the way to some promised lecture on Renaissance art or the like, Reggie would declare he had a 'capital idea', and would bang on the roof of the cab to demand a change of direction.

We went to Harrods department store, on one occasion, to see their new moving staircase. There were shrieks from some of the women on it and indeed from Reggie, but I loved it. Staff at the top handed out brandies to anyone adversely affected. Reggie went up and down several times, claiming he felt faint at the summit and required a reviving drink. For Reggie, participation in the world was merely a sport. He didn't want to change things or to be in charge; he just wanted to enjoy himself.

On a particularly hot summer's day Reggie took me on a steamer down the Thames for a little 'cool air'. As soon as we boarded the boat I forgot all the rules and took off my hat. Oh, the surge of excitement as I felt the air on my bare head.

Reggie smiled at me.

'It's not for you, is it, my lovely cousin?' He looked out across the river.

'What isn't?' I asked, distracted by the sun on the water and a young man with a particularly fine moustache who was rowing past.

'This life. You're like one of Father's wretched butterflies pinned to a tray. You need … I know … you need to go to Rosherville Gardens! We shall go immediately.'

'I do? We shall? What are they like?' I asked, breathless at the thought of anything new, anything out of the ordinary.

'My dear,' Reggie declared, 'the gardens are *the* place to spend a happy day.'

The diversion must have been planned, for we had no sooner spied the small, crenellated tower that marked the gardens than Reggie was waving to someone waiting on the dock.

Frank Rutherford was probably the most beautiful person I had ever met. He was a little older than Reggie and considerably taller. Beside him Reggie seemed quite the boy. Frank was clean-shaven, with dark hair that curled almost over his collar, and his eyes were the most astonishing blue. There was something so perfect about him. 'Where did you meet such a man?' I whispered to my cousin.

'In the Phigaleian Room at the British Museum,' smiled Reggie, 'standing before the battle between the Lapiths and the Centaurs. Indeed, I had some trouble at first distinguishing him from the rest of the statues.'

'Mr Rutherford, what a pleasant surprise!' he called out. 'May I present my cousin, Miss Valentine Grey?' He handed me down on to the dock.

As Frank took my hand I suddenly remembered.

'*Cheer, Boys, Cheer*!' I declared.

'Capital idea,' replied Reggie and both men let out a whoop.

I laughed. 'No, the play, Reggie. You said you saw a Mr Rutherford in a play called *Cheer, Boys, Cheer.* Are you that actor, Mr Rutherford?'

Frank bowed low. 'Guilty as charged.' He looked at me. 'Are you appalled?'

I shook my head. 'Not at all. My mother was an actress.'

'In that case,' said Frank, linking one arm through mine and the other through Reggie's, 'we are practically family. I shall be Frank to you and you shall be my Valentine and no one we know shall be more surprised than me.' Frank began to move us into the gardens. 'Come along, you two, pleasure awaits. Welcome to Gravesend!'

Reggie shuddered. 'Such a ghastly name. Imagine being forced to reside in Gravesend. I'd rather die.'

Frank laughed. 'Dear Reggie, you are too sensitive. It is perfectly possible to live anywhere for we have joy in our hearts – and, well, we shall all end in the grave one day.'

Leading the way into the pleasure gardens, Frank suddenly let go and clapped his hands. 'Let's plan our deaths. You first, Valentine.'

I shook my head. 'I've never thought of such a thing.'

'Oh, but you must,' declared Frank. 'We owe it to our friends to at least go in an interesting manner. How dreadful to have nothing to discuss at a funeral. I long to die young and be mourned terribly by my friends. Do you not think to die with potential would be splendid?'

Frank did not wait for a reply but commanded Reggie to fetch us a picnic from one of the stalls near the entrance, which we ate on a small patch of land known as The Wilderness. We drank some ginger wine and before long Frank was lying on his back singing a silly song. He was such a performer. I had never been to a play, but I imagined what it would be like to see Frank on stage.

It was Frank who brought up death again that day.

'I'm very fond of Lieutenant Gale,' Frank said. 'I mean his death. He made the most marvellous double gondola, two canvas baskets suspended from a balloon that he used to fly above Rosherville for the amusement of the crowd. He would set off in his contraption and, when he was at a good height, he lowered the longer gondola about thirty feet and climbed down a rope ladder to set off fireworks from the smaller basket. Tragically . . . ' Frank's voice lowered, 'he was troubled with a fondness for fine wine. He died in France, carried away, utterly intoxicated, in the rigging of his balloon before falling to earth from a great height. His body lay undetected for several days.' Frank nodded with great satisfaction. 'Perfect. A dramatic death but with a hint of amusement for everyone left behind. I should like that.'

'How unkind,' declared Reggie, 'you will leave the rest of us to mourn.'

Frank shook his head. 'My intention is that you should die laughing.'

Reggie lay down on his back and looked at the sky. 'I think your death sounds like jolly hard work, Frank. I intend to pass away in my bed and cause no trouble to anyone. Though I'd like a brilliant funeral.'

'And you, Valentine?' asked Frank. 'How will you meet your maker?'

'I don't know,' I replied, 'I try never to think of it.' I looked out across the gardens and back to my two friends. 'If there are places like this, times like this in the world, then I don't think I shall want to die at all.'

'Indeed,' agreed Reggie, 'and at the very least let us promise not to die without giving plenty of notice. I can't imagine anything more ill-mannered than dying without letting your friends know.'

After a few moments Frank sat up, leaning on one elbow, and looked at me.

'Do you know, Valentine, there used to be a place just here where women could rent male costumes, sailors and the like.' He looked me up and down and I blushed to be examined so openly. 'You're tall. I think you would have looked splendid. Pantaloons, a blue jacket and a rakish hat.'

He paused to look at me, but before I could say anything he was off on another jaunt. 'The tower! We must climb the tower.' Frank was up and off, disappearing to climb the stairs of the small watch tower. Reggie and I followed him up and arrived at the top to find him looking out across London. It took my breath away to see the river Thames rushing out beyond the gardens towards the open sea. Where might one go on such a mighty river?

'Look at us,' cried Frank. His voice carried out across the gardens as he bellowed, 'We are kings of the world and we shall rule all that we survey!'

To be a king and to be handsome. To not sit indoors and wait for life to come calling with a suitable gift. I longed to cry out and not be silent. I suddenly realised that Aunt Caroline's rules had reached in and taken hold. How had I allowed that to happen? I looked out over the gardens. They were probably well past their prime by then but I had never seen them before and I thought the lake was beautiful. I could not recall such beauty since I had ridden across the plantation on Papa's horse with his arm around my waist, holding me and keeping me safe. I had a sudden stab of homesickness. For the first time in two years I could smell the scent of blossom on the air as a breeze blew in from the river. The lowering sun burnished every colour with a golden tint and we breathed deeply. Then Frank was off again.

'Death to boredom!' yelled Frank to the gardens.

'Death to banality!' shouted Reggie.

Frank turned to me. 'Make a command,' he urged.

'Death to black!' I called to the air without thinking.

Frank and Reggie laughed. 'Death to black?'

'Black clothes,' I explained, looking down at my own garments. 'I hate them.'

'Death to black clothes!' we all bellowed in joyous unison.

At that moment a rather sombre couple appeared on the top step behind us. Frank turned upon them like a policeman.

'No black. There is to be no black up here. Have you not heard the decree? Colour, only colour.' He shooed them down the steps, all the while claiming he represented the garden authorities and that the poor couple had broken several regulations. Only his good nature, he said, was preventing him from issuing a fine.

Frank was giddy with power and delight.

'The maze!' he shouted once we had descended from the tower. 'You must see the maze.'

Frank and Reggie seemed to disappear the minute we entered the confusion of hedges. I found myself alone and quickly became disorientated. I looked up, hoping for some indication of where to go, but every turn seemed to lead to a dead end. There was supposed to be a small boy on a stepladder keeping an eye on everyone but I couldn't even see him. I became more and more anxious and started to half run along the narrow paths. Where were the boys? I called out their names but heard nothing back. Turning a corner I banged straight into a young man who was running towards me. Slightly taller than me, he put his arms around me to prevent my falling. I looked up at him – surely it was the young moustached man who had been rowing? – and in an instant he kissed me on the cheek. Then he stood back, grinned, looking terribly pleased with himself, and whispered, 'You are indeed lovely,' before running off again.

By the time I at last reached the gypsy tent at the centre of the maze I was all confusion. I ran out, wanting to tell Reggie what had happened, but he and Frank were leaning up against a wall, laughing quietly. I had the sense that I was interrupting something and paused before they saw me. Frank called my name.

There weren't many firework displays at the gardens any more, Frank said, but that night must have been a gala occasion. We stood together, me between my wonderful friends, while we watched the flares and rockets burst over the gardens, their colours reflecting in the waters of the Thames. Maybe life in London wasn't so bad after all? When we left, some fellows at the bar were laughing and ordering drinks. Just for a moment I saw myself, dressed as a sailor, drinking and laughing with them.

# Five

The chances of my ever being allowed to swagger like a sailor appeared slight. I was soon to come out of mourning and in the following February I would turn eighteen. Two months later I would, apparently, be ready for my formal introduction to society. By now my aunt had worked relentlessly on me for nearly three years. I could play the piano well enough and converse about literature appropriate to ladies. My dancing remained shockingly poor but I knew enough about the rules of etiquette to engage in both the art of conversation and that of silence. As the nineteenth century turned to the twentieth, I would officially be available on the marriage market. Nothing since the death of my papa had ever made me more depressed.

This, of course, meant that we needed new wardrobes. Aunt Caroline was preparing for the onerous duties of chaperone and threw herself into the task of clothing me appropriately. I confess I was still terribly hard work for her. On one of our many shopping expeditions, we were just crossing New Burlington Street for a final fitting at Mme Swaebe's when a woman in bloomers came past, bold as brass, riding a bicycle up the street. I thought she was glorious.

'Isn't she wonderful?' I exclaimed. 'Could we get some bloomers, could we?' I begged.

Aunt Caroline pulled me away. 'Valentine, how many times must we go over this? A gentlewoman never looks back after anyone in the street and certainly never stares. And she does not wear . . . ' She could not bring herself to say the word.

I wanted bloomers, I wanted a bicycle, I wanted excitement.

None of these things was mentioned at dinner. Indeed the four of us, Uncle Charles, Aunt Caroline, Reggie and I, struggled for conversation at the table. Often it was Reggie who took it upon himself to keep things from flagging.

'Johnny Longbottom was telling me a marvellous story today,' he would begin. 'Apparently there is a market town, I don't know precisely where, but a considerable market town in which there is a club of fat men. They don't come together as we might at White's to chat about this and that . . . but to celebrate their corpulence. Apparently the main room of the club has two entrances—'

Uncle Charles cleared his throat loudly.

'Reginald, I wish to talk to you about something important—'

Reggie attempted to carry on. 'The two entrances are of quite different sizes. One is a door of a moderate size, and the other, a pair of folding doors.'

'Reginald. I want to talk about South Africa. The mining boom in the Transvaal seems unabated and . . . ' Neither father nor son was listening to the other, but at last Reggie stopped.

'There is a considerable fortune to be made by an able young man and . . . ' Uncle Charles paused to look at his boy. 'Do you know nothing of South Africa, Reginald?'

Reggie shrugged and gazed at the ceiling. 'South Africa, let's see . . .'

I hadn't really been paying attention. I would often sit at the table and snatch glances at the footmen. Once they had served the meal they would stand quite still in uniform, waiting to be needed. They looked smart in their livery and I wondered if it was comfortable. How nice, I thought, to get up every day with no concern about what to wear, but how odd never to speak.

'Reginald!' Uncle Charles's sharp tone brought me back to the table. Reggie touched my foot with his and I felt a slight shiver of anxiety. There was much talk about South Africa throughout London and in the papers; talk of a mining boom and of a possible war. Reggie had no interest in politics but he did love spectacle and, as it happened, he and I did know something of South Africa because we had secretly been with Frank to see a show about it at Earl's Court. Reggie had first spotted it in the paper.

'Listen to this, Coz: *Savage South Africa, a vivid, realistic and picturesque representation of LIFE IN THE WILDS OF AFRICA!* I do love capital letters. It makes it so much more exciting. *A sight never previously presented in Europe, a horde of savages direct from their kraals* . . . We have to go. There is no question but we have to go. Can you imagine anything more thrilling than savages?'

*Savage South Africa* at the Empress Theatre in Earl's Court was the talk of the town. Frank knew someone in the show and got the three of us tickets. The climax of the entertainment was a re-enactment of the Shangani Patrol, when a major and some British soldiers in Rhodesia were separated from the main body of troops. They rather heroically sang something patriotic as they were cut down by the Matabele, whose war cry swept like a husky whispering wave across the hushed audience.

Reggie did not tell his father that I had been to the show. Instead, in answer to Uncle Charles's question, he teased me, saying archly, 'South Africa? I went to a marvellous exhibition at Earl's Court. They have a replica of a, what do they call it, Valentine?' He turned to me and smiled. 'Bless you, how would you know?' Reggie drummed his fingers on his temple as if trying to remember. 'Kaffir kraal, that's it. It's a sort of native hut and for sixpence you can crawl in and see how the blacks live. You should have seen it, Mama.'

Aunt Caroline raised an eyebrow in response.

'There were these two young women who were deeply interested in the savages and one of them said she wanted to kiss a savage to see what it was like.'

Uncle Charles, knowing his son was trying to shock, carried on stolidly drinking his soup.

'So,' said Reggie, enjoying his mother's discomfort, 'she picked out a swarthy native and told him that she wanted to be kissed. He, of course, had no idea what she was saying and started to dance. Well, she signed for him to stop and then stepped forward and kissed him on each cheek. He got the idea at last and caught the young lady round the waist and imprinted such a resounding smack on her lips that she was glad to make her escape. I can't tell you how everyone roared.'

As Reggie wiped away tears of laughter, his mother put down her spoon.

'I find it hard to credit, Reginald, that you would wish to attend such a dreadful thing. Charles, speak to your son.'

Uncle Charles removed his spectacles and distractedly cleaned them on his napkin. He was trying to work something out.

'I do not understand why some women take pleasure in touching these black persons. If the savages were a collection of astronomers or physiologists, if they were in any way noted for their brain power, they would create no interest at all among women of this kind. It is not a pleasant thing to say but this Earl's Court show does not appear to have demonstrated the delicacy of women.'

Reggie nodded. 'Perhaps the conquering race need saving from themselves,' he ventured, as Uncle Charles attempted to take the floor.

'I don't know why you must upset your mother with these things and certainly Valentine is far too young to hear of such matters.'

'Ah well, Father,' soothed Reggie, 'I am like tea and my true strength and goodness will not be properly drawn out until I have had a short time in hot water.'

Uncle Charles began to speak but instead he laughed.

'You are a hopeless fellow, my son,' he said, smiling affectionately at his boy. He shook his head and patted Reggie's hand.

I thought that would be the end of conversation about South Africa at Inkerman House, but it turned out to be just the beginning.

One evening in October we heard the paper boy beneath the gas light on the corner calling, 'War against the Boer!' and soon South Africa was the only topic at the dinner table.

'I was speaking to Sir Charles Newton today,' Uncle announced with unusual enthusiasm even before the first course had been served.

'The Lord Mayor?' enquired Aunt Caroline.

'Yes, of course the Lord Mayor.' Uncle Charles seemed irritated, as though he were suddenly under some pressure the rest of us could not understand. He paused to nod at his wife in apology and carried on. 'It seems Colonel Boxall has laid a plan to the Mayor to raise a volunteer regiment for South Africa. And Sir Charles has asked me to arrange a meeting with the masters of City companies, merchants and bankers at the Mansion House, so that the City may allocate the necessary monies.'

'You must be delighted, dear, to see the City of London taking such a lead in patriotic movements,' replied Aunt Caroline, determined to override even the slightest frisson of unpleasantness at the table.

'Indeed,' agreed Uncle Charles, 'it is a splendid opportunity to give citizen soldiers a chance to serve their Queen alongside the regular forces of the army and the troops from the Colonies.' He put down his fork and challenged his son. 'Don't you think so, Reginald?'

Reggie sighed and threw his hands in the air in a clear signal of surrender. 'I don't know, Father, you know I don't know. I take no interest in these things.'

'Well, you should. It's time you took an interest in something. I expect my son to be eager and ungrudging in his determination to help his country in her hour of difficulty.'

No laughing at Reggie's antics tonight, I was thinking as I kept my head down.

'Except she isn't in difficulty,' protested Reggie. 'It's some Dutchmen causing trouble thousands of miles away and they are nothing to do with us.'

'Nothing to do with us! Nothing to do with us!' exploded my usually mild-mannered uncle. 'What is the matter with you, boy? Do you feel nothing for the Empire?' Uncle Charles ignored the bowl now placed in front of him by a footman and instead banged the table as if he were on a podium. 'Do you feel nothing for your magnificent heritage won by the courage and energy of your ancestors? The British Empire is the greatest empire the world has ever seen and God himself has handed it to us in sacred trust. The advantages of British rule – the incalculable benefits of just law, tolerant trade and considerate government – extend to every race brought within its sphere. There has never been a better moment to be an Englishman and it is time you stood up and played your part.'

'Played my part? What on earth am I supposed to do?' asked Reggie, carefully adjusting the sleeve of his jacket into a more pleasing shape. 'Sing madrigals?' It was a fateful question and I think we all knew it.

Uncle Charles stood up and carefully laid his napkin on the table. Harris gave the tiniest of indications and the staff stepped back from serving the meal. No one moved. All you could hear was the clock ticking in the hall.

Uncle Charles cleared his throat and looked at me before continuing. 'As my dear brother used to say, "Life will always be to a large extent what we ourselves make it." Sadly, my dear Reginald, you seem disinclined to agree. As of today it is decided that the City of London will equip and transport to the seat of war in South Africa a regiment of volunteer marksmen one thousand strong, complete with weapons and transport, and this very morning, my boy, you volunteered.'

Reggie was white with shock. His father turned to depart.

'You leave in the New Year,' declared Uncle Charles before the door closed behind him. Aunt Caroline did the only ill-mannered thing I ever saw her do – she fainted into her soup.

# Six

Uncle Charles's involvement in the raising of the volunteer force for South Africa changed everything at Inkerman House. Gone was the tomblike quiet, for now messengers came night and day with queries that required instant responses. The doorbell rang so continuously that some of the servants practically took to sleeping in the hall. Aunt Caroline, with much encouragement from the ladies of the Primrose League, decided that England could not manage without her. As a consequence, she forsook my education to become an instant expert on soldiers' needs and a linchpin in the drive to defeat those who sought to diminish the Empire. She spoke to someone who knew someone who was doing something important and before long, to her immense satisfaction, she was drafted to help the Lady Mayoress herself organise and issue uniforms. The Guildhall, that ancient and dignified place, was soon to be turned into a warehouse issuing kit of all kinds. Desperate to do anything other than sit at home, I offered my help, but the very idea of having an unmarried woman dealing with men's trousers made my aunt feel unwell.

Just before Christmas came Black Week, with news of British defeats by the Boers in a number of major engagements. If there had been any hope of Reggie changing his father's mind, that hope was gone. For lack of any proper employment, I began to read the newspapers avidly. The key towns of Ladysmith, Mafeking and Kimberley were under siege. Maps were printed and faraway names became commonplace to everyone. It was generally agreed that 'any fool' could see that help was needed and needed urgently.

Reggie joined me in the drawing room as I was poring over a map. I must confess I was rather enjoying becoming an expert on the war. It was the most exciting thing that had happened since my arrival in England. I was just thinking of nipping up to the nursery to get out the tin soldiers so I could enact the battles whose maps were printed in every edition, when I looked up and saw him.

Reggie was distraught. He held his head in his hands, muttering, 'I can't go, Valentine, I just can't.' He slumped down into a chair.

On the surface there seemed to be nothing to prevent his departure. The volunteers were given the most cursory of medical examinations, which Reggie, who never exercised and deliberately gulped for air throughout the procedure, had passed without any trouble at all.

He had been appalled. 'There was a fellow next to me who was so hard of hearing he looked the wrong way the entire time the doctor was talking to him. He only realised he had to cough because the doctor gripped so tight, but it turns out, deaf as he may be, he's got nothing better to do so he's in. Dear God, I could be fighting alongside someone who can't even hear the enemy coming.'

My cousin was holding the commemorative shilling he had

been given to mark his enlistment. He had received the proverbial 'bob' on New Year's Day when the first batch of volunteers were sworn in at the Guildhall by the Lord Mayor, with five aldermen and sheriffs in attendance. Uncle Charles had been present, which I knew was almost more than could be said for his son. Reggie told me he had arrived in a fur coat, fresh from seeing in the new century, and had no recollection of his enlistment whatsoever. Maybe it was better that way.

Along with the coin, he had been given a stamped postcard addressed to *The Lord Mayor at Mansion House*. On it he was to provide his measurements for hats, boots and other necessities but the card still lay blank.

'You do seem to fit the bill, though, Reggie.' I came over and sat on the footstool to comfort him. I had read through the list of requirements that had been printed in *The Times*. It had seemed so easy to become a soldier and now I chanted: 'Between twenty and thirty, a bachelor ...'

'Of course I'm a bloody bachelor ...' Reggie was about to launch into a further tirade when his face lit up. 'Does it really say "bachelor"? Well then, you must marry me, Valentine. Today, if possible. If we were married I would have to be excused. How long does it take to get to Gretna Green?' He got up as if to order the carriage immediately.

'Don't be silly,' I replied. 'Sit down. We can't get married.'

'Why not? Her Majesty married her cousin. It happens all the time with royalty and the less well educated.'

I ignored him and continued with the soldierly requirements. 'It also said it would be useful if you can "ride *effectively*".'

I looked at my whimpering cousin and did not think effective riding was likely. The nearest I had seen him to a horse was sitting in the back of a hansom cab.

'Can you,' I asked, 'ride effectively?'

'Effectively?' Reggie snivelled. 'Are you mad? I don't like animals. I sneeze and start to itch and they seem to know. I've only to approach one of the blighters and they start to kick and bite. I don't even like them in paintings. There are whole galleries of Stubbs' paintings in the Royal Academy that I have to avoid.'

'Didn't they check that you can ride?' I asked.

'There was some test up at Albany Street Barracks near the park but it was hopeless. My school chums Sewell and Loveless came to watch me and they were crying with laughter. I wasn't alone. There were quite a few chaps who simply couldn't stick to their horses the moment the order to trot was given. I held on all right until they gave me a gun. "One or the bloody other," I said, "not both at the same time." What were they thinking? Anyway, no one is interested in whether I have a good seat. Father is putting up lots of money and that's all they see when they look at me.'

'I thought you had to belong to a volunteer regiment already in order to go?' I asked.

Reggie waved his hand at me. 'Well, I did belong to something or other, some rifle thing, but it was only so I could dine at the HAC.'

'The HAC?'

'Honourable Artillery Company, perfectly charming house with a splendid dining room and rather fine cricket facilities.'

'Do you play?' I asked, amazed.

Reggie managed a small grin. 'Don't be silly. Lovely people wearing white and running about. Nice tea, too. Anyway, I liked it for an outing.' Reggie brightened for a moment. 'Actually the dress uniform is rather fetching. I have a good leg, you know, everyone says so, but I never went and did any of their damnable drilling.'

I surveyed my handsome cousin sitting inconsolable on Aunt Caroline's favourite chair. He was brilliant company, a wonderful raconteur, a superb dresser – but it was fair to say he did not look like a man about to ride to the rescue of the Empire.

'It won't be for long,' I said soothingly.

'A year, Valentine, the enlistment is for a year. A year! In khaki!' He smiled gamely. 'It's not a good colour for anyone.'

'They say the war will be over in no time. Everyone is saying that it is the British Empire against thirty thousand farmers. The Boer can't possibly win. And you have no ... what do they call it?' I tried to remember. 'No pressing matter that stops you from going.'

'But I do, Valentine, I do.'

'What?'

But he wouldn't say.

I tried to speak to my uncle. Maisie told me not to knock on his study door before supper but I was determined to put Reggie's case.

'Yes?' came the terse reply.

I summoned my courage. 'I want to talk about Reggie, Uncle.'

'Do you know how to kill a butterfly, Valentine?'

I shook my head.

'Best way, once you've caught it of course, is to pinch its thorax – that's this bit here in the middle – between your thumb and forefinger. It takes a little practice to learn the proper pressure but it stuns them immediately and then they can't damage themselves, do you see? Then you slide them into an envelope and bring them home. Once you get them back here you need to help them relax. Dead insects can be jolly brittle and you want them to lie nicely for the display, so you pop them in a jar with a bit of sand, bit of carbolic acid and let them relax again. Then, you take the thing . . . '

Why were we talking about dead butterflies when Uncle Charles's son was so obviously in trouble?

Uncle picked up a dead swallowtail on the table with his tweezers and moved it towards a drawer that stood open. 'Put it in place and fix a pin right through the middle of the body between the wings.' He pushed the pin in hard and the dead creature hovered in place.

'Actually these are all from South Africa. Look at this.' Uncle Charles opened several drawers as he searched for something.

By now I was quite the expert on the war. I knew perfectly well that South Africa was made up of four colonies – two British ones called Cape Colony and Natal and two Dutch Boer ones called Transvaal and the Orange Free State. I did not need any further explanation, but when Uncle mentioned South Africa it dawned on me that I might make more headway with Reggie's case if I got him to talk about what was happening out there.

'So is it really the Dutch fighting against the British in South Africa?' I asked innocently.

Uncle Charles, his back to me as he fished around in a bottom drawer, snorted. 'The wretched Dutch happen to have found a lot of gold, really by chance, but of course they can't manage to mine it by themselves so lots of Englishmen rushed to help.' Uncle stood up and faced me. He was as cross as I had ever seen him. 'Now the Boers call these Englishmen *Uitlanders* or foreigners and, although they frankly cannot do the work without them, they refuse to give these fine fellows any say in anything.'

Exasperated, Uncle Charles continued. 'The Dutch take the *Uitlanders*' taxes but the President of the Transvaal, that dreadful

Mr Kruger ... *that man* ... will not give the English, the hard-working English, the vote in his absurd little state. We are fighting for nothing less than Englishmen's rights.'

'But can't Mr Kruger choose what laws he likes in his own country? What's it to do with us?'

Uncle Charles smiled at my innocence. 'My dear child, you need look no further than your own dear father in India to realise that the British are the best, the most humane, most honourable race the world possesses ... The best thing for Mr Kruger and, indeed, for everyone is for him to get out of the way of the British Empire.'

He looked as if he was going to pat me on the head, so I seized the advantage. 'Uncle, I wanted a word about Reggie. He is really very ... Even if they are farmers, there'll still be fighting and I don't think he ... '

'You are a kind girl, Valentine. I am aware that my son is a delicate soul but it won't do. It won't do at all. There is no pressing matter to prevent him leaving for South Africa at short notice and he is to go.'

So he did understand. How cruel he was then!

'But—'

Uncle Charles pointed to what looked like dead leaves. 'The *Junonia tugela* – the African Leaf Butterfly. One of the finest dead-leaf mimics in the world. See, it has the most splendidly coloured upper wing but when it is resting, when it closes its wings, it looks exactly like a dead leaf. Even something this delicate, Valentine, can keep itself safe from predators.'

'And if nothing kills it? How long does a butterfly live?' I asked, slightly bitterly.

'Only about a month, my dear, about a month. But what a month of beauty.'

'Uncle?'

I knew he was not really an unkind man, my uncle. Surely, if he really knew how Reggie felt . . . ?

'Yes?' he said.

'Aren't you worried about Reggie?' I blurted. 'It's a war. What if they lose?'

Uncle had never been in the army. His eyesight had always been poor but he stood upright as if he were undergoing a military inspection himself. He turned on me sternly.

'No one in this house is interested in the possibilities of defeat; no such possibilities exist. They cannot exist. Reginald is going to serve the Empire and return a man. It *will* make a man of him. I know it is hard for you, Valentine. Please know that I am trying to do my best for him. God knows, he cannot go on as he has been doing. You don't understand, Valentine. There is *talk*.'

I did not understand what he meant, though I realised there was no more discussion to be had. But as I headed for the door I had a question.

'Uncle, that butterfly on the island? The one that's a foot wide.'

'Yes?'

'Would you catch that by the thorax?' I asked.

Uncle chuckled, relieved to have got back to a subject about which he felt comfortable. 'Possibly, or I might just shoot the wretched thing.'

I came away having accomplished nothing for Reggie – and wondering who would shoot a butterfly.

Soon all the talk in the house was of how we should all be proud of Reggie. There was an endless parade of visitors through the house all of whom seemed to know just how to see off the Boer. Colonel Sir John and Lady Talbot, good friends of my aunt and uncle, were much involved in the preparations and as a consequence seemed to be present at almost every meal. Tradesmen came and went at the kitchen door like an army already on the move and Cook did her best to keep up.

While the men planned South Africa's future, the women found time to plan for me. When Aunt Caroline and Lady Talbot withdrew to the drawing room I could hear them discussing my imminent introduction to society.

'She's tall and slim, and much prettier than I had been led to believe,' whispered Lady Talbot.

'A blessing,' agreed Aunt Caroline, 'for so far we have no news of any monies.'

They moved on from my looks and apparent poverty to the revelation that Lady Talbot was determined to go to South Africa herself. Lady Talbot was older than my aunt. She seemed pinched and withered to me, like a dried herb fit only for storage.

'I have six or seven weeks of unoccupied time at my disposal and thought I would go back out to the Cape to see if I could be of some little service,' she explained to my aunt. It seemed many of the society ladies were hurriedly packing summer dresses, parasols and feather boas and heading south in the hope of undertaking a little light nursing. Even better, they might arrive just in time for the victory celebrations. 'Sadly the colonel is wanted here in London but he will trust me as his little "envoy".'

Clearly war was a more social affair than I had realised. I heard Colonel Talbot assure Reggie that South Africa was a fine place for a young man to indulge his fancy. 'If a Dutch girl gets a chance at an Englishman, old or young, poor or rich, she doesn't wait to be asked a second time.'

The truth was that everyone's preoccupation with the raising of the volunteer force meant my life had changed beyond all measure, and for the better. Aunt Caroline was busy and, released from my lessons in the drawing room, I suddenly found that no one was paying attention to what I did or where I went. One morning, the front door was open as I passed on my way to my room. Everyone was out – Uncle greasing the wheels of war, Aunt Caroline seeing everyone was dressed for the occasion and Reggie doing what he did most days – drowning his sorrows in some watering hole or other. Maisie was on her hands and knees, scrubbing the front steps with a donkey stone. Over her dark head I noticed the sky. It was one of those fresh wintry days where the air feels sharp on the lungs but there is a hint that spring will return. I stepped out on to the pavement.

'Your hat, Miss Valentine, shall I fetch your hat?' called Maisie anxiously.

I shook my head and looked up and down the road. A green Harrods delivery van had pulled up nearby and the horses stood restlessly waiting to move on. A boy buttoned up in a navy jacket was running towards the park with a kite. No one was looking at me. I walked along the black iron railings in front of the house, my hand slipping from one to another until slowly I reached the last. My feet wanted to continue but my arm dragged behind me, still grasping the final metal bar.

'Miss Valentine!' called Maisie. 'Valentine!'

Ignoring her anxious cries, I slipped my hand from the railing and, bare headed, carried on up the road, to the corner where Park Lane cut across. I could see right into Hyde Park. Somewhere in there, I knew, was Speakers' Corner where men stood on soap boxes and said what they thought. I looked back. No one except Maisie was paying me any attention. I was free.

'Valentine!' she called.

I didn't go much further on my first outing but gradually I widened the circle. I walked at first but pretty soon grew bolder and once I even took the dark green Number 42 omnibus all the way to the Seven Sisters Road. I saw the tavern in Tottenham where a woman on the bus told me that seven sisters had planted seven elms before they went their separate ways. What would it be like to have a sister for these adventures? I wondered, but it was thrilling, too, to be away from the house all alone.

I also worked out how to return to one of the places where I was happiest. Aunt Caroline got her hats from the very smart Lincoln & Bennett in Piccadilly. For my aunt, the considerations involved in such a purchase were intense and my relentless fidgeting in the shop a terrible distraction. She had quickly learned to park me along the way in Hatchard's Bookshop where, like a child in an emporium of sweets, I wandered about in awe. Papa had had many books but not like this.

Now by myself in this glorious place, I discovered Frances Willard's *A Wheel Within a Wheel*. Miss Willard was the leader of the Women's Christian Temperance Union in America but it was her advocacy of the bicycle that excited my thoughts. My heart pounded when Miss Willard declared that she had 'made myself master of the most remarkable, ingenious, and inspiring motor ever yet devised upon this planet' and said that I should 'do likewise'. I could think of little else.

Soon after, one morning at the breakfast table, Reggie and I were quietly eating while Aunt Caroline toyed with the tiniest morsel of toast. Uncle was reading dispatches from the war office and tutting continuously.

'Have you seen this, my dear?' he enquired of his wife, who seemed agitated and did not respond. Uncle Charles continued. 'From the front. Apparently horses are dying at an alarming rate.

Anyway – Colonel Knox, you remember Matthew? He has had a capital idea. Bicycles!'

'Bicycles?' I said, rather too eagerly.

'Yes, you know, bicycles. Well, they are getting more and more efficient. Send a man out on a bicycle and he can get about more quickly than the infantry. He can carry more, useful for sending messages.'

'Charles . . . ' tried Aunt Caroline.

'I should like a bicycle,' I said, but it was as if I hadn't spoken at all.

'Might be tricky drawing your sword,' commented Reggie quietly.

Uncle Charles smiled. 'Yes, but nevertheless I can see the sense in it.' He nodded, clearly pleased with the idea. 'Bicycles don't get diseases, you can't shoot 'em, don't need to feed 'em. I shall look into it today. Yes, bicycles. Capital idea.'

'Charles!' Aunt Caroline spoke a little louder than usual.

'What is it, dear?'

'I was thinking about Lady Talbot going to Cape Town. About her going to help. I was wondering . . . I mean I could . . . It occurred to me that . . . '

Uncle Charles patted her on the hand as he stood up to depart. 'My dear, of course you want to help. Everyone does. Why, they say even Her Majesty has commissioned large-scale maps specially so she can follow each skirmish despite her sadly fading eyesight, but it is out of the question for you to go out there. You must stay here.'

My uncle went off to find indestructible two-wheeled horses and Aunt Caroline departed for the Guildhall. Her life was not her own. She might have held sway over me in the drawing room but she could not do as she pleased. She could not decide anything for herself other than the style of hats and gloves. How odd to send men thousands of miles away to fight for the right to vote in someone else's country, when neither my aunt nor I had a say in anything back here at home.

Perhaps Reggie sensed the rebellion stirring in me, for he smiled and winked. 'No one has made plans for us today,' he whispered. 'Shall we have an outing?'

We slipped out and caught a cab to St James's Hall in Regent's Street. I had been to the great hall before to hear an organ recital with my aunt, but this time we went to one of the smaller halls on the ground floor near the restaurant. Even I had heard of the Moore and Burgess Minstrels who had been resident there for years, but of course I had never been allowed to watch this large company of men with their faces blackened and their lips lined in white. There was Mr Interlocutor and Mr Bones and then, best of all, came our Frank!

How different Frank looked in this black make-up. Such a transformation. Of course, I knew that it was Frank, his walk and his physique were unique, but otherwise he was quite disguised. The minstrel show was a wonderful mix of laughter and song and Frank did an act with a fellow called Percy Sawday. It involved acrobatics on a bicycle and I watched in amazement as he and Mr Sawday whizzed around the stage together on a single two-wheeler. Frank somehow managed to place one hand upon the bicycle saddle and raise his whole body up in the air while Mr Sawday sat on the handlebars, pedalling backwards, as they cycled in great wide circles. It was so clever that it had some of the men in the audience whistling in appreciation. This was not bicycling, it was flying.

Reggie and I practically bounded out of the theatre and bumped straight into the colonel's wife, Lady Talbot. It seemed she had been arranging a concert for the volunteers in the upper hall.

'Mr Grey. Miss Grey. You will forgive me for enquiring,' she began when she saw us, 'but is Lady Grey aware that you have spent the afternoon at the minstrels?' She turned to Reggie. 'Is this how you occupy your young cousin, Mr Grey, while your aunt and uncle are about the serious business of preparing for war?'

Reggie blushed and then quickly recovered himself. 'Lady Talbot, I depart imminently for the front. I'm sure you can understand that at such times a young man's fancy might turn to a little light relief before he faces what may be his ultimate challenge.' He removed his hat and bowed deeply. 'I would not wish to cause my mother any further anxiety by revealing such a need to her.' He gave a sigh. 'Forgive me, I . . . I may require a moment to myself.'

It was an acting performance worthy of Frank. As he stepped past me, Reggie whispered, 'Come to the artists' entrance as soon as you can.' He replaced his hat and headed for the door.

Lady Talbot looked most concerned so I passed a few moments' desultory conversation with her in the fervent hope that she might heed Reggie and not tell Aunt Caroline where we had met. A minute or two later I headed to the artists' entrance at the back of St James's Hall. Behind a wooden ledge inside the door sat an elderly man in a grey waistcoat and wire spectacles. He looked at me over his glasses and then stood up, clearly startled.

'Heavens, if it isn't Miss Elizabeth,' he declared. 'Elizabeth Perreau.'

It took a moment to realise that he had mistaken me for my mother.

'No, it can't be,' he continued, 'but you are so like her. Just the image of her, you are.' He shook his head in wonder and smiled. 'Oh, she was an actress of the rarest sort. Could play anything you like. One minute a thing of beauty, the next a terrible old hag.' He glanced at me quickly. 'I mean that as the greatest compliment, Miss ... Miss?'

'Valentine Grey.' She was my mother I explained, realising how little I had ever spoken of her.

'Silas Wilson.' He gave a small bow and I could see he was a little shaken.

'You here to go on the stage, miss?'

I laughed. 'No, no, Mr Wilson. I don't think I could dissemble at all.'

He gave me a long look. 'It's in the blood, Miss Valentine. It's there if you want it. You couldn't be Miss Elizabeth's child and not have the skill.'

I was both flattered and startled. I was my father's child, I thought.

'I'm here for Mr Rutherford. Frank Rutherford.'

'Oh yes, indeed. Charming fellow. I wouldn't normally let a young lady in but seeing as ... anyway, down the corridor, third on the right ... with Mr Sawday.' He shook his head again and sat down.

I took my time wandering down the corridor. Just walking about unescorted still seemed strange and gave me a slight thrill. The dressing-room door with Frank's name and that of Mr Sawday on it was ajar. I pushed it open to find Reggie kissing a black man.

# Seven

There was an advertisement for Pears soap at the time that showed a black boy washing himself. The child emerged from the bath with his body white but his unwashed head still black. It was what Frank looked like in the dressing room. His shirt collar was off and the open buttons at his neck revealed pale skin beneath his coal-black face. He smiled sheepishly, the whites of his eyes startling as he let Reggie go.

'Ah,' he said, 'probably should have locked that door, Reggie.' Frank moved to the sink and began to wash his black features away.

Reggie sank into a seat in the corner. He could not look at me. I don't think I was actually as surprised as perhaps I was expected to be. Did I know already? Many things charged through my mind as I leaned against the door jamb.

'Is this your pressing matter? The one that should stop you going to war?'

Reggie nodded, shame clouding every feature. 'I can't leave Frank. I just can't. I think I'll die.'

Frank dried himself with a towel and turned to me, fresh-faced and white once more. 'Nothing has changed, Valentine, we are still the same,' he said quietly.

Reggie was pale. He reached into his waistcoat pocket and pulled out his enlistment shilling. He began flipping it slowly in his hand – heads, tails, heads, tails, as if fate would decide. Frank put his hand on Reggie's shoulder and squeezed it gently.

'What shall we do, Valentine?' my cousin asked, finally looking up at me, anxious, as if I knew the answer.

I had no idea. I stood for a moment and then surprised us all by asking, 'Frank, will you teach me to ride your bicycle?'

Frank didn't seem at all taken aback by the suggestion so we went upstairs to the great hall at St James's. It was a vast place with room for two thousand people. If I had to learn indoors then this was the place to do it. A recessed orchestral gallery lay at one end, while an alcove at the other contained the large organ Aunt Caroline and I had come to hear. Light flooded in from the Gothic windows decorated with what looked like orange and yellow scrolls of paper. The great celebrations for the New Year were over and the orchestra had packed up, leaving a wonderfully empty stage. It was here, under a massive vaulted ceiling held up by gilded ribs intersecting on a brilliant red background, that I learned to ride a bicycle. It was here, watched by groups of sculpted figures holding scrolls inscribed with the names of Mozart, Handel and Beethoven, that Frank Rutherford handed me my independence.

The first thing we discovered was how impossible my dress was for the task. My long, billowy skirts were utterly impractical and my corset made pedalling and breathing a ridiculous combination. Clearly I was in need of some more rational costume. I knew what Aunt Caroline thought of bloomers but something had made me decide it was a day to blow caution to the winds. Both Reggie and Frank, cautious about my dressing-room discovery, were minded to let me do as I pleased. I persuaded Frank to let me wear his stage costume. He and I went back downstairs and when we re-emerged Reggie was clearly startled. I was tall and we had had no trouble with the fit.

'Valentine, you look, you look—'

'You look so like Reggie I could kiss you,' declared Frank.

I pushed him away, laughing, and Reggie grabbed me by the waist.

'Frank,' he asked, 'who was it that said, "The influence of the costume penetrates to the very soul of the wearer"?'

Frank smiled. 'Mr Wilde, I believe.'

Reggie nodded. 'Indeed, dear Oscar.' My cousin took both my hands and held me at arm's length. 'Fit for the Greek galleries of any museum,' he mused. 'Now you be careful with her, Frank. Don't allow the outfit to let you forget you are dealing with my cousin,' he added as we began our bicycling studies. 'My *female* cousin.'

Reggie was not at all sure about the lesson. He disliked anything with even a modicum of danger and kept warning Frank that I might get hurt. Nothing, however, was going to stop me. The stage was set and so was I. Reggie found a stool and sat mostly with his hands over his eyes, watching through his splayed fingers.

It was a boy's bicycle and it took me some time but my riding lessons with Bahadur had stayed with me. Anyone who could gallop across the Assam countryside had to have some idea of balance. Frank held the back of the leather saddle and ran beside me as we circled round and round on the wooden stage.

'Go on, Valentine, you're doing it.' He let go and for a brief moment I was in charge, but then my left hand played me false. I turned at an acute angle and away I went sidelong, machine and all, into the proscenium arch and landed on my right elbow.

Reggie ran to me. 'Oh Frank, what have you done? Valentine, Valentine! You've killed her.'

Although my elbow felt like a glassful of chopped ice, I sat up and laughed.

'I nearly did it,' I said triumphantly.

Now Reggie was cross. 'Why must you be so adventurous, Valentine? Honestly, you scared me half to death. It's so unnecessary. Why can't we all just sit? Read a book or something? Do what English people are supposed to do and spend an hour on the weather?'

Frank helped me up. 'It's fine. You will be fine. She'll be fine.'

He lifted me back into the saddle, saying, 'We shall do it in order. First learn to pedal, then perhaps to turn. Dismounting is useful and once you can get on by yourself, why then you shall have charge of this great beast. Decision and precision, that is the key.'

We started again and slowly, bit by bit, first with physical and then with moral support, I began to conquer that most mysterious metal animal. As I pedalled faster and faster past my cousin with Frank cheering by the side, I could feel the power pushing through my legs. Each turn of the wheels was pulling me further and further from the life I had been living. It was bliss. It was the nearest to flying I thought I would ever feel.

Mr Wilson stood in the wings, watching and nodding.

It was with great reluctance that I changed back into the confinement of my own clothes and we went for tea at Callard's in Regent Street. It took me surprisingly little time to get used to the idea that Reggie and Frank wanted to be together. When you saw them sitting side by side it just seemed right. It seemed natural. It might appear shocking to others but I have no other way to explain it. If I know nothing else from Papa then I am certain that life with love in it is better than life without.

The boys had cakes with cream but after I had worn trousers, my corset felt more restricting than ever and I could scarcely breathe, let alone eat. Back in my skirts I felt helpless and hopeless, suffocated. Now, when we had had so much fun together, we none of us spoke.

After a while, Reggie announced miserably, 'I have to go. I am due at the Guildhall for my uniform.'

Frank and I decided to keep him company and on the way we passed a photographer's. Frank insisted that we go in and have our portrait done. The photographer said he only did sitters on a Monday and we would have to return, but no one ever refused Frank anything once he was set on a plan. Frank sat in a fringed chair with Reggie and me flanking him, while behind us a drape of curtain hung beside a pot plant on a stand. Reggie had his hand on Frank's arm and I, wearing one of Aunt Caroline's cast-off hats, looked quite the society lady. The magnesium flash filled the room. Then the boys had pictures done together, both looking so handsome and so happy.

After that we went to the Guildhall. I had never been there before but even I could tell that the old place was not itself. It had the most peculiar air. Goods were heaped everywhere and people were calling out instructions. Long tables had been set out in a giant T shape in the centre of the hall. Behind them racks of pigeonholes stood stacked five sections high, one above the other. Boots and shoes sat in the top compartments and the rest was slowly filling up with clothing for both land and sea. Measurement cards had been pinned up for each man and a crowd of perhaps thirty people were checking the cards and transferring kit into the correct pigeonholes for the 64 officers and 1,675 men of other ranks. It was an impressive operation, this raising of a troop to fight seven thousand miles away in just seven weeks. At one end of the hall a sort of shop had been created where clothing was stacked according to size.

A Mr Kent seemed to be in charge and he had the most detailed knowledge about what might be needed.

'Size eight boots? They're small. He'll need four pairs of 10½-inch socks,' he responded in answer to a question.

Once sorted, the kit was made up into a parcel for collection and it was to pick up this package that Reggie had been summoned. Along with his boots and clothes he received the Freedom of the City of London from the Duke of Cambridge, who was then, I think, the Colonel-in-Chief of the Army. I watched Reggie sign the roll of freemen and thought it a curious choice for him.

'Any questions?' asked the sergeant in charge.

'Yes,' said Reggie, 'when do I meet my . . . uhm . . . horse?' It was the thing he most dreaded.

'Horses being provided in Cape Town,' replied the sergeant looking at his lists, 'by a Mr Abe Bailey. They say we shall save twelve thousand pounds by not transporting them there. Makes sense to me. Born and bred there so they'll be ready for the front. It can take three to four weeks for a horse to get fit after a sea voyage. Anyway, don't let that worry your head, young man, you're set for the cycle corps.'

'The cycle corps!' repeated Reggie as we left. 'The cycle corps! Do I look like an acrobat?'

Frank laughed. 'Be better off sending Valentine instead.'

We parted from Frank, who had to go back to the theatre.

There was a heavy mist on the way home and by the time we returned we were wet through. Despite the dreadful weather the front door was open. Maisie was standing there weeping and we could see a policeman talking to Harris at the door of Uncle's library. Uncle himself was silhouetted in the gaslight, looking most strange.

'I said death would come to this house!' sobbed Maisie. 'I did say. She would wear black for too long but I never meant it would be her. I never meant it.'

I should have learned by then that death does not come as you expect it. That it did not always arrive with a warning, allowing you to prepare yourself at the bedside of the soon to be departed. It was Aunt Caroline. It seemed she had been crossing Piccadilly when, no doubt looking to the right as she gathered up her skirts in the correct hand, she had been hit by a delivery van coming from the left.

'He was taking ribbons to a haberdasher in Reigate,' cried Maisie, who despite her grief had been able to gather quite a lot of information. 'Ribbons! I can't think what the rush can have been.'

I heard Reggie take a deep breath and then he dropped the parcel of clothes he was carrying. It thudded on to the marble floor. Uncle Charles nodded as though we were guests he had been expecting. He moved towards his son with his hand out, as if offering to shake it. Reggie stared at him and suddenly fell to his knees. Maisie and Harris rushed to help Reggie and seemed almost to prompt Uncle Charles to make room for him in the library.

The policeman, abandoned in the hall, walked towards me.

'Someone will have to see to matters,' he muttered. 'There'll be papers to sign.'

'Yes, yes, of course,' I said and took the details.

After that everything happened with astonishing speed and, even more extraordinary, I found myself in charge. It wasn't difficult. There was a rule for everything and fortunately most of it was in my aunt's household guide. The ladies from the Primrose League called and gave much advice and Uncle Charles handed over the arrangements to the funeral director who had buried his father. Invitations were ordered from Webster's, whose premises practically overlooked the fateful spot where Aunt Caroline had met her end. I already knew where to order suitable mourning clothes. Reggie? Reggie did nothing. Helped by me and Maisie, he retired to his room.

I made sure the photographer got a nice picture of Aunt Caroline laid out in her coffin and helped Maisie tie black crape on the bell knob so that no one would ring and upset the quiet. Lady Talbot arranged the pallbearers and assisted me in making sure that no one was omitted from the funeral invitations. I did not know what my aunt would have made of the fact that my first great social responsibility was seeing her into the next life. The Lord Mayor sent a telegram expressing his sorrow at our loss, which he declared had been incurred while my aunt was engaged in the great effort for the war. It was kind, and after that Aunt Caroline was spoken of as having died doing her bit for the nation, which seemed preferable to a violent encounter with a tradesman.

The night before the funeral I was rushing about making sure the house was fit for visitors. Maisie was polishing the stairs, slowly climbing up on her hands and knees, stair by stair, to achieve the perfection Aunt Caroline would have wanted. I found Reggie's parcel of soldier's clothing on the hall table. The paper had split from its fall and a small window of khaki was just visible. I knew this was not something Reggie could cope with now so I picked it up and took it to my room.

Before we knew it, the carriages were calling to take us to the family vault at Highgate. All the staff lined up outside the house to see us off, their heads bowed with respect. Reggie did not speak.

'Have you seen Frank?' I whispered as we sat down.

Reggie shook his head. For all her rigidity, Reggie had loved his mother and she him. I cannot say that I had loved my aunt but I knew she had truly meant well by me. She had taken me in and struggled to help me and I was, at least, grateful. The worst of it was that I could not bear Reggie's sorrow. His grief brought back all my own half-buried feelings of loss that I constantly tried to control and we both wept as he buried his mother and I, in some way, my papa. We both wept more than I suspect anyone thought agreeable. Perhaps to counter this, Uncle Charles was the absolute model of propriety. He made sure that every detail of the funeral procession was perfect. He wore the black band around his hat with dignity and made all the right responses in answer to the guests' solicitous enquiries. It is possible that he had not loved his wife but they had been married a long time and he seemed, if anything, bewildered to be without her. His respectful farewell to her convinced me of one thing – never would I settle for a union so utterly lacking in passion. I thought of Frank and Reggie and of Papa's instruction to feel deeply or not feel at all.

Reggie got drunk at the reception and began loudly quoting Tennyson to anyone who would listen.

'*Half a league, half a league, Half a league onward, All in the valley of Death Rode the six hundred* ... And why would they do that? Madness. Nothing but madness, ladies and gentlemen.'

Maisie and I took him up to bed before he could disgrace himself further. He lay on his bed and sobbed like a small boy.

'Your mother wouldn't want you to carry on so,' soothed Maisie, trying to get his boots off.

Reggie pulled me to him and said most earnestly, 'You have to understand, Valentine. I saw him on the stage, that shining creation, and my heart would never settle again.'

It could have been my father talking about my mother.

'I can't go, Valentine, I just can't,' he repeated.

And it was clear to me that he couldn't. That he was afraid, that he was not suited to the task and that no one who loved him would force him to go.

Uncle Charles continued with his war work but he seemed distracted. I don't know how long it was after the funeral, three weeks perhaps, that he asked to speak to me.

'My dear Valentine, thank you. You have been wonderful. I do appreciate it. Please, come into the drawing room. I want to talk to you.'

I sat down but he remained standing, looking down on me.

He cleared his throat with the slight cough I realised I had grown used to, even fond of. 'I have something to tell you.' He paused and I thought for a moment he was going to stroke my cheek, but he did not. 'I have decided to go away,' he said. 'To New Guinea, in the Pacific ... to find that butterfly. The big one.'

I was so surprised I couldn't think of anything to say except, 'When?'

Uncle looked rather surprised himself. 'Soon. As soon as possible.'

'Why?'

He smiled. 'It's your father, Valentine.'

For a brief second I thought he had received some news. That Papa had survived and was coming for me or, even more strangely, that somehow he was now in New Guinea.

'And you. What you said. I envied him, you know,' continued Uncle Charles, now turning and looking at himself in the mirror over the mantelpiece. 'Marrying that beautiful girl and heading off like that. I've been such a dullard but I had a duty, you see, and I think it is time I . . . ' He glanced at me in the looking glass, sitting behind him.'You, Valentine, have made me want to have an adventure before it's too late and I die here. It ought to be a law that life must not be boring. You told me that and so I'm going.'

Slightly embarrassed now, he turned back and said, 'I couldn't have gone while Caroline . . . She wouldn't have . . . couldn't have . . . '

Then briskly as if wiping his hands of his old life and me, 'I shall make arrangements for you. Caroline has . . . had a sister in Sussex . . . You met her at the funeral. You'll be fine. Caroline . . . Lady Grey, she liked being Lady Grey . . . Lady Grey did a wonderful job with you. She would be proud.'

He patted me and I went to my room with my head reeling. I lay on my bed, so full of rage that I was almost calm. Aunt Caroline was gone, Uncle Charles was leaving, Reggie was off to war and I was to . . . I was to what? Be shunted off to yet another relative I did not know in yet another strange house?

Reggie's bundle of army clothing lay partly open on the end of my bed. I felt it with my foot and it ripped a little more. The khaki jacket spilled out of the hole. Slowly I sat up and reached for the parcel. I placed it on my lap and one by one removed the contents. The fabric was rough and new. I laid it out on the bed as if an entirely flat person were asleep upon the counterpane. I stood looking at the uniform for a long time. I thought it would fit me. After an age I took off my own clothes. The trousers were jodhpur-like, becoming slimmer at the knee. The tunic fastened with brass buttons to a round high collar. A stiff, creaking, brown leather belt pulled it fast just above two large patch pockets. The puttees were confusing. I knew that these long strips of cloth were to be wound from knee to ankle to protect the lower leg but I did not know how they fastened. I put my trousered leg up on a chair and was attempting to wind the garters on when Maisie slipped into the room. I stood up, startled.

'You should knock,' I declared, angrily.

Maisie gazed at me silently. 'I never knocked before,' she replied.

'Well, things are different now,' I said.

'I see that.'

Without another word she knelt down beside me and, just as she had helped me a hundred times before to subdue my skirts and corsets, she began to settle the puttees into place. Silently she fastened them and reached for the sturdy pair of lace-up ankle boots that lay on the bed. The leather was tough and unforgiving but I pushed my feet in and Maisie tied the laces into a neat knot. A wide-brimmed hat, pulled up at one side, was next.

As I put it on, Maisie gently turned me towards the full-length mirror.

*The influence of the costume penetrates to the very soul of the wearer.* I knew in that moment how literally clothing made the man.

I could see that a transformation as simple as changing a suit of clothes could transport me to another, more privileged world. I lifted my arm and then my leg. Unencumbered by stays, bodices, skirts and petticoats, my body was free to move as I bid it. This suit of khaki, this soldier's garb, was the key to another world.

'We would have to cut your hair,' said Maisie, pulling my hair back behind my neck as if it were already gone.

# Eight

Just two days later Uncle Charles left for New Guinea. There happened to be a boat heading in the right direction and he saw no reason to delay. He bid Reggie a stiff farewell, with instructions to bring back honour for the family and to dispatch me as soon as possible to stay with Aunt Caroline's sister.

'When will you be back, Uncle?' I asked.

He shrugged as he pulled on his gloves. 'New Guinea? Long way. Reggie'll probably be back first.' He paused for a moment and looked at us both.

'Valentine, I . . . be careful, my dear. I'm sorry.' I'm not sure what he was sorry for. We were both sorry. He looked to Reggie and then back to me.

'Please make sure Reginald departs with honour. There is honour in this house and he has a duty. We all have our duties. I have done mine.' He looked meaningfully at Reggie and then, clutching his hat in both hands, awkwardly leaned forward to kiss me on the cheek. Without thinking, and even though I was angry with him, I flung my arms around his neck and hugged him to me. I don't know that anyone had ever hugged Uncle Charles. When we parted he was clearing his throat and busily blowing his nose. He shook hands with Reggie and then without looking at either of us again he was off, in a parade of hansom cabs bearing Wardian cases, butterfly nets and trunks. The house was stiller than even he might have liked.

Reggie kissed me and went straight to Frank.

We all knew he was due to depart for Cape Town in the morning but, at midnight, the house was hushed and empty. Maisie and I sat silently on the stairs waiting for him. I think we knew when he left that he would not be back. We went into the kitchen and Maisie got out the scissors while I sat quite still, and without saying a word she cut my hair. My womanhood that Aunt Caroline had worked so hard to shape fell on to the kitchen floor. Soon my neck felt bare and exposed. I kept running my hand across the back of my head and I wept.

I wrote to Aunt Caroline's sister to say that I had suddenly been called to India to look after my father's affairs and then Maisie led me upstairs and dressed me in Reggie's uniform. This time she took a strip of sheeting and wrapped it around my breasts so that they lay flattened and unnoticeable. Then she helped me into my new disguise. When she was done we stood looking in the mirror at the young man who appeared.

I looked in the glass and, dare I say, I believe I fell in love with myself. I could feel my restless, passionate soul calming. I did not want to be a man but I did want to go where a man could. I did not want the life my aunt had planned for me. I felt myself step into the freedom and glorious independence of masculinity.

'I could take a fancy to such a youth,' confided Maisie.

'It is madness,' I whispered.

It was a misty morning when I stepped out to move across the murky channels that separate male and female spheres. Under the gloom of a single streetlight, anyone passing might have seen a soldier kissing his girl goodbye. I had nothing of my old life with me except the small photograph of Reggie, Frank and myself tucked into my breast pocket. Maisie went inside and closed the door of Inkerman House as you might close a chapter in a book. The hard new heels of my boots clicked across the pavement. I hadn't the nerve to hail a hansom cab and so I walked to the barracks at Bunhill Row.

The air was cold on my newly shorn head but the idea that I could wander anywhere that my curiosity might lead me was so intoxicating that all other worries left me. Just being able to stride across the pavement was enough to make me feel quite light-headed. My legs seemed elongated, as if they now stretched out for ever. Nothing confined them, held them back from covering the pavement in great loping strides. I felt the rough fabric of my trousers brushing on my legs and it made me grin, as if the very idea of having legs at all were new. My walk even sounded different – like someone on the march, not a creature timidly tiptoeing through life. The heels of my boots made a thudding noise that echoed against the railings of the houses I passed. I thought of Reggie, of the men I knew, and I tried putting my hands in my pockets – ha! How comfortable that was. What a splendid way to walk. I had never thought of hands as heavy but how happily they rested on my thighs. I tried a little swagger and a small whistle, a noise I hadn't even known I could make. In just half an hour of walking I had become quite the lad.

It was, however, as I got closer to my destination that my hands emerged from my pockets, that my puckered lips once more fell into a thin line of doubt. I knew I must be in the right place, for there were an immense number of soldiers gathering and my anxieties returned with a gallop. I felt certain I would be the object of everyone's attention. Surely anyone I passed would stare at my legs. I skulked in a corner and stood in the shadows of a lamp above a door, only half daring to look out. I don't know how long I waited there but after a little while I realised that no one was looking at me at all. The place was teeming with men of all types and sizes and the only person to catch my eye was a sergeant who happened by with a checklist.

'Name?'

'Uh ...' For a minute I couldn't think. What was I doing? 'Grey,' I replied, which was the truth.

'Grey?' He ran his finger down the list. 'Reginald?'

I nodded. 'Yes ... Reginald.' It came out sounding like the smallest pipe on the St James's Hall organ. 'Reginald,' I repeated more gruffly. He looked up from his list. I forced myself to hold his gaze firmly.

'Sure?' he enquired with a slight smile.

'Yes.'

'Inside! Get your kit then,' he barked, suddenly turning fierce before moving on to the next poor soul. I realised there were too many men for anyone to stand out. Even my light voice and hairless face did not mark me out as unique. It was quickly clear that, despite the supposed age restriction for recruitment, many a young lad and the occasional old buffer had managed to sneak into the regiment unchallenged. Gingerly I moved away from my hiding place and towards the bright light leading to the hall, where I found the still cocoon of my previous life was shattered. A rabble of men was arriving from all quarters. Inside were volunteer soldiers mixed with an assortment of relatives and hangers-on. The atmosphere was slightly hysterical. The explosion of jingoism following the declaration of war had left the nation giddy with excitement and not much discipline. I had never heard noise like it.

Everywhere there was activity. Weapons were issued from the Tower of London and each man was provided with two kitbags – one for the sea voyage, one for land use – into which everything deemed necessary for a year's campaign was to be packed. It all seemed such a lot of clobber. Everyone was busy either organising or being organised and I soon found myself drawn into various lines to receive more and more things to carry. I had always thought of myself as strong, yet by the end I was beginning to stagger under it all. I was seriously wondering if I were fit enough to manage this ruse.

'Grey!' called the issuing clerk. 'You forgot your rucksack.'

'My what?'

'Cycles, ain't you?'

I nodded. Cycles! Yes, I was cycles. How exciting. Who would not want a cycle? I was cycles.

'You need this,' he declared, uninterested in my flash of excitement. He passed over a capacious carrier that I later learned had been suggested by an Alpine climber in our section. I cursed the fellow, for now I had three bags, a greatcoat, a belt for bullets called a bandolier, a gun and a bayonet to deal with. I struggled to put half the unfamiliar baggage across my shoulders and suddenly I felt the weight of what we were all supposed to do. I remembered Colonel Talbot and his pride in Reggie going off to battle in the name of Queen and country. We were to defeat Mr Kruger and his men. The responsibilities of the Empire lay on my shoulders. I almost had to laugh at the idea. I had never fought anyone and how on earth were you supposed to do it carrying all this gear?

'Excuse me, Mr Boer, I just need to put some of this down so I can shoot at you.'

Panic rose in me and I turned to ... I don't know what ... run perhaps, or find some gentleman who would be kind enough to carry the kit for me. I bumped into a fellow volunteer and immediately dropped my bayonet with a great clatter on the stone floor.

He was struggling to keep hold of a large box. 'Steady on!' he cried. Instead, I bent down to pick up the fallen weapon and tripped over one of my kitbags and sent the poor man flying. Small packets flew in a great arc from his box.

'Blast,' he cried and scrambled to gather up his cargo. 'Don't stand there, please! Excuse me! Sorry! Blast! Yes, yes, pardon my French.'

I rushed to help but only caused more confusion as I leapt between the legs of soldiers.

'How many have you got?' he called out to me.

'Six,' I replied.

'Splendid.' He smiled at me as we stood and replaced the precious items back in his box.

He put out his hand. 'John Jackson. Britannia Soap at the Empire's Service.' Jackson reached into his jacket pocket and produced a business card with his details and a picture of a bar of soap.

'My card,' he said with a flourish. Everything about Jackson was fulsome. He cannot have been much more than in his early twenties but he was one of those men who already carry their father's body. Somewhat plump with a rosy face, he had hair that barely did the duty of covering his head; none at the front and what there was at the sides had been swept across the top of his head in thin, carefully laid strands which were now seriously awry. He had a gigantic moustache that might have been borrowed from the walrus itself. Indeed, his moustache was so bushy it was a wonder it allowed him to eat. Yet eat he certainly did, for even though his uniform was new every button protested at its closure.

I glanced at the cream-coloured card. 'You're from Lancashire?' I said as if it were the most surprising thing in the world.

'Was,' said Jackson firmly. 'I'm a London man now. Factory in Warrington,' he tapped the side of his head, 'brains in London. So, Cycle Corps – and you?'

'Me what?' I replied stupidly.

'I say, you look a bit . . . '

'Grey,' I said.

Jackson laughed. 'All right. I was going to say green but you do look a bit grey. You all right, lad?'

'Fine. I'm fine,' I stammered. 'Reginald Grey. I'm known as Reginald Grey.' This time the name did seem a little easier.

'Cycle Corps?' he repeated, helping me to gather my fallen bayonet.

I nodded. 'Bicycles. Yes, bicycles as well.' I puffed out my chest slightly before remembering it was one of the many things I meant to hide. 'I can ride a bicycle,' I declared proudly.

Jackson slapped me on the back and I almost dropped the bayonet again.

'Splendid news. This way.'

Jackson already seemed to know everyone and everything. He marched through the crowd handing out his packets calling 'Britannia Soap at the Empire's Service, gentlemen!' and telling me 'how marvellous' it all was.

'Why marvellous?' I panted.

'Why, Grey, this is the greatest business opportunity this

country has ever seen. Do you have any idea what the possibilities for soap are where we are going? Half those Boers will never have heard of the stuff and as for the natives . . . Well, it beggars belief. And if they don't want to wash? What then?'

I had no idea.

'Candles! Who doesn't want to see in the dark? Even the unwashed and ungodly require light. My card!' he called out to a passing officer before giving a half-salute and a bar of soap to the somewhat surprised gentleman in khaki.

'Soap and candles?' I said stupidly.

'Of course,' Jackson boomed, 'anyone who makes one would be a fool not to make the other. Gone hand in hand for generations. It's all about boiling in the end.'

Jackson's enthusiasm pulled me along. He helped me to believe that we were off to do great things. To fight for the rights of the *Uitlanders*; to bring civilisation to the Boer – or at the very least to bring them soap.

That night there was a service at St Paul's and I sat, one among many, hearing how God was blessing my enterprise. As we marched back to barracks I began to feel I was part of something. At first my pace faltered as I tried to find the rhythm of the men but soon I was stepping along like the best of them. It felt wonderful to march together like that. I couldn't help but feel proud. There were hundreds of people shouting encouragement despite the pouring rain. The men around me were excited and kept calling out that they would 'bring a lock of Kruger's whiskers' when they returned. At one point a policeman rushed at me. I thought for a second that the game was up there and then but instead he wrung my hand, with a fervent 'Safe home again!'

We arrived in barracks where we were 'told off' to different companies. We were twenty in the Cycle Corps. A supper was provided for us but I could not eat. A rough-and-ready chap from Camberwell called George Sheridan had got a card game going a few feet away. There was much deep laughter and the jingle of coins. The day had been unlike any other. I was exhausted and could hardly speak, which was a good thing as that night I lay down in a basement of the Queen's Westminster Drill Hall without a mattress, straw or blanket on the bare stone flags. Lights were out by quarter past ten with a shouted order that no man was 'allowed to leave barracks without special leave signed by an officer'. I lay with my head on my new coat next to my new comrade. Jackson seemed to do everything with huge enthusiasm for he fell into an instant sleep, snoring as if he were advertising its benefits.

All of England, every class, every type lay on that floor for our last night's rest in our land – artists, plumbers, silversmiths, painters, a varnish tester, piano players, paper hangers, warehousemen, grooms and coachmen, collar makers, candle makers, the butcher, the baker ... I remembered sleeping as a child with the men when we hunted, but there I had lain between Papa and Bahadur. This was different. I did not know the people in this hall, their smell or their sounds. Papa, for all his ideas about me being able to shoot and ride ... would he think this was a good idea?

I wanted to sleep but I could not. The men smelt of something unfamiliar: leather mixed with the musty smell of the rough clothing. We had had a busy day and there had been no chance to wash. No basin to splash our faces in. Perhaps I too smelt differently. Amid the deep male snores, not far away I could hear a lad crying quietly. I felt cold seeping into my body and could not tell if it came from the floor or from fear. Then bit by bit the clothes I had donned with such relish seemed to grow uncomfortable. My boots chafed from my enthusiastic marching and the binding round my chest seemed to have wound itself tighter. What was Reggie doing? Could he have slept here in my place? I got up silently to seek some privacy and found a small set of public stalls off the hall. The place reeked as if dogs had been relieving themselves upon the floor. One fellow was on his knees emptying his nervous stomach into a pan. None of it was the smell of Her Majesty's heroes.

I found a stall with a lock and entered. I took off my belt, my jacket and shirt and released my breasts from their restrictions. How odd they looked already. Flattened and out of place. I looked down – my naked top so female and my lower half entirely alien in my boy's clothes. Could my mother have played such a part? I wanted to go back to Inkerman House and yet could not think what for. To sit once more in silence waiting for something to happen? There was nothing there for me. This was my chance. I lowered my trousers, determined to steady myself, but as I sat down I realised here was something I had not even thought of. How would I manage such basic matters? I leaned my head against the wall and quietly wept for my foolishness. As I wept, I looked down at my abandoned jacket and saw something in the pocket. It was the photograph of myself with Reggie and Frank taken that day I had learned to ride a bicycle. I reached down and opened the pocket. The photograph was new and both the boys seemed to shine from it. I looked at Reggie and knew that I had no choice.

# Nine

The curtains were drawn tight. With no light leaking in from outside it was impossible to know what time it was. A small electric lamp by the bed cast a faint beam on the drapes. Great folds of velvet, they were too full for the window and fell down from the rail on to a window seat, spilling away in a wave of burgundy. They looked theatrical, as if they hid a great show about to start. Perhaps he was in a play, Reggie thought groggily, or a church, for the place was heady with the scent of incense and the dark mahogany of the bedpost gleamed rich with polish.

He turned his head to see Frank sleeping beside him, his long hair dark on the white pillow. Reggie reached his hand across the soft cotton sheets and touched Frank's cheek gently, daring to place his hand upon a work of art. The art did not move. Slowly Reggie roused himself and sat on the edge of the bed. He had not spent the night in Frank's flat before and took his time to absorb it all. It was a small but lush two-room place in St James's just round the corner from Jermyn Street. He thought how often he had strolled near here to purchase a shirt or boots from his favourite shops on this road without once thinking of what other pleasures might lie so close at hand.

The flat, like Frank himself, was a concoction of theatrical splendour. There was not much of anything but what there was was sumptuous. Even the bed was a stage for drama. Frank had somehow managed to squeeze a large four-poster into the small bedroom. Curtains embroidered with mythical hunting scenes hung in great swags around the mattress. Through the bedroom door to the small sitting room Reggie could make out an upright piano with sheet music. Candles of every size and shape stood in any kind of container that might ever have been contrived to hold their light steady. Books lined the shelves either side of an ornate fireplace upon which stood banks of invitations past and present. It was a set. The set, perhaps, for a particularly risqué sort of play, possibly even one in French. Reggie, who had lived in the commodious lap of wealth all his life, thought he had never seen anywhere more beautiful. He reached out for his trousers which hung on the end of the bed and removed a watch from his pocket.

'Christ!' he declared loudly.

'Played him once,' murmured Frank from the bed. 'Seemed rather a nice life to me. All that walking on water, turning water into wine, twelve fellows knocking about with you all the time.'

Reggie sighed and Frank reached out his hand.

'Don't begin the day by sighing, Reggie, dear. Time enough for that when the omnibus to work breaks down.'

'It's eight o'clock, Frank. It's eight o'clock,' repeated Reggie.

Frank looked bewildered. 'In the morning?'

'Of course, in the morning,' replied Reggie.

Frank rubbed his eyes and pulled himself upright enough to

lean against the bed-head. 'Heavens, so this is what that hour feels like,' he said slowly.

Reggie got out of bed and began searching the room for his abandoned clothes. 'I was supposed to be at the station.'

'I thought you said you weren't going?' Frank continued, lolling against his pillow. He looked calm but his voice was tense. 'I thought we agreed ... last night. You said you can't—'

'I know, I know. It's just ...' Reggie began pacing at the end of the bed. 'Oh, Frank, my father. He's always been so disappointed in me. He never says but ... I don't think I can do this, Frank. I can't just not go. There'll be talk. What will people say? They'll know. They'll know everything. It's not good for either of us. I want to protect you too. You have to understand. I have no choice.'

Reggie pulled on his trousers and as Frank began to sense his earnestness, he reached out for him.

'Who cares about talk? Reggie, you cannot go to war. You are not suited. They have shooting and everything.'

'I have a duty. Besides, everyone says it will be over before we get there.'

'You can't be certain of that,' declared Frank loudly. 'Haven't there been wars that have gone on for a hundred years? Besides which, you and I are not dutiful. If we were we wouldn't be here at all. Please.' Frank knelt and put both hands on Reggie's shoulders. 'You'll die. All right, you might not die but I'll die without you. Please, let's at least talk about it. Have coffee. We'll go and have coffee at a little place I know. Don't rush off.'

'But the train ... I'm late,' persisted Reggie.

Frank smiled. 'If you must go at all, let's at least send you off in style. Coffee first. It's not too much to ask.'

By the time the two men stepped out into the street Frank was at his most charming. 'It's a splendid little shop. You'll love it, Reggie,' he babbled. 'It's full of marvellous morning characters. They sell the genuine produce of Mocha and not some other dismal concoction. All sorts go there. Why, we might meet anyone.'

The exterior of the shop seemed smart, all gold lettering and gleaming lamps, but inside Frank led the way down a set of treacherous steps into a low-ceilinged room divided into stalls with narrow tables and hard seats. The place was steamy and coffee rings on every surface suggested many past breakfasts. The walls were decorated with hat-pegs and a single battered advertisement in bright green which showed a most competent woman on a bicycle. There was a slight hint of lace under her long skirt as she managed to keep a large picture hat on her head and her bicycle well in advance of two gentlemen pedalling some way behind. Reggie thought miserably of Valentine. What was she thinking now about him missing the train to go off to war? How could he so disappoint everyone?

Frank sniffed the air appreciatively, as Reggie slumped down into a chair.

'Do you not think the smell of coffee is enough to transform a morning into a little slice of heaven?' he asked no one in particular as he ordered from the woman behind the counter and joined Reggie. It was odd for Reggie to see Frank sitting at the less than pristine table. Even though he had dressed in more of a hurry than usual, Frank looked, as ever, immaculate. Had Beau Brummell himself happened upon them he might have admired Frank's elegance. But it didn't overcome Reggie's anxiety. He sat drumming his fingers on the table while Frank chattered away and sipped his coffee as if nothing untoward was happening.

'You'll love it round here when you get to know it,'

pronounced Frank. 'Lovely place, Jermyn Street. Named after Henry Jermyn, Earl of somewhere or other. They say he had "dissolute morals". Certainly he never married. Perhaps he too was one for a wander in the Greek rooms at the British Museum. They say the great Sarah Siddons sat in rooms here for her portrait.'

Ignoring the handful of customers seeking a quiet corner to start their day, Frank threw his head back and proclaimed:

*'Come, you spirits*
*That tend on mortal thoughts, unsex me here,*
*And fill me from the crown to the toe topful*
*Of direst cruelty!'*

He stopped as suddenly as he had started and turned to Reggie, at last sincere. He spoke as softly as possible. 'I wish that I were unsexed. That you could have me for your own. I should happily be a woman for you. Reggie, you cannot go. It would be the direst cruelty.'

'Oh, Frank. I am in agony,' whispered Reggie, almost weeping. 'Do you think I want anything more than to sit here with you and while away the day? But I do have my duty and ... I don't know what I was thinking. Where did I think I would hide? I can't hide. I need to speak to Valentine. I cannot have her of all people think me a coward. I have to go home, get my uniform.'

They took a cab to Inkerman House together. As they headed through the streets of Mayfair and the houses became grander, Frank grew more and more talkative. He looked out at the cream porticos and polished front steps of the moneyed classes and though this was far from his world he kept chatting as if he and Reggie were on an idle little adventure.

'Doesn't Lord Mansfield live near here? I met him once. They say he has quite fallen for a chap who works shifts in some wretched little tailor's den. I believe the tailor has poor health but it brings out something protective in Lord Mansfield and he simply adores him,' he said, but Reggie wasn't listening.

The cab stopped in front of Reggie's home and Frank was silenced at last. Reggie turned to him and gently placed his finger on Frank's lips.

'Wait for me,' he said.

'Reggie . . . ' began Frank, but Reggie descended from the cab and went inside.

Even with Reggie's father abroad they both knew it was not appropriate for Frank to enter the house. Reggie was not gone long before he returned and seated himself back beside Frank in the cab. He was pale and agitated.

'Something terrible has happened,' Reggie murmured. 'It's Valentine.'

'Is she hurt?'

'No. Oh, Frank . . . she has gone.'

'Gone where?' asked Frank, bewildered.

'In my place,' explained Reggie, almost unable to say the words. 'She has gone in my place to war.'

'How is that possible?'

'Dressed as me,' wailed Reggie. 'She's dressed as me.'

Frank gave a low, appreciative laugh. 'What a splendid girl.'

The cab driver called down to them, 'Where to, gentlemen?'

'I don't know. I don't know,' repeated Reggie. Suddenly he brightened as if he had a thought. 'Where would she go, Frank? How do people go to war?'

'I have no idea,' Frank replied. 'It's a long way, isn't it? South Africa? I suppose I'd go by train and then by sea. Where do you go to the sea?

'The sea. Southampton. She must've gone to Southampton.' Reggie banged suddenly on the roof of the cab. 'Victoria Station. Victoria Station,' he called.

Although the first rush of morning was over, the station was still full of the bustle of travel. Under the high arches, in the grey light of a dull day, men and women went about their business. Whistles were blowing on distant platforms and the station-master had just finished his round of seeing to the main trains of the morning. Reggie raced through the crowd of cloth caps and bowlers, bonnets and shining silk toppers. Frank ran after him and watched him scour the concourse for anyone in khaki.

'There's no one here,' yelled Reggie in despair. 'No soldiers at all. Where are they? Where the hell are they?'

Frank grabbed Reggie's arm. 'I don't know but I know they are not here. Sit for a minute. Have a think. We cannot rush all over London like this.'

A woman carrying a large bunch of flowers eyed them suspiciously as Frank pulled Reggie towards a wooden bench. They sat down and for a moment were silent. Here was the Empire in action. Here was all human life interlocked in a gigantic, nation-wide and complex railway timetable, which revealed all the possibilities of technical progress. But all Reggie saw was the time.

'It's gone eleven,' he groaned. 'They'll be halfway there by now.'

'To South Africa?' replied Frank. 'Isn't it an awfully long way?'

'What am I going to do?' moaned Reggie, holding his head in his hands. 'Oh God, I'm such an idiot. How could I let this happen? She's going to go to war. Valentine!'

Frank reached over and stroked Reggie's arm. 'It's not your fault,' he said.

'It is. It is,' moaned Reggie. 'I have to do something. Tell someone.'

Frank looked at his lover and then asked quietly, 'Why?'

Reggie looked baffled. 'What do you mean, why?'

'Why do you have to do something?' asked Frank again. 'Reginald Grey was due to go to war. Thanks to your cousin, Reginald Grey has gone to war. You are free to stay here.'

'For God's sake, Frank,' Reggie exploded, 'she's a woman.'

Frank spoke calmly and with great determination. 'But she is not just any woman. You've seen her. She is a bicycling Amazon. All Valentine wanted was an adventure. Don't take that from her. Think of it. She has her liberty. How splendid! What a gift you have given her. She doesn't want to sit about in the drawing room waiting for someone to come home and tell her about life in the outside world. She wants to live it. She wants to bicycle. The world needs women like her. She will become a hero, a legend. Valentine is not someone destined for seclusion. She needs to stride out and now she can. She will leave her imprint on history. The Joan of Arc of her regiment. The Boadicea of her troop. I never met a woman more suited to going to war than Valentine – or a man less suited than you.'

It was a fine speech delivered with all the ringing assurance of Prince Hal leading his men to victory.

'But someone may discover her,' protested Reggie.

'Indeed, they may and then she will come home and everyone will be agog to hear her tales. Why, she could take to the stage and make her fortune.'

Reggie was silenced by this notion. Perhaps she wouldn't be gone long. Perhaps it would be rather jolly for Valentine. Reggie, who did not want to go to war, sat and thought. Near the bench a woman was choosing a book from the lending library. She carried a parasol although neither rain nor sun seemed imminent under the great iron canopy of the station. She sighed, for she was heavily corseted and appeared to find the action of selecting some reading material extremely taxing. Beside her hung a blue poster with gold lettering on which a woman in a smart gold dress appeared to be playing a typewriter as if settling to a fugue on the piano.

'We live in the most astonishing time,' continued Frank. 'Don't let Valentine miss out. She has done something grand for you, now let her get on with it. It's hardly a dangerous mission. It's a bunch of farmers. She'll be back in a month with a grand story to tell. Think, she could teach or work, typing or at the telephone exchange, and have her own rooms.'

Frank paused and then sniffed the air. 'Can you smell that? It's the cooking school opposite the station. Smells good.' He turned to Reggie as a locomotive emblazoned in gold livery shaded in black steamed up noisily at a nearby platform.

'Life is good. This is our chance, Reggie, to have the world leave us alone. Your father is away. Valentine is having the adventure to end them all and we – why we can do as we please.'

'We can't . . . I can't . . . ' muttered Reggie.

Frank began tapping his feet on the floor with barely contained excitement. 'But you can. It's all so splendid,' he said with passion. 'Look at where we are. All life is here and all you have to do is plunge in. We could go anywhere. Take the train and breathe the kind of clean air London can only dream of. We could go to Epping Forest to lie down among the pine cones and inhale their scent. Perhaps we could get a house in some genteel and desirable village – I hear even Croydon has a certain charm. Look at the possibilities. Gipsy Hill sounds divine, or what about Herne Bay? We could live by the sea and every day be made heady by the air. I love the railway. Travelling at speed stirs the soul of all.'

Frank had become like a small boy, giddy with excitement. 'Look, a London-to-Brighton train.'

Reggie put his head in his hands. 'What have I done, Frank?'

Frank stood up and pulled Reggie to his feet. 'You have liberated your cousin and now you must do the same for yourself.'

Frank pulled Reggie with him as he plunged into the thick of the busy station. 'Think of getting lost in that crowd. All that pushing and shoving, finding yourself up against a porter or a clerk newly arrived from his dull home in his dull little town. Feeling the breath with liquor on it in the early morning or the slight cough of the anxious gent who wishes he were more of a man about town. It is thrilling. Curates and schoolmasters or dangerous footpads eyeing your watch. You don't know what you will find getting lost in a great crowd of men.'

Frank dragged Reggie into the throng, calling out, 'Live now! Grab life by the throat.'

Outside the station the sound of a Salvation Army rally could be heard. Through the entrance Reggie could see a man in a peaked cap holding a banner while someone else stood on a wooden box and proclaimed news about God. Frank pulled him forward.

'Waterloo!' cried Reggie suddenly.

'Stop thinking about war,' yelled Frank.

'The trains to Southampton,' shouted Reggie above the hubbub, 'I think they go from Waterloo.'

'Reggie, you cannot go to war,' Frank yelled as he plunged into a fresh crowd of passengers decanting from a train. 'There is too much to live for!'

'Frank, Frank! Wait!' called Reggie after him. 'I have an idea.'

# Ten

By evening we were in Southampton. It had been a day like no other. By six we had been on parade. There was no hairbrushing, no endless preparations for the day. We were simply up and out. How hopeless if Maisie had been with me. There would have been nothing for her to do. I had never been outside in a London street at that time of the morning and despite my body being stiff from the hard floor, the experience gave me new energy. It felt illicit. The night was passing but it was still dark with the street lit only by a fitful moon and I had felt a surge of renewed determination. I looked around and saw a young, lean red-headed fellow staggering, just like me, under the weight of baggage for a year's campaign. A General Inspection followed. I looked beside me: we were very stout, dressed as we were in two suits of clothes to ease our packing. We were young. Perhaps we could manage after all.

General Kelly Kenny had looked us up and down and declared he was 'delighted with the turnout'.

'Passed muster then, Grey!' boomed Jackson with delight, and I was pleased, I who had never thought of passing anything.

Our kitbags were loaded on to cream and green Harrods furniture vans before the march to Nine Elms railway station. Despite the hour, crowds had yet again gathered. Enormous crowds. It should've taken just over an hour to the train but the noise and enthusiasm of the people meant that the march took almost three and a half. Flags waved and women tried to dance with the marching men. We were heroes who had done nothing. It felt wonderful and I was carried along. I was all dressed for my part and had no idea how long the play would last. I don't suppose anyone thought then of the many who would not return. It was not a real war we were going to fight; it was a teatime war that would be over before we knew it. We would make Her Majesty proud. Our entire country would be grateful. We volunteers, none of whom knew much of fighting, would save the day. Of course the truth was that I might as well have been playing soldiers with Maisie. It was all pretend.

It did not take long for my renewed excitement to wane and for serious doubts to wash over me once more. My determination was like the tide, endlessly ebbing and flowing. I don't know what I had thought when I set out. I had not imagined that I would get this far. Perhaps I had half believed that Reggie would come home, realise my plan and come after me, but with each hour I journeyed I began to understand just what I had done. How foolish I had been to embark on such a scheme without really thinking it through. I knew we were by the sea because I could smell it in the air. This was madness. Unless I did something about it very soon I would be leaving Britain.

Trains had brought soldiers from all over the country and now there was an ever larger crowd of us. We were lined up and herded into a vast shed where a breakfast had been provided by an unknown benefactor. Some fellow in a top hat insisted on making a speech that concluded with a gift to each man of an insurance policy of one hundred pounds each.

Jackson stroked his moustache. 'Splendid,' he declared. 'Shan't need it, but a jolly nice gesture. Soap. Britannia soap!' he called out as we were moved forward.

I sat, provided with soap and insured against death, but I could not eat as I listened to the great murmur of men around me. It should have been a familiar sound from my childhood with Bahadur, Papa and his men, yet I was surprised to realise that I had grown accustomed to the light chatter of women. This low hum of men was entirely alien. Perhaps even months of contemplation would not have prepared me for this ... lack of freedom. And I, who had railed against the lack of choices in Aunt Caroline's drawing room, now had even less power to decide. No one was interested in my doubts or views on anything. No one was interested in me at all. I sat where I was told. I was dressed in what they had given me. I ate when they decided it was time. I moved when told to move and when they gave the sign, I, Private Reginald Charles Albert Grey, CIV Cycle Corps, marched in front of one khaki-clad soldier and behind another up the gangway of a troopship bound for Cape Town.

The *Ariosto* was a newish ship, I learned later, built originally for passage between Sweden and Hull. Now she was in war service and equipment filled every space, making her look too small for the hundreds of men attempting to board her.

'A fine-looking vessel,' declared Jackson admiringly. I expect she was, with her black hull and a single red funnel, but I could not think about such things. My expanded step had once more shrunk to fearful lady size but I was not alone. My fellow soldiers' tread too had slowed by the time we crept one by one on board. It was all very well to fight for England but it was something else to leave her behind. I realised that I had become attached to the place, begun to think of her as home.

'Find your mess!' yelled an officer.

'Sorry? What?' I replied, struggling to clutch the handrail and not lose all my kit into the water below.

'This way, Grey!' called Jackson, immediately seeming to know the way as the great mass of men began to divide into groups: a many-headed hydra splitting into the dozens of smaller serpents who filled the ship to repletion.

Jackson, a man of relentless enthusiasm, somehow managed not only to carry all that was required but to hand out business cards as he walked. He disappeared up ahead of me as swathes of men crowded in front of me. No one stood aside to let 'a lady' pass and I was bumped and jostled in a way that had never happened before. A stout, sweaty man with his hat askew pushed ahead of me, his breath heavy with drink.

The swaddling around my breasts was still too tight and my breathing once more felt corseted. No one knew or cared that I was Reggie Grey's cousin who had signed up on a whim because her life was a little dull. I was simply a tiny part of a vast khaki mass that needed to be crammed on board. Now I was not afraid of discovery; I was afraid of never being noticed again. Perhaps, I began to think, this might be the right time to announce the truth. This jolly game had been played out and possibly I should now say that I was Valentine Grey and really I needed to get the train back to London and sit in the ladies' carriage if no one minded very much.

As I waited my turn to descend below, I saw a slight, bespectacled fellow standing on the deck. He was thin and pale with a small fine chin and soft green eyes. I had noticed him before in the hall in London. Despite his neat, almost ginger moustache you could see the boy in the man. His eyes were scouring the dock, searching for something. As he did so he banged the wooden railing with his hand impatiently. He seemed uninterested in 'finding his mess'.

'Go on, you little nancy,' boomed someone behind me. It was the loudest voice I had ever heard come out of a human being. How dare someone speak to me like that! I turned to remonstrate and looked into a sea of faces. It could have been any one of the men all around me. Everywhere voices echoed at this deeper pitch. Everything, every noise, every movement seemed to bang into me with force. Men jostled each other, seemingly unconcerned if they knocked a fellow over in the process. Unable to go against the tide, I grabbed on to the metal railings and began my descent below. It took all my concentration to balance my need to hold on with a desire not to drop either my rifle or my many bags. I realised how little in the last two years I had been required to depend upon my body. I had not been trusted to get in and out of carriages or on and off horses or even, sometimes, to rise from my seat unattended. I was horrified to realise that I had become weak and unsure of myself when I, who had never once fallen when hunting with Papa and Bahadur, nearly slipped and fell.

'Steady,' called the loud voice again. A large hand reached out from below me and pushed me back towards the ladder. It held me in place until I once more had a good grip and could finish my descent.

'Thank you,' I replied, turning to speak to my saviour. It was the Camberwell card sharp from the night before: Sheridan, George Sheridan. He was not a tall man. In fact I was possibly even an inch or two taller, but he was wide and seemed to be made entirely of muscle. If a bulldog were to take human form then I imagined he would fill a uniform exactly as Sheridan did.

I could think of nothing to say except, rather hopelessly, I remembered Reggie's advice about conversation:

'If a lady and a gentleman have not been formally introduced, they should never engage in conversation, except, oh joy, on board ship, where the world, for reasons I cannot fathom, descends into a social abyss. There a "good morning" or "good evening" and a slight but graceful bow will suffice.'

Certain none of that would do, I nodded to my saviour and murmured that I was 'grateful'.

'Think nothing of it, my lad,' he laughed. 'Might as well start the journey in my debt.'

'I'm . . . Reginald,' I murmured.

'Reggie!' he boomed. 'A pleasure, a pleasure for you certainly and possibly one for me. We shall see. George Sheridan.' He reached out to shake my hand, his iron fist gripping mine as if he meant to keep it. I looked down and realised foolishly that I wore no gloves. That we none of us wore gloves. How ridiculous. His flesh touched my flesh, a man I did not know, and it made me shiver.

'Do you play cards, Grey?' he asked, but there was no time to answer for I was not the only one to stumble on the ladder. Just then the bespectacled fellow from the deck tumbled into view having missed the final step of the descent. He was, if possible, a man even less certain of his footing than I was. His glasses flew off under a wooden table.

'Bugger,' he declared as he fell with a thud at Sheridan's feet. I moved to retrieve his spectacles and he almost pushed me away.

'I don't need any help,' he raged as he groped under the table.

Sheridan laughed. 'Excellent. So far our mess is made up of me, a lad who looks twelve and a blind man. The Boer must be pissin' themselves.'

This was, apparently, our 'mess'. Jackson was already putting his things away so we had clearly arrived. Everyone was hanging hammocks and I was considering where to place mine when a boy's head suddenly appeared upside down through the hatch. He hung there like a monkey at the zoo, banging the metal ladder with a tin cup and shouting excitedly, 'She's leaving! We're off!'

Our belongings abandoned, everyone rushed to the deck to say one last farewell to the mother of the Empire, to England. Below us on the dock, mooring ropes were slackened to small cheers and the strains of a single, vaingloriously blown cornet played out bravely, disregarding the torrential rain.

Several gentlemen connected with the regiment came to bid us 'farewell and God speed'. One of them was a colonel who kept telling us that even 'expecting the worst' was an honour, which wasn't exactly heartening. I looked along the railings at all the young men and wondered if they felt honoured or whether they too had felt tremors of panic rushing through their veins. George Sheridan muscled in next to me as we stood listening to the colonel repeating how he 'would like to have gone with us had it been possible'.

'Looks perfectly fit to me,' muttered Sheridan, scratching at the stubble on his chin. 'I can't think why not.' He wandered off, asking if anyone fancied a wager on the exact length of our journey. I found myself stroking my own chin and wondered at its hairlessness for the first time.

A band of Grenadiers on the quay struck up 'Auld Lang Syne', followed by 'God Save the Queen', flags were waved and the crowds began yelling, 'Give it to the Boers'. I don't think there was a single emotion which my body was not subjected to that afternoon. It seemed ridiculous but now I felt so swelled with pride that tears welled up in my eyes. We were going to do something just, we were going to set things right, and in that moment I honestly believed that there was no race of people on earth better suited to do it. I even believed that I would be able to play some part.

I was thinking these patriotic thoughts when there was a cry from below.

'Two secs! Two secs! Just a jiffy.'

The gangway was about to be hoisted away when a soldier bearing our own regimental markings could be seen running towards it carrying all his kit. The wooden bridge was already slightly aloft but he reached up and pulled himself on to it so that it swung back to the boat bearing him with it. There was a great cheer as it banged into the side and he leapt neatly to the deck beside us. Everyone applauded. He took a deep bow and I thought how Reggie would have loved it.

The latecomer stood up with a great grin, clearly pleased with himself, and instantly I knew that we had met before but I could not think where. He was, and I think there is no other expression for it, 'devilishly handsome'. Despite what must have been a strenuous climb aboard his hair remained immaculately parted and the waxed ends of his moustache were still resolutely smart. Where the rest of us wore our uniform as issued from general stores, his appeared to have had the hand of Savile Row upon it, fitting him with an elegance even the colonel had not mastered. He saw me looking and stuck out his hand.

'Thomas Sidney Cooper, barrister, late of the Inner Temple.' I put my hand out and he shook it vigorously. 'Actually not just late of the Temple, pretty much late everywhere. Can't think why they were in such a hurry. I don't suppose the Boer are great time-keepers. Sorry, Private Cooper I should have said, although that will take some getting used to. And you are?'

He looked at me intently.

'I'm Private Grey,' I answered slowly, still unfamiliar with the sound the name made in my mouth.

He slapped me gently on the back with the word 'Excellent' as if he were genuinely pleased. Cooper: he made you smile just to look at him. He had an air of casual confidence which led him to carry his rifle as if he were planning to lean on it rather than shoot with it. As he touched me I realised where we had met. He was the young man who had kissed me in the maze. I was sure he was. I recalled the touch of his moustache on my cheek and the way he had grinned at me. Now he walked along beside me, not knowing me at all.

'Look at all this,' sighed Cooper in admiration as the melee of men crowded the railings, waving and calling out. 'Fifty-three volunteer battalions giving up their men – a true citizen force. Isn't it incredible, Grey? Stay home and mind the chambers! How could anyone even think such a thing? You done much armying before, Grey?' he asked.

'No. Not really.'

'Me neither,' said Cooper. 'Actually, only just made up my mind to join. Last minute sort of thing. Lucky some bugger didn't want to go. Still, what can be the trick to it, eh? We ride, we shoot, we're English, I've a smattering of French, perfect Italian ... that ought to do us. Got to be more fun than Chancery, which is the devil's own work, I assure you.' Cooper smoothed the ends of his moustache with his thumb and forefinger. 'Family seeing you off?' he asked.

'No, they—'

Cooper shook his head. 'Of course not. Nor mine. Just as well. Father would be in a right old to-do about me leaving the firm.'

'Have you not told him?' I asked.

'Oh, he'll notice soon enough. Splendid stuff. Splendid stuff.'

Exactly what stuff was splendid was unclear but in Cooper's presence it really did feel as though all would be well.

The gruff soldier who had lost his glasses appeared on deck now, wearing them. He stood beside me scanning the crowd as if he searched for someone. As we pulled away a number of women stood crying and waving goodbye.

'Is your girl down there?' I asked as he looked and looked.

'No,' he said and turned and said sternly, 'We have work to do. We have come to be soldiers, not shilly-shally about with girls.'

I looked at the women on the dock and thought that perhaps what was truly splendid was to be waving from above and not weeping down below. To be off doing and not just waiting for it to be done. Not to be shilly-shallying about.

Along the railings some poor, terribly thin fellow was making himself even thinner by heaving over the side. The other men were roaring and teasing him about being sick in the harbour. He was unfortunate in having no real chin to speak of, a widow's peak of thin hair, a sharp nose and a weak mouth, below which his face rather seemed to give up and collapse down to his neck.

The monkey boy who had called us to the deck had been larking about. He was a tiny whippet of a fellow, hardly out of short trousers and full of the energy of youth, but for a moment he stopped beside me and clutched the railing. Looking back at the quay, he murmured, 'Do you think we'll be all right?'

Cooper shrugged and put his arm around the lad. 'Who knows?' he said. 'Man proposes, God disposes.'

'Sorry?' I said.

'Ludovico Ariosto. Italian poet. Name of the boat actually – *Ariosto*. Funny name for a boat,' he mused. 'Marvellous poem about the splendid Bradamante – one of the greatest female knights in literature. She fights better than the men and wields a magical lance that unhorses everyone it touches.'

Cooper looked at me and I turned away.

By three o'clock we were heading out to sea, the last notes of 'Soldiers of the Queen' and 'Goodbye Dolly Gray' lingering on deck long after we lost sight of land.

'Thank heavens,' declared Cooper, puffing on his pipe. 'We are rescued from the brink of bathos.'

'Brink of something,' agreed Sheridan, surveying the horizon one last time before nodding with satisfaction and turning away to suggest a further wager to someone.

I lingered on deck for ages and by the time I had got below almost everyone had already packed away their kit and commandeered a place to hang their hammock. I realised John Jackson had not been on deck to say goodbye. He seemed intent on helping everyone stow their bags.

'Did you not want to say goodbye, John?' I asked.

'Only my mother calls me John,' he said softly, before returning to the tasks at hand.

Each mess had a nine-foot table with a single plank on each side for a seat. At the end of the table, hooks had been fixed to the side of the hull. These were for small articles, while above there were larger ones for hammocks.

Had the Primrose League been in charge of the matter, the sleeping arrangements would have been discussed for days. A sub-committee might have been formed with many ladies declaring they 'didn't really mind but it might be best if . . .' Here, however, in my new world of men, no one discussed the arrangements. Everyone just got on with it by themselves and because I didn't get on with anything, all the hooks were taken by the time

I was ready to claim my place. Even the young lad, who went by the name of Haddock, was ahead of me. My only option was to sleep on the table and my one comfort was in knowing that Reggie could never have managed such a thing.

Our mess, who would eat and sleep together, was under the charge of Corporal Chivenden. The corporal gave me some heart, for he seemed to be a genuine soldier who might know something of military life. He stood ramrod straight, barking at us and holding himself aloof from the men in his care. My mess. These were some of the men I would come to know best. It could as easily have been another seven fellows plucked from any walk of life, for the hold was full of men of all sorts and conditions – the sons of dukes slept and drilled shoulder to shoulder, for there was no room in between, with the sons of cooks. For some the newness lay not in their clothes but in the mixing with their superiors and inferiors. It took a while for some to stop giving orders and others to stop taking them.

'Right! Tea!' barked Corporal Chivenden.

'Capital,' declared Cooper, whose father was a belted earl. He sat and began refilling his pipe.

Chivenden eyed him in silence until Cooper at last looked up. No one had moved.

'Two sugars,' said Cooper. The silence continued until he said, 'Ah. Different plan to the one I had in mind, is there?'

It soon became clear that the accents with which we spoke might be varied but our dress and duties were the same.

Any thoughts anyone might have had about finding a scrap of privacy or comfort on board were soon as distant as our last glimpse of the Lizard lights. There was nowhere to sit but on the plank seat where four of us squeezed next to each other. The first night we sat at the rough table saying little.

Chivenden gave a small talk.

'Right, this is it. Take a look around. This is your mess. This is the group you will have to learn to depend on. I suggest you get on with it.'

The glorious Thomas Cooper, from the Inner Temple, barrister; George Sheridan from Camberwell, comedian, juggler and card sharp who worked the halls and somehow managed to make the war pay; John Jackson, Lancashire soap and candle manufacturer, so full of life and determination; the boy, Billy Tudor Haddock, too young to be anything at all and whom we might as well have killed ourselves; the fellow with the ginger moustache and glasses was Benjamin White, of Westminster, a painter, according to the list; myself, apparently the son of Lord Grey; and finally, there was Pattenden. Michael Pattenden, the thin, balding man of middle years who had caused such merriment by being sick before we had even reached the sea. A gentleman's valet, but no gentleman himself. A man I would come to hate more than the Boer.

We, who in truth had nothing in common, now united. I sat with them and no one looked at me askance. I thought for a fleeting second that perhaps I could manage this great performance, this mimicry of a man and then I realised with horror that I had not been excused since the morning. I needed to go to the lavatory.

I found a 'monkey closet', as Cooper called it – a cubicle in which to do the necessary – and, much relieved, I returned to go to bed. At first I had bemoaned my failure to secure a hook for sleeping but that first night I saw that I had perhaps not done so badly. What hammocks there were had been slung so close together that the occupants overlapped. As they lay in their scooped beds, the men's resting places swung in ordered ranks from side to side with the roll of the ship. Pattenden, as the outer man, might have thought he had gained some triumphant space but with each alternate movement his whippet-like body was squeezed tightly against the framework of the vessel, while the great mass of John Jackson, on the inside, hung perilously over the open hatchway leading down to the hold and the sergeants' mess.

I lay on my back with the men swinging inches from my face, feeling the wooden boards of the table along the length of my body. Questions crowded into my mind. Was Reggie, even now, coming after me? Would there soon be word to the ship's captain to remove me from this place? This strange place: a pungent mix of oil and coal from the boat blended with stale tobacco smoke, the whiff of damp socks and unwashed bodies, male bodies pressing menacingly close. Even in their sleep the men made deep, rumbling noises. I wondered how I might ever keep my true self disguised.

I quickly learned, however, that men take life more easily and straightforwardly than women. The truth is – no one thought to question me and so I went unquestioned.

Our gear was simple. There was one large tub, a bucket, a large tin dish, a tin can for soup, meat and beer and an earthen jar for drinking water between us. In addition each man had a knife, fork and spoon, tin plate and pannikin. Each day two of us would be chosen by Chivenden to fetch, serve, wash, clean and tidy for the mess as well as fetch the joint from the stove and the bread or biscuits from the bakery. The bread quickly ran out but the hard biscuits were decent. Jackson, who could never get enough food, was thrilled that we were to get jam three times a week.

'Three times a week,' he beamed, 'for nothing! This is the life! Old Tommy Atkins has to buy his at the dry canteen.'

I knew so little that I thought Tommy Atkins must be some poor mug in another mess rather than the general name for any common soldier in the army. I soon understood how they looked down upon us as volunteers and how we in turn sought to be a cut above, even if only with rations of jam. We were all heading to fight the Boer. We had a common enemy but first the men seemed to need to divide into smaller loyalties. There was only a foot of space between each mess yet it might as well have been the Rubicon, for no one crossed from their side to another. The closest one to us, No. 8, George Sheridan quickly nicknamed the Girls' School as they seemed unable to agree on anything without much squabbling. It did not take long for us to feel most superior to our neighbours.

Our little group seemed to find a way of working from the beginning. Young Billy Haddock was not the brightest but he knew he was the runt of the group and, wishing he were more of a man, showed willing at everything. His hairless and boyish face by comparison helped make me seem positively manly. As for the rest: George Sheridan, although not an unkind fellow, saw to himself first whenever possible. Pattenden, it turned out, had been a gentleman's valet to Lord Briggs. When his lordship had volunteered so too had Pattenden, thinking not so much of service to his country as of ingratiating himself with his master. Sadly, the authorities had thought otherwise and now Pattenden found himself shipped off to war while his lordship remained behind, presumably unpressed and unserviced, sorting telegrams in Whitehall. Pattenden had been in service all his life and at first seemed bereft and unable to function, but he and Thomas Cooper quickly found mutual comfort in the one being allowed to perform the odd service and the other being served. Thus my dear friend Cooper became one of the few privates to have his own batman. Ben White? He kept to himself and I hardly spoke to him.

Once we had settled to our chores and grown used to the newness of it all, I would dare to say there were those who found the voyage out almost monotonous. On the whole, it was much the same every day. We had physical drill or, rather, tried to tie ourselves in knots as the ship rolled and we rolled with it. The games were childish – leapfrog, skipping and other silly sports. I never tired of it, for I was rediscovering my body. In Assam I had been allowed to run and jump and fall in a heap as I pleased; now I was free again to trust my own limbs. I loved the feeling of pushing my legs to run faster, jump higher, and I began to get a reputation for being rather good at our shipboard games. Although, as Cooper pointed out, unless we were planning to jump over the Boers or skip beside them, they probably weren't a lot of use.

'What did you come to war for?' asked Sheridan.

'Why, for the girls. Isn't that why we're all here, eh, Grey? We heard there would be girls.' Cooper punched me on the arm and everyone laughed.

'You got a girl at home, Grey?' asked Pattenden, looking at me with an intensity that left me a little uneasy.

'Yeah, he left her there with his beard,' jeered Sheridan. Sheridan did not have a moustache or beard himself but a slight stubble that looked as though no razor could quite keep it at bay. 'What are you – a brown or a white meat man? Leg or breast?'

Everyone looked at me and I don't know what I was thinking but I blurted out, 'I have a girl. I have a photograph of my girl.'

The men gathered round as I produced from my pocket the photograph of myself with Frank and Reggie.

Cooper gave a low whistle. 'She's a looker all right. You'll have to introduce me when we return.'

I blushed and put the picture away, announcing boldly, 'I'm not worried about girls at home. I hear if a Dutch girl gets a chance at an Englishman, old or young, poor or rich, she doesn't wait to be asked a second time.'

The others laughed and I soon saw that laughter was the key. I ducked down and Cooper jumped over me and the leapfrog game stopped the chat. My best response to everything was to become brazen, and with each passing day I was less and less the woman I had been trained to be.

The sea stretched out interminably before us and I think we half forgot why we were headed south. The only nod to our real job ahead was that the doctor gave a lecture on field dressings and occasionally we had a little practice in shooting at a barrel swung from the bow of the ship.

Jackson picked up his gun as if it weighed nothing. He put the rifle to his shoulder and aimed at the barrel.

'This will only be useful,' he hissed, missing for the umpteenth time, 'if the ruddy Boers are hanging about made of wood.'

'Yeah, and we head towards them on the ran-tan,' added Sheridan.

'On the what?' I asked.

'Ran-tan. You know, "corned", drunk, off our heads. What's the matter with you? Just because you don't have a beard yet doesn't mean you haven't had a drink, does it, you little toffer?'

'Get on with the rifle practice, you lazy bastards,' called Corporal Chivenden.

The heavy Lee-Enfield rifle kicked back into my shoulder with a force that made me think of the cart hitting Aunt Caroline. Did it hurt? Did she feel the pain? I tried to steady the gun. I did not remember Papa's guns weighing this much. It took all my strength to hold the thing level.

'You all right, Grey?' sneered Pattenden. 'Too heavy for you? Think you could actually hit anything with that gun?'

'This? I don't need a gun. I could kill with my bare hands,' I swaggered.

The men stopped and looked at me.

'How would you do that?' asked Haddock, wide-eyed.

I had no idea why I had said what I did. It was a piece of foolishness. 'Why, I'd crush their thorax.'

Cooper agreed. 'That would certainly do it.'

Having settled the point, I then calmly turned and, without taking much aim and by a complete fluke, hit the barrel clean in the middle.

There was an appreciative silence, broken when young Haddock, who didn't always follow a conversation but who clearly remembered someone had mentioned drink, suddenly piped up with, 'I bet I can drink more than anyone.'

Poor Haddock. While I looked like an adolescent boy, he actually was one. He had the sweetest face. Bright eyes, a little light blond fluff on his top lip, and skin that looked fresh from a mother's care. He confessed early on to being just fifteen years old, but he did so with great bravado.

'They never spotted me. Thought I was easily of age,' he boasted, his young face barely filled with enough potential to see he might one day make a fine man.

'Sergeant never even gave me a second look,' he added.

For George Sheridan, Haddock's boast was an immediate invitation to a wager. Sheridan bet on anything. In his leisure hours he was able to turn whatever part of the *Ariosto* he found himself in into a floating Monte Carlo. Everywhere you went during the day you could hear his voice calling out, 'Fifteen, twenty-four, thirty-one, sixty-one, top of the house,' or, 'Two to one on the lucky seven. Any more, gentlemen?' Then at night he did his rounds: 'Collecting debts, laying bets, gentlemen.' It was Sheridan who decided to bet Haddock's staying power against mine.

'The two young lads, Haddock and Grey, drinking competition,' he announced without once checking to see if Haddock or I deemed it a good idea. Haddock looked uncertain and Ben White shook his head. Ben was a man who did not like games.

'Winner gets half a crown,' added Sheridan to clinch the deal.

'Hilarious,' said Jackson, slapping me on the back and nearly sending me flying.

Pattenden scoffed at me. 'He'll barely manage half a pint, the shivering Jemmy.'

Each mess was issued half a pint of beer per man with the evening meal. Sheridan, already holding many debts from across the boat, quickly rounded up a tub full of the stuff. Hammocks were usually slung about seven so that night to keep out of Chivenden's gaze, everyone proceeded to make a show of their night-time preparations. I sat hunched in a corner feeling sick. I had never had alcohol of any kind and had no idea what to expect, but I was sure it wasn't going to be good. A great crowd had gathered. Men seemed to be everywhere – hanging from the hooks, swinging in the hammocks, sitting on the floor, the tables, any space where a man might squeeze himself.

'Final bets!' called Sheridan. 'Make your final bets.'

'I'll have an alderman on it,' came the cry as the last bits of money changed hands.

Cooper had decided to act as my second and was rubbing my shoulders as if that somehow might prepare me to take on more drink. How odd that no man had ever touched me and now I sat among many with casual hands upon me. Haddock looked so anxious I had half a mind to just fall to the floor and let him have the victory, but I did not. Perhaps I was beginning to be man enough to want to win this foolish battle.

We began quite slowly, sipping. I had thought the first taste might make me retch but I was surprised. I'd never had so much as a sherry before but I liked this. I liked it a lot and easily downed the first cup. Egged on by the men, Haddock and I soon began chucking whole tin cups of quite flat beer down our throats.

As I drank, I realised that my nerves were disappearing. A pleasant sensation like honey was pouring through my veins. I didn't really care about anything.

'One! Two! Three!' called the crowd as the tally mounted but I didn't mind the noise.

I think Haddock slowed down first. His eyes looked bright and he took to muttering 'I am a man' as he alternated gulps of air with the drink. Jackson stood guard over the boy and tried to help him. Before long, we were both clutching the table with one hand and drinking slowly, as we stared glassy-eyed at each other. I don't know how many cups we drank. I know that I slipped to my knees at one point, only to have Sheridan raise me swiftly with his foot. He had big money on the matter and didn't want it over too soon. I didn't mind. I didn't mind anything and it was marvellous.

'Steady, Grey. Mind over matter. You can do it,' said Cooper and I heard the echo of Papa.

At last Haddock stopped drinking entirely and just stood swaying. At least I think he swayed. The whole room swayed and the lights seemed more beautiful than Rosherville Gardens. I was tired and wanted to lie down, lie down on my table.

'Just one more half, Grey,' Cooper whispered in my ear, 'and the victory is yours.'

Victory? What was that? What victory?

Those who had bet on Haddock were trying to get him to be sick so that he might start again, but Cooper was quick. He pulled a half-pint from the tub with his own cup and passed it to me.

'Grey! Grey! Grey!' chanted the men, banging the hull, the floor and any other surface that might let them beat out their enthusiasm. The beer foamed slightly as it came towards my lips and I suspect as much fell down my front as down my throat, but down it went. I stood blinking as Haddock fell to the floor, out cold. I looked at him for one brief moment and promptly fell on top of him.

Someone placed both of us, like fallen Greek soldiers laid upon a shield, side by side, upon the table. I woke in the night to find Haddock weeping, and without thinking, I put my arm around his shoulders and pulled him close. He was no more a man than I was.

'I ain't half going to fetch it from my mum when she finds out I've been drinking,' he wept.

'Does she even know you've gone to war?' I whispered.

'No,' he sobbed. 'I mean, probably now she does.'

I stroked his hair. 'She may have other things she wants a word about before the drinking.'

In the morning I felt sicker than I had ever known possible. Every roll of the boat seemed to move in the very opposite direction to my brain but I was victorious. It was a ridiculous triumph and yet I was so very pleased. The change in me had begun.

'Well done, Grey! Good man!' fellows I didn't even know called out. Even Pattenden said, 'Didn't think you had it in you, you little macer.'

I had swallowed more alcohol than a boy, and somehow that made me a man.

The only person from whom I could feel disapproval was Ben. We brushed against each other as we fetched the day's meat together.

'So you are conscious now, are you?' he enquired.

'It was just a bit of fun.'

Ben suddenly turned and held me by the shoulders. I thought for a moment he was going to shake me. 'It wasn't fun. It was pathetic. You shouldn't ...' He stopped speaking and turned away with a look of disgust.

Feeling unwell, I headed for fresh air on the deck. Cooper stood puffing on his pipe and contemplating the horizon. He smiled as I approached.

'Ah, the fallen warrior is arisen.'

We stood in silence looking out to sea.

'Ben thinks I'm pathetic.'

Cooper nodded. 'Ben seems a less than joyful fellow. He's an artist, isn't he? A painter? We must unlock his good nature.' He turned to look at me. 'We have quite an odyssey ahead, Grey, so a little light relief may be essential. Do you like Homer?'

I shrugged. I did not think he had ever come up in conversation before.

'I thought it was fun and now I feel foolish,' I muttered.

Cooper began to quote.

'*I'll tell you a secret ... The Gods envy us. They envy us because we're mortal, because any moment might be our last. Everything is more beautiful because we're doomed. You will never be lovelier than you are now. We will never be here again.*'

# Eleven

Everything about Frank's rooms, as he himself explained, was intended to 'excite the nerves and dazzle the senses'. Frank seemed to be a man in little need of sleep. Reggie often woke to find the small world that he and Frank inhabited was illuminated by the electric lamp that stood on a table beside the bed. He could not get used to the glare. Lord Grey had not allowed electricity in Inkerman House and Reggie felt exposed by the brightness of the new lamps.

When he turned out the lights, so as to be lit only by the flames of the fire, Frank would tease him.

*'Men of Science, you must aid and tell us, if you please,*
*How we shall make our charms withstand such glaring lights as these,*
*For if the Ladies find these lamps still turn them pale and wan,*
*They'll lead a feminine Crusade 'gainst EDISON and SWAN!'*

Reggie lay with his back to the light and his body cast shadows upon the curtains that shut out the world around the four-poster. He liked them. Diana, the huntress, ran across the folds through a sacred grove of oak trees in pursuit of some hapless creature. Tall and slim with her hair pulled back from her forehead, she wore a short tunic so that she might run with ease. Her hand gripped a large bow and across her back was strapped a quiver full of arrows. A deer ran by her side, which was odd for it seemed just the sort of creature she might be hunting.

'She was a goddess to everyone, you know.' Frank's voice drifted across his shoulder. 'Not just the Romans.'

Reggie turned and smiled.

'Did they keep some gods just for themselves then?' he asked.

Frank nodded. 'Oh yes, there were quite a few gods who really only dealt with the upper classes.'

'And how do you know that?' he asked.

'I know everything,' intoned Frank sagely. 'I have a book.'

He held up the volume he was reading.

Reggie read the title out loud. '*Enquire Within Upon Everything*.'

'Indeed,' replied Frank, assuming the voice and manner of a man about to astound the world from the stage. 'Ladies and gentlemen, for your delectation, Mr Frank Rutherford will now amaze and delight by answering any question whatsoever posed to him by a member of the audience not known to him previously.' He pretended to point out into the darkness. 'You, madam, yes, you. Have you an enquiry for Mr Rutherford?'

Frank shoved the book at Reggie and whispered, 'Go on, ask me anything.'

Reggie laughed and tried to push the book away. 'I'm not awake yet.'

But it was clear that Frank wanted to play the game. 'Please,' he implored.

'All right, all right.' Reggie pulled himself up so that he rested against the pillows and opened the book to a random page.

'What are ... *Dr Kitchener's rules for marketing*?' Reggie looked up bewildered. 'Surely that can't be the same Kitchener who has gone to war?'

Frank shook his head. 'I shouldn't think so at all. This one is all stale fish and tough mutton. I shouldn't have thought that soldier chap has time for all that. No, this Kitchener will tell you how to toddle home in triumph after dealing with tradespeople and his principal advice is to pay ready money for everything and only deal with respectable people.'

Reggie read the passage in question and laughed. 'So it is. My goodness, Mr Rutherford, how very impressive.'

Frank clapped his hands with pleasure. He pointed once more into his imaginary audience and called out, 'Yes, you, sir, in that shocking jacket, what is your question for Mr Rutherford?'

Reggie closed his eyes and the book simultaneously, then rather dramatically opened both at the same time. The book fell open at a section on health.

'How, Mr Rutherford, might one remove freckles?' Reggie looked again. 'How might one remove freckles? Oh, for goodness' sake.' He was about to search for another entry but Frank placed his hand on the book, pretending to be in a great trance of recollection.

'You will require half an ounce of lemon juice, one ounce of Venice soap and a quarter of an ounce each of oil of bitter almonds and ... no, don't tell me ... *deliquated* oil of tartar. Apparently this filthy mixture when placed in the sun will take on the consistency of an ointment which, heaven help us, you rub into the affected area after washing it in elderflower water. I can't say I shouldn't prefer to be blemished with freckles.'

Frank smiled and turned on his side to look at Reggie naked beside him. He reached out and gently kissed his lover's shoulder.

Reggie continued to flick through the book. 'Why do you bother to learn all this? You sound like my mother. You can't possibly care about all this nonsense.'

Frank kissed him again. 'You have freckles. On your shoulder.'

'Do I?' replied Reggie, not looking up.

Frank stroked Reggie's arm as he looked intently at his few tiny blemishes. 'I wouldn't change them for all the world.'

'Have you ever thought to marry, Frank?' asked Reggie, suddenly.

A great guffaw exploded from Frank. 'Marry? Me? Why on earth would I do that?'

Reggie shrugged. 'I don't know. Because one is supposed to. Because it is expected.'

'I think it would be dreadful.' Frank seized the book and began to riffle through the pages until he found what he was looking for. 'Listen to this. *The wife who will establish the rule of allowing her husband to have the last word, will achieve for herself and her sex a great moral victory*!'

Frank threw the book down upon the bed. 'Can you imagine such a life? Some simpering woman spending all her time never having a view of her own and letting you think whatever you like?' He pulled Reggie to him. 'We shall not marry, you and I. We shall stay here. In this bed. This will be our world and no one will trouble us.'

Now that Reggie had abandoned the idea of living anywhere else, he began to feel more at home. He liked the little drawing room, but he preferred to retire to the bed so that they might draw the curtains and lie in the half-darkness, dreaming of the life they might share. They talked of a country idyll, though neither had any notion what one might 'do' amid nature.

'Perhaps we might have a stream to bathe in,' sighed Frank. 'I should like to see you in a stream with the water rushing past your waist.'

Frank had never been happier and he did everything possible to ensure that Reggie felt the same. In the daytime, when they lay together and talked, everything was wonderful, but come the evening Frank would have to get up and go to the theatre and Reggie would sit alone in the flat. These were not good hours for him. Often he would lie on the bed and it would not take him long to begin berating himself for his weakness. He should have gone to war; he should not have let Valentine go. Even his 'great idea' to protect her was no doubt doomed to failure. He tried to picture her among her fellow soldiers but Reggie had so little experience of such a life that he could not even imagine it.

On many occasions, Frank would return to find Reggie lying down, staring at the curtains. The sight of Frank's cheery face always pulled Reggie up from his melancholy, and before long laughter would once more echo about the flat. It was hard to be gloomy in Frank's company. For him, all the world truly was a stage. Some evenings he would read out loud from the *Arabian Nights*, while seated on a cushion in front of the fire in the cosy drawing room, wearing nothing but a turban and a silly accent. Frank had many books, including a beautiful leather-bound volume on the Renaissance, which Reggie loved, and a book of *Illustrations of Homer and Theocritus* that Reggie could hardly believe.

'Where did you get this?' he exclaimed as Frank sat beside him, turning the pages.

'It's quite the talk of the town,' enthused Frank.

The illustrations were photographs by a German gentleman called Baron Wilhelm von Gloeden. It seemed that in the last twenty years he had been pioneering open-air photography in quite a unique manner. He specialised in photographs of naked boys in bucolic settings, many of them local farm lads and fishermen on the island of Sicily. Frank was particularly taken with one composition entitled 'Two Seated Sicilian Youths'. Two young men sat upon some foreign hillside looking insolently at the camera. Behind them the sweeping vista of a Sicilian bay curved away into the distance. One of the lads wore a sheet as a loose toga to reveal his smooth, hairless breast, while his companion was entirely naked with merely a headband holding his tousled brown locks in place and his left knee coyly bent to preserve his modesty.

'How can they publish such things?' marvelled Reggie.

Frank looked at him sternly. 'I don't know what you are suggesting,' he said. 'These are, and I quote, "ethnographic studies of young natives of the island of Sicily" and who but the most filthy-minded might find cause to quibble with that?'

On other evenings they would lie in each other's arms on the floor before the fire. Here they would talk of beauty and passion and how they might devote their lives to seeking them out.

'Must be dull having relations with a woman,' Frank whispered, his lips brushing Reggie's. 'Always in the dark of the bedroom.'

'Is that the only place they do it?' murmured Reggie, entirely content.

'If you're lucky.' Frank sighed. 'It must be dreadful never to have pleasure just for itself but instead forever to be lying back and thinking of England. Our lives are so much more exciting.

They say there is even a brothel near the Regent's Park Barracks on Albany Street where a soldier may be had for ready money.'

Reggie sat up, agitated. 'Would you go to such a place? Don't go to such a place.'

Frank pulled him gently back down. 'Ssh, why would I go anywhere when I have you here at home with me?'

Reggie lay for a moment looking at Frank's beautiful profile. Then he pulled himself up and put his arms around his lover's back. He rested his head on Frank's shoulder and sighed. How much he loved the smell of Frank. It had never occurred to him before that a man might smell so wonderful. He took a deep breath and they sat for some time until Reggie said quietly, 'Sometimes I envy Valentine, out there exploring.'

Valentine was always present in the rooms, as if she lived there. Frank kissed Reggie's hand and then stood up to pull him to the bed.

'We could explore somewhere dangerous,' he suggested, his voice rising with infectious excitement. 'Yes, why not? We don't have to stay here. Why, we could go to the East End and find a Jew who will have us to dinner where we shall eat heaven knows what.'

He pushed Reggie back on the pillows and smiled at him.

# Twelve

I was getting away with it. Perhaps all I had to do was swagger a little and drink a lot and I was a man. If not a man exactly then at the very least I was Bradamante, the fearless female knight of Ariosto. I could do anything I wanted, it seemed, and once I realised I just had to fall in and follow orders, I could do that as well as the next fellow.

In the pecking order of our mess Haddock was now at the bottom of the pile but instead of abusing this, the men surprised me by treating him kindly. I suspect that while they now saw the man in me, they had also seen the boy in him and it brought out the best in them. We were all young, probably only a few years older than Haddock. I was glad to find that the men had protective instincts. It brought out finer feelings in everyone except Pattenden, who had no such feelings at all.

My youthfulness still evoked teasing but even that seemed less aggressive, and so the first days passed. Gradually I lost my fear of being found out and started to relax a bit. I think I must have looked odd walking for I started to take pleasure in much longer strides. I loved leaning back in my chair or putting my hands in my pockets. What a thing to be denied to women! Pockets! I noticed that Cooper always sat with his legs wide apart and I tried to copy this, but he looked at me strangely, and I drew my knees closer together. Perhaps that would come. Other things I adopted with no trouble. I knew to 'show a leg' at morning reveille and to pronounce coffee 'corfy' and to have it thick and sweet for breakfast with bully beef and biscuit. I learned to play nap and whist and to shrug off losing two shillings every time Sheridan had a hand. They were just games but I could see these were ways in which we were getting to know each other – and, not least, seeing who could be trusted to play a fair hand and who needed to be watched.

We sighted the Portuguese island of Madeira and I remembered how often I had seen the drink passed round at table and never once thought of the place from which it took its name. The world was full of places whose names I knew and which I had never thought I might journey to. I clutched the ship's rail and trembled with excitement to think how far I had come from the railings of my uncle's house. How I no longer had to look at the world through plate-glass windows but could almost taste the scent of the sweet foreign grasses blowing in on the sea air. The ship was never without noise and it made me realise how much of my recent years had passed in near silence. Each British vessel we passed received raucous cheers. The *Kildonan Castle* steamed past, and another day we spotted the great Anchor liner the *City of Rome* in full majestic sail, though neither brought us news. Would the war be over before we could do our bit?

We moored at St Vincent Harbour to take on coal but none of us was allowed ashore. Our failure to leave the boat, however, did not deter the local populace. Within half an hour the *Ariosto* was surrounded by swarms of small boats hanging on our port side, manned by natives who slung baskets up on deck and did a roaring trade in oranges, tobacco and bananas. The weather was moist and warm and the air loud with shouts and laughter.

'Smells like Covent Garden,' yelled Cooper, catching an orange thrown up to him from below. He threw it straight to Ben, calling, 'Don't you think it's beautiful? The colour?'

For a moment Ben couldn't help himself. He smiled but then he quickly recovered, put the fruit down and walked away. Cooper looked at me and raised his eyebrows.

We pressed to the deck sides, cheering as the local men dived for coins. Their bodies were sleek and their dark skin glistened, just like men in the heat of Assam where they'd worn little but a loincloth. I think I was too young to see how handsome they were.

Pattenden did not think them lovely. 'Bloody hell!' he shouted as he tried to beat them from the deck with a stick. Cooper and Jackson grasped him none too gently, removed the stick and threw it into the sea. Would that they had thrown the man instead. I stood by doing nothing and instantly felt like a helpless girl again. An island fellow climbed halfway up to the deck and offered me a bottle of local rum. I bought it using some of my winnings from Sheridan and slipped it quietly into my pocket. This will make me a man, I thought.

Once away from St Vincent we began to settle down again, with some of us trying to learn Dutch from 'the red book'. Cooper had no patience for it.

'It's been written by some pompous old pedant,' he complained. 'The pronunciation is maddening and the explanations are worse.'

Ben too was uninterested. 'I thought the plan was to stop the place being Dutch, not chat about it,' he declared. The hint of good humour elicited by the orange had quickly faded.

But I quite liked the feel of another language in my mouth and was happy to spend my hours learning to say *landbouwbedrijf* for farm and *koe* for cow. That anyone might trust me to learn another language at all seemed remarkable.

When not called upon for some task I revelled in being allowed to sit alone, cross-legged, in my sea togs – khaki drill and fisherman's cap – on a coil of rope on the spar deck, reading or simply staring out to sea. As we steamed south into the broad Atlantic, the sun shone bright but not too warm from a blue sky scattered with fleecy clouds. The topmost peak of Tenerife winked at us over a deep blue sea with white crests blown by what Jackson told me was 'a crisp nor'easter'.

My introduction to alcohol had given me a taste for it and I would sit sipping at my secret supply of rum, letting the rough liquid soothe any troubles that still rose in my chest. Soon calm would descend and I would look out to sea, marvelling at the size of my horizon. Occasionally I spied flying fish and sharks in the distance and I knew that, no matter how high she might climb in her Primrose League, no woman could ever know such freedom. I breathed deeply, unencumbered.

One night I was sitting as far aft as possible to watch the moonlit wake that followed us, when Ben unexpectedly came over. He sat down without speaking, stretching out his long legs in front of him, pretending to look at the sea, but each time I turned my head I could tell he'd been staring at me. Then suddenly, he reached out and picked up my left hand. He held it in front of his face, turning it back and forth until I pulled it away. It didn't do to be examined too closely and I decided that brooding, moody Ben was, like Pattenden, to be avoided.

Sheridan, however, was my easy, bluff gambling friend. A pound of tobacco was served out as a present from the ship's owners to each man and, as Sheridan said, it seemed a shame to let it go to waste. He taught me to smoke, laughing as I coughed and coughed through the first attempts. I persevered, never wanting to fail at something new – besides which, I liked the feeling each successful puff provided as a warmth spread through my limbs and body. With Sheridan's laughter and encouragement from the hammock above, I also learned to hold my nerve when the rats ran across my feet at night. Soon I was so accustomed to sleeping fully clothed that I forgot it was usual to undress before bed.

And then one day I swung down into our mess and saw Jackson, Cooper and Pattenden standing there completely naked. I had never seen such a thing. In our uniforms we all blended together but now it was very clear that not all men were equal. Jackson was covered in the most astonishing amount of hair, while Pattenden was pale and stood with his hands on his thin hips like a feeble sugar bowl. Cooper was rather strategically holding a book but the others stood as bold as if they were clothed. Jackson lifted his leg up on to the bench seat and put his hand on his knee.

'Ah, Grey,' he declared, as if I were simply late for tea.

I couldn't speak. I felt colour rush to my cheeks. I could neither look away nor stop looking. There was no doubt that in some instances I would never pass for a man.

I blushed and stumbled and Pattenden looked at me strangely.

'Birthday suit L4N,' he announced.

'L4N?'

'Looking for nits, you idiot boy,' he jeered. 'The mess are to report for bathing parade.'

'Naked?' I asked foolishly.

'No,' mocked Pattenden, 'in ball gowns.'

The game was up. I felt sick and could feel my face getting hotter. I started to pull back, putting my hand over my mouth. I wanted it all to stop right now.

'Look, chaps,' I managed to squeak out.

'Grey! Colonel wants you.' Ben, blessedly fully clothed, suddenly appeared.

So now the colonel wanted me . . . I turned quickly and left the mess. My heart pounded. Up until now I had successfully hidden all my personal needs in my small cupboard but this 'parade' could not be done in that private space. Perhaps the colonel already knew and wished to spare my blushes. Would he expose me in front of the men or be more kind? Could they not simply set me off at Cape Verde to catch a boat heading the other way? What was the punishment for my strange and inexplicable crime? I wondered if Reggie would be made to go after all. My mind raced, muddling, stumbling over things. The uniform was still good, a little grubby but I had hardly worn it. Perhaps Jackson could deal with the stains. With each step towards the colonel I realised how much I wanted to stay. I felt infuriating girlish tears rising up and my throat closing, but I swallowed and tried to gulp down my fear.

On deck, a big man sitting in a chair had his sleeve rolled up over a fleshy arm. He was grimacing as he received an injection. This was Colonel Mackinnon. I had never spoken to him but had seen him on deck. Corporal Chivenden stood beside him, overseeing the medical orderly.

'Grey!' Corporal Chivenden barked as I saluted with a trembling hand for what I was sure was the final time.

'Yes, sir.'

Chivenden checked a list. 'Ah, yes, you are in distinguished company. Colonel Mackinnon, the orderly officers and ninety men including yourself will be the first to receive an injection for enteric. Nasty business, enteric – attacks your stomach.'

I nodded, trying to fight back tears, now of relief.

'You don't have to have it,' counselled the Colonel kindly, seeing my face, 'but if you do, you will need to be confined to bunks for the day.'

It was still my secret. No one knew. I simply nodded and rolled up my own sleeve. The orderly gave a stab with a syringe followed by a dose of some hot, obnoxious fluid and I retreated back to the mess, where mercifully everyone was once again clothed. Cooper let me have his hammock and I lay down, sweating with relief. Over the next few hours, my right arm swelled and ached so that I could hardly move. For an hour or so I had a splitting headache which was followed by a horrible feverish night during which I wished men in general and my cousin Reggie in particular at the bottom of the sea. The injections were given in batches until the entire company had been dealt with. Some recovered quickly but others were not so fortunate. By the next morning half the company were sick. Grown men turned into small boys, shivering as sickness swept over them. I was lucky and had nothing but a sore arm.

The rolling sea prevented the portholes from being opened and the stench around the mess was shocking, for those affected found they could not even keep down the plainest cup of broth. Those who were not so sick tried to help by offering some soda water or straightening a hammock. Well schooled by Bahadur in the comforts of cleanliness, I went to look for some cleaning things and in a tall cupboard beside the sergeants' mess found what I was looking for. I also found Jackson.

'What are you doing, Jackson?'

The large fellow was shivering, and clearly not from fever. His round face, creased with anxiety, was partly hidden as he attempted to tuck his huge frame behind an old mop. His feet had clashed with a tin bucket as he pressed his knees towards the back of the cupboard. He looked ridiculous.

'I can't do it. I can't do it,' he kept repeating.

He was beside himself. I put my hand out and touched his arm. 'It's all right. I don't suppose anyone really wants to fight.'

'Not that,' he hissed. 'Do you think I give a damn about the fighting? It's the injections. I can't do the injections.'

Jackson, a man so full of life he could barely fit in his uniform, was frightened. Frightened of a man with a needle.

'It's over before you know it,' I said. 'Look at me, I'm fine.'

But he could not do it. Every man has his place of fear.

'I don't need it,' he kept repeating. 'I have soap. Soap. Cleanliness is next to godliness. Do they not know that?'

I hid Jackson from the orderlies and that cupboard later did duty for me too. From it I got a bottle of carbolic disinfectant and some soda, mops and brushes. Jackson gave me soap. I became the efficient nurse of our mess.

I grew quite bossy, sending sick men to crawl on deck into the cheerless mist and rain while I cleaned floors, emptied the sundry buckets and scoured out the lavatories. Everyone was so wretched that their gratitude for my service further solidified my place below decks. They lay looking pathetic as I cajoled them into drinking some light broth or wiped their brows with a damp cloth. It was only Pattenden who made me uncomfortable. He seemed clammier than the rest, as if something truly nasty were seeping out of him. I took him a tin cup of water and put my hand under his head to raise him up a little. He stared at me as he sipped. I turned to go as he lay down again but he grabbed my wrist. He was surprisingly strong for someone so unwell.

'You have very soft hands,' he said. I didn't know what to say. After a moment he closed his eyes and I didn't bring him water after that.

And in my cupboard I quietly cleaned myself as my monthly visitor had arrived and I needed rags.

Jackson's fears seemed justified when one poor chap in another mess did not survive. Chivenden said he had died of pneumonia but everyone blamed the inoculations. He had been one of the oldest on board. None of our mess knew him and the first we learned of his death was when we were called up on deck on parade. As his body was brought forward wrapped in a shroud, the engines were stopped. They had throbbed and hummed so incessantly since we had left port that the sound of an entirely still vessel was unnerving. I thought for a moment I had gone deaf but then the ship's bell tolled and a volley from the firing party made some of us jump. As the last post on the bugle sounded, the body was committed to the deep with a splash, a prayer and a murmur from Jackson: 'I told you it wasn't safe.'

It was our first taste of death. Perhaps it encouraged our celebration of life, for there was a big party when we crossed the line of the Equator, with fireworks and rockets and all the men cheering. The sailors had an odd way of celebrating. Several of them dressed up in sacks and blackened their faces, and one great strapping man played Father Neptune. They chased and caught those of their crew who had never crossed the Equator before and held them on a chair, smothering their heads in a black, greasy fluid with a whitewash brush. Then they ducked them in water and let them go.

Three of the sailors dressed as women and went about the crowd, teasing them with long hair they procured from mops and swaying their hips in a suggestive fashion. It was a show, something Frank might have done. Was he making them laugh even now in St James's Hall? Were he and Reggie wondering what had become of me or were they sitting in a little tearoom somewhere, simply glad not to have been parted?

Everyone laughed at the men on deck whose heads had been dunked.

'Virgins!' called the older men to their juniors. The young ones looked more dead than alive and spent the next day grumbling because they could not get the sticky stuff out of their hair. What a way to celebrate travelling so far. I thought then how curious men are.

# Thirteen

It was a scorching summer day when we docked at Cape Town. After twenty-six days at sea the rain and chill of London seemed part of some other life, something that had been washed away in the heaving waters of the Atlantic. The beauty of the place silenced us all. The rough sea was finally subdued by the towering castellated rock of Table Mountain, and now lapped gently against the shore; a wild creature tamed by contact. The sun was low in the afternoon sky and seemed to make the mountain shimmer with gold, while in the distance other peaks gleamed purple and blue. No wonder men had come here seeking riches. The town stood out white as it lay nestled between sea and rock.

As we disembarked in our best serge tunics and trousers and our broad hats, a group of young women in white muslin presented each of us with a handful of muscatel grapes. They giggled and blushed and told us it was 'the Tommy welcome to the Cape'. I thought how foolish they looked. There was a war going on and this was the best they could do. Being female seemed ridiculous.

'Stupid women,' I muttered.

'Rather lovely though,' declared Cooper.

One of the simpering girls reached forward to give me a kiss on the cheek but Cooper stepped in front of me and received it instead. I thought of the women who had tried to kiss the natives at Earl's Court and wondered if I were now as curious to my own sex.

The voyage between London and the Cape and all those days out of sight of land made being ashore surprising. I felt as if my life in London had been spent breathing mud and looking out on the world through fog. Perhaps it was the firm sound of my now familiar boots upon the ground as I strode about my business on the docks but this, at last, I said to myself, was air, this was oxygen. The docks were crowded. The *Kinfauns Castle* was also newly arrived and men poured from her deck. The talk was that they had had a more luxurious passage than ourselves, and the breast of every man in our mess swelled with pride at our fortitude.

There was no time for sightseeing. As the ship emptied out on to the docks, men flailed about in search of lost kit. Everywhere you looked you saw great lines of men on their knees with everything they possessed laid out before them. We knelt on our greatcoats, trying to create some order in our sea-crumpled belongings as officers tutted along the line. Soon Corporal Chivenden sent our mess to seek out the cycles that had travelled in on another ship, the *Gaul*. Twenty-three cases had been shipped but at first we could find only three. Jackson boldly led our invasion of the docks to look for the missing cases. I began to wonder if Jackson was actually a very thin man who merely looked rotund because his pockets were always full of his products. We were quick to follow in his giant shadow and soon found the gear scattered over a wide range of wharves, hidden under tarpaulins. Haddock was an agile young monkey as he climbed up above bales of fodder, guns, military stores and goods of all descriptions to cry out, 'Here's one! Here's one!'

Jackson and Sheridan broke open wooden cases with their bare hands, while Cooper had somehow procured a cup of tea and sat blithely drinking it. Once the cases were unpacked we found we had so many disparate pieces of metal that no one could think how they might be transformed into whole bikes. Somehow we managed it and once the cycles were assembled it was Sheridan who could tune them like grand pianos. We worked and laughed amid clouds of coal-dust and crowds of good-natured kaffirs gathered to watch.

'Blimey, darkies everywhere,' muttered Pattenden, as one of the black men retrieved a nut that had rolled from Sheridan's grasp. 'Hope they don't think we've come to fight for them.'

By the time we had found all our missing parts, Haddock had discovered one of the four Vickers-Maxim field guns that had been presented by the City of London. He sat astride the barrel, pretending to fire at all comers.

'Look out, Mr Kruger,' he yelled, 'I'm on my way. They say the Boers have Creusot guns,' he called excitedly, 'and that there is one they call Long Tom with a range of ten thousand yards.'

'Yes, but it is fired by peasants,' laughed Cooper as Sheridan spun the wheel of one of our completed bicycles.

The docks were heaving as we made our way through to our camp. Military trucks roared and the pavements teemed with soldiers of many nationalities – Canadians, Australians and New Zealanders mixed with the English and the Scots and even a few Irish. Some said that the Canadians had travelled twelve thousand miles to get to Cape Town and fight for the Empire.

Bit by bit we began moving the cycles to Green Point camp, which lay at the foot of Table Mountain some two miles from the docks. It had a wonderful view of Table Bay, off which about forty large transport vessels lay anchored. A village of tents had sprung up as men in puttees and khaki milled about, trying to make sense of where they found themselves. Not everyone was to cycle, and horses were pegged out everywhere, whinnying for grass. Green Point was poorly named as it seemed to be made entirely of white sand. The wind pulled at well-driven tent pegs and guys, and the air was thick with clouds of fine blown grit. It got into everything and soon there was sand in our food, our drink, our boots and even our hair. But by nightfall the wind would quieten and the lights from the ships in the bay were almost romantic.

Mail from home had been given out, but hardly anyone in our mess had received any.

Pattenden had a letter from his sister and Jackson some business missive from a Lancashire partner. Perhaps Maisie or even Reggie might have sent some word? But no – and the pang of disappointment was acute. Haddock had a letter from his mother which lay unopened for an age until Cooper asked him if he wanted to hear it read. Haddock nodded. It was written by a neighbour and the language was slightly stilted but as Cooper read aloud, tears fell unbidden down the boy's face. His mother had discovered where he had gone and she wanted him home. I knew we should have made him go back. Instead, Jackson reached out and ruffled his hair.

We sat in silence. A gloom had descended upon us and it was hard to shift. We went into town.

All along Adderley Street, before the steamship companies' offices, silent fellows loafed about in the corduroy trousers and flannel shirts of the miners of the Rand. These were the British working men we had come to fight for. These were the *Uitlanders*, the foreigners, the *Roineks* to whom the dreadful Mr Kruger, President of the South African Republic, refused to grant equal rights. We had come to fight for their rights yet many of them were clearly not waiting to see how we fared. Inside the offices they thronged the counters several deep, desperate to depart. They said twenty thousand had escaped from the Transvaal. Down to the docks they filed steadily with their bundles, hoping to be penned in the black hulls of homeward liners. As they waited for ships, they choked the lodging-houses, the bars, the streets in one huge demonstration of the unemployed.

'Why are they not staying to fight?' I asked Cooper, bewildered. 'Why do they not volunteer like us? What about their rights?' I thought about my conversation with Uncle Charles and his confidence that we had come to get these men the vote.

Cooper smiled. 'My dear Grey, they don't want rights. They want one hundred pounds to buy a cottage and marry a girl. If they can't have that then they'd rather go home.'

On the corner of Strand Street stood the Grand Hotel. We all had some purchases to make. Cooper went to see if he could buy some proper Three Castles cigarettes, of which he was inordinately fond. Haddock was collecting the cigarette cards inside and Cooper had promised him one on our return. We separated, Ben, as ever, to mind his own business and I to buy a quiet bottle or two to keep in my tent. When I returned to the hotel veranda I stood rolling a cigarette of my own, thinking nothing of smoking it in the street. I stood with my legs wide apart, still swaying a little in my head from the long journey at sea.

Cooper returned and we went into the Grand to get a meal. The talk in the hotel was of little else but the war. Uniforms of many regiments jostled at the bar with those recently returned from the front, who were distinguishable from the newly arrived by their silence. Pale, distracted businessmen in dark suits chewed on cigars in corners.

Jackson was already in their midst, handing out his cards and samples. He was smiling and laughing as if he had found his purpose.

'I don't understand Jackson,' I said innocently. 'He talks of nothing but money.'

Cooper nodded. 'Then he has come to the right place. You know what they say – *war seldom enters, but where wealth allures*.'

I did not know anyone who said that. I did not really know anything.

'Do you have a quote for everything, Cooper?' I asked.

Cooper looked abashed. 'I suppose I do. Perhaps it saves me having to think.'

At the desk several men had arrived with tents and camp beds. They too were volunteers but without a regiment; men who had come simply to fight. They seemed to have neither book learning nor experience but were demanding to see someone with authority to grant railway passes so that they might 'go to the front'. Even to me, who had done the maddest thing of all, their arrival with no plan seemed utter lunacy.

The food we had been given both at sea and at the camp had been good but had lacked variety. Cooper led the way into the dining room and sniffed the air appreciatively.

'This, my dear Grey, is the business.'

We sat down and I noticed him quietly stroke the linen-covered table with his hand, and I knew I was seeing a man expressing deep pleasure. He ordered wine and it was wonderful stuff, a deep rich red that glowed in a decanter on the table. I drank it down and felt the now familiar sensation of calm spread across my back. Cooper watched me as I drained my glass and poured another.

'*I have very poor and unhappy brains for drinking: I could well wish courtesy would invent some other custom of entertainment*,' he said quietly. 'Othello,' he explained. 'I wonder what Shakespeare knew of being a black man? I wonder how it was that he could imagine being someone else entirely?'

Cooper looked at me and I did not reply, but looked back at him with a steadiness no woman would have allowed herself. He was beautiful. I felt an unexpected sigh rise in me and I thought for a moment he was going to say something. His hand reached across the table but in the end he simply broke off some bread and looked away. For a companionable moment the two of us sat listening to the solid rhythm of a large grandfather clock whiling away the time. There was not silence for long. Like the town, the hotel was full to bursting. If the *Uitlanders* were dashing to escape then in equal measure the London shipping offices were besieged by people who wanted to be 'in on the excitement'. Any number of society women had lost all sense of what my aunt would have thought seemly and were now arriving to do 'a little work' for the war. Once here, they were apparently busy demanding the best hotel rooms, organising tea and dinner parties, enjoying daily canters on the lower slopes of Table Mountain, charity bazaars and soirées, and fighting over the officers.

'Blasted women,' Cooper seethed through his soup, 'coming over here and getting in the way. Think they can potter about the wards in flounces and furbelows hindering the nurses and irritating the patients. Can you imagine *that* looking after you if you were feeling a bit peaky?'

Cooper pointed to a woman who had just arrived. She was a formidable-looking creature dressed like royalty about to open or close something. I realised she was with Ben and that together they were surveying the dining room. With horror, I saw that it was Colonel Talbot's wife. Ben spied us and in a moment she was sailing towards us with Ben lagging behind, looking apologetic.

'Reginald? Is that you?' she enquired loudly, peering at me through a lorgnette.

'Yes, it is,' affirmed Cooper.

I tried to get to my feet and it was only then that I realised quite how much wine I had consumed.

'Lady Talbot,' I slurred before sitting back down with a slight bump.

Cooper managed to be far more measured. He bowed his head and introduced himself. 'Private Thomas Cooper, your ladyship.'

'Her ladyship stopped me in the street,' mumbled Ben.

'The uniform!' declared Lady Talbot, clearly pleased with herself. 'I recognised the uniform and, well, we can hardly stand on ceremony now that we are all here to fight the good fight. I have become quite emboldened, have I not, Private ... uhm?'

'White,' replied Ben.

'White, yes. I went straight up to him and said – what did I say, Private?'

'I, well, I wasn't really ...' Ben appeared mortified to have brought this woman to our table.

Lady Talbot ploughed on regardless. 'I said, you, young man, are a City Imperial Volunteer and therefore you must know Lord Grey's boy, Reginald, and of course, I was right and here you are.'

'Here we are,' agreed Cooper affably.

Lady Talbot paused. 'You look different, Reginald.'

Cooper cleared his throat. 'Perhaps the boy has become a man.'

'A man,' I repeated thickly.

'Yes,' echoed Ben.

'Are you here with . . . Colonel Talbot?' I finally managed.

'Sadly, no,' sighed his wife, happy to have the focus back on herself. 'The colonel remains in London on pressing business but I did not think that precluded me from setting off and seeing what needs to be done. I am blessed with a most understanding husband and so I have, rather boldly some might say, set off alone.'

Cooper smiled. 'And tell us, how do you intend to share your accomplishments with the good people of the Cape, Lady Talbot?'

Lady Talbot gave a great sigh of pleasure. 'Ah, I plan to teach the Dutchwomen of the Cape how to cook. Through the kitchen I believe we may cause them to see sense. I'll write to your uncle, Reginald. Tell him you are well.' And with that she was off.

I thought I would be sick there and then. I looked at Cooper to see what he had made of the encounter but he seemed unaware of my anxiety.

'Sit, Ben,' he encouraged, indicating a chair.

Ben shook his head and was preparing to leave when Cooper removed a small box from his pocket. It was made of a dark wood and as he placed it on the table Cooper slid the lid back to reveal an array of small blocks of colour.

'Have you seen this?' he asked.

Ben hesitated. Apart from our slightly odd encounter on the deck, he had made no moves of friendship during our journey and seemed intent on keeping it that way, but he was drawn to the box.

'Where did you get it?' he asked quietly.

'Very nice little shop about five minutes from here.' Cooper sipped his drink. 'Oh, and these,' he added, casually pulling some pencils and watercolour brushes from his pocket.

Ben pulled his chair up to the table and looked at the box. Cooper laughed.

'It's the bloodiest thing. I thought the box looked so nice. It was only after I bought it that I remembered I can't jolly well paint. I don't suppose it's any use to you, is it?'

Ben nodded quietly.

The men sat either side of me, Ben absorbed by the tablets of colour, Cooper delighted with everything, finishing his wine and lounging with his arm over the back of his chair to survey the room. Such a handsome fellow, so strong and capable. He carried such an air of confidence that I suspected he would look splendid wherever he was. A man to fight beside.

There weren't any more dinners like that. Instead there was nothing but hard work and I silently thanked Papa for bringing me up to be strong. Each of us carried a bandolier charged with a hundred rounds, a full haversack and water bottle, a belt with a pouch and a frog for the bayonet, a carbon filter attached to a lanyard, a pair of field glasses, a knife and a compass. On our bikes we each had a rolled-up mackintosh tied to the handlebars, our rifle on a bucket attachment with a Turner carrier behind taking the rolled-up greatcoat and Alpine rucksack, and a blanket strapped on at the back of it all. As if that weren't enough, the bikes themselves were heavy – 28 lb. These were not the agile machines on which Reggie's Frank had taught me. These were great beasts that would have been difficult enough to ride on the Ripley Road let alone the loose sand at Green Point. It turned out Ben couldn't ride at all so he was subjected to much ribbing, which meant my first clumsy efforts were rather overlooked. Jackson spent his free time running alongside Ben, holding the saddle of his cycle until he 'got the hang of it', as the Canadian troops liked to say. It made us laugh and Ben slowly began to smile. It didn't take long until we all had the hang of it. Certainly we got fitter with each day as we practised mounting and dismounting and taking messages backwards and forwards in full kit.

'I'm sure we'll outpace the infantry with our wheels,' said Haddock enthusiastically as we walked the quarter of a mile to the water troughs to wash the service mess tin and regulation cutlery. The stew for the evening had floated in much soup-like gravy whose fatty nature had been tempered only by sand. The beef had required considerable chewing to get it down and I was glad to stretch my legs.

I was on my way back to the tent for a restorative sip from my diminishing bottles of alcohol and just passing one of the ambulance wagons, when Pattenden appeared behind me. I didn't even notice he was there until he suddenly pushed me forward so that I landed upright against the giant back wheel. For a slim man he was surprisingly strong and he used his body to trap me against the spokes. My forehead banged against the stretchers tied above the wheel and a gash above my right eye began to bleed. I tried to lash out at him with my arms but he held me tight.

'On your own, Grey?' he hissed.

'What the hell, Pattenden—'

'Thought you could get away with it, did you?' he continued. 'I knew. I knew from the way you put your shoes on.'

'My shoes?'

'Oh, you can tell a lot by shoes.'

His body pressed against me and, even with the little I knew of such matters, there was no mistaking his intention. His right hand began to rip at my trouser buttons while his left pinned my neck against the top of the wheel. The steel edge cut into my cheek and, try as I might, I could not get free of his grip. Button after button, he forced them open and as his hand prepared to slip inside I forgot all about being a man and screamed.

I don't know why Cooper had come back, but in that moment he appeared and seized Pattenden by the collar. Cooper, that gentle, literary man, turned him round and landed a punch that threw my attacker to the ground. He looked set to finish him off.

'Please, Cooper, please.' Pattenden put up his hands to fend off any blows. 'I was doing it for the mess. I'd found out and I thought we should be sure.'

'Sure of what?' demanded Cooper.

'Grey, he's a—'

'He's a what?'

Pattenden looked at me and even in defeat he almost smiled as he jeered, 'A mandrake, a molly, a bugger ... he's a bloody sodomite.'

'And you thought you'd just check, did you?' Cooper loomed over the prostrate man. 'Sure you weren't interested yourself? Hmm? Fancy a bit of that soft cheek, did you?'

Pattenden tried to laugh. 'No, don't be absurd. It was for the mess.'

Cooper picked him up by the scruff of the neck and held him inches from his own face. He then dropped Pattenden back on the ground and turned to leave.

'Come on, Grey,' he said over his shoulder, 'concert to go to.'

I left, buttoning my flies. One thing was certain. I was man enough to know that Cooper and I would never mention the matter again.

# Fourteen

One night, when Frank returned from work, Reggie had descended into such gloom that he did not even turn his head in greeting. Frank pulled the curtains back from the large bed and looked down at his lover, but Reggie did not look back at him.

'Do you think what we do is wrong?' asked Reggie at last.

Frank's rage was instantaneous. 'Wrong! Wrong!' he shouted, until the woman downstairs banged on the ceiling with her broom handle. Frank sat on the edge of the bed and held Reggie down by his wrists. His voice was low and intense and his face was contorted with fury.

'Don't you ever say that in here. Don't you ever say that again.'

Reggie had never seen Frank enraged and it both frightened and thrilled him. Suddenly Frank let go of him and sat up. 'How can it possibly be wrong for me to use my own body to love?' he asked in a whisper.

It was late the next afternoon when Reggie sat up in bed, rubbing his temples against the previous night's excesses. Frank, whose whole life revolved around late nights, seemed unaffected. He floated about in a Japanese silk dressing gown, preparing coffee and humming a song from his latest show. The heavy curtains remained closed against the day and the only light came from a low fire and the usual incense burner glowing on the mantelpiece. The woman in the flat below was Irish and Frank could not stand the smell of the meals she cooked. Often, when he returned drunk at night, he would loudly berate her for 'ruining' his life.

Frank placed the coffee on a small table and sat down stroking his gown with the back of his hand.

'It is possible that I am in love with the Japanese. I think the whole world should throw out the mahogany and embrace peacock feathers. Charles – you know, Lord Hartnell – was telling me Harrods has a chair in the Oriental style that is a sonnet in ivory.'

Reggie smiled. 'Shall I buy it for you?'

Frank shook his head. 'No, my dear Reggie. I may seek to be uplifted by beauty but I do not seek your money to do it.' He paused and, as if to make his point, added, 'I love you, Reginald Grey.'

Reggie looked away and picked up his coffee.

'They were saying at the theatre last night that a man was arrested outside the Criterion bar for suggesting "something unspeakable" to a gentleman.'

'What do you suppose it was that he suggested?' wondered Reggie.

Frank smiled. 'I couldn't say. It was, after all, "unspeakable". Did you know men met there? I had no idea. Shall we go this evening?'

Reggie did not reply. Frank stood up and moved to the side of the bed. He pushed back Reggie's hair and gently stroked his head.

'Come with me, Reggie. You cannot simply stay here.'

Reggie looked up at the beautiful man. 'Why not?'

'Because,' said Frank gently, 'there's a whole world out there.'

After Frank had finished work that night, they did go to the Long Bar at the Criterion. They sat below the gilded ceiling where Sherlock Holmes and Dr Watson were said to have met and drank American cocktails. Reggie was enjoying Frank's ability to mimic almost any man in the place and he had almost begun to relax when he noticed a familiar-looking fellow standing at the end of the bar. The gentleman was small and white-haired and might have gone unnoticed in the crowd had he not held himself with a remarkable ramrod stiffness. He stood impossibly erect, chatting to a young officer in Guards' uniform. Frank was just starting an anecdote when Reggie caught sight of the man's face in the mirrored wall. It was Colonel Sir John Talbot.

Reggie was about to look away when he saw the colonel had noticed him. It was hard to say which of them felt more awkward. The colonel glanced away for a moment and then turned back, giving Reggie a slight nod.

Drunk as he was, Reggie got to his feet murmuring, 'Excuse me, Frank. I just have to . . . '

He made his way to the bar with the careful tread of a man who has lost the easy steadiness of sobriety. Reggie reached the bar and coughed slightly.

'Colonel Talbot, I believe.'

The colonel seemed disconcerted. 'Yes, yes. Grey, isn't it? I thought you were off? Already gone with the regiment.'

Reggie took a deep breath. 'Yes, uhm, a slight delay. The slightest of delays. A family matter.'

'Your mother. Yes. Dreadful business. Good. Good,' emphasised the colonel. 'Every man needed. What about your friend?' he asked, pointing towards Frank. 'The one without a moustache.'

Reggie paused. 'He uh—'

The colonel did not wait for a reply. 'Do not trust a man without a moustache, Grey,' he intoned. 'Always a rum sort.'

Reggie, horribly aware of the light blond down which was all that seemed to wish to grow on his face, nodded and backed away, declaring, 'Indeed. Good to see you, Colonel.'

'Safe journey,' the colonel replied. He downed his drink and departed without another word to anyone. The young officer he had been standing with watched him go and said nothing.

Reggie wound his way back to the table.

'We have to leave,' he hissed.

Frank was bewildered. 'Why? What?'

'I can't be here,' Reggie said urgently. 'Don't you understand? I can't be anywhere.'

The alcohol mixed with the unfortunate encounter had turned to temper by the time Reggie and Frank got into a cab. Reggie turned to Frank in a fury.

'Why do you not have a moustache?' he demanded.

Frank was bemused. 'Reggie, whatever is the matter?'

'Don't you know people will talk if you don't have a moustache?' Reggie practically shouted. 'Why must you be clean-shaven? Must you make a statement about everything?'

Frank tried to soothe Reggie by placing a hand on his knee but Reggie shook it off. Frank kept his voice calm. 'I am clean-shaven,' he explained, 'because I work in the theatre. I may be called upon to play any part, even a woman sometimes. I can't have a moustache for my work.'

Reggie slumped back into the darkest corner of the seat.

'What have we done, Frank?'

'Oh, Reggie, please,' begged Frank, slightly irritated. 'Not again.'

Reggie could hardly speak. 'Don't you understand? I cannot go out. We didn't think it through. Reginald Grey is supposed to be at war. I will not be able to go anywhere. What were we thinking? It will all go wrong.'

Frank tried to suggest many outings after that, but Reggie was afraid, both for himself and for his beloved cousin. He felt claustrophobic within the small flat's walls, yet he did not dare go out for fear of being recognised. Reggie slept away the evenings so that by the time Frank was home, ready for bed, he could no longer lie still. He paced the room as his mind raced.

'Oh, Valentine. I should find out how she is,' he repeated over and over. 'Frank, how can we get word to her?' Some nights he would fret for hours. 'Oh, Frank, what am I to do? I cannot live the life my father wishes for me with every day the same, every suit of clothing identical, a dull life where nothing ever surprises – and now I cannot live this life either.' Then he would stop and consider himself in the mirror. 'Perhaps it's not too late. Perhaps I can still join up. Join a regiment and go and find her. There must be other regiments where I might, you know, manage. Where it's not so much the fighting as the willingness to make a bit of a show of it.'

One early morning, just as the sun peeped into the tightly veiled apartment, Frank, exhausted with Reggie's distress, had an idea.

'We need to have a party,' he announced. 'If you cannot go out into London, why then London must come to you. Let's make a list.'

Frank sat down and wrote a list of all the most entertaining people he could think of, with his own and Reggie's names proudly at the top. When he was done he clapped his hands. 'You'll need to dress up.' Frank eyed his lover expertly. 'What part shall we make you play?'

Reggie shook his head. 'I could never dress up like you do,' he said. 'I could never be someone else.'

Frank dismissed the worry. 'Nonsense. It's just a frock. We're all born naked and after that it's up to us.' Suddenly his eyes shone. 'I know, a trapeze artist! We could get you one of those bodysuits they wear, and the little skirt.'

Reggie stopped his pacing. He was half appalled and half thrilled by the idea. Once he had seen a wonderful trapeze act at the Holborn Empire, with the acrobat whirling and swinging so high up that for a brief while he had not been able to tell if it were a boy or a girl. Confusingly, it turned out to be a boy pretending to be a great female gymnast and the lad concluded his gymnastics with a song that had the refrain 'Wait till I'm a man.' Later he had seen the young artist in full white tie and tails leaning on the arm of a common sort of fellow in a cloth cap, as if he had no strength at all and needed his companion's support just for the act of walking.

'I should be very exposed, Frank, in such a costume,' Reggie whispered anxiously. 'Can I not be something else? Can I not be a soldier?'

Thus it was that Reggie for the first time in his life came to wear Her Majesty's uniform. The word went out to Frank's acquaintances that a 'Boer War Party' was to be held in his apartment and that participants should dress 'appropriately'. The many men, and it was only men, who attended took this instruction in varying ways. There were those, like Reggie, who were rather obviously dressed as Guardsmen in brilliant red tunics and tight-fitting black trousers; there were simple privates (mostly men who liked to obey orders) and several full colonels (mostly men who liked to give them), and even a delicate man of fifty, whose most striking feature was his tiny hands, who lay on the bed pretending to be wounded. He spent the evening like an exiled and impoverished princess, refusing to rise from his recumbent position and peppering his conversation with dramatic French. 'My protectors,' he called from among the silk cushions to anyone who would listen, 'be brave. We must not fall into *une vie de désespoir.*'

Frank had outdone himself. He was dressed as a Dutch girl and insisted on being addressed as 'Dolly Dutch'. It was a wonderful costume complete with long blonde plaits tied with blue ribbons, a white cap and a matching pinny over a bright red dress with short sleeves and a lace trim that fell just below the knee. His legs were encased in dark stockings and he had even managed to procure wooden clogs for his feet. It was the triumph of the evening.

Everything had a military feel. Halfway through, Frank had even arranged for a telegraph boy to deliver 'a message from the front'. One of Frank's music hall friends played the piano and he sang a new song they'd written about all the news from the war being 'Double Dutch'. It was met with wild applause. Even in the tiny room Frank was brilliant and Reggie felt proud of him.

As the evening wore on and more drink was consumed, however, the mood seemed to darken. There was much muttering about the Theatre and Music Halls Committee closing down a Moorish bath scene at the Empire because it was 'too suggestive'. Of what, no one would say out loud. Frank stood at the mantelpiece in his plaits and clogs talking to a man dressed as a Boer farmer.

'But where can you meet a real soldier?' he was asking.

The farmer sipped his drink. 'That's easy. Hyde Park of a night time. The place is awash with them.'

Frank looked up to see Reggie standing by his side.

'All right, my darling?' he asked.

'What were you saying?' Reggie asked.

'Idle talk,' replied Frank. 'Don't get involved. It's the sort of thing could lose us the war.'

The room gradually thinned out to leave only the most stalwart of revellers. Five or six men lay sprawled on chairs and on the floor, setting the world to rights. Frank had removed his wig and sat with his male head poking out of his female guise.

'But I should like to do something,' one of the men was saying. 'I should like to help Her Majesty, it's just—'

'—you'd be so hopeless,' chimed in another.

Everyone laughed but Reggie looked serious. 'It makes me feel hopeless,' he said quietly.

Frank reached out and took his hand. 'I saw a play once about the Sacred Band of Thebes. They were soldiers in Greek times made up of one hundred and fifty pairs of male lovers – each couple had an older fellow and his younger paramour. I think the idea was that soldiers would fight harder and better if they fought alongside a lover.'

'What happened to them?'

Frank's voice lowered into story-telling mode. 'They took part in the battle of Chaeronea. It was a terrible battle and when the rest of the army turned and fled, the three hundred men of the Sacred Band remained and fought to the death. When the general they had fought against came upon the corpses heaped together in defeat, he said: "Perish any man who suspects that these men either did or suffered anything unseemly."'

'Might we have such a band again?' asked Reggie. 'I would fight for you, Frank.'

'And I for you, Reggie.'

The room was silent.

'We should do something,' said someone. 'They say the town of Ladysmith is still under siege and yet we sit here.'

'We are useless Uranians,' said another.

'We are not useless,' said Frank, getting to his feet. 'We are glorious. We believe in the glory of passion. We believe in the inspiration of emotion. We believe in the holiness of love. The world may sometimes scoff at us but we know we have noble hearts that are true. We should not just do something, we should do something splendid and we shall.'

It was a stirring speech for a Dutch girl.

The party slipped away into the night and Reggie soon fell into a deep slumber. Frank covered him with a blanket, changed into a dark suit and slipped from the flat. It was still dark enough outside for secrets to be abroad as he left Jermyn Street and walked swiftly towards Hyde Park.

# Fifteen

We had just begun to get used to life at Green Point, to the mix of tropical sun and sandstorm, when Haddock appeared at the tent flap carrying a small piece of paper.

'We got orders,' he said, looking very pleased with himself.

'Orders for what?' I asked from my cot where I lay smoking and daydreaming in the heat.

Haddock shrugged as Cooper looked up from his book, showing half an eyebrow of interest.

'Young Billy, did it not occur to you before you set off from home that our entire job as the Cycle Corps is delivering messages? Did you not wonder how you might deliver messages if you can't read them?'

Haddock looked at him rather blankly. 'I can deliver 'em. I don't need to read 'em. They're not for me, is they?'

Cooper smiled. 'No, indeed.'

He took the note from the boy and looked at it thoughtfully.

'Well, there we are,' he said quietly. 'We depart in half an hour. Kit and caboodle.'

It was to become the familiar rhythm of soldiering life – hours of endless tedium followed by short bursts of intense activity with no explanation as to why such commotion might be useful. Where were we going and why? But they were pointless questions. Several groups had already moved on. The Canadian Artillery, who had been camped beside us, had started off two days before and envy had been left behind in the dust of their departure.

I struggled to pack everything up while Cooper sat watching and puffing on his pipe.

'I can't get it all in,' I moaned.

'Clearly no one has advised you of the three critical categories of packing,' he mused. 'One, absolute necessities; two, absolute necessities which are not quite so necessary; and three, absolute necessities which it is absolutely necessary to leave behind.'

If I had ever imagined heading for the front, I don't suppose starting at a railway station had been part of the picture. Perhaps I had imagined men trudging over the Alps behind Hannibal and his elephants, footsore soldiers marching behind Alexander on his horse. Catching a train with a bicycle seemed, well, odd. We stood waiting to board as if it were all some rather marvellous charabanc and any minute we would stop at the buffet for a nice cup of tea and a scone. What distinguished the journey from any other we might have taken in the past was that none of us had any idea about the destination. Perhaps we were to travel all night to reinforce the troops heavily engaged around Arundel. Everything was conjecture, nothing was certainty and everyone accepted it. We were six to seven hundred men with twenty officers who got to the station at 6.45 only to find the train was not leaving till 9.55. It was the army life of hurry up and wait.

Aboard the train, once all our kit was piled in, there was room for five in our compartment and Cooper made it clear that Pattenden should find somewhere else to travel. Four of us had seats while Haddock sat on the floor on the rucksacks.

'Third class, eh?' smiled Cooper, throwing himself on to a seat with a smile and patting the place beside him for me. 'Who would have thought it could be so marvellous?'

It shouldn't have been fun. Our business was serious, but in truth we were a merry party, knee-deep in belts, haversacks, blankets, cloaks and water bottles. There was teasing and games and shared cigarettes. Even Ben had relaxed a little and now was rarely seen without his box of colours, sketching and painting.

'So, Grey,' started Sheridan, 'when are you going to grow up and get a moustache?'

'Why, what would you wager?' I retorted, taking a gulp of white wine from the neck of a passing bottle.

'I shall grow a moustache soon. Maybe even this week,' declared Haddock with certainty.

'Yes, and you'll be running the regiment as well,' Sheridan teased as he reached out and pushed Haddock flat against the rucksacks. The others threw their hats and anything else to hand on top of him. It was easy being with the men. There was no secret spite born of some petty jealousy, no sideways sneer of superiority about a hat or the colour of a gown or who said what about whom. If anyone had something to say to another fellow, he just said it and the air was clear. I had no moustache and it was fine. We lay in great heaps across the seats, not caring whose arm touched another's leg. I felt as though I had grown into a large creature with many limbs who could fight off all comers.

The sun set as we coursed through the mountains that surround Cape Town. Rumours raced up and down the train –

that Kruger was stopped, that his real plan was to take England . . . Chivenden came to check on us.

'The news is good, lads,' he beamed. 'They say the Boers have lost heart and are retreating in all directions, with our cavalry following them up and not even giving them time to collect their horses. They reckon our troops are now within thirty-five miles of Bloemfontein.'

'Where? Where is that? Bloom, what was it?' demanded Haddock excitedly from the floor.

'The capital of the Orange Free State, you ignorant glock.' Sheridan cuffed the boy gently on the head.

Haddock ducked away and laughed. 'Well, I don't know, do I? I'm from bloody Whitechapel.' He pulled himself up to look out of the open window. 'Do you think we'll see a leopard?' he asked.

I loved Haddock's excitement. It made us all feel good and he could get excited about almost anything. Cooper reached into his pocket.

'Got that card you wanted, Haddock.' He handed over a cigarette card bearing a drawing of Lord Roberts.

'Fantastic! Thanks, Coops.'

He was a boy as easily pleased by a cigarette card as by a leopard. He was a boy.

At night there were two bunks each side with Haddock still on the luggage, but it was better than the sand of the tent floor or the rough table on the *Ariosto*. We slept well and by morning the sun was rising over the open veldt.

The air was fresh and the heat not too bad. It felt as though the train was pulling up an incline between hills, making for a corner round one of the ranges. I looked out of the window constantly, feeling that when we got round the next bend we would at last see something, but each time we arrived we saw only another incline, two more ranges and another corner. We kept on travelling and saw only the same vast nothing we had seen before. Everything standing desolate under the unbroken arch of the sky.

'Stunning,' sighed Ben, rubbing his spectacles and reaching for his pencil. Cooper had indeed unlocked Ben with his small box of paints. Ben knew about colour and he in turn opened our eyes to the colours around us.

'No bloody green,' moaned Jackson, 'place has got no bloody colour. You should see Lancashire. Climb Pendle Hill and you see green for miles and miles. This place, bloody nothing.'

Ben smiled and said quietly, 'My dear chap, you're not looking. It's just that all the colours harmonise. Look again. Look at the sand. It's tawny, the scrub is silver-grey, there are crimson-tufted flowers like heather, black ribs of rock, puce shoots of strange plants, violet mountains in the middle distance ...'

'Blue fairy battlements that guard the horizon,' added Cooper dreamily, and indeed so it seemed, for above all the empty space brooded the intense purity of the azure South African sky.

Ben took out his small wooden box of paints and began to mix them for us so that we might see how colour had no boundaries.

'Hardly anything is just black and white,' he explained. 'In almost everything one hue blends into another.'

In his box, Indian yellow, emerald green, cobalt blue and cadmium red all lay in little compartments. He spat upon some paper and made them run. Everyone always called him Ben. The others went by their surnames but perhaps White was not suitable for the artist in our midst. He gradually relaxed and through his eyes we learned to see the grand landscape.

At the rare railway stations we occasionally saw a corrugated-iron store or perhaps a score of small stone houses with a couple of churches. There seemed to be little enough stock – here a dozen goats browsing on withered sticks, there a trio of ostriches, high-stepping, supercilious heads in the air, wheeling like a troop of cavalry and trotting out of the stink of that beastly train, but of men we saw little. Occasionally at a bridge there might be a couple of tents guarding the railway route or sometimes, at a culvert, Haddock, shouting out with glee, would spot a black man, in straw hat and patched trousers, standing with his hands in his pockets watching the train. None of it suggested war. Yet war it was. It was whispered in the air. The train moved with a gathering rush, an electric vibration that you could feel through your whole body.

We finally detrained at De Aar at five in the morning after nearly three days on the move. We went into camp and pitched our tents, which were immediately battered by the usual sandstorm. We were now sixteen men to each tent and because of the size of the place there was no choice but to have Pattenden rejoin us. Cooper no longer made use of his services. I watched my friend burn his pale, soft hands as he attempted to make the tea, I watched him learn to do for himself and I knew it was on my account. Pattenden stopped trying to help and sat back looking lost. I didn't care. I carried the reminders of the man on my face.

A little town of white tents sprang up and about them moved a great mass of identical men. Signal flags blinked from the rises, pickets with fixed bayonets dotted the ridges while mounted men in couples patrolled the plain, the dip and the slope. De Aar was hot and an awful place for sandstorms and, to make things worse, they always came on about dinnertime.

'Splendid place,' announced Cooper cheerfully as we ate.

'You're mad,' muttered Jackson, beginning to loathe the endless filth.

'Not at all,' said Cooper, as sand swirled around us. 'Absolutely no need for salt or pepper, saves a lot of bother.'

We had time here to become acquainted with the curiosity of this land's climate. There were glorious sunrises and sunsets where a burst of colour announced the rapid change as day plunged into night or rose from the darkness in an instant. I remember violent thunderstorms, burning gusts of wind, clouds of blinding dust and summer lightning flashing on the horizon when the night was fine and clear. Even at night none of the stars was familiar. If this was British land then it hid its origins well.

We were in enemy country now but we saw no sign of them, yet the talk grew that an attack would take place at night. A low level of fear bubbled quietly through our days. I began to realise how easy it might be to talk oneself into anxiety. The nights were glorious, warm as the hottest August evening in England, but just before sunrise the air would grow chilly and damp with dew.

The terrain was unknown to us and strewn with boulders, and in the last hours of a weary outpost watch it became easy to imagine that the Boer hid behind them in droves. I, who had not been allowed to fend for myself in any way, now fended for the men who slept. I was alone with a gun and my imagination fought me at every turn. Those were the times when I most wished to be Valentine again.

Ben and I were fetching water. It had become a habit that we would go together and complete our personal washing on the way. We were easier with each other. What had started gradually was cemented one afternoon. As we returned from our chore we heard laughter from behind the tent. Sheridan and Haddock were excusing themselves in what seemed like an astonishing flow of water. I pretended I hadn't seen them but Sheridan called out.

'Come on, Grey, see if you can hit past that tin can. Haddock's nowhere near.'

'I'll get it, I'll get it,' shouted Haddock, holding himself on display as if it were the most natural thing in the world. 'Hey, Ben,' he shouted, 'come on, it's a wager.'

Ben looked at me. 'I'd rather not. Sorry. I suppose I'm a bit fastidious but, well, I prefer solitude for these . . . matters.'

He turned to me, his face anxious, and he was tight-lipped as we walked round to the front of the tent.

'Look, it's very awkward. I know I'm a fool but I really can't,' he explained. He pulled out his cigarettes and handed me one. We lit up as he hesitantly continued, 'Oh dear, these are the very things about me that my wife despised.'

'Your wife?'

'Yes. I do not want to be that sort of fellow, the sort who likes a great show, and I was wondering . . . well, it would be an awful kindness if when I needed to . . . you know, well perhaps, I mean you seem to be a private fellow too . . . whether we might stand guard for each other? Keep it private, do you see?'

And so it was that I had a guard for my moments of necessary privacy. It was the greatest relief to me that Ben was a gentleman. One day, as we looked over the brilliant sunlit plain we thought what we saw was impossible – snowflakes driving towards us. It was a swarm of locusts, their gauzy wings fluttering in the sunlight, but I did not see the beauty. Instead I began to shriek as some of the creatures landed on our sleeves and on our trousers. I tried to brush them from my hair, my face. Ben grabbed me and pulled me close.

'Stand still,' he urged. I buried my face in his shoulder and the horrible swarm engulfed us before passing on.

I knew they were gone when the light whirring sound they made moved away. I looked up, embarrassed.

'I'm so sorry,' I muttered.

Ben looked at me intently.

'What?' I said, mortified by my behaviour and uncomfortable with his gaze.

He motioned for me to be quiet. 'Ssh, you have one on your sleeve. Don't move,' he said. 'Look at it closely. It's not your enemy. It's beautiful. Astonishing. Look at that incredible latticework of lines across its back. Green with slight red and black markings. What an exquisite creature, an engineering wonder.'

After a moment the locust tired of our attention and flew off. Immediately Ben took out his small box of paints and sat down to recreate the visitor. When he was done, the image was so real it was a surprise that the creature did not flutter from the page and depart as well. I looked at him with the same intensity he'd given the insect. Ben was gifted. He should never have volunteered. His bicycle riding was poor, his rifle skills hopeless and his chest wheezed at every turn in the breeze.

'Why did you come, Ben? Why are you not sketching some smart woman in her drawing room?'

For a while he didn't reply, then, just as we had nearly reached the tent, he stopped and put his hand on my arm.

'My wife left me,' he explained quietly. 'She took my boy. She took James. Went off with some fellow she met. She said that no man should spend his time "colouring in". That I was not man enough to do a proper job. Not tough enough. I thought she'd stop me, come to the docks, but instead here I am to show her otherwise.'

'But if she has some other fellow now,' I began gently, 'I mean, what if it doesn't do the trick?'

He shrugged. 'I shan't mind if I die.'

We had been at De Aar for a while when out of the blue a fellow from London turned up, riding one mule and leading another. He was cheerful, full of life and rather like Jackson, confident that war had been declared so that he might make his fortune.

'Cooper!' he called, 'Cooper!' as he approached in a cloud of dust.

Cooper looked up from his rather ineffective attempts to wash some clothes.

'Good Lord, Hawks!' he exclaimed. Cooper looked at me and said firmly, 'You remember Harry Hawkins, Reggie. We were at school with him.'

Hawkins leapt down from the mule, holding out his hand. 'Reggie Grey, is that you? I heard Coops was here but you'd be the last man I'd peg for a volunteer. I mean no offence but you were never really the sporting type. Bit more of an ... well, art gallery fellow.' He looked at me and added, 'Not really filled out, have you?' It was a question that required no answer. He slapped me on the back and proceeded to spend the next ten minutes catching up with Cooper and demanding tea.

Cooper looked at me over the boiling kettle and said nothing. I felt anxious. If Cooper had been to school with Reggie, why had he not said? Why had he not mentioned it? If he knew Reggie, then surely ...

On his pack mule Hawkins carried a large mahogany and brass camera with twin lenses.

'Not sure I was the fighting type myself but didn't want to miss out on the fun,' he explained as he assembled his equipment. 'Then these American chaps, Underwood, were looking for photographers for the war. I thought it can't be that bloody difficult so here I am, ready to immortalise you boys as heroes of the nation.'

'Excellent publicity,' declared Jackson, rubbing his hands and preparing some suitable packages to appear in the pictures.

'But we 'aven't done anything yet,' protested Haddock. 'We 'aven't even been shot at.'

Hawkins grinned. 'Splendid. Don't want any blood in the pictures. Far too upsetting for everyone. Why, my work will appear in magazines read by ladies. Now then, let's see. We could start with you,' he said, pointing at Haddock. 'You look young enough to make every mother weep.'

We treated the afternoon like a day off. I had traded my coat for a bottle of whisky from an Irish sergeant and Jackson had got hold of some cake. We drank and ate and smoked as we spent the afternoon staging photographs, first on the veldt and then on a kopje. Hawkins had permission from the colonel, who said it would be good for the regiment if everyone at home saw how brave we were. Cooper turned out to be terrible at dying while I, it seemed, had a natural flair. Perhaps I had something of my mother's theatrical skills, for I fell to the ground in mock death with no trouble at all. It made the others cry with laughter. Hawkins snapped the picture as I lay motionless on the veldt brought down in my prime by the wretched Boer. Then we all went back for a beer.

I strode beside Cooper as we returned. 'Cooper,' I began, 'about Harry and—'

'Best leave it alone,' he said gruffly. 'All is well, Grey, all is well. Remember, take what comes and don't worry,' and he walked on with Hawkins.

Did we look like soldiers? Perhaps. Were we ready for war? Absolutely not.

# Sixteen

Just for the fun of it, Frank had shown the manager at the Holborn Empire the Dolly Dutch costume from the party and found 'she' had promptly been booked as an act. Over at the Alhambra, Kipling's *The Absent Minded Beggar* was pulling them in and Frank's theatre wanted some of that: a crowd supporting the boys doing their bit in the Boer War. Dolly was to be the centrepiece in a new show, and Frank spent long hours at the theatre getting the songs and the routine ready.

Sundays he had free but to Reggie's intense frustration, each week Frank would go out first thing, saying only that he had 'some business' to attend to and that Reggie should 'relax and not worry' until he returned in the early afternoon. But those times were the worst. Frank would not explain where he was going and Reggie's mind became more and more tormented as he waited alone for his lover to return.

One Sunday, sick with imagined jealousies and ignoring the risk he was taking, Reggie slipped from the flat just after Frank had departed. Frank was several hundred yards ahead when

Reggie turned into Jermyn Street and he was only just in time to see him hopping on the red omnibus towards London Bridge. Reggie hailed a cab and instructed the driver to pursue the vehicle. Through the narrow window of the cab Reggie watched with mounting concern as Frank changed buses twice more and they headed east along the river. Gradually the landscape changed into a portrait of London that Reggie had never seen before. There were dozens of cheap lodging-houses, public houses, beer shops and dance halls. Here everyone seemed to live in each other's pockets with no concern for the noise they might be making. Street vendors hawked their wares in the crowded streets. A drunk banged into the side of the cab, demanding money from Reggie. He looked away and saw a young street sweeper leaning disconsolately upon his broom, clearly defeated by the piles of manure that steamed in the street.

'You sure about this, sir?' called the cab driver to Reggie for the umpteenth time.

'Drive on,' instructed Reggie tersely, reaching for a handkerchief to place across his nose.

At last Frank descended from the bus and began to walk towards the river. Reggie paid his fare and skulked after him. The streets were narrow, with houses so poorly made that they seemed to lean on each other for support. Children played in the street while women in long aprons went about their work. Reggie passed a young tired-looking woman sitting on a step, holding a wriggling baby in a short dress. The child tried to escape his mother's grasp as she held him by the back of his clothes to stop him falling in the muddy street. Reggie looked away and down at the pavement and saw that his once shining shoes were now black with filth.

Almost at the river Frank turned down a street too small even to admit a horse and cart. Reggie hung back, not wanting to be discovered. Here the houses lay in each other's pockets. Frank was clearly familiar with this strange place, for he waved to someone and then, without a pause, let himself in the front door of a shabby terraced house. Reggie's breathing was ragged. Almost blind with jealousy, he stumbled up to the door where Frank had entered. The entrance confused him. There was no bell or knocker and he wasn't at all sure how he was supposed to alert the occupants to his presence.

'Just bang,' called a woman across the way. 'They's in.'

But Reggie couldn't do it. He stood undecided on the doorstep. His mind raced. He loved Frank with such a passion that he would never recover. It was a terrible weakness, he knew, and he could not bear to discover that Frank did not feel the same. He stepped away from the door, feeling light-headed and unwell. An old curtain was drawn across the window at street level and Reggie could not see into the house, but he could imagine it all. Frank was beautiful. Who would not want to be with him? The theatre and its bars were full of opportunities. What had he been thinking? Frank had promised him nothing.

Reggie began to pace up and down the narrow alleyway. A dozen times he went to knock upon the door and end his torment but each time he withdrew his hand. He walked to the end of the street, determined to depart. He thought of leaving, but there were no cabs to be had in this godforsaken place. He was lost. A small boy sitting on a step watched him as he returned once more.

'What you scared of?' asked the child.

Reggie looked at him and did not know what to say. He wasn't scared. He was terrified.

Perhaps an hour passed before at last Frank opened the door to leave. He stood and stared at Reggie without speaking.

'What are you doing here?' he whispered urgently, looking over his shoulder into the house and trying to shut the door a little.

'Who is it?' called someone from inside.

'What am I doing here?' demanded Reggie, by now in a rage. 'Why, I think I am the one who is entitled to ask you—'

Suddenly the door swung wide open and there, dressed in a long skirt and wrapped in a woollen shawl, stood a small, wide woman with a smiling face.

'Who is it, Frank?' she asked again.

Frank turned to her. 'It's my friend, Mr Grey. Mr Grey, Reggie, I should like to present you to my mother.'

Reggie, a man never lost for words, could hardly manage the basic greetings.

'We have to go now,' said Frank.

Frank's mother invited them in. Through the door Reggie could see that she lived in a single room, about ten foot square. Frank was suddenly in a hurry.

'I have to go,' he repeated.

Mrs Rutherford stroked her son's cheek. 'Of course you do.' She turned to Reggie and looked at him, openly curious, but all she said was, 'He's a good boy visiting me.'

Frank kissed his mother and set off at a pace down the lane. Reggie bowed to a bemused Mrs Rutherford and ran after him.

'Frank!' he called.

Frank walked so fast that Reggie could hardly catch him and it was some time before he could touch his arm.

'Frank, wait.'

Frank turned to him, his beautiful face drawn, white with fury, eyes hard.

'What the hell are you doing spying on me?'

'I wasn't spying, I—'

'Following me all this way and now you've seen it,' exploded Frank, arms flung to the sky. 'Satisfied?'

Reggie was bewildered. 'Seen what? I don't know what you're talking about.' Miserable, he tried to take Frank's arm but his lover pulled away. 'Frank, you have to speak to me. I wasn't spying on you – well, yes, I was, but it's because—'

'Because what?' Frank stopped and faced Reggie, his whole face suffused with anger.

'Because I thought you had a lover,' Reggie replied quietly. 'And I couldn't bear it.'

They had reached a path along the river and Frank's pace slowed until he stopped by the water's edge. He drew breath and turned and looked at Reggie and spoke slowly, evenly.

'Reggie, I do have a lover. I have you.'

It was all Reggie could do to stop himself from throwing his arms around Frank. Instead he started to weep.

'Then why the secrecy?

Frank sighed. 'I didn't want you to see, Reggie. I didn't want you to know.'

'Know what?'

'Where I come from.'

Reggie and Frank walked on past a warehouse where goods were being loaded and unloaded. Men in working clothes heaved heavy crates as if they weighed nothing. Reggie was grateful that for once he'd just thrown on a coat, that he had not dressed with his usual care. Even so, he attracted looks from the men on the road.

Frank spoke quietly. 'My people are toshers, Reggie, have been since my grandfather. There aren't as many as there used to be but my brother Jack still goes down.'

'Down?'

'To the sewers.'

'Why?'

'For the valuable things that get lost down the drains,' explained Frank. 'There's a manhole cover in our backyard. He goes out the back and down to work just like my father did.' Frank shivered. 'I couldn't do it for long. Couldn't stand the smell.'

Reggie could not imagine such a thing. He looked down at his feet and wondered if even now some fellow was underground, beneath him, searching through the sewers. 'Is it dangerous?' he asked.

Frank shrugged. 'I suppose. Jack carries a pole, about eight foot long, with an iron hoe on the end to check the firmness of the ground. He's pulled himself out of the quagmire with it before now. It's dark and there's rats and you've got to know the tides, where things get carried by the water, but sometimes he comes up with half a sovereign and then he's happy with his whack.'

'Who would drop half a sovereign in a sewer?' asked Reggie.

'Some toff like you,' said Frank.

'What do they think of you being in the theatre?'

Frank laughed. 'They don't know. My mother thinks I drive an omnibus.'

'Why do you not tell her?'

Frank shrugged. 'I don't know. She likes to think of me working the buses and I did use to once upon a time, but then I met someone in the theatre and he ... I don't think she'd like the life. She'd think it wasn't nice. All that dressing up and pretending. I don't want her to be disappointed.'

'And why did you not tell me? About your mother? About where you go?'

Frank gave a slight smile and touched Reggie's shoulder. 'We are literally from different worlds. I have stood in the sewers below, waiting for someone like you to drop coins on my head. We are not cut from the same cloth, Reggie.'

'*Enquire Within Upon Everything*,' said Reggie quietly, turning to Frank. 'You worry that you won't know something. That someone will find you out.'

Frank nodded. The two men stood and looked out across the Thames. A boatman was pulling hard on his oars for the opposite shore while a pair of seagulls screeched above. The air was full with the sounds of life.

'I cannot stay inside any more,' said Reggie quietly.

'No,' agreed Frank.

Reggie turned to him. 'But I don't know what I am to do. I cannot leave you, Frank. I thought perhaps . . . '

'Yes?'

Reggie, who had spent a lifetime avoiding too much sentiment, was now so choked with it he could hardly speak.

'I had thought that perhaps we might tire of each other if pressed into constant company but it is quite the opposite. I can no more leave you than stop breathing.'

Frank and Reggie did not touch. They did not dare.

'Nor I you. It will be all right. I promise,' said Frank.

They went back to the theatre, walking silently and then taking a bus, the kind Frank might have driven had life been different. They did not speak as they left his world behind. They went back to the Empire, where Frank's new act was due to open at the end of the week. The place was quiet and the stage door-keeper was reading Saturday's *Daily Graphic*. A large photograph of Field Marshal Lord Roberts took up almost the entire front page as the paper celebrated the recent relief of Kimberley by the Cavalry Division.

'Good news this, gents,' said the old fellow, looking up from his paper. 'General French says, "All well and cheerful." They say it's a turn in the tide. Perhaps they'll be home soon.'

'That would be splendid,' agreed Frank.

The theatrical gatekeeper turned the page and moved on, his interest in the war entirely satisfied. 'I see Mr Benson's *Henry V* is well received at the Lyceum,' he mumbled. 'Now there's a part. If I weren't too old . . . '

It was unclear what the fellow might do if he weren't too old: whether he might fight the Boer or merely don some Shakespearean armour for the paying public.

Frank murmured something sympathetic and headed to the dressing rooms.

'Do you really think so?' asked Reggie, following along behind. 'That the tide is turning and Valentine might be back soon?'

Behind the scenes the theatre was full of acts in various stages of rehearsal, comedians, even cats and dogs from some animal act. Through the open door of one of the small dressing rooms a weary voice could be heard instructing, 'Stand with your feet further apart. You're supposed to be a man about town, not your bleedin' auntie.'

Frank took Reggie into the small changing room next door and put him on a seat in front of the mirror.

'What are you doing?' asked Reggie.

Frank waved his hands in front of Reggie's face as if he were transformed into a mighty magician. His voice became low and mysterious.

'Reginald Grey cannot go out for he is not supposed to be in town, so Reginald Grey must disappear!'

With a knowing look he took a black tin box down from a

shelf, opened it up and went to stand behind Reggie. The two of them looked at their reflections. Reggie had grown pale and thin since his seclusion in the flat. The collar of his shirt seemed to belong to another, bigger man and even his hair had lost its lustre. Beside Frank's athletic beauty, Reggie looked unwell. Frank put his hand on Reggie's shoulder and smiled.

'You, my beloved, cannot stay hiding in the flat for ever and so' – Frank waved his hands once more to assist the magic he was about to perform – 'we shall simply assist your disappearance.' He searched through the tin and removed several wax pencils, some gum and what looked like a nest of brown hair.

It took about half an hour for Frank to do his work. The mat of hair was glued and shaped to Reggie's chin so that soon he had a rather neat, almost naval beard. His hair was parted differently and trimmed so that it now swept across his head, giving him an entirely new look. The clothes were next. While Reggie stared at his disbelieving self, Frank scrabbled through a large trunk full of costumes before producing a tweed jacket and some woollen trousers. Reggie's immaculate, Jermyn Street shirt and Savile Row suit were laid aside and soon he was dressed in an outfit that would not have made Frank's brother Jack uncomfortable. In trousers cinched tight with a wide leather belt and a collarless shirt with the sleeves rolled up, he looked quite the rough fellow.

Reggie stared at himself. This was not some toff who might misplace half a sovereign down a drain. This was a bearded working man who might toil a week for such a sum.

'Let me see your hands,' commanded Frank and Reggie dutifully held them out before him. They were pale and white and even he could see that these were not the hands of the man he had now become. Frank rubbed a dark stick of greasepaint across Reggie's knuckles and then gently massaged the make-up into his skin. When he was done, Frank stood back and looked at his work. He chuckled.

'Nature's face improved by art. You are my bit of rough,' he said with excited satisfaction, pulling Reggie from the chair so he could kiss his newly made lover.

They were cautious at first with the new disguise. They went out late at night, feeling safest under cover of darkness. As if encouraged by the change, Reggie's own beard began to grow and soon he did not need the false hair on his chin. He became accustomed to the looser clothes and even began to enjoy the freedom the costume gave him. He would sit in the flat and put his feet up on the fender of the fire as if the manners of the drawing room meant nothing to him. He began to eat more, realising how often his fashionable clothing had stopped him from overindulging. Frank was busy with rehearsals, but after dark Reggie dared to collect him from the stage door. He would don his new uniform and slip through the streets, an ordinary working man.

Gradually, he and Frank grew bolder. One Sunday morning they arose early, before Frank was due to head off to his mother's, and went to watch the men who daily braved the cold waters of the Serpentine in Hyde Park. Reggie sat upon the grass, enjoying the novelty of not worrying about the dirt on his trousers. Frank, tired from a busy week at the theatre, lay down, but Reggie sat up watching men of all kinds removing their clothing and returning themselves to their natural glory. In the still grey light he watched a young rough transformed as he stripped and entered the lake. Reggie watched him move swiftly and cleanly through the water like a mythical Greek hero. When he returned to the shore, the young man must have felt the admiring gaze, for he turned to preen and looked straight at Reggie, who suddenly took a great breath of surprise and pulled back.

'What is it?' asked Frank.

'That man,' whispered Reggie. 'I think he's one of our footmen.'

'It's all right,' soothed Frank, 'he does not know you. You're as rough as him in your disguise.' He leaned forward and whispered in Reggie's ear, 'Though much lovelier.'

Reggie wasn't so sure.

As he and Frank moved in their twilight world, Reggie began to realise that the two of them were not alone. They attended meetings of the Order of Chaeronea at the home of a man called George Cecil Ives. Frank described these secret gatherings as the 'usual mix of poets and priests' but here Reggie was surprised to meet like-minded fellows from every walk of life.

Some of these men had come to cheer on Frank's first appearance as Dolly Dutch, which was a triumph. Reggie no longer waited at the stage door but had taken to standing backstage, watching the performance from the wings. He stood in a crowd of all sorts – men dressed as women, women as smart men; one, he was thrilled to see, with a top hat and fur-trimmed velvet cape thrown over the shoulders of a red hunting jacket, was the celebrated Millie Hylton. A tiny man dressed as a sergeant major stood beside a female ventriloquist. Rather confusingly, she carried a small male dummy on her arm and kept practising his patter while they waited, so that it was hard to know who was speaking. Reggie leaned against the wall and drank it all in. Here was a world where appearances were just that. People could change; no identity was fixed and no identity was disparaged. No one in the theatre worried about what Reggie might be to Frank. Here was love of every sort and they blended in. Reggie could feel the roughness of the brick wall at his back and he rubbed his shoulders against it. He felt unencumbered by anything.

The house was full and when the curtains were raised everyone stood for the National Anthem. The usual loyal and patriotic toasts were given and responded to with a vigour that almost shook the place. Then some burlesque actor put on a drama in which he played all the parts, making quick changes with astonishing skill. There followed a mix of serious and comic singers, a patter man, some sisters doing step-dancing, a bizarre child baritone and a red-nosed comedian overfond of the line 'I was accused by a policeman of being funny – found guilty, ladies and gentlemen.'

The first half closed with Reggie's favourite moment, when an American illusionist caused his wife to entirely disappear. The Vanishing Lady was a sensation. By the time the audience had recovered from that and had a few interval drinks they were ready to be enthusiastic for Dolly Dutch. She was preceded by some crackling black and white photos from the front presented by Animatograph, in which various young men in uniform were shown being heroic. It was projected up against the dirty white backdrop, accompanied by a stirring rendition of 'The British Grenadiers' and then Frank's Dolly music. By the time Frank came on the audience was in a fiercely patriotic mood.

The skit involved Frank, dressed in his clogs, Dutch frock and plaits, emerging from a farmhouse to meet a British soldier. The skirt of his costume was attached to Frank's hands by thin strings. As soon as the soldier appeared he pretended to go into shock, pulling the strings to make his skirt rise up. Underneath he wore large bloomers decorated with tulips and as he ran about in a flustered pantomime of the hysterical female, real flowers fell from pockets in his petticoat. The laughter began in great waves, after which the little Dutch girl fell in love with the Tommy. It ended with a massive finale with many actors dressed as soldiers singing a song:

*The boys are coming home?*
*Did they get all the gold?*
*No.*
*Then send them back.*

Reggie loved the piece and was often heard singing along lustily from the wings. For the finale the farmhouse had to be moved swiftly off the stage so that the 'military men' might do their marching, but one night the large set refused to budge. Two men heaved and pulled at it from behind until one of them called, 'Oy.'

Reggie looked about, horrified to realise they were calling him. Reluctantly he moved behind the set and put his shoulder to the scenery.

'Undo that one and hold it till I say,' hissed one of the workers, indicating a rope attached to a cleat. Reggie hesitated but he could see Frank darting looks to the wings and waiting for something to happen, so he unwound the thick hemp and held it tight until the signal came to lower a large flag from above. It caused delighted hysteria among the audience and Reggie could feel his own chest swell as if he too had triumphed.

Dolly Dutch was a sensation. Afterwards there was a collection for 'the boys' at the front and many coins were gathered. Frank left the theatre in a crowd of well-wishers and after that Reggie was there every night. He pushed and pulled scenery, undid, lowered and raised ropes and his hands grew strong and tough. Dolly was hailed as patriotic. It was war work, said Frank.

# Seventeen

The word was that it was a bloody business out there, but not for us. Everyone agreed that it was galling to be so close to scenes of such epoch-making events and not to take part. Corporal Chivenden hinted at mysterious strategic movements in the near future and assured the company that there was still plenty for us to do. Nevertheless, Haddock and Sheridan, in particular, chafed at the continued maiden innocence of their rifles. In this huge and alien country I rode reconnaissance out on the plains, where occasionally I glimpsed trains creeping along the railway, laden with troops or stores for the front. From the distance you could not tell whether the men on board were Boer prisoners, British wounded or refugees heading south from Kimberley to Cape Town.

My legs grew strong and my face brown. I still took quiet pleasure each time I swung my leg over the saddle of my bicycle and set off. No one accompanied me, no one needed to watch out for me. Each time I left the camp behind there was an exhilarating sense of freedom and excitement. Often I would light up a cigarette as I rode, king of all I surveyed. One day I rode to within five miles of the Boer laager, where outpost shots were exchanged daily and where some officers had narrowly escaped capture. I saw no enemy but word was that a group of about thirty Boers had been seen on the same road that afternoon. On my return, caught by the sudden darkness that immediately succeeds sunset in South Africa, my cycle suffered a puncture from one of the sharp mimosa thorns that littered even the best roads. I walked, pushing my iron steed, feeling my breath become laboured at the thought of meeting 'the enemy'. In my mind they had become something other than human.

We were moved to a slightly larger tent, which meant we could finally lie down without our feet resting on another man's chest. It was just as well, for Cooper was beginning to be troubled with his feet. Either his boots did not fit well or he was less used to physical work than anyone. Certainly he didn't know how to look after himself. Here was a man who had been tended all his life, and left to his own devices even some of the basics seemed to elude him. His great book learning meant that he was a man who knew many details about the world around him and nothing about himself. His feet began to swell and then to develop small sores. He said nothing and, worse, did nothing. The smell of infection began to rise. Jackson gave him soap and I got hot water to bathe them but now that Pattenden was not allowed to attend him he would let no one help. It pained me to watch him struggle. Many a time he caught me looking at him, with me willing the distance between us to be less, but we said nothing. We did not even mention the photographer, Harry Hawkins, who had known Reggie at school. So much more was unspoken between us than was ever said.

'*Ex Africa semper aliquid novi*,' he muttered. Out of Africa always something new.

The only cheer in that time was indeed something new and unexpected. It was Haddock's duck. Most of us were asleep one night when a giant rainstorm hit. It washed through the tent with a ferocity we had got used to, leaving behind the usual sodden clothing and ruined diaries. This time, however, where Haddock's bed had been, the weather also deposited a small bundle of dark and light grey fluff. It was a baby duck or rather, as Cooper corrected us, it was a type of duck known as an Egyptian Goose. A duck pretending to be a goose, a baby goose impostor. Quite where it had come from was uncertain but where it was going was clear. Haddock scooped up the shivering creature in both hands and held it to his chest.

'She must be terrified.' He was almost sobbing with pity.

'She?' questioned Jackson.

No one checked but 'she' it was. Haddock named the duck Bessie after his mother and thus Bessie joined the troop. He fed her insects and grass and she quickly took to following him in the day and sleeping on his chest at night. She was the softest thing there ever was, even though Jackson used jokingly to chase her around with a mess tin and threaten her with the oven. I watched Haddock stroke her; he was too young to worry that it might make him less of a man.

One morning the order to move out once more was given. I had tried to get some Condy's Fluid for Cooper. It was something I knew was helpful to soothe tired feet, but nothing about our life was predictable and I found the horses had been washed in the bright reddish-purple liquid overnight. There was none left. The fluid was intended to conceal the horses, and it had discoloured them white and grey. It left the men responsible drained of colour as well, and we headed north into the Orange Free State in our new camouflage looking as if ghosts marched to battle.

'Nothing but bloody farmers!' was the disparaging cry you heard up and down the ranks.

'They're not even professional soldiers,' echoed young Haddock.

'Neither are we,' muttered Ben.

Of all of us, Haddock was the keenest to 'get stuck in'. He reminded me of the smallest of our dogs on the hunt in Assam, always ready for a scrap. So far our biggest problem seemed to be finding the war.

The first sign of battles won or lost that we spotted were the empty cartridge cases littering the ground. The fact that there were so many testified to the slowness of the advance and the severity of the fighting. Soon we saw the remains of neatly planned military lines – trenches, gun emplacements, sangars, wire entanglements, tents left standing, shelters constructed out of bushes and small trees, but there were also many human signs of haste. A plate lay with a fork, abandoned; a half-washed pair of trousers, one leg still in the water. There was tobacco, bags of bullets, rice and coffee beans, and Chivenden let us take what we liked.

As the CIV headed north, shots were often heard in the distance but much of our day-to-day anxiety centred on food. There were no regular supplies for the ordinary soldiers, let alone the volunteers, and looting farms became common practice for all of us. Drinking water too was an issue and the struggles made everyone often weary and unwell. Soon tents were no longer provided. We made whatever bivouacs we could manage and when the rain fell steadily we seemed to live in a lake.

By the Easter of 1900, they told us we were on the move for

Bloemfontein but then it was taken by Lord Roberts before we could get there. Haddock was devastated. How he longed to liberate somewhere in the name of Queen and country.

'Where to?' became the boy's repeated question as we travelled.

The answer was north. We were going to Bloemfontein after all. As Cooper explained, 'It is the law of South Africa that the Boer drive the native north and the English drive the Boer north but now the Boer can go north no more.'

'Why not?' I asked.

'Tsetse fly and the fever. So if the Boer must perish, he sees it as his duty to perish fighting. That makes for a formidable enemy.'

We headed God knows where, the men ever marching and we cyclists pedalling messages up and down the ranks. It rained hard all day and the drifts across the river were impossible to cross. The wagons were up to their axles in mud and the horses, not seeing what the Empire had to do with them, often refused to go on. We were the tiniest part of a large black column which rolled ahead and behind us.

Everything was upside down. It might have been spring in England, but here it was autumn. Now there was no dust. Just mud. Endless mud that caked everything and sucked our boots and the tyres of our bicycles down into the ground. Every step was exhausting, every turn of the bicycle wheels strained our legs and all around we heard the squelching sound of men moving forward.

'*A horse! A horse! My kingdom for a horse!*' quoted Cooper, trying to lift our spirits, but no one had time for literary references. His books were left behind. All manner of things were discarded in our wake as we took nothing but the most essential items with us – for me, bicycle and liquor.

Across the rolling veldt moved cavalry and guns. Sometimes we came in sight of the railway line where slate-coloured trains puffed along packed with khaki and occasionally a Maxim at the tail of it all. They were heading north, while hospital trains carrying pale faces and bandaged limbs headed south. The bandolier of bullets we each carried had proved a heavy weight on the chest and many of us now wore them around the waist or slung old pouches anywhere at all to try to balance the equipment. We were no longer the smart troop who had disembarked at Cape Town but absent-minded beggars who managed as best we could. Cooper had cut his boots to allow for his swollen feet, and my tunic bore the signs of many encounters with thorns on outpost duty. The sun burned the scars on my forehead, so I had taken to wearing a strip of fabric around my head to protect them.

Cooper smiled at me and said I was 'quite the gentleman in khaki'. But I began not to care what I looked like. I traded my rucksack for a half-bottle of homemade alcohol that fitted neatly into my jacket pocket beside my photograph from home. I could now manage without much food but I could no longer get through the day without a drink. Gradually I gave away whatever I had for whatever filthy liquor I could find. I hid it all from Cooper, from Ben, from everyone.

More men from around the world joined us as part of our brigade – the Ceylon Mounted Infantry, the Derby Regiment and most of the Canadian Dragoons. Ceylon, Derby, Canada – how far everyone had come. By the time we reached Bloemfontein, we could hear the guns. The fighting was some twenty miles away. Gradually we grew nearer. At first it was merely a few shells falling among the Derbys but our artillery soon found their range and silenced the guns. Then two of Loch's Horse were killed.

I had been pretending to be a soldier for months. Now, at last, I had to pretend to be ready. The order came to move into battle formation. I downed what alcohol I had left and we began advancing. The guns were behind us while ahead Brother Boer held two kopjes – one on either side of the line of advance. The guns began their booming work, each blast thudding inside me. Poor Ben's breathing turned to wheezing and Haddock gave tiny cries of fear which echoed every blast, as he clutched Bessie to his chest.

Jackson called out encouragement.

'Come on, fellows. Who do they think they are?' He shook his massive fist and laughed at the hidden enemy. 'Why, we shall crush them.'

It was a good question. Who did they think they were? I did not know the answer. We had seen almost nothing of them. They were mythical men who threatened the Empire; who apparently sought to destroy 'everything your father fought for'. Guns were going off all around as if there were men who knew who they should be aiming at. Orders were given for us to leave our bikes in a battle stack and lie down in a field, which we did. Boer shells passed endlessly overhead but they landed well behind us and were more a source of wonder than of fear. We were there for so long and many were so exhausted that some of the men fell asleep. In the midst of battle they slept. We watched the shrapnel burst beyond us and listened to the continuous purring of the Maxims, the evil tapping of the dreaded pom-poms and the sharp rattle of the musketry. A great cloud of dust burst upon the hilltop and two guns went off with a double boom.

'Like a right and left at partridges,' muttered Cooper.

'This is better than watching W.G. hit three successive

boundaries from the best Australian bowling,' declared Sheridan. 'Anyone fancy a bet on the next hit?'

A shell burst among a flying group of Boers. A laugh rang out from our side.

'This is sport with a vengeance,' decided Jackson, sitting up and getting out a cigarette. A fellow from the City lay beside him and they began discussing financial options for a factory John was planning. In the distance there was a flash and glitter as the men ahead fixed bayonets, ready to kill at close quarters. Artillery fire came faster and faster. We could see the stretcher bearers with their stiff burdens scrambling away and yet we did not move.

Ben sat up, drawing what he saw – the puffs of smoke and flares over the brown veldt all done in great sweeps of charcoal. Haddock sat beside him, holding Bessie tight. At last we had arrived at battle yet we seemed to have come as audience. Cooper lent me his field glasses and behind the rocks I caught glimpses of the enemy faces, their hats and rifles. They were just men and boys like us. Perhaps I should tell someone, tell them that these were not the villains we had been led to believe. I think the alcohol had made me lose all sense. I looked up and noticed an extraordinary thing. The hollow we lay in was alive with butterflies. Camberwell Beauties darted and fluttered in the sunshine while shells whistled and shrieked. A butterfly landed on my arm and was perfectly still. It was, I thought, a Painted Lady, a brilliant orange and gold with white and brown markings. I reached out and crushed its thorax with my fingers.

'Why did you do that?' asked Ben.

I shook my head. 'I don't know.'

When the guns quietened, we marched on. I walked past the body of an English soldier. He was clearly dead but he lay on the ground with his eyes open as though he saw me. He had a thin well-trimmed moustache and was so well groomed that he looked as if he should be going somewhere, as if he had an important appointment.

'He is dead,' I said stupidly.

Cooper looked away. 'It is the one thing that we will all eventually have in common.'

At first the men behaved well, trying to buy bread from the Boer women, but when they were refused the thefts began. In one of the endless villages that we marched through, a woman tried to shoo us from her door but Pattenden pushed past and seized some tinned fish and jam from her kitchen. He did not intend to share but Jackson grabbed him by the neck and we fell upon it as if it were the most glorious food of the Grand Hotel, little caring who it had once belonged to.

Soldiers were like locusts lighting upon anything that might sustain us. A young woman stood in her doorway watching as we passed. Her house stood beside a property that had been commandeered for an officers' mess, so no one dared steal from her.

'How much?' called Pattenden.

She shrugged and looked at him. 'How much do you have?'

I didn't know what he meant. How much for what? How did Pattenden know that she had anything for sale? Pattenden reached in his pocket and produced a coin. He flipped it in the air and she caught it. She turned and went inside, leaving the door open.

Cooper grabbed Pattenden's arm. 'Don't do this. The food is bad enough. Can't you ever behave well?' he asked.

Pattenden laughed. 'Behave well? But I am behaving well. It's not for me. It's a gift.' He turned slowly and looked at me. 'A gift for Grey to make up for any old misunderstandings.'

'What gift?' I stammered.

Ben shook his head. 'No, Pattenden, leave the poor girl alone.'

Pattenden smiled and patted me on the shoulder. 'I'm trying to help the boy. Poor thing has yet to find his beard but surely it is time he found a woman.'

Sheridan and Haddock began to laugh and push me forward.

Pattenden jeered at Cooper. 'Think Grey's not man enough?'

Cooper reached out to grab me. 'It's not that ... it's just ...' He looked at me and sighed. 'Let me speak to the boy a minute.'

Cooper pulled me away from the others. Haddock was laughing more than anyone, perhaps out of relief that he was not the youth Pattenden had decided to pick on.

'I don't know what's going on,' I whispered urgently.

'No,' replied Cooper. 'I know. Pattenden has paid for you to ... to be with that girl.'

'But I ... I can't.'

'No.' Cooper looked as though he were going to stroke my arm but stopped himself. 'Just go in. Shut the door. Find some way to ... It'll be all right.'

I turned back to the men. They were all looking at me. Ben turned aside and began to walk away, up the road. I wanted to go after him, but instead I moved to the door of the small house and went inside, to the sound of laughter.

'We'll wait right here!' called Pattenden.

'I'm next!' added Sheridan excitedly as I closed the door behind me.

The young woman, almost exactly my age, wore a plain dress and had her hair swept up into a bun. Everything about her suggested defeat. The dress was ragged and her hair was too thin to stay in place. She was pale and lined with exhaustion. I stood looking at her.

'Come on then,' she said in heavily accented English.

The house consisted of a single room in which all life was conducted. There was a small stove, a chair and in one corner, a bed.

It was only when she moved to the bed and sat down to undo the buttons of her dress that it dawned on me what was meant to happen.

'Wait!' I called, leaping across the room to stop her. 'I ... we ... ' I put my hand on hers and held it fast. She looked up at me.

Conscious that the men were listening outside, I lowered my voice.

'What is your name?' I asked in halting Dutch.

She looked surprised. 'Sarel.'

'Sarel,' I repeated.

There was a thump at the door.

'I can't hear you,' called Pattenden.

'I can't do this,' I said urgently in English.

Sarel gave a half-laugh and replied brokenly in my own tongue. 'All the men can do this. Boer, British, what's the difference?' Suddenly she reached out with her free hand and grabbed the fold of fabric between my legs. She squeezed and squeezed again, looking confused.

I nodded. 'No, I really can't do this.'

Still holding her hand, I sat down on the bed beside her. Was this what any man could do? Buy a woman? It had never occurred to me. Who did this? Not Cooper surely? Gentle Ben White? Bahadur? Would Bahadur purchase a woman's favour?

More thumps were delivered to the door. 'Shall we come in and help?' shouted Pattenden.

'They cannot come in,' she declared, looking afraid.

'No. No,' I agreed.

'The men leave me alone because the officers have what they like,' she explained.

I shook my head. 'I don't understand.'

Sarel smiled. 'No. All men are the same. It doesn't matter what uniform they wear. They will give you whatever you want if you give them yourself.'

Suddenly she pushed me back on the bed.

'Make a noise,' she said.

'What kind of noise?' I asked.

She demonstrated a moan.

I let out a low noise.

'Louder!' she commanded, rolling me about on the bed and lying on top of me. I moaned more and she began pushing me up and down on the bed. It made me giggle.

'Ssh!' she said, trying to sound cross but sniggering at our play-acting.

Without warning, she called out, 'Oh my God!' as if in a state of complete amazement.

'What?' I cried.

'Ssh!' she repeated, still trying not to laugh. But then we both began laughing loudly and moaning and crying out and thumping the bed.

I was young. I had not thought about sex at all. After a short while we stopped making any noise, and I thought how nice it was to lie there for a moment in that still room. To lie upon a bed and hold a woman's hand. She smelt good. A woman. How I longed to stay and shut the world away. How dreadful to have to pay for such a nice thing. Sarel smiled at me and stroked my hair back from my forehead and I thought how lucky men were to have a woman treat them like this. Whose hair would I wish to stroke if I had the chance? Tears began to roll down my cheeks as if all my exhaustion were leaking from my body.

There was a knock at the door.

'Are you all right, Grey?' It was Cooper. I could hear the concern in his voice.

Reluctantly we rose and shook out our clothes. Sarel looked at me shyly.

'I do not understand,' she said.

I smiled. 'Neither do I. I thought I did but not any more.'

We moved to the door.

She picked up a framed photograph from a small table. It showed a young man of perhaps fifteen, Haddock's age. He wore two bandoliers criss-crossed over his chest and a large wide-brimmed hat. He stood between a couple of bearded fellows but looked too small and too young to lift the large gun that rested in his hand.

'My brother, Izak,' she explained. She put the picture down and quietly asked, 'Do you go fighting now?'

'I suppose so,' I said.

'Do you need anything?'

'Drink. Some drink. Whisky?'

Sarel moved to a small cupboard and took out a half-empty bottle of brandy. She looked at it. 'We had it for medicine. Seems no point now. There is no curing anything.'

I took it and put it in my pocket. She reached out and ran her hand across my cheek.

'Do not shoot Izak, will you? Do not shoot my brother.'

'I'll . . . no.'

I lit a cigarette and then we casually opened the door and I went out. Sarel leaned against the frame as if she were exhausted.

The men stood in a small group waiting for me. Our play-acting had clearly silenced them. Sarel gave a loud sigh of contentment. I was not at all sure of the correct method of farewell.

'You have been most kind,' I said.

Sheridan pulled up his trousers and threw back his shoulders as he headed for the door. 'My turn,' he called cheerily, but as he moved towards Sarel an officer appeared from the mess and frowned at us. Sarel moved quickly inside, shut the door and bolted it.

As we walked off, both Sheridan and Pattenden seemed quite out of sorts, but for different reasons. Cooper put his arm around me and squeezed my shoulders.

Some fifty men were unfit to march and were left behind. Cooper should have gone nowhere but he sat upon his bike so casually that no officer thought to have him relegated to a sickbed. I should have been his friend. I should have told someone that he was not fit but I was selfish and glad that he stayed beside me. That night as I lay among the sleeping bodies of the men I knew so well I thought about them in a new light. How innocent I had been. I ran my hands across my unfamiliar body and wondered what might happen if my friends ever knew the truth.

We moved on. At a river, which river I have no idea, a river – the Orange, the Vaal – at some river the Boer at last lay in front. All was rumour. So far we had heard fighting; we had even seen fighting, but we had not participated. Now word came that it was to be our turn.

'I hear there are ten thousand Boers,' exclaimed Jackson excitedly, 'and twenty-five thousand guns.'

# Eighteen

Dolly was a triumph in every regard. The newspapers were ecstatic, while some men in the audience were so taken with the Dutch girl that they sent flowers to her, and she even received a handwritten marriage proposal at the stage door. Dolly's act was enlarged; there were Dutch windmills, prop cannons and all sorts of stage paraphernalia that Reggie became responsible for. Each night after the show there was a heady round of celebration and champagne. Society people came to call, including some who had been in Reggie's circle. No one, however, suspected that the bearded stagehand might be someone they had once known.

Frank and Reggie had, in effect, swapped places. Frank was quite the swell and he could not have been happier. One night Reggie presented Frank with a small wrapped parcel, pretending it was one of the many gifts sent backstage. Frank was sitting in his chair by his make-up mirror, laughing about something that had happened during the show. He had just removed the last traces of Dolly and his face was clean and shiny, ready for a night of amusement. He casually unwrapped the present while sipping at some champagne. His laughter faded at the sight of the elegant silver card case with Frank Rutherford, Esq. etched on the lid, and when he opened it and saw the words *For Frank. For ever. Reggie* on the inside cover, tears sprang to his eyes.

In truth, Frank had known many men. It was something he and Reggie never talked about. Frank's work had brought many liaisons to his door and it had never occurred to him that he might settle for just one. When he had first spied Reggie in the museum he had been struck by his cheerful young face, but he had been a boy, a boy to dally with over lunch. Now Frank looked up and saw the man before him and he knew that he would never leave. Reggie smiled at him.

'It wasn't meant to make you cry,' he said gently.

'Come here,' replied Frank, putting his hand out to his lover.

Reggie took Frank's hand and allowed himself to be pulled into the older man's embrace. He stood for a long time gently stroking Frank's hair and then they went home to the safety of their rooms.

Reggie enjoyed his work behind the scenes more than anything he had ever done before. He found he was comfortable with the gang of working-class lads who worked alongside him. They mimicked his accent, but they respected the way he pulled his weight. He began to learn that the exact timing of the pull on a rope or the reveal of a particular scene could generate a wave of applause through the audience. For the first time in his life, he felt the power of his hands to do something useful. He felt strong. He loved the camaraderie of the stage crew, the rough jokes, the sense of belonging, of feeling useful. Some nights he would sit up in the flies above the stage, looking down on the entertainers, hearing the laughter and feeling as though he ruled the world. The heat from the lights wafted upwards and in it small motes of dust played in the air. It was as foreign as anything he had ever known. How he loved the Empire.

But buckets of champagne and compliments, and jolly camaraderie could not keep the news from the front at bay. While Frank sat drinking and taking off his make-up and costume, Reggie read the news reports and realised the war was not going well.

'I should go, Frank. I have to go, don't I?' Only activity and alcohol kept his cousin out of his mind, but as soon as he stopped, as soon as he sat quietly, Valentine would be there. The truth was that he was a coward, he knew that. He was a fraud.

One night after the curtain had fallen on a particularly appreciative audience, Frank was dressing to go to the Criterion. If anyone had ever wished to advertise the glamour of a man wearing white tie and tails, then Frank would have been their model. He wore it as if he were born to it. This was the time of night when Frank came to life. His body, still pumping with adrenalin from his performance, was that of a sprinter ready for the race. He checked his hair in the mirror and smiled. He had never had such success, such adulation, and could not bear that Reggie, who had already sunk several glasses of champagne, sat brooding in a corner. He longed for them both to enjoy the moment.

Frank turned and raised both arms as if to hug the very idea he was about to propose. 'We must have an adventure,' he declared. 'One that would make Valentine proud.'

Reggie looked up and the sight of Frank caught his breath, for his lover had never looked more beautiful.

Frank, clutching one open and one fresh bottle of Dom Perignon, hurried Reggie out of the dressing room. At the stage door a hansom cab stood waiting. He gave the driver an address with which Reggie was unfamiliar.

'You sure, sir?' the man called down from his perch.

'Sure?' replied Frank loudly. 'Sure? I am not only sure, I am rich.' He reached into his pocket and pulled out a wad of notes which he waved briefly, indicating to Reggie to get in. The two of them tumbled past the disapproving driver and his horse and on to the leather seat.

'The impertinence,' Frank muttered at the driver's back.

'Where are we going?' laughed Reggie.

Frank hushed him. 'You have to speak lower, my love. Otherwise, the driver will know that you are a bugger and the game will be up. I think it's the drink makes your voice high. You should not have any more after this.'

Frank waved his bottle and, rather than lower his own voice, shouted out of the window to anyone who would listen, 'We are off to foreign parts; we are off to travel the world down the old Ratcliffe Highway.'

'Which bit of the world might that be?' enquired Reggie, intrigued as Frank struggled to remove the cork from the new bottle of champagne.

'Why, we can go where you like. It's all on the Highway,' explained Frank, as flamboyant and dramatic as if he were playing Dolly and conducting a tour for those not fortunate enough to attend the theatre. 'You've got your Spanish and Maltese sailors at the Rose and Crown down Wapping end; there's a place just by Wellclose Square where you can get a fine drop of German or Lawson's – now that's run by a German, but you find your Swedish sailors in there. Other places there's Greeks, Italians and there's The Bell, a music hall just for Sambos. You should see those black men when they laugh in the dark. It's like a house full of teeth.' The cork flew from the bottle and ricocheted into the roof of the cab, banging back into Reggie's nose.

'Oops, sorry,' muttered Frank, 'war wound.' He took a great gulp of champagne and gestured wildly to the open window. It was dark now and the occasional gas lamps did little to illuminate the route. Reggie saw flashes of public houses and a few passers-by, but he could not work out where they were going.

'I haven't even mentioned Paddy's Goose,' continued Frank, 'which used to be packed with half the tramps and thieves of London, although lately the law has been bothering them and they say it is a little dull. There's your Yiddishers along Whitechapel, of course. Oh yes . . . ' Frank banged the side of the cab with appreciation for his native surroundings, 'from the City to Limehouse we've got everything along here. You Mayfair people have nothing like this.'

Reggie disliked it when Frank mentioned any differences in their station but he kept quiet and just watched this strange, exotic creature beside him with a mix of irritation and wonder. Then he grabbed the open bottle and glugged some champagne.

'I tell you what, Reggie,' continued Frank, 'when we're done we could stop at the Emporium and see if they happen to have a tiger. How much do you suppose they'd want for such a thing? I bet I could afford one.'

They were both very drunk, but Reggie remained quiet and let Frank prattle on.

'Dolly can buy what she likes now,' babbled Frank. 'Why, at this rate I shall be as rich as your dear father, Lord Grey himself.' He loomed close to Reggie's face. 'Do you think he would like to meet me then? Perhaps he would like a tiger. When my father was a boy, a tiger from Bengal, I think— Is that a place? Ben Gal. Sounds like a fella's name. Anyway, it escaped from its box at

Jamrach's. They have every kind of creature you can imagine but they don't often have a tiger. The wretched animal carried off some passing boy ... passing to where I know not, but not a good day for him, I should say, and Jamrach came running up and thrust his bare hands into the tiger's mouth, forcing the beast to let his captive go.' Even in the confined space of the cab Frank did a fine job of enacting the horrifying scene.

'What happened?' asked Reggie, his eyes wide with wonder and alcohol.

'I believe the boy sued and the tiger became ... well, either a popular attraction or ... a rug. I forget which,' slurred Frank, losing interest.

Reggie looked out of the cab window. An even greater darkness seemed to have settled on this part of London. The streets of terraced houses were squeezed among an overcrowded network of canals and railway lines, of lead works and coal yards, factories, shipyards and workshops. He had heard stories about Limehouse: tales of mysterious murders in foggy riverside alleys, of sordid opium dens, of innocent English girls lost in a dangerous underworld controlled by some evil Chinese genius. Limehouse belonged to the sordid and dangerous spaces of the East End. He flexed the muscles in his arm. He was strong now. Perhaps he could have gone to South Africa. Perhaps he could fight.

As they got closer to their destination, Reggie thought he saw small oriental figures with pigtails and little black hats scurrying through the dark. 'Chinese sailors,' whispered Frank dramatically. 'From the tea ships. Perfectly nice fellows but not as good as your regular sailor if you want a bit of love and attention. They don't seem as keen.'

At last the cab came to a halt in a narrow street of three-storey terraced houses. Public houses and corner cafés threw out their lights into the dank and dark road. Reggie felt frightened and thrilled. The air had strange spices in it, scents of food, and, perhaps it was fanciful, but Reggie felt he could almost hear sex and violence throbbing below the surface.

Frank obviously knew his way around these streets as he strode off quickly, beckoning Reggie to follow. Down a little passageway they went, until they emerged on a dingy corner. A shopfront carried Chinese letters either side of a door that had once been red, and above it was the name *H. Doe Foon*. A horse and cart bearing many newly arrived trunks from the ships rattled past, pushing Reggie and Frank up against the door. There was strangeness here and Reggie tried to feel emboldened by it. The place reeked of the sea and sweat and sawdust and Frank reached into his pocket for a handkerchief to place across his nose.

Reggie laughed out loud. 'Aren't you funny about smell?' he remarked.

'It's terrible,' coughed Frank.

Reggie took a deep breath of the polluted air. 'I think it's marvellous. Makes me feel alive.'

'*The accumulated scum of humanity gathered here, washed, as it were, from somewhere else*,' quoted Frank.

'So why have we come?' asked Reggie.

'We have come,' declared Frank, walking backwards and luring Reggie onward with his hands, 'to leave London behind.' He turned and raised his arm in the air with a triumphant cry: 'Follow me, my hearty, to the Orient.'

Frank almost danced down a narrow passage that barely admitted a single figure. It was dull and empty and wound round shabby properties with dark doorways and sightless windows. A few strange signs in Chinese script suggested these were boarding-houses or perhaps shops for an alien people. But there was no one there now. At last the meandering alleyway ended in a squalid cul-de-sac. Frank lurched towards a small wooden door and banged loudly on it.

'Johnny!' he called. 'Where the devil are you?' He stepped back a little to look up into the dark curtained windows above. 'Johnny!' Frank called again. 'Johnny Chinaman. Splendid fellow,' he explained to Reggie.

After some time, a weak light appeared in the dirty window above the door, coming from a single oil lantern. When the door opened, it revealed a small Chinese man in a cloth coat and baggy trousers, with flat slippers. This ageless soul with hard, staring eyes was evidently Johnny. Silently, he held the door open for Frank and Reggie to enter. The low ceiling made Frank duck slightly as he led Reggie down a set of creaking stairs into a small room that reeked of something sweet. Reggie stood still, in the gloom and smoke. Eventually he made out several men lying on ancient couches or on mattresses on the floor around the dim flame of a smoky lamp. Beside it sat an elderly Chinese woman, toasting on a long wire tiny lumps of what looked like thick brown dung. What was this place?

'Welcome to Paradise,' announced Frank, throwing himself down on the end of a couch covered in red silk. Johnny bowed slightly and then handed Frank what Reggie thought looked like a broken-down flute with a tiny bowl at the end. With his long supple fingers Johnny crammed something into the bowl and Frank grinned at Reggie and then began to suck hard through it at the smoky little flame.

As Reggie's eyes became accustomed to the light he saw that Johnny's patrons came from every part of London. In the corner he felt sure he recognised some fellow from his club lying beside a man who looked as if he might be known to the police. Other than the old Chinese woman, the room was all men, of all ages. No, he suddenly thought, one patron deep in the shadows might have been a society woman.

Opium. Reggie might have lived a life of indulgence in the past but he had never tried opium. He had heard of it, of course, and had wondered what it was like, but he had no idea how to get started on it; the Chinese woman had to help him. He sat himself down on a low couch. He had arrived in a state of some agitation but it was not long before he felt as though his limbs had turned to warm jelly. He could feel himself drifting in and out of consciousness. He was lying down, staring at the ceiling, as he drifted between euphoria and a state where his whole being became a blank. His breathing slowed until he felt as if he both floated above and had sunk deep into the couch upon which he lay.

Occasionally he thought he heard Frank's voice winding around him in the gloom.

'We are travelling the world, Reggie. Did we not, after all, meet in Greece among the greatest beauties of the ancient world? Did those young men not stare at you, their stone turning to flesh as you gazed back?'

Reggie thought of the wonderful carved boy with the broken arm in the Phigaleian Room. In his mind he held him and nursed him back to health. He and Frank walked with the boy through a landscape peopled with beautiful young Sicilians wearing togas and with vine leaves in their hair. The boys smiled as they passed until Reggie lay down under an olive tree and slipped away into sleep.

Reggie did not know how long they spent in the cellar of the

Chinaman, hours perhaps. When they finally crawled up from their exotic sojourn and were released into the cul-de-sac, it was as if the whole world had turned yellow. A thick fog hung so heavily in the streets that it made Reggie cough as soon as he reached the air. His mouth was so dry he could hardly speak. He turned to Frank and saw that his pupils were mere pinheads of black. Frank seemed disinclined to move at all so Reggie reached out for his hand and pulled him down the alleyway, stumbling towards the street where the cab had dropped them. It might have been morning, but the fog was so thick that even the single gas lamp on the street corner could not overcome the gloom.

The driver was long gone and these were not the sorts of streets where cabs happened by, looking for a fare, nor was any omnibus minded to ply a nearby route. The local warehouses and the docks were waking up and labourers and stevedores were ambling past en route to work. A couple of large young men loomed out of the shroud of fog. It was impossible to know if they were up early or late. They were swigging from a bottle so it was unlikely that they were heading for work. One of them was shouting at no one in particular.

'... and while brave young Englishmen go off to fight for Queen and country,' he yelled, 'the bloody Chinese take their jobs and ...' It was with these words that he spied Reggie and Frank just stepping into the pool of yellow light beneath the lamp post.

'Well, well, well,' said the man, hitching up his trousers and moving closer.

Reggie pulled at Frank's arm.

'Let's go,' he said urgently, but Frank was lost to his dreams.

'Ssh,' he said, melodramatically placing one finger on his lips, 'I'm from round here. You don't understand. It's fine. They're fine. We're all fine.' He turned to face the men, placing his hands firmly on his hips. 'Hello, lads,' he said, giving a mock bow in the men's direction. 'I wonder if I could trouble you to direct me and my friend to the Highway?'

'Well, if it ain't a couple of mollies out and about,' said one of the men, as they moved closer and began circling around Frank.

Reggie, suddenly clear-headed, moved forward to try to protect him. 'Now then, gentlemen, no need for trouble here. Frank!'

Frank waved Reggie away, turning his back to the men. 'Trouble? How can there be trouble? I am Dolly Dutch. Every night at the Empire, twice on Saturdays.'

Frank began to do the dance that had made him so popular in the West End but this was the East End and he seemed unaware that the audience was not ideal.

'You taking the mick?' growled one of the men.

'Stop doing that,' said the other, but Frank continued to jig on the street. As he did so his new silver card case fell from his pocket and one of the men picked it up.

'Nice,' he declared, opening it up and looking inside. 'Esquire, is it? Look at that, we got an esquire doin' a little dance for us. Do you want to dance with me, eh, molly?' he taunted.

The mixture of drink and drugs had left Frank incapable of sensing any undercurrent of danger.

'Why, I'd be delighted,' he declared, stepping forward towards the man.

'Look,' tried Reggie again, 'you probably know his family, the Rutherfords? They're,' Reggie struggled to remember the word, 'toshers, near ... Wapping.'

He finished his explanation just as the first fellow delivered a punch right to Frank's stomach. A knee was next. It crunched into Frank's nose as he bent double in pain. Reggie ran forward to defend Frank, only to find himself thrown to the kerb by a punch from the second labourer. He rose as fast as he could and managed to land one blow on the man who had the card case. The silver gift flew through the air, and landed with a thud on the street.

Reggie had grown much tougher in his time backstage. He fought like the Jamrach tiger to protect Frank but when the larger of the two assailants deliberately smashed his bottle on the lamp post and came at them, Reggie stood frozen. Then as the broken edge of glass came towards him, he shouted 'NO' and ducked in horror – but Frank didn't see it coming. He just stood there. Reggie turned and watched as it sliced into his lover's beautiful face. For a moment Frank looked faintly surprised before screaming and collapsing in the gutter, blood pouring from his cheek. Something stirred in the fog, and the attackers gave Frank one final kick where he lay and ran off, shouting to each other in triumph.

Reggie crawled over the dirty cobbles. Frank's face was crimson with blood. He did not move as Reggie picked him up in his arms and carried him like a baby, away from this terrible place.

'Take me home,' moaned Frank.

Reggie shook his head. 'No, let's go where you'll be safe.'

He carried Frank all the way back to the main highway. He carried him through such thick fog that most of the time he had no idea where he was going. At last he waved down a cab heading for the City. The driver, horrified at his cargo, worried about his cab but some kindness in him prevailed and he helped Reggie lay Frank gently upon the seat. When they finally arrived at Inkerman House, Frank was no longer conscious. The driver helped Reggie pull him from the cab and rang the bell for them. The door opened and a shaft of light cut through the grey air. Reggie, with his lover in his arms, looked up into the face of his father.

# Nineteen

The order came at 3 a.m. and with empty stomachs, thirsty throats and fearful hearts we headed into the flowing river. Now, Chivenden told us, we were not messengers but fighters. Our bicycles were of no use and lay behind us in a great heap. Fighters? I held my gun above my head as we trod through the waters. Could I shoot a man as well as I shot a barrel? Could I kill someone? The answer was probably not. I was afraid but I also knew that I had my brandy from Sarel with me. That was my secret. That was how I would survive.

And then suddenly, here was what Haddock had once longed for – action at last. We were being shelled with pom-poms and big guns but we just moved forward, too tired, too hungry, too foolish to do anything else. The noise alone should have woken us from our sleep-walking. Our artillery pounded away at the Boer trenches in front and the din was relentless, as if my own heartbeat were on the march. As we reached the opposite bank, our wet clothes clinging to us, I saw men advancing ahead of us protected by the steep banks of the kopje. We could not have had a better view of the charge if we had been watching it at Earl's Court. One of the men stopped in his tracks. He seemed to take a great breath, draw his body up to its full height and reach out with both arms as if taking the final shape of Jesus on the cross, then he crumpled to the ground. We were drowning in the landscape. On our left rose tiers of hills; in front a huge green hill blocked our view, with other hills crowding behind like a regiment gathering in the wake of its general. Everywhere rose walls of red-brown kopje, endless fields of rough grass littered with boulders, more veldt.

Sheridan pointed ahead. 'The enemy are over that rise.'

The enemy? Who were they? I could not see. Was it Izak? Did Sarel's brother lie in wait for us? Could I kill him? Would he kill me? This was madness. I closed my eyes for a moment and lay upon the bed with my enemy and she smelt good and we laughed.

A snarling roll of musketry broke not from the rise ahead, but far to our left.

'What's that?' I called in fear.

Cooper reached out and put a steadying hand on my shoulder.

A thunder of galloping orderlies and hoarse yells of command filled the air: 'Advance! In line! Wagon supply!'

And with a great rattle the batteries tore past us, wheeled and unlimbered as if they had broken in half. The wagons were next. I could see them gathered round the guns like medical men round a patient in an operation. The first gun barked and Haddock looked to Sheridan for comfort. In the distance you could see mounted men scurrying up the slopes of the big hill opposite. Our guns still thudded and thud came the answer. We crouched, frozen.

'Where's it coming from?' cried Pattenden in anguish. I looked at him. He was frightened, more frightened than anyone, and I am ashamed to say it made me bold.

'You little Jemmy,' I sneered.

'Away on the right,' Ben yelled, pointing.

We moved forward. Still we had no idea what part we were playing.

'Limbers!' came the cry and from halves the guns were whole again, and wheeled away. Down went a length of wire fencing, and on we went as shots scored the soft pasture beyond. We passed round the edge of a brown hill and joined our infantry in a broad green valley. We moved on but it was all the same – more ridges rising above us freckled with innumerable boulders. The Boer guns seemed to boom without pause.

We did not know it then, but when it was all over these very battles would be restaged in America. Twice a day General Cronjé himself would appear with six hundred veterans to show the world what it had been like. They would pretend to fight and the Boer general Christiaan de Wet would conclude the entertainment by escaping on horseback, leaping thirty-five feet into a pool of water as if it were an African river. People were dying and one day it would make a piece of theatre.

There was the sound of a shell coming towards us, a faint whirr at first which built into a furious scream, then a white cloud that flung itself on to the very line of our batteries unlimbering on the brow. Whirr and scream – another dashed itself into the field between the guns and limbers. Another and another, only now they fell harmlessly behind the guns, seeking vainly for the wagons and teams. More shells were bursting now on the clear space to the rear of the guns between our infantry columns. All the infantry were lying down. So well folded in the ground that I could hardly see them, they were swallowed by the veldt, eaten by the soil we fought for. Ball after ball of our own white smoke alighted on the kopje, trying to find the right length – the first at the base, the second over, the third on the Boer gun. By the fourth the gun flashed no more.

Sheridan seemed to follow the triumph as if he had a wager on each shot.

'Hurrah,' he called. 'Look, Haddock, look.' But the boy, at last in the thick of the fighting he had sought, said nothing. He seemed as though he had just awakened from a long sleep and had yet to recall his whereabouts. Cooper took his pipe from his pocket and bit down upon the stem.

Now our guns sent forth little white balloons of shrapnel, to the right, to the left, higher, lower, peppering the whole face of the hill. There was a roll of rifle fire that echoed like the ungreased wheels of a farm cart. As the guns rang out faster and faster we saw mounted men urging their horses up the kopje and over the edge. Shrapnel followed so that some dived and came up no more. The Boer gun opened up again and the third or fourth shell pitched clean into a wagon with its double team of eight horses. It was full of shells. We held our breath for an explosion. But when the smoke cleared, the wagon simply lay on its side with a wheel in the air. Our batteries bayed again; and again, for a moment, the Boer guns were silent.

'Attack!' came the order.

We who had done nothing but watch, now moved forward as the guns flung shrapnel across the valley. The time had come for us to take to the stage and play our part.

Ben looked to the sky. 'Why is it so dark?' he asked.

It was astonishingly dark for the gods, no doubt enraged by our behaviour, now sent down a sheet of rain from the eastern sky. With the first stabbing drops the horses turned their heads away, trembling, and, being of more sense than any human, no whip or spur could bring them up to it. I have never known rain the like of that on the South African veldt. It drove through mackintoshes as if they were blotting paper. The air was filled with hissing; underfoot you could see solid earth melting into mud, and mud flowing away in water. It blotted out hill and dale and enemy in one grey curtain of vapour. You would have said that the heavens had opened to drown the wrath of man. It should have given us pause but through it the guns still thundered and the khaki columns pushed doggedly on.

The infantry began to open out among the boulders with the reserves following up behind. Ahead of us on the stone-pitted hill, a storm of lead burst forth. Haddock, at last awake to the danger, threw himself behind a boulder. He lay curled in a ball with his arms over his head and we left him. Pattenden too tried to hide but Sheridan was having none of it.

'You are not a boy,' he cried, hauling the terrified man to his feet and pushing him forward, on into the fray.

Ahead, more men had chosen rocks to be their refuge. In all the melee you could still hear bullets flicking round them. Many were still on the move and here and there a man would stop and start before dropping limply as if the string that held him upright were cut. No one was immune. A colonel fell, shot in the arm. A major was left at the bottom of that ridge, his pipe in his mouth and a Mauser bullet through his leg, yet the regiment pushed on.

Still I had not been called upon to fire. I carried my useless gun on and on. Another ridge was won and passed but all that lay beyond was a further hellish hail of bullets. More men down, more men pushed into the firing line, more bullets in the air. They beat on the boulders like a million hammers; they tore the turf like a harrow.

'Christ, will this cursed hill never end?' cried out Ben, whose breathing was so laboured it could be heard above the battle.

Cooper took Ben's gun and we both sat him down so that he might rest for a moment. We tried to stay by his side but we were in a field of hell, sown with bodies. The dead lay behind us while ahead the world was edged with stinging fire. A broken line of Boers appeared directly in front of us.

'Fire!' yelled Jackson but I could not. I was close enough to see their faces and I madly scanned the line for Sarel's brother, Izak. They all seemed to carry his face.

'What's that?' cried Pattenden, terrified.

It was the bugles. They rang out across the hill. Perhaps I need never shoot. My heart pounded not with fear for my own life but that I might take someone else's. I was not a soldier. I could not be a soldier. I did not know how.

'Fix bayonets!' Staff officers rushed forward from the rear, imploring, cajoling, cursing, slamming every man who could move into the line, but it was a line no longer. It was a surging wave of men all inextricably mixed. With so many officers down, Jackson seemed to take command, yelling advice and dashing about, assisting anyone who needed it. There were men everywhere firing carbines, stumbling, leaping, killing, falling, all drunk with battle, shoving through hell to the throat of the enemy. And there beneath our feet was the Boer camp and the last Boers galloping out of it.

'Look! Look!' yelled Sheridan.

Squadrons of mounted men were storming in among the retreating Boers, shouting, spearing, stamping them into the ground.

'Cease fire!' came the order, echoing from man to man. 'Cease fire!'

It was over. Weeks and weeks of endless travel, endless waiting, ending in half an hour of lunacy. Pursuing cavalry and pursued enemy faded out of our sight. When at last I could loosen my hands from their grip on my gun, I realised that night had fallen, so swiftly and unnoticed it was as though the stage manager of our show had been mistaken about his choice of lighting. We were stranded, a mob of ill-assorted soldiers standing on the rock-sown, man-sown hillside, victorious and helpless in equal measure. My hands shook as I tried in vain to light a cigarette. Out of every quarter of the blackness leapt rough voices.

'F Company!'

'Sussex here!'

'Over here!'

'Over where?' followed by a trip and a heavy stumble and an oath.

'Doctor wanted 'ere!'

'Help for a wounded officer! Damn you there!'

Gradually I could make out in the inky blackness that the world was now divided into two realms – men who moved and those who did not.

'All wounded men are to be brought down to the Boer camp between the two hills,' called Sheridan into the night. The dark was against us now. Cooper and I bent down to a Sussex man whose leg sat at odds with his body. We lifted him between us and turned down the face of the hill. We could see nothing and stumbled, searching for firm rock, losing our feet in ankle-wrenching holes, scrambling down five minutes at a time with only a single yard completed. I fell and banged my head and when I looked up I thought I saw the dead rise. South Africa had become a land of phantoms, a place where a train could vanish into an invisible fold in the ground. A ghost train peopled by ghostly men drenched in Condy's Fluid.

'Grey!' shouted Cooper and, putting down our injured charge, he ran to me. 'Grey, are you all right?'

I nodded, unable to speak.

By the time we stumbled to the foot of that precipice it felt as though a week of nights had passed, and yet it was not even eight o'clock.

At the bottom of the slope were half a dozen tents, a couple of lanterns and a dozen wagons – huge, heavy veldt-ships lumbered up with cargo.

Off the break-neck hillside hoarse cries still dropped.

'Wounded man here! Doctor wanted!'

'Three of 'em here!'

'A stretcher, for God's sake!'

'A stretcher there! Is there no stretcher?'

The wounded were brought down any way that could be thought of. Slung in a blanket came a captain, his wet hair matted over his forehead, brow and teeth set, lips twitching as they put him down, gripping his whole soul to keep it from crying out. He turned with the beginning of a smile that would not finish.

'Would you mind straightening out my arm?' he asked Sheridan. The arm was bandaged above the elbow, and the forearm was hooked under him. Sheridan bent over the officer.

''Ere, 'old out your 'and.' There was a terrible crunching sound followed by the slightest of whimpers from the wounded man.

'Got it,' said Sheridan gruffly, his hand coming up wet and red, and the supine body quivered all over.

'What?' said the weak voice as the smile struggled to come out again, but dropped back when he understood what had happened. 'Have they got my fingers too?'

We covered him with a blanket, wringing wet, and left the

man to soak and shiver. He was but one out of more than two hundred wounded. For hours every man with hands and legs toiled up and down, up and down, that ladder of pain. Perhaps the worst of it, the thing I will never forget, was that as men died, Boer or British, across the wasteland they were united in their final cries for their mothers.

By heaven's grace the Boers had filled their wagons with the loot of many stores; there were blankets to carry men in and mattresses to lay them on. They came down with sprawling bearers, with jolts and groans. Would day never break? Man by man they brought them down. The tent was carpeted now with limp bodies. With breaking backs the fittest heaved some shoulder-high into wagons, while others they laid on mattresses on the ground. In the rain-blurred light of the lantern – would that piercing drizzle never cease? – the doctor, the one doctor, toiled on. Cutting up their clothes with scissors, feeling with light firm fingers over torn chests and thighs, cunningly slipping round a bandage, using a captured rifle for a splint, tenderly covering up the crimson ruin of strong men.

Cooper in particular made no distinction between the wounded enemy and his own comrades. To the men who in the afternoon had been lying down behind rocks with rifles pointed to kill him, he gave his water, his strength and what comfort he had left. Haddock had not fared well in the fighting. He was not hit but the poor boy shook as if the ground were still beaten by the guns. We were able to find a space for him under a wagon. His pet duck Bessie had been kept safe in one of the carts that had followed behind, and Cooper went to collect her. I had just fetched a lantern to calm Haddock's terror when its light gave me sight of Jackson.

In all the horror, in all his dealings with the dead and dying, he had not faltered. He had seemed indefatigable, a man made of iron on whom we could all depend. Now in his arms he carried a dead young man as if he were a baby. The dead boy was beautiful and I could see no mark on him nor could I tell if he had been friend or foe. There was no blood but there was no doubt that he lay dead in Jackson's arms and my big, brave brute of a friend wept.

George Sheridan made a fire in the gnawing damp and cold, and organised the unwounded Boer prisoners to sit around it. We had captured about forty prisoners and for the first time I saw the Dutch fighters up close. They were rough, bearded men of all ages. Big and loose-limbed, shabbily dressed in broad-brimmed hats, corduroy trousers and brown shoes, they looked us straight in the eye with no fear. One of the men sat rubbing a hot sore on his head with a coin and no one said a word. I saw a bearded grandfather pull his grandson of no more than twelve years close as they both quietly gave up their guns. He stroked the boy's head as if to soften the blow of defeat.

We were almost friendly. The Boers had fought their best, and lost. They were neither ashamed nor angry. Everyone was most polite, thanking each other as if we had gathered for tea.

For a long while we thought we had lost Ben. No one could find him and we went back time after time to look among the dead. It was Jackson who found him leaning against a boulder. Blood had poured down his face from a wound and had dried into a nut-brown mark. His hand was still sweeping across a page of his notebook with a piece of charcoal but instead of capturing what he saw, now he just made wide streaks of black. It took us a moment to understand what had happened. The man who had taught us to see the colours of the country could no longer see them at all.

'Grey,' he cried. 'Grey.' It was both my name and perhaps the colour he saw. 'This is not right,' he called into the night. 'I wanted to die. I wanted to die.'

'What kind of God does that?' asked Cooper bitterly, as we helped pack up Ben's things and roll away his drawings.

'I haven't seen God all day,' replied Jackson.

'She won't have me now,' whispered Ben to me as I stroked his head and tried to place a fold of cloth over his blank eyes. 'She'll never have me now.'

'Ssh, ssh,' I kept repeating for there were no words left.

He was led away to the railway.

At last we had dropped down to sleep or as near as any man could get, when there was a rattle and a crash. A hundred men betrayed their nerves by springing up and reaching for their rifles. On the ground lay a bucket, a cooking pot, a couple of tin plates, and some knives and forks, all emptied out of a sack. Beside them, descending from the wagon, Cooper.

'Sorry, lads. I beg your pardon. They told me there was a box of cigars here. Does anyone know if the boys have smoked them all?'

Apart from Ben's departure, our mess was blessedly still intact and we moved on. We were not dead but we were dead tired and filthy. You could only guess that we wore boots by the huge balls of stratified mud we wore around our feet. Eyelids hung fat and heavy over hollow cheeks and sharp cheekbones. More miles, who knew how many. Haddock was silent now. Where once he had loved to cycle beside the big guns, spattered with earth and spinning mud from their wheels, now that they were war-worn and fresh from slaughter he did not look at them. Letters arrived from wives and mothers seven thousand miles away and those of the dead lay in a pile unopened. No one wrote to me. No one knew where I was and perhaps, I thought, Reggie did not dare. I rarely thought of him any more. I was him and there was no room for two of us.

The news that Mafeking had been relieved caused only the smallest cheer. We did see an engine decorated with flags, but we had begun to forget what we had come for. Other place names came and went, but our minds were on our empty stomachs. Sometimes we had a little dried fruit but we often went twenty-four hours with no food. Many had some injury or other from the endless motion and everyone was very done up. I had perhaps an inch or two of brandy left and I kept it by me, waiting for the moment when I dared finish off the bottle of 'life preserver'. At each stage more and more sick were left behind. Some days Cooper's feet were so bad that we contrived to pull him on his bicycle between Jackson and myself. I should have given him my bottle. But I was not kind.

'This is not a proper war,' grumbled the regular soldiers who had seen action before, and certainly it was not a war anyone could understand. The regulars had been accustomed to wars with headquarters or at any rate to wars with a main body and a concerted plan, but this conflict had neither. Ahead all you could see was the stiff, unwieldy, crawling tail of an army. Indians tottered and staggered under green-curtained doolies. Kaffir boys guided spans of four and five and six mules drawing ambulances, like bakers' vans. Others walked beside wagons, curling whips that Jackson declared would dwarf the biggest salmon rod round the flanks of small-bodied, huge-horned oxen.

Sometimes we stopped at a farm. I remember a place where the Mounted Infantry caught thirty horses and ransacked the house. There was a lot of looting. The men stole anything – a white shirt, a shawl, a kettle, a thin driving coat, even a sun bonnet. The farmers were all off fighting and their women watched us silently. It was a pretty place, white with a tin-roofed veranda held up by slim white pillars overlooking a wide lawn. I ran into the drawing room where Cooper was having rare sport at an old piano. I went to grab a silver candlestick when I saw the mother of the house standing in the doorway, looking at me, and Cooper stopped his tune. Behind her, two small children played with their toys in the passage, oblivious of what was happening.

Sheridan, carrying a chicken under each arm, called from the window, 'Grey! Now!'

I have no idea what I had thought to do with the candlestick – exchange it for drink, no doubt – but I put it back down on the mantel, muttered an apology and Cooper and I fled. I who had been taught to do everything correctly had become a stranger even to myself.

We no longer knew or perhaps cared where we were, although some said we were heading for Jo'burg. I don't remember all the places where we slept or even where we skirmished but I do remember Doornkop. It was at Doornkop that I lost Cooper and began to lose myself.

# Twenty

It was always when I awoke that I marvelled briefly at where I was and who I was. I would rise up from my sleep and for a brief moment I was Valentine again. I might have been in any bed waiting to see what the day might bring. A day with Papa and Bahadur, or Reggie and Frank. A morning awakening with Maisie. Sometimes I ran my hands across my body as if to remind myself of its female form. I had stopped wearing a strap across my breasts. They had shrunk and faded away, as had my monthly bleeding, as though the girl in me were truly departing.

Haddock shook me and I blushed as guilt swept across my face.

'It's Jackson,' he pleaded, almost crying. 'I can't wake him. I took him his tea but he won't budge.'

Jackson, big Jackson, the man from Lancashire who was going to change the world with his soap and his candles, was burning with a high temperature. We had seen enough of it now to know what it was – enteric fever, one of the great scourges of our daily life. Along with dysentery and pneumonia, it was doing great service to the Boers in felling the British. As well as the fever, Jackson's nose began to bleed. It was a sign we had been warned about and we needed to be quick.

We were not far from a military hospital and Sheridan and I managed to commandeer a Cape cart to take him, us and our bicycles. Cooper wanted to come but his feet would not allow it. He lay on his blanket almost incoherent with pain and we left him behind. We had heard of men succumbing to the fever but neither Sheridan nor I had expected to see so many men sick with it. The hospital, such as it was, consisted of rectangular wooden structures with tin roofs fitted together so that they were easy to dismantle, transport and re-erect. These temporary marquees, full to overflowing, had been erected on every square patch of land. Everything about our lives was temporary. Everything suggested people simply passing through. Everything except the graveyard, which was filling even as we arrived.

There were twelve wards with perhaps a dozen beds in each. We found a medical orderly of the RAMC and begged him for a space. The sergeant in charge was a rough sort of Tommy – kindly, sturdy, bullet-headed, foul-mouthed and with no apparent medical training or bedside manner.

'I've had seventeen hundred men through here in the last six weeks,' he sighed. 'If I had a bed I'd give it to you but you see ... ' He waved his arms around to indicate the full ward. 'We're up to twenty-five or thirty deaths every day from enteric and only one from wounds. Was he inoculated?' he asked.

I shook my head and the orderly shook his. 'All I'm saying is that no one who was inoculated has died of the bloody disease.'

The journey had roused Jackson and he tried to get out of the cart. 'I'm fine,' he mumbled. He began to walk but only managed a few yards before he fell into Sheridan's arms.

'Am I wounded?' he asked.

'No,' soothed Sheridan, 'you are sick.'

Jackson shook his head. 'I will not fall foul of some ridiculous microbes. Britannia soap will not allow ... I will be wounded honourably on the battlefield, although not so wounded that it interferes with the ladies, you understand,' he concluded, and passed out.

We waited till at last a bed was found, found because the previous occupant no longer needed a bed at all.

'Try and keep him cheerful,' advised the sergeant. 'They need cheerfulness and good spirits. I reckon despondency kills more than disease. Keep cheery; you never know, you might cure your friend.'

And with that he was off to the next patient.

Some well-meaning ladies swept through, enquiring if Jackson wanted writing paper, but we said it seemed unlikely and they moved on.

That night Sheridan and I sat beside Jackson's bed, listening to the prayers for the dying being read over a patient a few feet away, to the incoherent raving of the fevered and the despairing murmurs of the weak and despondent who had lost both hope and heart. The ward was crowded; the fleas innumerable and irritating. Those with dysentery had been worn to a mere skeleton and their eyes held that pathetic deer-like expression of the very sick. There had been a sister in charge but she too was now ill and the single doctor was drowning in work. At least the beds were comfortable and had spring mattresses and slats. I almost wished for a slight fever that I might lie in one too.

I went to find somewhere private to relieve myself and on my way back a fellow in a side bed called out to me.

'Sister, please!'

He was young, as young as Haddock and thinner than a boy might ever imagine he could be. He had red hair and freckles. Ben had red hair. Would his son grow up to look like this? The poor boy was delirious with fever and reached out for my hand.

'Where is the sister? Are you the sister?' he cried, squeezing my hand.

'I am a soldier. I am Reginald Grey.'

'I thought you were the sister. I want you to take my things. Give them to my mother. Please.'

He reached under his covers and pulled out a small red tin. Lots of men had them. They had been sent, filled with chocolates, from the Queen to celebrate the New Year. Queen Victoria's face was embossed on the lid but she looked away from us. Away from what was happening.

'Take it now,' he urged.

'But you mustn't give up, you must . . . ' I knew it was pointless. Death marched through the tent in a hurry.

'Don't let me die alone,' he whispered. 'Promise? I don't want to die alone.'

'I promise,' I answered.

He squeezed my hand as his fever swept him back to blessed sleep. I sat with him for some time listening to his breathing, urging it not to stop. I looked across to where Jackson now lay in the same ragged state. I knew it was my fault. If I had not hidden him, he might have had the inoculation. The sleeping boy stirred. I slipped my hand free that he might lie more comfortably and that I might light a cigarette. As I struck the match I looked at my hands. Until that moment I had not noticed the change in them.

I remembered the day that Ben had examined them on board ship. He had held them up against the blue sky and my hands had been pale and soft. They had not been fit for a soldier. Now, when I looked again, they seemed to belong to someone else. Carrying heavy kit and gripping the bicycle handlebars across impossible terrain had coarsened them. I turned my hands over as if I had never seen them before. There were calluses and ragged flaps of skin around my broken nails. Dirt had become ingrained in the creases and the flesh had been browned in the South African sun. I tried to trace my lifeline in the palm of my hand but it was so obscured that I might almost be dead. My hands were as alien as anything to be found in that strange landscape.

The boy breathed quietly while all around me men lay sick and dying. Men. This was a place of many men, many officers. There must be stores full of supplies nearby. There had to be drink somewhere. I don't know what had happened to me: I had gone from finding pleasure in a small tot of rum to being unable to think of anything else. I was consumed by the need to obliterate my thoughts with alcohol of any kind. I no longer feared death – I feared life without a route to oblivion.

Forgetting my promise to the boy, I stood up and stepped outside the tent. Army life was the same wherever I went. Men were busy being busy and preparing for the unpreparable. Here that included digging graves for men not yet ready for them. Piles of earth stood beside a great pit where, for the sake of speed, many men would meet their maker in a great band of brothers. I found the supply tent on the very edge of the camp. It was of a size similar to the marquee sixteen of us and our cycles had once slept in. It had been a long while since I had slept under cover, a long while since I had done anything civilised. The tent was piled high with boxes of all shapes and sizes which spoke of wonderful things, of sugar and coffee, tea and biscuits. I thought of having tea at Callard's and how odd I would look now in a picture hat.

The sergeant in charge was a great bear of a man who clearly had not had the same trouble finding food as the rest of us. Among his many supplies a razor had failed to feature and he wore shaggy whiskers that spilled out over the fat folds of his face. For some the war was clearly less troublesome than for others. He was sitting at a desk going through mounds of forms, and beside him a large bottle of Scotch whisky stood open. The amber liquid looked like gold to me.

'Paperwork!' he snapped without looking up.

I stood there and stared at the bottle.

'I want whisky,' I said calmly, 'and cigarettes.'

He laughed and looked at me. Slowly he reached for the bottle and deliberately brought it to his lips and drank, never once taking his eyes off mine.

'Whisky is for officers. You ain't no officer.'

I thought of Sarel. Men will give you whatever you want if you—

'No, but perhaps I have something that you want,' I said.

He smirked at me and licked a drop from the neck of the bottle.

'You'd need something pretty spectacular to trade, my boy. Where you going to get that, eh? Seems to me you've barely got a shirt on your back.'

I reached for the top button of my jacket and it fell away in my hand. It bounced on the ground and rolled away, and I watched it until it settled almost under the sergeant's foot. It had been shiny once and I wondered if I could be bothered to pick it up. The sergeant's shoes were clean. He had not marched a thousand miles. My eyes wandered up his body as if I had all the time in the world. He did not take his eyes off me. The light in the tent seemed to catch the colour of the whisky and after a moment my hands continued down the line of remaining buttons as I undid my jacket, one fastening at a time. He watched me and shook his head.

'Pretty boy. Don't think I'm not tempted but I can have any lad I like for a packet of bourbons and I—'

He stopped mid-sentence as I removed my shirt, gave a slight cough and then licked his lips. 'Well, now, that would make a nice change. A very nice change indeed.'

He got up and moved towards me. As he got closer I could see remnants of food in his beard. I had not eaten and I remember wondering what was caught in his whiskers. Was I now so low that I might eat food from a man's beard?

'A whole bottle of whisky and two packets of cigarettes,' I muttered.

He nodded and pushed me back against a wooden case just high enough for me to sit down. He did not speak but reached for my belt buckle. My trousers dropped to the floor, too big now to stay upon my hips. He smelt. I had got used to the smell of filth, to the bitter residue of gunpowder in the air and the burning stench that rises up from injured flesh and assaults the nose, but this was worse. He stank of gluttony and greed. He pressed his mouth upon mine and I thought I could smell bread. He fumbled for his own trousers and soon he was upon me. For weeks I had expected pain but not this. This, I thought, was worse than dying, for I was awake and in that moment knew what I had become. I no longer cared what might happen.

For a moment I thought something had happened to him for he gave a great cry and then seemed to collapse upon me. If he were dead, I thought with a surge of excitement, then I could take what I liked. I had a brief fantasy of bearing away great crates full of things for the men, for my boys, but after a few seconds the sergeant shook himself upright again. He moved away, doing up his trousers and laughing. He sat down and drew a great gulp of Scotch from his bottle.

'Very nice change indeed,' he repeated.

I looked down at my legs. My trousers were round my ankles, lying in thin folds over my almost worn-out boots. Blood was seeping from me and running in small rivers down my thighs, which were sticky with mess. I pulled my trousers up and cinched them once more with my belt. My hands shook and I could hardly fasten my shirt and jacket but I had not lost sight of my intention.

'I want my things,' I said without emotion.

He nodded and reached into a small case behind him. He took out a full bottle of Scotch and two packets of cigarettes and placed them on his desk.

'Give you some bully beef if you come back in an hour for another ride,' he offered.

I shook my head and took my reward. Outside, life was going on just the same. Everyone was busy doing nothing much at all. I felt ill and a sudden anger rose in my chest. I was in terrible pain and found it difficult to walk straight. But my overwhelming feeling was sheer rage against Reggie that he had not been man enough to keep me from this.

# Twenty-one

I found Sheridan under a tree, grinning all over. He pointed to a stash of goods at his feet. There was some vermicelli, a packet of blancmange powder, orange peel and two bottles of beer.

'Look what I got. Some poor fellow died in the end bed and there was no one there to take care of his stuff. There's even an old newspaper from home.'

Sheridan shared with me but I did not tell him about my secret supplies. Instead I sat with him under the tree, drinking a dead man's beer. The newspaper was only about a month old but already so mutilated by constant unfolding that in parts it was scarcely decipherable. I read anything and everything – the weather, who had raced who at Sandown, what was being said of summer fashion and all the details of a mysterious murder in Water Lane, Brixton, and we drank and drank.

By the time I returned to the boy, the boy I had promised I would not allow to die alone, he had already passed away. The blue army form that was to list his treatment hung blankly at the end of his bed. He had died before the doctor had seen him. He had died without me. His name was Seamus Duffy, an Irish lad from London. His body was sewn into a blanket and buried with nineteen other men in a pit. Sheridan and I took his shoes, a sweater and the red tin which he had so wanted returned to his mother.

We knew then that Jackson might die, that Jackson who had been afraid of nothing except a needle might be killed by his own fear. We had no choice but to leave him behind and hope for the best. We abandoned the Cape cart. There would be trouble, but we did not have the energy to return with it. It was a long ride back and we were slow, for we had not one but two punctures from the wretched mimosa thorns on the road.

When we returned, Cooper was captaining a cricket match from a chair.

'What ho!' he called cheerfully. I could feel the dried blood on my thighs. I rounded on him.

'You will see a doctor about your feet! You will and I will not hear a word against it.'

Feminine tears sprang unbidden to my eyes and I thought I would sob.

'All right, all right,' replied Cooper, somewhat startled. The match continued. Haddock sat watching with his duck. Since the battle Haddock had done what the rest of us could not – he wept without pause and poor Bessie endured his grief.

Perhaps you know the sound of a boy weeping with unbearable grief but you cannot know what it is to mix that noise with the echoes of war that do not leave you. In the still of the night Haddock cried as a backdrop to the guns in my head which continued to shriek and whistle. I could hear the thud and bang, boom and phutt, whizz and pound and yet that is not enough to tell you the noise they made. The blood of every man felled had left their bodies and now beat and echoed in my ears. The devil himself rode to get me. Cooper did see a doctor but the exhausted medic simply gave him two No. 9 pills that he said would cure anything and moved on.

It was late May 1900 and we were nearing the gold-mining centre of Johannesburg. Across our route lay the formidable Klipriviersberg Range. In its midst was Doornkop, which the Boers had occupied in force. We ran up against yet another cursed river, this time the Klip, I think, which lay about four kilometres to the south of where we were heading.

Perhaps lessons were being learned, for now the force fanned out. Orders had been received from Lord Roberts that no longer were we to use the frontal attack the Boers had come to expect. Now we were to take a leaf from their book and spread out to attack from all sides. After dark, temperatures now fell below freezing yet in the inky night we moved forward. Those in charge seemed to think we volunteers had done well and we were to be rewarded, rewarded by being given a place of honour in the front line: the honour of dying first. I was ready. I was also drunk.

We had the honour but no real idea as we advanced to take the kopjes that stood between us and glory. The Mausers and pom-poms were busy exchanging fire across us. Several men fell before we had gone many yards and shells passed over our heads to burst among the men behind us. They were Highlanders, men in kilts. Men in skirts and me in trousers. Death before, death behind, death patiently seeking our measure, each of our steps uncertain. Sheridan, knowing Haddock could not manage another battle, strode ahead of the boy, acting like a human shield.

The Boers had set fire to the brush and for part of the distance we had to run through flames. What meals we could have cooked. Now we were the meat and we ran. Hot, cold, hot, cold, would we ever be a normal temperature again? Once through the fire we lay down, waiting for the machine-gun section to soften the way ahead. The Boer replies landed right on the battery, killing horses and knocking over an ammunition wagon. For a second our gun was a whirl of blue-white smoke, with grey-black figures struggling and plunging inside it. Then the figures grew blacker and the smoke cleared and in the name of wonder the gun was still there. A burst of a shell and the battery wheeled about, the legs of the eight horses pattering as if they belonged all to one creature.

Through the smoke I thought I saw a man hold up a cross as if to bless us all.

'No atheists here. No atheists for the Empire,' I called out.

Somewhere in my mind I knew that he was simply taking the elevations for the guns but it looked like a priest giving his benediction. Over the noise you could hear the major sing out, 'Two thousand!' and then, 'Number four!'

The gun hurled out fire and filmy smoke, then leapt back, half frightened at its own fury, half anxious to get a better view of what it had done. The shot was long.

'Nineteen hundred,' cried the major. Same ritual, only a little short. 'Nineteen fifty,' and it was just right. Just right for whom? Who stood there at nineteen fifty? Whose story was now over? Field and mountain guns, yard by yard, up and down, right and left, carefully, methodically sowed the place with bullets. The hillside began to turn pale blue with the smoke of burning veldt. A beautiful blue; I had time to think it was a beautiful blue. Ben should have seen it. Then in the middle came a patch of black.

At first it was small but it spread and spread till the huge expanse was all black, bordered with the red of the ever-extending fire. Death to black! God help any wounded enemy who lay there.

Crushed into the face of the earth by the guns, we heard the rattle of the rifles; we heard the rap-rap-rap-rap-rap of the Boer Maxim knocking at the door. I could smell eucalyptus as the gum trees were stripped bare by the rifle fire and the trees wept. I could hear the pom-pom – the most blood-curdling of all the weapons.

Perhaps in the end it was our inexperience that saved us. In the uphill charge that followed, the Highlanders did as they had been trained to do and walked slowly uphill towards the enemy while the deadly shower from above ploughed up the ground at their feet. In ten minutes they lost a hundred men. We watched in horror.

'Bugger that,' declared Sheridan. Chivenden was nowhere to be seen and orders were few and far between. Sheridan took charge.

'Right, we're not going up the bloody hill to be slaughtered like that. Short rushes, everyone, in small groups. Cooper, you lead the first lot to that boulder and I'll cover, then we'll go on ahead and you cover and so on. Pattenden, you stay with me.'

'But I—' began Pattenden.

'With me,' Sheridan repeated. 'Slow and steady, not some bloody big target.' He paused for a moment and then added, 'Haddock, you guard this rock just here. This rock is very important so I need you to wait here.'

He carefully placed the boy in the safe embrace of a small crop of boulders. He stroked the lad's hair and then we moved forward, making our way from boulder to boulder up the hill. No doubt what we did was amateurish, but it seemed to our novice minds that those who knew what they were doing were dying fastest.

As we rushed from one grey rock to another seeking sanctuary I stepped on some poor fellow's dead body. I realised he had been in the mess beside us – the Girls' School – but I knew nothing about him. I had lived alongside him, marched with him and I did not know him. The men swept past me but I did not follow. I stood watching the Indian stretcher-bearers moving to and fro across the battlefield with their green doolies, picking up the British wounded. They had volunteered from India, from my beloved India, and I could not think why they had ever wanted to leave.

I lowered my rifle and stood there. I knew that however far we had travelled for this moment, I could not and would not ever fire my gun. A brilliant flash filled the air. Shrapnel and blood rained. At first I felt nothing. I simply stood there feeling, if anything, surprised before I became aware of a sensation of boiling water pouring on to my side. The entire hillside seemed to turn brilliant white as my legs gave way and I fell to the ground. In slow motion I could see the battle continuing around me as tingling echoed and surged through my body. My breaths were short and painful and for a moment I lost consciousness.

I awoke with tufts of rough grass against my cheek and warm blood on my side. The battle was over. Whether it was won or lost I had no idea. I had been hit by shrapnel and the whisky bottle in my pocket had smashed. A great shard of glass had gone into my side and at first I wondered if I were dead. I lay looking at the grass beside me. An ant, a tiny ant, looked startlingly black as he crawled up a blade of grass. He was going about his business as if we had not interrupted him at all. Could the dead see ants?

'Valentine! Valentine!'

I turned my head and saw Cooper stumbling across the slope towards me.

'Valentine, dear God, Valentine, I'm coming,' he called in a panic. His feet were so poorly that the act of running was too much for him. His boots slipped on loose rock and he tried to regain his footing but he did not have the strength. He struggled to stand upright and for a moment stood motionless in pain. It was enough for a Boer, who did not know or did not care about the rules of war, to release a single rifle shot. Who was he, this invisible man who hid from us? Perhaps a farmer? Was it Izak? Whoever he was, he was the enemy whom we had derided as unprofessional and amateur, who could not withstand the might of the British Empire. He was a good shot. His bullet hit Cooper in the back and for a moment my friend paused, looking almost annoyed. His back arched and he dropped his rifle before falling to his knees and then on to his front.

I could not quite get up so I crawled the final yards to reach him. I turned him over and his khaki chest was red. I thought of Reggie, wearing his red waistcoat, enacting death in the drawing room. It was a play. Just a play.

My own pain forgotten, I gathered Cooper in my arms and kissed his forehead, his cheek, his hair, any part of him on which I could rain down affection. I no longer cared about who or what I was. I no longer cared about anything. He smiled and almost laughed.

'Are we come to this, my dear?' he said.

'You knew, didn't you?' I whispered.

'Reggie sent me to look after you. Not doing a very good job, I'm afraid.'

'You are the best.' I was weeping.

'And you make a fine man, Valentine. A very fine man indeed. You should be proud, Bradamante ...'

Cooper's eyes began to close and I pulled him closer, kissing his face. 'Stay with me,' I begged, holding him close. 'Cooper, please! You kissed me in the maze, remember?'

Cooper's eyes fluttered open and he gave a small smile. 'It was Reggie's idea and I didn't mind. I rowed up to meet him. You were so lovely.'

My sobs shook us both.

'Ssh,' whispered Cooper. '*I'll tell you a secret ... The Gods envy us. They envy us because we're mortal, because any moment might be our last. Everything is more ...*'

He gasped for air and could not speak. I pulled his cheek against mine and whispered back, '*... more beautiful because we're doomed. You will never be lovelier than you are now. We will never be here again.*'

Cooper gave a great shiver and said, 'Tell my father I am sorry. Valentine, I love ...'

And with that he was gone. Just like that. One minute a man filled with learning and delight and the next, nothing. Nothing at all. Madness filled my head and I clutched Cooper's body, screaming, 'This is not right. We should not be here. What are we doing here? We do not belong here. Go home. All of you. Go home!'

I gave a long scream of despair. I don't know who came to stand by me. I don't know who stopped me. I don't know how I got back to the camp. I told no one about my injury. I couldn't. If I had been taken to medical treatment the game would have been up. Sheridan and I buried my beloved friend at the foot of a peach tree. As there was no chaplain with the force, nothing was said and the wind whistled and took away his spirit. At last Sheridan lifted me to my feet and we left dear Cooper behind.

I patched myself as best I could. There were many shrugging off small wounds and I was not alone in my apparent stoicism. I was neither admired nor unique. We marched on without Ben or Jackson or Cooper. We marched on across spent cartridges, across Boer articles left in hurried retreat, across the dead and the wounded. We awoke to hoar frost glistening on our blankets in starlight. Our hands were bitterly cold and numb as we attempted to pack our kit. I don't know why we moved forward. I could harm no one. Great waves of regret now poured through my thoughts and I began to question everything. I thought about the day I had picked up Reggie's parcel in the front hall at Inkerman House. Had he left it there on purpose for me? Had he connived to have me take his place? Why had he sent Cooper? Of all men to send to die.

We marched up along the valley and through the passes commanded on all sides by rugged heights that make Pretoria one of the strongest military positions in the world. We tramped down the broad high road, round the shoulder of some low hills and saw the trees and spires of the Boer capital in the distance. Lord Roberts' column, with the Guards Brigade leading, marched along the valley road to receive the final surrender. By noon we were being served the unheard-of luxury of bully beef and a biscuit per man, but I could not eat. Then the whole of the 21st brigade formed up and we marched into the town.

The square was crowded with a mass of horsemen, smart, clean and bright in khaki dress. Civilians were kept back by a row of soldiers who left a passage clear for us to march through. Here we were in the great impregnable fortress, arsenal and stronghold of enemy power. There were many ladies in brightly coloured dresses who waved as we passed. Officers told us that everyone was 'beastly proud'.

The pipers ceased and massed bands of the Guards began to strike up with 'The Boys of the Old Brigade'. There was a burst of cheering as Lord Roberts appeared on horseback and moved in front of the pedestal for old Kruger's statue. He had a proud fatherly smile and we all thought our battles were done, that we would march next for the sea and for home.

'We won,' said Sheridan, holding Haddock close.

'Won what?' I asked.

We got back to camp in a thunderstorm and, most bizarre of all, discovered that the post had at last caught up with us. There was a letter for me, or rather a letter addressed to Reggie. I could not think who it might be from and sat holding the envelope for an age. When at last I slit it open I found it was from the photographer, Harry Hawkins. It contained some photographs. There was Cooper refusing to be good at playing dead and there was me dying so well on the veldt. Harry did not know that Cooper was lost. He sent him his best wishes. I put the pictures in my pocket and slept in a puddle. Many of the men got very boozed for we all thought our journey was done but it was not. It was only the beginning.

# Twenty-two

Lord Grey could not have been kinder. The doctor was sent for. Frank was laid in the guest bed where the fine cotton sheets were soon soaked with his blood. The maid and the footman brought towels and bandages were ripped from old linen. Water was boiled and liniment brought from the chemist. All night the lights burned in the house. Reggie sat by Frank's side and held his hand as the great gaping wound on his face was cleaned and stitched with black thread. It was an angry red and swollen gash that started just below his left eye, ran jagged across his nose and split his upper lip. Mercifully his eyes were spared, but they lay beneath deep ugly swelling. Frank, now senseless on chloroform, was unmoved by the activity around him and all the while Lord Grey, who stood quietly in the doorway watching, did not ask his son a single question. Reggie stared blankly at Frank, beautiful Frank, now turned into a Mary Shelley nightmare.

It was the following night before calm was restored to the house and at last Reggie was persuaded from the sick room for a moment's rest. Lord Grey took him to his room. He called for a bath to be brought and in front of the fire he did something he had never done before for anyone: he washed his son. He peeled away the dirty old clothes of his son's disguise. The filthy bundles were taken away to be burned; fresh, soft shirts and trousers were laid near the fire to warm. Lord Grey helped his sad, silent son to climb into the steaming water. As Reggie lay back, eyes closed, his father cleansed the dried blood from his son's hands and face, gently shaved away his beard and once more saw his boy appear. When he was clean and his hair combed, he gently helped him from the bath, towelled him dry and dressed him. Lord Grey would allow no one else to help him as he tended to his broken child. When at last a little of the Reggie of old had appeared he helped him downstairs to his study. Soup was brought and Reggie ate slowly, staring ahead.

Finished, Reggie sat staring at the floor.

'Would you like a drink?' asked his father.

Reggie shook his head. He wanted nothing. Lord Grey cleared his throat. 'I want to . . .' he said quietly. 'The thing is, I had a letter from Lady Talbot. From Cape Town. She says she saw you, and my wife's sister writes that Valentine never . . .'

The truth was Lord Grey did not understand any of it. He did not know why Reggie was even in London or who the injured man was. He had so many questions he did not know where to begin.

He tried a different tack.

'I came home early,' he began, perhaps thinking an explanation of his own actions might help, but when Reggie began to weep he stopped, uncertain how to proceed. He rose from his chair and moved slowly to stand beside his son. Now Reggie's entire body was convulsed with sobs and his father reached out and softly stroked his head.

'Ssh. We shall make things right. Whatever it is, we shall make it right,' he repeated over and over.

After that Reggie could not stop crying. The doctor was called again and prescribed something to calm him. Now in his old room, Reggie slept too while downstairs Lord Grey paced and wondered if he could indeed make sense of things. He needed to know what had happened. Where was Valentine? Who was the man with Reggie? Why was Reggie not in South Africa? The confusion in Lord Grey's head was unbearable and he missed his wife with a sorrow of which he had not known himself capable.

It was a week before Frank could even sip at some weak tea. He had lost a great deal of blood. He was pale and hardly spoke. When at last he did it was to ask for a mirror. The gash from the broken bottle had been stitched as neatly as any doctor could have managed but the wound was uneven and would be unlikely ever to heal fully. The doctor kept Reggie sedated in his room, so for many hours and days Frank lay alone in the grand house. Lord Grey came in each evening, asking only after his health and never seeking an explanation. When not with Frank, his lordship sat by his son's bed, taking his meals there and sleeping in a chair until Reggie got up.

It was the young footman who first engaged Frank in conversation. His name was Chandler and he had felt he had the measure of Frank from the moment he arrived at the house. It had irked him to care for such a fellow and as soon as he was able he let Frank know he had not gone undetected.

'Seen you at the Serpentine, ain't I?' he said one morning. 'And at the Criterion.'

'I don't know you,' said Frank, eyeing him evenly.

'Oh, you do. You do,' replied Chandler.

Reggie came in just as the conversation was in mid-flow.

'What do you want, Chandler?' he demanded.

'Nothing, sir. Just commenting on how many times I seen Mr Rutherford about the place. It seems we both take the odd stroll in Hyde Park of a late evening, if you know what I mean.'

Reggie frowned. 'You can go now, Chandler.' He waited for the man to leave and then asked, 'Hyde Park?'

'Reggie,' Frank said weakly, his lip making it difficult to talk. 'I was trying to find a soldier. It wasn't for what you think. I was trying to send a message to Valentine. I felt responsible. I would never betray you.'

Chandler watched it all and stalked the patient, darting into the room whenever Reggie left. It did not take him long to begin mentioning money to Frank. He wanted a 'little something' to keep information to himself. He didn't want anyone to go 'upsetting' Lord Grey or thinking anything 'untoward' about his son. It was in the midst of such a conversation that Lord Grey entered the room. He did not fully understand what was happening in his house but he knew blackmail when he heard it. Chandler was dismissed on the spot and Lord Grey himself saw him off the premises.

Frank knew then that he had to leave. That trouble would only come to Reggie if he stayed. Some of Reggie's clothes had been laid out in the room for him and it was with great difficulty that he arose in the night, dressed and slipped out into the street. He went to the only place he could think of – the Empire. The theatre was dark but there was an overnight man on the stage door. The man was old and distracted, reading the paper. He didn't see Frank's face. Frank went to his dressing room and turned on the light.

He sat down before the mirror and looked himself full in the face. He was as broken as an ancient statue. His wound, like a bolt of lightning, split his face in two. Frank ran his hand over his features. It was monstrous. The singular beauty that he had once possessed was banished for ever. He ran his finger along the cut that the bottle had made and tried to smile, but the pain was too great. He reached up to the shelf for his metal box and placed it on the table. Slowly he opened it and looked at the sticks of make-up that lay inside. He removed a brown stick and carefully ripped some paper from the end. Then looking in the mirror, he began gently to apply it to his wounds. It would not stick, for tears streamed down his cheeks.

Frank had not been at the theatre long when there was a knock at the door. The night watchman called through it to say Frank had a visitor. Thinking it might be Reggie he left the dressing room and went to the stage door. There, stood Jack, Frank's brother. He was a coarser version of Frank. He stood, discomfited by his surroundings, clenching his cap in his hand.

'Hello, Frank,' he said.

'Jack.'

'So it's true then?' muttered Jack, looking everywhere but at his brother.

'Come away from here,' said Frank and led his brother down to the stage where it was quiet. He sat down on a wicker prop basket and waited for his brother to speak.

Jack began with the obvious. 'You been cut up rough,' he said.

'Yes, I have,' agreed Frank.

The brothers, who had never had much in common and whom life had gradually driven further apart, sat in silence until at last Jack reached into his pocket.

'Funniest thing,' he said. 'I mean what are the chances, but look what came my way.' He produced a silver calling-card case and held it up for Frank to see. Frank inhaled sharply. 'Under a grating in Limehouse. Not the sort of thing those Chinese fellas normally drop. Couldn't read it, o' course, so I gives it to Lanky George. Thought there might be some reward in it and that. He says the name and I think, what are the chances? So I goes to the address as George tells me is on the cards inside and some woman downstairs, she sends me 'ere.'

Frank could not bear the smell of his brother and he could not bear to have him here in the theatre.

'Have you told Mother?' he asked, forcing himself to stay calm.

Jack shook his head. 'Thought there might be a reward in it and that,' he repeated.

'Why should I give you anything? I'm not giving you anything, Jack,' said Frank, trying to hide his temper. His own brother.

Jack stood up and looked down at him. 'I always knew, Frank,' he sneered. 'Even when we was little. You're a disgrace.' Jack flicked open the case. '*For Frank. For ever. Reggie.* 'Ave I got that right? That what it says, Frank? Maybe this Reggie wants the case then. Wants to see me all right for it. I bet I could find him. I found you, didn't I?'

Jack snapped the case shut. Then he turned and walked away so swiftly that it took Frank a minute to start after him.

'Jack, wait!' But his brother was gone. Frank chased up the stairs to the stage door and out into the street. He could not see him so he ran to the corner. A policeman was just crossing the road and Frank, wearing no jacket or hat, caught his eye.

'In a hurry are we, sir?' he demanded.

'No, I—' Frank stopped. He looked at the surly policeman and in that moment his life was over.

Frank was arrested for 'effeminacy'; for wearing make-up. His explanations about the theatre and his scars might have washed with the sergeant on the desk had Chandler, the footman, not been brought in at much the same time. There was said to be a place near the Regent's Park Barracks on Albany Street where a soldier might be had for ready money and Chandler had been arrested in the vicinity. It did not take him long to give his former employer's address. When he spied Frank waiting to be dealt with he tried to gain some leniency by telling all he knew.

The investigation led the police both to Frank's flat and to Lord Grey's house. The officers were most polite. They did not want to disturb Lord Grey but a list of names had been found in Frank's flat. It seemed to relate to some party held on the premises and it included his son Reginald. While they were certain some 'mistake had occurred' they wanted to ensure that no trouble came to his family. Lord Grey thanked the officers and closed the door before walking to the stairs and sinking slowly down on the bottom step. Valentine's step. He had to do something.

# Twenty-three

The taking of Pretoria, capital of the Transvaal, and Bloemfontein, capital of the Orange Free State, did not cause the Boer to surrender. If they had believed in rules then Cooper might have lived. No one made any effort to keep us volunteer soldiers informed or fed. Our clothes and our spirits were in rags. Many of the men were now just bone from the knee down.

Sheridan had secured a pair of peculiar white moleskin leggings in Pretoria. He said they were 'cut saucy over the trotters' as he paraded his new fashion, trying to make Haddock smile. Some had covered themselves with a shapeless garment of grey-blue shoddy cloth while many patched their khaki serge trousers with anything they could find. The bitter and biting wind mixed with solid, pitiless and marrow-chilling rain washed the very heart out of us and easily penetrated through the parched leather of our boots. Each fold hardened until the skin beneath peeled and tore. We were in such a sorry state that it took a loaf of bread, not news of a victory, to lift the general gloom. Add to this a chronic belittling of distances by the officers, who seemed to ignore all bends, contours and curves in the way ahead, and you had a troop disheartened to their core. The officers did all the measuring with a ruler while the regiment did all the marching with their feet.

The Boer had begun building sangars – rough circles of stone in the rocky crevices of the mountainsides from which they shot at us at will. I was cycling beside a man who suddenly crumpled and fell as a bullet hit its mark and I simply rode on. The wagons broke down and there was neither kit nor grub. Orders were given that each man must fill his water bottle or face punishment by an officer. It was a sign of weariness that many simply could not be bothered. But still we pushed forward, clearing the land and opening its slopes to British civilisation.

We dragged ourselves on, having eaten all our private chocolate, smoked all the baccy and used all the matches. We were forbidden to catch chickens even if they ran across our path with no owner in sight, and nor were we allowed to buy them from the farms we passed. We knew that other regiments had been told the same but did so anyway.

'We amateurs are more regular than the regulars,' muttered Sheridan.

It was freezing cold without blankets. Sheridan had been made tent orderly, which was surely a sarcastic post for we had no tent. He had developed toothache and could hardly speak. We marched twenty-six miles still with no water and nothing to eat. Thirty of our men fell out but the Shropshires lost seventy and we were told we should 'feel proud'. We visited a camp held by Colonel Howe. It was entrenched all around yet they had lost over six hundred horses and oxen to Boer shellfire and the stench was terrible.

I spent my time transferring kit belonging to men who had

succumbed to one illness or another, seeking stores and delivering such mail as arrived. Occasionally I saw Pattenden and sometimes he spoke. He hated the fact that we had seen his fear and witnessed his cowardice on the field.

'Where's your great protector then,' he jeered one day, 'the dashing Cooper? Oh, I know, dashed on some hillside, isn't he?' He gripped my wrist and squeezed. 'Not protected now, are you, Grey?'

I tried to pay him little attention. I had enough to think about, for the wound in my side would not heal. Rather it began to swell and fill with vile pus, and each night I attempted to find some moment to clean and tend it. I would look down at my wound and see my female parts. Now I bled only from my side. Somehow I had become unsexed.

I grew weaker and weaker but my exhausted frame looked no different from that of the men.

Skirmishes occurred with a regularity that made them almost routine. Without much thought, I would shoulder a hundredweight of bike and kit and move to lie down as a shell burst where I had just been. Sometimes the whole regiment rose as one and there would be a great sweep up a fire-scarred mountainside, none of us pausing to lie down and fire. We ignored the rain of bullets that swept through the ranks and mowed down man after man. We achieved our object and presumably the officers thought the heavy losses were a fit price to pay. For the men I can tell you there was no thought of dying for country or for Queen; there was no high sentiment, it was simply the next day, the next hour. We were ready to die for we felt dead already.

The deprivations mixed with constant danger brought out something terrible in each of us, something dark and unkind. If we had already learned to steal from strangers we now learned to take from our own. Pattenden began to move in on the boy, on Haddock. I should have done something. How Cooper would have railed at me, but every day I battled with the thought of simply giving up. Of confessing all, so that I might lie in a bed with white sheets and be cared for.

At first I saw them together in the distance. Perhaps, I reasoned, it was chance that Pattenden was standing waiting when Haddock returned from duty on his bike. Then I noticed that sometimes he and Haddock shared a mug of tea or a cigarette. When Pattenden saw me he smiled but it was a smile that warned me to stay away. He walked over to me and roughly removed the bandage from my forehead. I did not speak as he slowly ran his finger along the scar on my face.

One evening Haddock could not be found. I think we presumed he had been sent up the line with post for the colonel, while the rest of us were on wood fatigue. A nearby field had a wooden fence and there was a great race for the nearest posts. In five minutes not a stick of wood was left standing for about a mile. It was as I searched for sticks that I found Bessie the duck had been left in the shelter of a tree hollow, in a small tent fashioned from twigs and a scrap of material off a torn coat. Haddock had taken great care to make sure she was protected. Pattenden appeared behind, looking flushed and excitable.

'Grey!' he sneered. 'You been waiting for me?'

'Leave me alone, Pattenden.'

He was about to pin me against the stump when he noticed the duck. Without another word Pattenden reached in and wrung the bird's neck. It was over in a second. No discussion, no thought. He wound the strip of coat that had protected her round himself as a scarf and slung her limp body over his shoulder.

When we returned to the camp Sheridan looked at the bird and then set about making a fire.

'She's dead,' he said to me quietly. 'There's nothing to be done.'

The duck did smell good. Even I thought so. We were half mad with hunger and the thought of such a meal was like a dream. Pattenden disappeared and then, just as we prepared to eat, he returned, buttoning up his trousers and leering at me. I was helping to consume his duck when the boy returned. Something terrible had happened to him. His trousers were ripped and he could barely stand. His face bore the kind of shock you saw in every moment of battle.

'All right, Haddock?' asked Pattenden, grinning at the boy as he slowly and methodically licked grease from a finger. 'Had a nice evening, have you? We've had the most delicious meal. Such a shame you missed it. Duck. A great big plump duck.'

Haddock stared at us and then turned away into the soaking dark. I went after him but as soon as I got beyond the tent flap I began to be sick. I vomited and vomited as if my stomach might expel what was left of my life. In the morning we found Haddock's body hanging from the muzzle of one of his beloved big guns. It swung in the breeze like a blade of grass on the wide South African plains.

Sheridan did not speak but followed me as I went in search of Pattenden. I found him filling his water bottle and called his name. As he turned towards me I pulled back my arm and punched him square on the jaw.

'Grey!' shouted Sheridan, as if to stop me. 'What are you thinking?' He picked Pattenden up off the ground and shook his head at me. 'That's not how you do it, Grey.' He held the man at arm's length and made a fist. 'Like this.' George Sheridan landed a punch that made Pattenden's head rock on his shoulders before he collapsed to his knees.

I looked at Sheridan.

'Ah, I see,' I said.

'Try again,' he said, hauling Pattenden to his feet. I punched the vile man so hard it shook my entire body. I had never understood why men fought each other in this way but now I knew the satisfaction of it. I could feel it course through my veins.

We buried Haddock on the veldt where he joined so many now lying beneath the blood-soaked African soil. Death surrounded us. And now it was in our tent, in our mess and some of it was our fault. I wished myself dead, and regretted each bullet that passed me by.

I received orders to ride fifty miles across the veldt to direct General Broadwood as to our column's intentions. The pain in my side meant I could no longer swing my leg across the saddle so mounting was difficult.

As I began to pedal out I passed a group preparing to execute a kaffir. The black native had been caught stealing a goat and was about to face a firing squad. He shook and would not stand still so they tied him to a cart wheel. As I turned away the sound of a single shot echoed across the veldt.

By now I had lost all pleasure in the bicycle. The thrill I had first felt circling the stage under Frank's command was long gone. The metal seemed heavy and hateful, the saddle cut into me. Now I longed to be like the Boer, who sat astride their horses as easily as rocking in a chair on a veranda. I even longed to be confined once more to Aunt Caroline's drawing room.

As well as my wound or perhaps because of it I now also had a fever. Sweat ran across my body as I pedalled forward. I could no longer think. I remembered the bear in London's zoological gardens who took Tuesdays off and thought I should like to do the same. I don't know how many miles I had covered when I saw the farm in the distance. It was a large, low building painted white and standing on a slight rise. It must have been the home of quite wealthy people, for an attempt had been made at a proper drive and white stone pillars at the entrance bore the name Wolfaardt. A few trees had been optimistically planted where a garden was perhaps intended. I fell off my bike and as dirt slammed into the back of my throat, I heard the sound of dogs racing across the yard towards me.

# Twenty-four

Frank's case came to court. Like a certain celebrated predecessor, he was charged under the 1885 Criminal Amendment Act and like Mr Wilde's his case was quite the cause célèbre. Dolly Dutch had brought Frank fame and the courtroom was packed each day with a mix of newspaper men, gossips and shrill young men who were supporting Frank as an 'unspeakable of the Oscar Wilde sort'. The management of the Empire distanced themselves from the matter, stating their regret at being 'deceived' about Frank's inclinations. His once loyal theatre following seemed to melt away as word spread about the 'horrible charge' laid at his door. There were debates in the papers about both the propensity of music-hall entertainment to lead to degenerate behaviour and the general 'disease of effeminacy' that was sadly spreading throughout 'modern cities'.

Elaborate rumours spread: Frank had a pink-ribboned poodle who had died of heartbreak now his master was in jail; someone declared that they knew for certain that Frank was actually Dutch, while another suggested that Frank's 'superior bearing' was due to the fact that he was really the illegitimate son of a member of the aristocracy who had since fled abroad. He was said to have been intimate with a great range of lovers, including a noted artist who could be found 'hung in the National Gallery', a member of a Brazilian trade delegation with a particularly outrageous moustache and several batsmen from a visiting Australian cricket team.

The initial cause of his arrest, the make-up, might have been overlooked because of his profession but the moment the police began to investigate his life in more detail the matter became more serious. The 'poets and priests' of his circle, mostly men terrified for their own reputations, were quick to bring allegations against him the moment their own names were mentioned. Several of those named on the list found in Frank's desk reluctantly admitted to having attended parties at Frank's flat. All, however, swore on oath that the moment they had discovered the 'improper' nature of his social gatherings they had departed.

Lord Grey's sole thought was to protect Reggie from the investigation. He pulled in favours, invited the editor of *The Times* to lunch at the House of Lords where the old newspaper man could see for himself how helpful Lord Grey might be with matters pertaining to Parliament. Then he 'bumped into' the police commissioner and reminded him what japes they had got up to together as boys at Marlborough College. Lord Grey had a wide acquaintance and did not rest until he had spoken with as many influential men as possible. When Frank's flat was searched, anything that might have related to Reggie was discreetly overlooked.

Soon it was the flat itself that became a focal point. Its décor and darkened, perfumed rooms were of service to the prosecution case and provided lively newspaper copy. 'The windows of his room were covered with stained art muslin, dark velvet curtains and lace curtains ... The rooms were furnished sumptuously and were lighted by different coloured lamps and candles ... The windows were never opened and the daylight never admitted.' The gossips drank in the details of an unnatural, shadowy world full of heady perfumes and exotic scents. Fresh air and light – the conduits of Victorian health and vitality – were absent. Even his reading material was presented in evidence. Curiously, it was not the ethnographic photographs of Sicilian boys that drew the most attention but the leather-bound book on the Renaissance. This was clearly the abode of a sexual deviant who shaped his domestic sphere on degenerate foreign ideas.

The Irish woman from the flat below gave testimony for the prosecution.

'And this street?' enquired the lawyer. 'Is it a rough area?'

'I should say not,' replied the offended woman, before adding, 'even though it is quite near the Houses of Parliament.'

There was light laughter.

'And who visited Mr Rutherford in these premises?'

'One night it was a soldier of the Royal Horse Guards,' she declared.

'And how do you know that?' enquired the prosecution.

'I could hear him go up the stairs – he had spurs on. No light went on in the rooms but he seemed to keep his spurs on all night.'

More laughter in the gallery.

The courtroom was shocked to learn that a telegraph boy from GPO headquarters had called late one night. The 'den of infamy' was not in an obscure back street where common street boys consorted; it was instead a place where one might find post office employees and soldiers in uniform.

The case went on for a week, gripping and appalling the capital as placards and newspapers shouted the details. In the court itself there was an almost comical delicacy to the proceedings. Not wishing to sully anyone present, the prosecution barrister spoke of his reluctance to drag into the light of day these 'foul loathsome slimy things that are hidden out of sight'. He was so reticent that at times it was almost impossible to know what he was talking about.

'I am sorry to have to put this question,' declared the lawyer, 'but I want a plain answer. You will understand what I mean. Now do I understand that the accused suggested something to you to which you objected?'

'Yes, sir,' replied the witness, anxious to do anything to avoid further scrutiny of his own life.

The barrister turned dramatically to the presiding judge. 'My lord, once again, a canker has been brought to light.'

It was left to individuals to determine exactly what the canker might have been. The trial became a ludicrous parade of people being asked to give clear testimony while simultaneously being expected to have the good manners not to go into too much detail. The world that Frank moved in was made to seem so murky that no clear picture of it would ever emerge in the confines of polite society. Frank's lack of facial hair, penchant for fashionable dress, his theatrical career had 'created a stage on which to play out his symptoms of degeneracy'. It was clear that Frank was an associate of 'men of vicious habits' and that 'the hideous crime' was a malevolent presence which haunted the city.

Throughout the trial, Lord Grey kept Reggie safe behind the great black door of Inkerman House, where the doctors continued to sedate him and he was not allowed newspapers for fear of 'exciting' his nerves, so he remained unaware of what

Frank was suffering. Every day Frank sat alone with a microscope on his life. He was silent throughout. Frank loved Reggie with all his might and rather than risk a single word that could implicate his absent lover, he preferred not to speak at all. He did not even lift his head to examine those who sought to condemn him. Perhaps, too, he dare not catch his mother's eye, for she sat at the back of the court, her shawl wrapped tightly around her. She came for her son but she did not know him. He did not, after all, drive an omnibus. Frank could not bear to witness her disappointment.

'See how he looks down at the floor in shame?' boomed the barrister. 'Any modern scientist will tell you that it is possible to read identity and character directly from the body. Is this not a Uranian we have here, a danger to us all? Every honest and wholesome-minded Englishman must grieve to learn how largely this French and pagan plague has crept like a weed into the healthy fields of English life, undermining the natural affections, the domestic joys, the sanctity and sweetness of the home. Indeed, it is against these very foreign influences upon our life that, as we stand here today, our own men are fighting in South Africa.'

Perhaps Frank looked down because he could not bear what the scar had done to his beauty. The stitches had been removed but it was still red and angry and spoke of dark deeds. The court artist drew him with an exaggerated, jagged line across his face, and when it was published in the *Illustrated News* Frank looked nothing short of monstrous. The disfigurement caused another ripple of rumours, the favourite being that he had been injured by a member of the House of Lords who had been forced to protect his honour with a rapier.

Despite all this, Frank still carried an air of distinction. When finally he was called to testify he rose slowly and shook imagined dust from his clothes. He wore an immaculate double-breasted frock coat in soft grey with trousers in a lighter hue. A neat handkerchief poked from his breast pocket and a well-wisher had provided him with a single flower that matched his tie and stood out upon his silk lapel. He did not know how to dress other than to strive for perfection. He stood with one hand casually draped over the wooden rail of the witness box, the perfect posture of a man wrongly accused. At last he held his head up but he looked only at the judge.

'My name is Frank Rutherford and I am guilty' – there was a single intake of breath from the court before he continued – 'of love.'

Frank said nothing else. He refused to curry favour with the judge by implicating anyone else.

His defence barrister was a fine fellow and he did his best. He even tried to introduce the idea that *sexual inversion* was an inborn condition. This was a new notion and he managed to persuade a couple of men of science to testify that there were those for whom 'inversion' was in their nature. But no one was minded to pay attention; it was clear from the beginning that the offence was too gross to admit of any excuse.

The prosecution summed up their case, declaring confidently, 'The universal truth, my lord, is that each man and each woman holds his virility and her femininity in trust for humanity and that to meddle with either is fraught with danger for the state and for future generations.'

It was a fine speech, a speech Frank might have delivered with aplomb. Instead he was sentenced to two years with hard labour.

The gallery roared their approval.

Frank stood firm and noble. It was clear he had guessed what the outcome would be and intended to face his punishment without flinching. He remained upright with his chin held high as he allowed the officers to take him from the court. But just as he got to the prison van he heard a small knot of well-wishers call out and his fortitude began to give way. As he stepped up into the van he faltered and almost fell. The press reported a final glimpse of him quite crushed and broken.

Lord Grey put down his newspaper and walked restlessly round the house. Despite all his best efforts he was not certain that Reggie was safe. The press had loved the story and were still circling. He needed to do something more.

# Twenty-five

I awoke in a bed, lying between clean white sheets. I stretched out my bare foot and incredulously felt the linen smooth on my skin. I took a deep breath and a hand touched my cheek. A black fellow was sitting quietly beside me. I started: I did not know the angels would be black. He smiled at me and rose from his chair.

I was clearly alive – but where was I?

I pulled my hands up out of the covers, and moved them over my body, exploring. Fresh bandages had been applied to my head and to the wound on my right-hand side. I noticed that I felt no pain. I was wearing a long white nightshirt. My clothes had disappeared. I looked around. The sun at the lace-curtained window illuminated a small room and I could see that I was in a narrow brass bed, covered in a red quilt. A dark mahogany chest of drawers with a flowery china basin and jug upon it stood against a wall opposite. There was a small chair padded in a faded floral print beside the bed. The windows looked out on to a veranda shaded with a reddish tin roof. I took in all this wonder but I did not speak. I could not speak. I watched the young man fill a glass of water from the jug.

He returned and, aiding my attempts to sit up, gently helped me to drink and then wiped some drops from my lips with a white linen cloth. The water was fresh and clear and I realised that I would not exchange such a drink for all the whisky in the world. He smiled and for a moment, despite my bewilderment, I smiled back. I had not even known I could still manage such a thing: that smiles might still lurk within me.

I guessed he was a servant for he wore a plain white shirt and rough black trousers but his feet were free of shoes. I had marched with many of the kaffirs as they herded oxen and took care of the animals. I knew some to be Zulu but I had never spoken to one, never sat close and examined their faces. His lips were thick and full, his nose wide and his skin as black as the night sky. It was difficult for me to tell but I thought he was probably not far off my own age. Here before me was one of the 'savages' people at Earl's Court had paid money to see. He put his hand to my forehead. The palm of his hand was pale, a lovely light brown colour, and it soothed me.

Then suddenly fear rose in me and I tried to start up. My messages! I had messages to deliver. Perhaps he was the enemy. Perhaps they wanted my messages. I should not be lying here! I tried to raise myself from the bed, scrabbling at the sheets with my hands.

'Who are you? What do you want?' I cried, finding my creaking voice.

But he did not say a word. Gently he pushed me back down on to the bed and laid his finger on his own lips to silence me.

'I have to go,' I declared, trying once more to get out of bed.

The young man was strong. He pushed me back against the pillows.

It seemed that while I slept the mistress of the house had kept out of the room, but now instinct drew her in and she arrived with a bang of the bedroom door. The boy moved away, once more putting his finger to his lips to indicate that I should be quiet.

Mrs Wolfaardt, as I was to find out, was not yet a widow, but perhaps she wore black in anticipation. In my slight delirium I thought: she is white and wears black and her servant is black and wears white, and that is how it was. Even at first glance it was clear that Mrs Wolfaardt was a formidable woman. Her long gown swept stiffly to the floor and was fastened tightly at the neck by a single piece of plain jet jewellery, her only ornament. Her hair was drawn back into a bun, and her face seemed set into hard misery. In all the time I was with her I only saw her smile once, but then I learned that she had little reason for good cheer.

'So, young man, you are awake?' declared Mrs Wolfaardt. She did not sit down but remained standing in the doorway, eyeing me from a distance.

*Young man?* How was this possible? I had been tended to, had my clothes changed, lay beneath the sheets for anyone to notice that I was as much a woman as I had ever been. I glanced at the servant, who stared at the floor and did not meet my gaze.

'Yes.' I attempted to hoist myself up on the pillows.

'Where are you from?' demanded my hostess.

'From?'

Mrs Wolfaardt was impatient. 'Yes, yes, where from? Are you stupid as well as English?'

I wasn't sure if I was to tell her. Was it a military secret? But I also wasn't entirely sure where I had come from or even where I had been going.

'I was in Reitfontein, I think. I was to head for the Klip, the river . . . I had messages.'

Mrs Wolfaardt clicked her teeth and gestured to her servant. 'Should've left him in the yard for the dogs. Where is your home, idiot boy?'

'Oh.' I realised we were having the sort of conversation I had forgotten about. One where one took an interest in another person and wanted to know something about them. Where two strangers met and engaged in polite chatter.

'London, although I was born in India,' I whispered.

Mrs Wolfaardt looked at me long and hard. 'London,' she repeated as if she could not conceive of anything more appalling. 'Hmm. Well, you are safe now.'

Safe? How ridiculous. How could anyone ever be safe again? Cooper had travelled to keep me safe and now he lay below a peach tree, for ever part of the great veldt. Haddock had not been safe and I did not know about Jackson. No one was safe. I could not lie here unprotected.

'When you are well you must go home. You do not belong here. You must go home.'

Home. It was such an incredible thought. Home. Where was that? But I agreed politely, 'Yes, I must go home.'

Mrs Wolfaardt turned to go but paused in the doorway.

'What is your name?'

My name. I could not think. I could not think what I should be called. The game was surely up.

'Grey. My name is Grey.' I glanced at the young man, who continued to look at the floor. What else my name might be I did not say.

'Umfaan, see to Mr Grey,' Mrs Wolfaardt ordered as she closed the door behind her.

I lay in the bed, washed and changed, my wound carefully tended to. There was no question that Umfaan knew my secret but it was clear he had not and probably would not reveal it to anyone. I had been given into his care and as far as anyone else was concerned it was one young man dealing with another.

I was weak and had lost a great deal of blood. I lay in that room for a long time, letting the sun rise and fall behind the lace curtains. I found no desire to step outside into the world. I was like a child doing exactly as I was told. I did not wish to leave the room. I did not wish to smoke or drink. I was entirely content in that small world. It was enough to feel safe, to lie and listen to the silence. Umfaan saw to all my needs and I let him. I let him without speaking. He would bring a bowl of warm water in the morning and quietly wash each part of me as if I were the most helpless infant. Slowly and carefully he removed the war from me.

Mrs Wolfaardt knew little about Umfaan but I discovered that he had come to the farm as a small boy. Something had happened to his family but no one knew exactly what because Umfaan did not speak. He seemed to hear all right and to understand but he never said a word to anyone. He lived his life on the farm as a silent servant of all work, and now that work included looking after me.

Occasionally Mrs Wolfaardt would ask me odd questions but I think I made her anxious. More often I would catch a glimpse of her on the porch outside my window, particularly as the sun was setting, looking out across the plains, waiting. I had not thought before what it might be like for those who did not fight, those who waited day after day for word of the battles. As I recovered I began to see the strain on everyone's nerves. You only had to hear one of the natives running across the yard or chatting in louder tones than usual and at once you thought there must be news. Mrs Wolfaardt would rush to the porch from any occupation, only to sink on to a chair in disappointment. We saw no newspapers and there was not much prospect of obtaining any. Wires were cut, railway lines were up, no word came.

Umfaan made me drink milk and slowly began to reintroduce my body to small meals. He helped me to sit up. He combed and cut my hair, washed me and changed my linen. I was a baby in his care who gave up all claim to control. I did not speak much but lay thinking about where I had been and what I had seen. Sometimes at night it was as if I were back on the hill at Doornkop. As if Cooper were running towards me again, as if once more he were stopped in his tracks by a single bullet and the blood spread across his body as he looked at me in surprise. The blood had no end to it but poured in great streams like the waving grass of the plains. I would awaken with terror and rise up to reach for my gun. At those moments Umfaan seemed always to be by my side. He would hold my hand fast and stroke my forehead as I sobbed.

During the day I lay thinking about what I had been told: that at the call of duty a soldier must obey, that he questions not the cause but cheerfully goes out to uphold the honour of his island land. I knew I should not simply lie there, yet lie there I did. I wondered about my London life. There had been snippets from other men's letters, the old newspaper at the hospital, but it had been a strange mix of information about life in England. How odd the things relatives thought important enough to write about – Southampton had beaten Everton 3–0 in some League match, Cambridge had won the boat race by twenty lengths and someone's Aunt Agatha had a nasty head cold. Occasionally we had read a report of what we ourselves were supposed to be up to as our loved ones repeated the 'good news' they had heard of our 'triumphs'. What of Reggie though? And Frank? Had my uncle returned bearing the world's largest dead butterfly? Had Bahadur come back to find me? Did anyone even know I was missing?

In my mind, I walked with the men in my mess. Jackson, was he alive? Ben, was he home, did his wife take him back? Poor Haddock. I sat with them all and I lived again what I had seen, what we had done. I thought of Cooper, of his wasted life, of his kiss and of what I would tell Reggie. I didn't want any of it ever again, and some days I passed entirely with my face to the wall, crying quiet tears. But then, slowly, in spite of myself, I began to heal.

I started to take notice and find small comfort in the things which once I had taken for granted: a house, a comfortable bed, clean clothes, food – such simple pleasures. It was all any of us wanted – Boer or Briton, friend or foe.

One day after lunch, judging me ready, Umfaan brought me a set of clothes belonging to one of the Wolfaardt boys – comfortable corduroy trousers, a soft shirt and waistcoat. Ignoring my protests, he dressed me and helped me pull on a worn pair of brown boots. Slowly I walked as far as the porch, leaning on his arm. It was enough to exhaust me. I was still sitting there alone in a rocking chair, my legs covered with a soft blanket, when Mrs Wolfaardt appeared for her early evening ritual, to scan the horizon. She started when she saw me and placed her hand over her mouth.

I tried to get up. 'Are you all right?'

'I thought you were Abraham,' she confessed, her colour returning. She helped us both to sit.

'Abraham?' I asked.

'My oldest boy. Those are his clothes. You have something of a look of him.'

All of her men, from Mr Wolfaardt and his elderly father to Abraham who was twenty and even the youngest lad of thirteen, all were at war, at war with the likes of me. I sat in the very place that they sought to defend. I sat where Mrs Wolfaardt waited each night for news of their safe return. I was up close with the enemy and we were all the same.

'Would you like a drink?' she asked.

I shook my head. I could smell a heady scent from some kind of sweet flower that wound itself around the porch railings and I did not want to stupefy my senses ever again. I thought I might never touch another drop of alcohol.

The ground around the farm was as plain as Mrs Wolfaardt's dress, yet she was a woman whose soul harboured surprising colour. We became used to spending a half-hour together each day upon the porch. I had returned to the pleasure of an evening cigarette and as the smoke curled away she talked of gardens and trees.

South Africa was a wonderful country to grow anything in. She showed me ten- or twelve-foot high pines that were only four or five summers old; mighty blue gums with towering pyramids of dark metallic green and gnarled old trunks, first planted when her youngest boy was born. It was a strange, broad, treeless land of barren rock and rolling veldt with few natural plants. There was mimosa along the river beds and sparse rough bushes on the sides of kopjes, yet plant an alien tree and water it and it would flourish as it never did in its native land. I saw myself lying in a field long enough to be covered over with flowers for ever. Mrs Wolfaardt talked of the butterflies that would come and tears slipped down my cheeks for a Painted Lady. If she saw them she did not say. But there was so much we did not speak of and it was still clear that my hostess did not quite trust me. Who could blame her?

The house was single-storey, with the servants' quarters and the kitchen at the back. The main hall was dark and narrow and lined with framed photographs of the family, which I studied: Abraham and his younger brother, Johannes, who stood beside his father and brother dressed for war with the face of a boy.

One day I wandered in, off the main hall, to Mr Wolfaardt's study. A small room, it was lined with heavy bookcases built around a large marble fireplace. The walls were painted a deep red, a colour I no longer took pleasure in. Above the mantelpiece hung an old Martini-Henry rifle. No gun had touched my hand for some time and I was curious to see the workings of this old piece, so I took it down – it was heavy in my hand – and examined the breech. Mrs Wolfaardt appeared at the door.

'Put that back!' she barked so loudly that I almost dropped the gun.

'I meant no harm,' I stammered, rushing to put the weapon back. I reached up and strained the not quite healed wound in my side. I gasped and fell back into a chair, still clutching the gun which swung and pointed at its owner.

'Put it back,' she repeated, her voice shaking.

'I can't, I'm sorry. My side—'

Umfaan rushed in and looked with horror at what appeared to be me holding a gun to his mistress.

'It's all right, Umfaan, I fell. It's nothing. I would not harm you. Either of you.'

Umfaan took the gun from me and returned it to its place above the fire.

'I meant no harm,' I repeated.

Mrs Wolfaardt took a deep breath. 'Don't ever touch that again,' she said firmly and waited till I rose and left the room.

But that changed our relationship. After that, oddly, it seemed to be all right for me occasionally to spend the evening in the master's study with Mrs Wolfaardt and Umfaan in attendance. He'd light the fire and sit against the wall while Mrs Wolfaardt and I enjoyed the flames. Mrs Wolfaardt was lonely. She told me about the Great Trek from Cape Colony in tented wagons that she and her family had undertaken all those years ago to come here and make a new life, of their dreams for a great farm where they could live as they pleased. She cursed the diamonds and the gold that she said had brought fighting to the land.

'What about the *Uitlanders*' rights?' I asked.

'Diamonds and gold,' she repeated.

Some evenings I told stories of India and of London. Of tiger hunts, cricket matches and tea parties, of hansom carriages and theatre shows. Not Frank's. I didn't mention Frank nor did I talk about family either. It all seemed impossibly long ago and far away. As Umfaan listened he carved small creatures from pieces of bone. Under his hands, delicate beings came to life. Just like I had, I suppose.

'Can you make me a butterfly?' I asked.

As I grew stronger I began to find small chores around the farm that I might help with. There was livestock to tend, milk to bring in and firewood to chop. The exercise did me good. I dressed like the Wolfaardt boys and I think perhaps I even began to sound a little like them. Gradually I was aware of using the odd Boer term and I suspect my accent began to mould itself to my surroundings. One morning when Mrs Wolfaardt asked how I was and I replied, '*Ek's goed, dankie*,' we both laughed at how easily the words had formed on my lips.

I began to feel as though I belonged. As if my other life had never really happened. Then one afternoon when I was bringing a churn to the kitchen door, I glanced through the window and saw Umfaan with one of the kitchen maids, a girl called Tombi. They were laughing as Tombi did something to Umfaan's hair. A great pang shot through my body and I realised with some amazement that I was jealous: I did not want anyone to touch Umfaan. I thought of him as mine.

Later that week we were in my bedroom. He moved to brush my hair and I grabbed the comb from his hand.

'I can do that,' I said curtly. I had been rude and brusque with him for a few days now.

Umfaan stood looking long and hard at me. I glared at him and then I leaned forward and kissed him. He looked startled, even affronted, and then he gave a slow smile and took both my wrists in his hands. The hand of another on my own flesh. For a moment terror seized me and I remembered the man, the sergeant with the beard. Shame poured through me that I could ever have sunk so low. I pulled away from Umfaan and stood taking deep breaths of fear. He looked at me and reached out his hand to touch my cheek. He put his head on one side looking at me as if I were an injured bird he had found in the garden. Gently he stroked my face and slowly pulled me back into his embrace. Now he kissed me back. Then, just as gently as he had tended to my broken body, but with the utmost seriousness, he undressed me and laid me down, never taking his eyes off mine. Now there was no pain, just gentleness and I drew back from some brink I hadn't even realised I stood upon. Afterwards he stroked my skin. I had seen too much death not to need to be reminded of tenderness. Perhaps he awakened Valentine.

How joyous the world seemed; how alive I felt in my body. I worked with a renewed energy on the farm. I dug the flower beds that Mrs Wolfaardt longed for as if I had no other plan than to see them bloom. I forgot about the war and about my part in it. At night I lay in Umfaan's arms and all was well. He was mine and I thought he felt the same about me.

I was nearly better when the soldiers came. There were only a handful but they were wide-eyed with hunger, their uniforms so ripped I could barely tell the regiment. The one thing I knew for sure when I heard Tombi scream from the milking shed and I looked out of the window was that they were British.

Mrs Wolfaardt was standing in the study, utterly immobilised, when I ran in.

'Give me the gun,' I called.

She hesitated for a moment and then grabbed the rifle from the wall. She thrust it at me and hurried to fetch a box of cartridges from a drawer.

I loaded it as if it were second nature and ran to the yard at the back. Across the way in the small barn, one of the men had Tombi up against the wall and was attempting to lift her skirts. Another had a chicken under each arm while the third drank milk from the churn with a tin cup, so fast that it poured down his front and soaked him.

I called out the sentence we had been taught to use if captured. '*Waar is jy vandaan?*' Where is your officer? but they did not reply so I fired the gun just above the head of the man on top of Tombi, peppering the wall with shot. He sprang back and dropped her to the ground.

'What the bloody hell—'

The men turned to me and I held the gun level at my shoulder. Umfaan stood beside me, weaponless but with his hands clenched defiantly.

'If you are hungry, we will feed you, otherwise please go,' I said calmly.

The man with the chickens attempted some bluster.

'Look, lads, it's a farmer with gun. 'Ow terrifying.'

Dressed in Abraham Wolfaardt's clothes, I realised I now stood as a Boer defending his land. The very land I had come to seize.

'No beard though,' said the man mopping milk from his mouth. 'Got no beard, have you? You too young to go to proper war, eh, little fella?' he taunted, holding out the cup.

I fired a careful shot and took the mug clean out of his hand.

As the mug clanged to the ground all three raised their arms and the freed chickens fled for their lives.

'All right, all right, no need to get shirty. We're off. Bloody Boer.'

The men began to slink from the yard and as they reached the corner of the house they passed my regimental bicycle. One of them turned back and studied me.

# Twenty-six

By the time Mrs Wolfaardt and I were marched into the camps, there were almost two thousand people living in the hundreds of white tents set up as far as the eye could see. The majority were women, with more than nine hundred children. The crematorium erected to the south-west blew the smell of burnt flesh into the camp. It was unbearable. The smoke was biting and cut into the nostrils as if some of our own flesh burned in sympathy. A group of children sent out to play had sunk down upon the ground and sat like little old men and women waiting for the end.

Mrs Wolfaardt wept. 'Surely God has forsaken us.'

Spring had come early to the Wolfaardt farm. It was August but in South Africa it was spring. My world continued upside down. I was a man by day and a woman with a lover at night. I had begun to help Mrs Wolfaardt plant her garden. She had many packets of seeds sent out from Europe, which now we began to plant out in the greenhouse. I loved the feel of the soil in my hands and the sun on my back. I was growing strong and well and foolishly I dropped my guard. I thought of nothing but the garden. How the air would be sweet with the smell of jasmine. I imagined that no palette could capture the colour: hibiscus with its small, purplish-pink flowers, a kind of lily in the deepest blue, Lion's Ear with tall spikes of bright orange flowers that attracted the birds, small Kirstenbosch flowers so bright they seemed to have been splashed with paint, carpets of Namaqualand daisies.

The soldiers had arrived in the afternoon. They were a mounted group of perhaps six or seven. I did not hear them come because I was busy with new life in the greenhouse, pressing tiny shoots into clay pots. I cursed myself. Why hadn't I kept the gun with me? There was no time to get it now.

'Grey!' Mrs Wolfaardt had screamed. The pot dropped from my hand and smashed on the stone floor. I ran but it was too late. The soldiers were in the house.

'There are no men here,' cried Mrs Wolfaardt, trying to face them down on the veranda as I came up.

'Grey, they think we harbour fighters,' she cried.

I found the corporal in charge. He was young, just a bit older than me, but full of himself. He reminded me of Pattenden. I planted myself in front of him. 'There are no men here.'

He stopped in the middle of poking into the pantry after some eggs that had taken his fancy.

'Really? You look like a man to me,' he said evenly, his English accent seeming so foreign to me now.

'I'm not a fighter. You don't understand, I—'

The corporal jabbed me in the chest and put his face in mine. 'No, you don't understand, sonny boy. If you Boer followed the rules this wouldn't be necessary but the place is crawling with your bloody guerrilla fighters. You have brought this upon yourselves. You have five minutes.'

'Five minutes to do what?' I asked.

'I don't really care,' he replied, turning to pocket a small silver trinket.

In the end, we didn't even have five minutes. Mrs Wolfaardt and I stood helpless near our beloved flower beds and watched our life die a terrible, agonising death.

'Where is Umfaan?'

'They took him and Tombi.'

'Took them where?'

'I don't know.'

In no time the fire, begun in the library, spread until the house was nothing but a torch. We watched as the meagre livestock was slaughtered. Next were the dogs. Numb, we saw the soldiers fell our new saplings, trample the flowers. They made us stand and watch until there was nothing left but a harsh smell and smoking ruins.

'You will come with us,' came the order from the soldiers. We piled our few salvaged possessions on to a cart and began to walk.

'You must tell them who you are,' hissed Mrs Wolfaardt under her breath. 'Save yourself.'

I shook my head and whispered quietly, 'I am not leaving you. We are together.' I put my arm around her and we walked into hell.

We were told to search for a tent with space for us. We wandered through a maze of abandoned people but there was no room. Each bell tent already held as many as a dozen people, with two and sometimes three different families sharing a single canvas dwelling. None had as much as a bedstead or a mattress. We learned that even fuel was scarce and had to be collected from the green bushes on the slopes of the kopjes by the people themselves. Many lacked even kettles in which to boil the drinking water they gathered from puddles and all were shrouded in grime. The smell in the air was unbearable. It was so rich a scent of death and filth that it was as though we tasted rather than smelt it.

Mrs Wolfaardt found a space for us at last when she saw her neighbour, a Mrs van der Poel, filling a bucket with filthy water and the woman took pity on us. She took us to her tent where three small boys were lying listlessly on khaki blankets on ground that was covered in ants. A woman I thought to be their mother lay on a small mat. A little girl of perhaps seven lay beside her, also ill. To add to their misery the tent was full of khaki lice.

'She has milk fever,' explained Mrs van der Poel, nodding towards the mother.

'But where is the baby?' I asked.

'It is a blessing. He is already dead.'

The mother stirred as I entered. 'I had no candle,' she whispered. 'He died in the dark. I had no candle.'

Mrs van der Poel now eyed me with suspicion. 'Are you a *hendsopper*, a hands-upper?'

'I don't know what you mean,' I replied, confused.

'Look around you,' said Mrs van der Poel. 'There are no men here. Just women and babies. The only men are those who have surrendered. I do not want a *hendsopper* in my tent.'

Mrs Wolfaardt shook her head. 'Mr Grey has surrendered to no one. He is my friend.' Mrs van der Poel didn't look convinced but she was too tired to argue.

We sat ourselves down upon the ground. I covered my mouth and nose with my forearms; I could not bear the smell.

'Let me wash the blankets for you,' I offered.

Mrs van der Poel shook her head. 'There is no soap. We are undesirables.'

I thought of Jackson and his quest to cleanse South Africa with his bars of Britannia. Perhaps he had been right after all.

'What do you mean?'

'We are classified when we come. Those who did not surrender or who have family in the commando are classified as undesirables and so we get no soap. The *hendsoppers* get a few extra spoonfuls of sugar, some condensed milk, sometimes, I hear, a potato. I hope they think it was worth it.'

That night we sat with other women from nearby tents. Like us they had been given minutes to get out of their homes, to collect their things. That was all, minutes. And then the Tommies, my comrades – I wanted to spit – had taken whatever they wanted and killed anything – ducks, geese, pigs – anything the women might have had a use for.

'Where are your men?' I asked.

Mrs van der Poel's eyes teared.

'I don't know,' she replied. 'They sent many away to, I don't know, Ceylon, we hear, and India, Bermuda, an island, St Helena, I think it's called, but now they take no more prisoners. They shoot them all. They say Lord Kitchener has ordered anyone bringing in a prisoner to give up half his rations for the prisoner's keep. No prisoners are taken. No one wants to starve and no one wants tales to be told.'

'Will they give up? The men?' I wondered.

Mrs Wolfaardt stood to put the kettle on her small fire with a vigour I remembered from when she ruled her property.

'Never,' she declared with ferocity. 'They can do what they like. We may see our own hungry children die before our eyes but the men must never give way. This shall be fought to the bitter end. I have to believe "all things will come to those who will but wait".'

How like Cooper that sounded. We needed him now; perhaps his lawyer's mind could have found some way out of this hell-hole. Everywhere we saw terrible suffering. I thought I had seen a lifetime's share, but this seemed worse than the battlefield. No one had volunteered for this. There were very few tents that did not house one or more sick persons, most of them children. Measles, bronchitis, pneumonia, dysentery and typhoid had invaded the camp with fatal results. Everything was needed but nothing was done. My own concerns seemed so trifling. I helped where I could but it was not long before I could contain myself no longer and I asked the question I needed to hear answered.

I lay beside Mrs Wolfaardt as we tried in vain to sleep upon the ground.

'Mrs Wolfaardt. In the morning I must search for Umfaan.'

Mrs Wolfaardt looked bewildered. 'Umfaan?'

'Yes, Umfaan,' I persisted.

'The boy?' she asked. 'But, Valentine, he is not here, or Tombi. They took them to a separate place.'

'I have to find him. Do you know if he has another name? Some second name so I can look for him on the lists?'

Mrs Wolfaardt looked at me as if I understood nothing.

'But, my dear child, you will never find him.'

'I have to try.'

'It is impossible.'

I would not let it go. 'Why?' I insisted.

'Umfaan just means "boy". It's what we called them all.'

Umfaan meant boy and Tombi meant girl. They might as well have been called Maisie.

# Twenty-seven

I stood in the queue for Mrs Wolfaardt while her food ration was issued – an ounce of sugar, some mealie meal, 1/18th of a tin of condensed milk, meat so chilled that, even after cooking, it had chunks of ice in it. I helped collect firewood on a kopje next to the camp and every morning I stood in line to fill her bucket with water brought from a river by cart. I thought if I concentrated on daily tasks, on helping Mrs Wolfaardt, I would be able to overcome my distress and my shame about Umfaan. I had been calling him 'boy'; I had almost commanded him to take me to bed. What did it mean? That I was naive and he was canny? That I understood nothing and he understood it all exactly? I was a white mistress and he was a black servant. I cared for him and surely he cared for me. Or was it like Sarel? Had my dear lover expected to be paid? I felt a shame and a terrible longing for him that nearly felled me.

Throughout it all, though, I couldn't let Mrs Wolfaardt down; she remained oddly resolute. And as the only man in our tents, I certainly couldn't sit still. I looked around our new surroundings and felt, over the days and weeks, my dull ache turn into rage. Rage against decay, waste and death.

I tried to help with the cleaning but it was an impossible task. Aside from the dry dust, lice were everywhere. Even the soldiers who guarded the camp had to take their leggings off, unwinding them like strips of bandages, and use broken glass to scrape the lice from their flesh. The rest of us were soon crawling with the detested bugs. In the end poor Mrs Wolfaardt had to cut all her own hair off. I watched it fall in clumps on the ground and thought of Maisie cutting my hair. I had felt liberated then, but now Mrs Wolfaardt wept for her lost dignity.

I thought my war days of mud and mindless brutality could not be beaten, but this was a different sort of cruelty and degradation. The toilet was horrible: a big hole with plank seats and sacking around it, where you climbed up on top of the planks and did your business; no newspaper, no rags.

Not everyone had Mrs Wolfaardt's resolve; many of the women tussled and fought. Theft was rife. One morning the woman in the next tent stole a skirt from our tent and walked off with one of the Tommies. She came back with some salt and we felt a mixture of disgust and jealousy.

And every day carts rumbled between the rows of tents to pick up the dead.

One evening Maria, the young woman in the next tent, begged us to sit with her. Pinched and dry-eyed, she sat on a small trunk containing all her possessions. Her baby in a little soiled cloth lay limply across her knee. On the cold earth sat a child of about four, so pale and emaciated that he did not seem human at all. In his trembling hand he had a jam tin filled with black, bitter coffee; in the other a slice of half-baked bread, heavy and clammy. It would be his only meal until the next day. Unaware of his mother's grief, he watched us as we in turn watched with reverent silence while his younger sibling drew his last breath. Maria neither moved nor wept. Deathly white, she sat there motionless, looking not at the child but far, far away into depths of grief beyond tears. All so that England might extend her Empire and that Paul Kruger might keep out that bogey the *Uitlander*.

I had never understood anything about strategy in all the time I had been engaged in the fighting, but now I understood perfectly. The aim was to cause ordinary South Africans so much suffering that they must long for peace, and force the government to demand it. The people must be left with nothing but their eyes so they might weep over the war.

Everywhere lay children with diarrhoea and dysentery, enteric fever, marasmus (a wasting away of the body), whooping cough and malaria, tiny creatures suffering convulsions.

One of the girls in our tent, Lyzzie, was seven but as frail and weak as a newborn and in desperate need of good care. She lay near the raised flap, gasping her life out in the heat. Suddenly, overwhelmed, I scooped her up and said I was taking her to the camp hospital. My manly stride was still allowing me to venture further in the world but now it was taking me to places I did not want to go. I presented myself and my bundle at the doctor's tent.

In pristine uniform – new boots and belt, fresh trousers and jacket – and with an equally fresh face, the doctor must have been part of a recent draft.

'How old are you?' he demanded of the child.

'She is seven,' I replied.

'If she is seven then she can reply for herself,' he declared.

'She doesn't understand you. She doesn't speak English.'

He shrugged, did nothing to relieve her suffering but said I could have some of the water they had set aside for the hospital, then he moved on.

'She is ill,' I called after him.

'Then her mother should not have starved her,' he retorted, without once looking back.

I returned to the tent with the dying child, having achieved nothing – defeated and useless. But Mrs Wolfaardt had a plan for me.

'You must go home, Mr Grey,' she said. 'I do not believe that England would want us to suffer like this. God's hand is too heavy for us. Please, go and tell them what you have seen.'

Mrs Wolfaardt set about the preparations. In spite of her determination, my departure was not straightforward. A man alone, away from the confines of the camp, was in danger. The Boer might shoot me for a spy and the British for a traitor.

'We could disguise you,' said Mrs Wolfaardt.

'Disguise me?'

'As a woman,' she replied, 'to keep you safe.'

I almost laughed in her earnest face.

And so it was that I once more donned female clothes: a woman who had been a man now pretending to be a woman.

I pulled on a skirt and blouse and placed a scarf on my head. Mrs Wolfaardt nodded her approval. I could not speak. She had become a mother to me; it was not what I had come to South Africa to find.

'You make a fine woman, Mr Grey.'

I walked from the camp through the scorched earth. Everywhere crops had been decimated and houses not only destroyed by fire but often blown up by dynamite so that not a stone was left unturned. In the field dead livestock lay rotting and feeding no one. On one farm, three hundred horses had been chased into a kraal and shot dead. Vultures wheeled and turned in the air through the dust of people on the move.

I thought of our happy mess who had headed north from Cape Town all those months ago. Of Haddock with his cigarette cards, sitting laughing on the rucksacks, and the rest of us – Jackson, Sheridan, Cooper – all crammed together, our thighs touching as if we were one. We had believed that we brought the honour of the Empire in our wake. Now I saw families huddled – hungry, sick, dying and dead. What would my kind fellows have said? Was this what we had fought for? I reached the railway line where trains passed with open trucks crammed with old and young under an unrelenting sun. Everywhere I looked, the British army, my army, were moving across the veldt like a plague of locusts. Anything that could not be eaten or transported was destroyed. It was the uprooting of an entire nation.

As I followed the railway line I saw a soldier push a woman back from the track. She fell, tumbled down the siding and did not get up. I ran towards her and nearly tripped in my unfamiliar skirts. I who had marched a thousand miles now could not walk. The soldier turned and roughly grabbed me by the arm.

'What do you think you're doing?' he demanded. He was young, younger than me.

'I'm British,' I said. I hadn't meant to and I don't know why it came out.

He looked at me clearly puzzled by my accent, which was no doubt much changed after so many months in South Africa.

'I'm from London. I need to go home,' and then I did a dreadfully female thing and fainted.

I awoke as the soldier was lifting me into a small cart pulled by a ragged-looking horse.

'Ssh,' he said quietly, 'you're all right now.'

He placed me on the seat and jumped up beside me.

'Been trying to help, have you?' he asked.

I nodded silently. I was dull and compliant, as if I had been drugged. We set off for the town, passing yet another burnt-out farm.

'Are there many like that?'

The fellow nodded. 'Almost all the farms and villages in both republics.'

'Where are the men? The Boers? Where is the fighting?' I asked.

'Ha,' he exclaimed with glee, 'we flush them out. It's as good as hunting grouse.'

I stared at him, unbelieving.

We arrived in Bloemfontein and the soldier stopped in front of a large public building. The city lay in a plain with low hills surrounding it. Here was the civilisation I had forgotten about: daily newspapers being sold at a bookstall, electric light and clean running water. The soldier stepped down and ran round to help me. I took his hand and leaned upon it as I slowly clambered from the cart.

'You'll need to see the sergeant in the hall,' he said, nodding to the front door. 'He'll arrange your transport.'

Then he bowed as if we had met on Bond Street and passed a pleasant afternoon.

I found the sergeant with no trouble. In a large public room he was busy instructing kaffirs to pull up the battered floorboards and have them replaced. I knew him the minute I saw him, even though he had his back to me. He was large and his uniform burst with his greed. He turned and looked at me. I wanted to run, run back to the camp, back to the people I knew. He was clean-shaven now but the folds of his fleshy face looked the same without his unkempt whiskers. Disgust filled my body and I was certain that he would know me as the soldier who had given her body for whisky. I thought he would tell everyone of my shame. He looked straight at me as I stood shaking.

'Can I help you?'

How could it be? How could he not know me? I felt ill.

'Yes, yes . . . I'm . . . ' I stammered. 'My name is Valentine Grey and . . . '

I had not said my name for so long that once I had spoken it all other words failed me. The sergeant frowned at me.

'Sorry, miss, you'll have to be quick. Can't stop. Got a new floor to get in here by this evening. We've had that many dances in here the wood has fair worn out. You're welcome to come along, if you fancy. I can get tickets on the cheap.'

A man appeared in the doorway. He had a long beard and was dressed in the traditional Boer style with a shabby suit and no tie.

'Oh, hello, here's another one,' sighed the sergeant. 'Yes?'

'Child,' said the man in thickly accented English.

'Pound and five shillings,' replied the fat officer.

'It is so much,' the bearded man muttered.

The sergeant blew his nose loudly on a handkerchief. 'Listen, I could be charging four quid, I reckon. I'm doing you a favour. You don't have to have it. Bury 'em in a soap box for all I care.'

The bearded man carefully counted out the money and passed it to the sergeant, who stuffed it in his pocket.

'You, kaffir, get him the wood,' he ordered and turned back to me with a wink. 'Nice little earner, this one. Floor's got to come up anyway.'

'I need to get to Cape Town. I've been . . . '

The sergeant fetched a young adjutant, fresh from home and yet to see any service. His uniform was sharp and clean and even his buckle shone. He clicked his heels at me and escorted me to the colonel, a small, rotund man, busy running his little empire. I waited outside his office.

'You should not have gone to the camps,' he said when at last we spoke. 'I'm afraid you cannot understand what is required, Miss Grey. I'm certain you meant well but now look at you. Lost your luggage, your papers and quite at sea out here.'

'But we cannot allow anyone to live as they do in the camps,' I protested.

The colonel paused and tried to be kind. 'Miss Grey, I can see that you have had a difficult experience and it has, I am sorry to say, made you slightly hysterical. What we are doing is the only humane solution to an intractable problem. There is no food for them in the fields. Surely you can understand that the women and children are safer in the camps? Apart from anything else, it is for their protection against the kaffirs.'

Here was a new excuse for this barbarism.

'Have you been in South Africa for long, Miss Grey?'

'A while.'

'Well, you'll know then that Mr Kruger has aroused the wrath and defied the might of the greatest world power that this or any other age has ever seen. But in a short time these two puny republics will cease to exist, for the old British lion is making its resonant roar heard across the veldt of the sub-continent.'

Terribly pleased with this speech, he adjusted his shoulders and slapped his silver-topped officer's stick on the palm of his hand.

'Now, you must go to that woman from the . . . committee . . . What the hell is it called? What's her name?' He rummaged through some papers on his desk. 'Ah, here we are – Lady Talbot. She can deal with you.'

Lady Talbot? Surely it could not be the same Lady Talbot?

They arranged to put me on the train to Cape Town. I was going home. I stood on the platform at Bloemfontein and as the train pulled in I caught sight of myself in the passing window. A slight, weary and sunburned woman stared back at me. I boarded the train and sat alone by a window, watching the world I had come to know slowly move away. As we departed, I saw the whole town spread out in the hollow of a rolling valley between Monument Hill in the south and the steep side of Newal Hill that guards it in the north. Peach and apricot trees were now a crowded mass of pink and white blossom and everywhere dark spires of eucalyptus and delicate green willows softened the grey galvanised roofs of the single-storey houses. It was more beautiful than it had a right to be. A two-spired Dutch church stood sentry for God and I wondered where he was.

Lady Talbot controlled her surprise at seeing me, as one might hope any well-brought up woman would do. She was wearing a complex gown that seemed to consist of many parts and a large, wide-brimmed hat that bore more flowers than Mrs Wolfaardt might ever dream of for her garden. I had forgotten about such clothes.

'Well, well,' she said as I was shown into her rooms. 'Miss Grey. What a surprise. I believe I saw your cousin—'

'Do you know about the camps?' I demanded. 'Do you know what is happening?'

Lady Talbot gave a slight smile. 'My dear, of course I know. Indeed, I am now chairwoman of the Bloemfontein League of Loyal Women and we are quite determined that every poor lost soul, whether British or Boer, shall have his grave marked.'

She examined me closely. 'We must find you something else to wear.'

She took me shopping and I did not speak. Once more I was corseted and restrained and I could not breathe.

Lady Talbot was determined to get me to tell her my story but I was afraid to reveal even the slightest detail. My thoughts were suddenly full of Reggie and what might happen to him if the truth were out. And what about Uncle Charles? I hadn't thought of him all this time. Would he even let me come home?

Cape Town's magnificent Mount Nelson Hotel, where Lady Talbot had a suite, was littered with knots of women spending hours organising a single tombola. Excitable young men fresh off the boat lined the bar, talking about the 'thick of it' and 'getting stuck in'. I dared not speak to anyone. I struggled to sound as English as I knew I ought and I was terrified that I might give too much away about where I had been and what I had done.

'Where is your cousin?' Lady Talbot kept repeating, looking at me crossly. 'I have enquired of the regiment and he seems to have disappeared. Disappeared entirely. It's most peculiar. You must be beside yourself with worry. And how did you get here?'

I answered her nothing. I was as mute as dear Umfaan, and just listened to the talk around me.

Now I heard the news from which I had so long been cut off. I learned that the Africans were being armed.

'The blacks have been told that if the Boers win, slavery will be brought back in the Cape Colony,' explained a journalist from *The Times*. 'They have been promised Boer property and farmsteads if they join the English, and the Boers will have to work for the blacks.'

'I want to find someone. Someone who helped me. A Zulu. He was taken away,' I explained.

He shook his head. 'I'm afraid that is out of the question. There are no records kept of the blacks.'

The night before my ship sailed, I sat on the wooden veranda of the hotel listening to the sounds of the African night. I now knew Umfaan had joined my list of lost men: Cooper, Ben, Jackson, Haddock and now an unnamed Zulu. There were dozens of camps where the 'black Boers' had been sent: about seventy encampments, some with British names like Balmoral, while others – Klerksdorp, Volksrust, Bronkhorstspruit – bespoke their Dutch heritage. The conditions were said to be worse, if that were possible, than at Bloemfontein.

The journalist left the next morning. As we parted he patted my hand. 'Please, Miss Grey, if you wish to do some good, go home and tell the world what you have seen.'

Lady Talbot saw me on to the boat but she did not come with me. She had more 'work' to do.

She handed me a small purse of money. Her final words of goodbye floated up from the quayside. 'Don't you worry,' she called, 'I shall find Reginald for you. I never fail to succeed once I have made up my mind.'

This time I had a cabin to myself. I slept in a bed. I lay there for almost the entire journey home. Home. Uncle and Reggie and Frank. I could not imagine what I would find and what I would do now. The ship left Table Mountain and the great bay of Cape Town; we passed the Equator, we took on coal at St Vincent and I saw nothing. The world passed me by. I was a female too feeble to go on deck. Lady Talbot had entrusted me to the captain but he did not approve of me. He did not approve of women who meddled in men's affairs. He did not care to have me at his table. And that was fine with me. I was sick and tired of men's business.

# Twenty-eight

Cooper had told me the tale of 'The Shirt of Nessus', a Greek legend about the poisoned shirt that killed Hercules. He was strong but his clothing killed him. Hercules' wife, Deianeira, gave him the fatal garment, daubed with the tainted blood of the centaur Nessus, by mistake. The poison burned Hercules, driving him so mad with pain that he threw himself on to a funeral pyre. When he tried to tear off the clothing it pulled his skin away. I was thinking of this as I stepped down from a cab outside Inkerman House.

I had taken off my fateful clothing but the Shirt of Nessus was still upon me. There had been no one to meet me at the docks. Why would there have been? I did not know where Reggie was or whether my uncle was still chasing insects on some distant island. I took a train to Waterloo Station and then gave the cab driver the address of the large, smart house where the Grey family lived. I stood in the street, uncertain what I should do next.

I did not know if I should ring the bell or seek out Maisie below in the kitchens. I stood for ages, not moving, until a young woman opened the door, her arms full of rags and a tin of brass polish.

'Oh,' she said.

I hesitated. 'I'm looking for Maisie.'

'I'm Maisie,' she replied.

'No,' I said more firmly. 'Maisie, the maid . . . the maid who works here for my aunt Ca . . . Maisie.' I tailed off.

The new Maisie let me in. I looked around the ever still and silent hall and then towards the stairs.

'Reggie? Is Reggie in?' I asked.

'Mr Reginald?'

I nodded.

'I never seen him. Don't know where he is. He ain't been here since I come. Must be weeks now.'

I could not understand. Where could Reggie possibly be?

'What about my uncle?' I persisted. 'Uncle Charles. Lord Grey?'

She stared at me. 'Are you Valentine?'

Valentine.

Yes. Yes.

I nodded.

'Heavens!' She put her hand to her mouth and stepped back as if I were possessed.

'My uncle?'

The girl could no longer speak. She nodded cautiously towards the library before running to the stairs and bolting below with a barely stifled shriek. I was left alone, drowning once more. I don't know how long I stood there trying to find the courage to knock upon my uncle's door. When I knocked, there was no answer but I was sure the girl had indicated he was inside. I tried again but still nothing, so I slowly opened the door.

My uncle sat, eyes closed, slumped in a leather armchair in the corner. The library had been turned upside down. Once organised cases lay helter-skelter, opened, tipped up on the floor. Butterflies lay everywhere, their brilliant colours a blanket of death. My uncle looked up at me as I approached. He seemed to have wasted away in the time I had been abroad. As if he too had marched many miles on an empty stomach with no hope of filling it. I knelt down beside him and placed my head on his lap.

'Uncle, I . . . I am home.'

'Oh Valentine, we have needed you.' He began to weep.

Words came from him in fits and starts as he struggled to speak.

'I thought you were away,' I said, 'searching for your butterfly.'

My uncle heaved with sobs. 'I couldn't do it. I was hopeless. I only got as far as France and then . . . I don't know what happened. I missed Caroline so much I couldn't move. When I finally got back everything was terrible. Reggie was in such a state, and that poor boy, Frank . . . I did not know what to do. The whole thing was being hawked in the street and everyone was inventing his or her own story. I wanted to help. I thought I was helping. Reggie would have been next, would have been called if they had found him. He is in a terrible state and I could not find you. I thought it was best but now . . . now I am so very uncertain.' His voice faltered and his hands shook.

'Where is he? Where is Reggie?' I asked, trying not to panic.

Uncle shook his head. 'I cannot tell you. It is awful. It is too awful but I thought it was for the best.'

Agitated, Uncle Charles stood up and then looked at his butterflies, as if surprised to find them on the floor. He sat down among them and would not address me again except to repeat, 'Too awful, too awful.'

What unspeakable thing had occurred while I had been away? I could not leave Uncle Charles like this so I went to the kitchen and got Cook to make him some broth. I would not let anyone but me take it to him. As I knelt beside him with the bowl the brilliantly coloured butterflies crackled beneath me. Uncle let me feed him small spoonfuls and then after a while he rested his head on my shoulder.

Everything seemed new. It was Harris's afternoon off and the footman who appeared was a stranger. Maisie, the new Maisie, I did not know, or the young man who helped me get Uncle Charles to his room, where I sat with him until at last he slept. The house was quiet, a quiet I was still not used to. The clock ticked in the hall. While I had been away, while people had been dying, while something terrible had happened to Reggie, while Uncle Charles had collapsed, the clock, solid and dependable, had carried on ticking. I pulled a cover over my uncle and left the room.

I slipped into the hall and climbed the stairs, finding myself marvelling at the gleaming wood beneath my feet. It all seemed so new, so impossibly clean. The door to the nursery was closed but it was not locked. I opened it and a shaft of light fell upon the old table. Ranks of soldiers stood in the gloom, their guns at the ready. I knew now what a horrible mistake they were making. That facing the enemy in great rows was almost certain death. I sat down beside them. They needed to find outcrops, rocks to hide behind, or the great pom-poms would wipe them away. I began to move them one by one to safer places, until suddenly with a sweep of my arm I threw them all to destruction on the floor below. I laid my head down upon the table and sobbed and when I finally opened my eyes a solitary toy soldier stood beside me, his gun trained upon my face. I wished he could shoot.

In the morning I could not find Uncle Charles. Harris thought he had gone out but he did not know where. The new Maisie helped me into one of my old dresses. It was black with a high collar which buttoned tightly around my neck. The skirt was full to the ground and I wore so many petticoats that I could not lace my own boots. I had forgotten how many fastenings there were and how impossible it was to manage on my own. Once I had been pulled and pinched I sat on the edge of the bed, invalided by my clothes. I wanted to take a deep breath and found it difficult even to do that. Maisie prepared me for the world, with a blue serge coat, a matching hat and black leather gloves. Once I was ready, however, I could not think where I should begin. Mrs Wolfaardt, Maria, Umfaan, Tombi, they all needed my help.

I sat uncertain and afraid. I had thought everything would be the same at Inkerman House when I returned; that I would have had an adventure and everyone else would have sat in the drawing room waiting for me; Reggie smiling at me, laughing at my stories.

I could think of no one who could help me other than Frank. Frank Rutherford. He would know where Reggie was. Perhaps I might find him at St James's Hall. Perhaps he was there singing a song in blackface and making everyone laugh. Perhaps he would take me to Rosherville Gardens and we would get lost in the maze. I left the house and stood bewildered for a moment. I could not think what omnibus I might take and could not manage to hail a cab, so I began to walk. It was so odd. My hands, accustomed to grasping the handlebars of a bicycle or at least having refuge in a pocket, seemed spare and useless. I wanted a cigarette. I had tucked some in the small bag Maisie had given me but when I stopped to remove them I saw a man staring at me. He kept on staring until I put the cigarettes away and moved on.

Silas Wilson, I remembered his name, was standing guard at the artists' entrance to St James's as usual, as if nothing had happened and no one had been anywhere.

'Miss Perreau,' he exclaimed, using my mother's name. Now I needed a mother and a father and a whole army. I was lost, more lost than I had ever thought possible. I did not bother to correct him. Names were no longer important.

'Mr Wilson, I need to find Frank, Frank Rutherford.'

Silas shook his head and scraped at an old pipe with a metal cleaner.

'Mr Rutherford ain't been here in months. Been in some trouble. Did you not see it? It was in all the papers. They say someone pulled some strings for him 'cos he didn't stay in long.'

'Stay in?' I echoed.

'Prison, miss. Fine actor like that. I should think the treadmill would have broken him. Still he only did a few weeks instead of the two years they said. Got to be someone havin' a word, wouldn't you say? Friends in high places and all that. Anyway, they won't have him back here.'

'What on earth did he do?'

'Turns out he was a fancy fella. You know, liked the boys. Still, I'm not one to judge. Been in the theatre game too long for that. Shame. Nice lad.'

'Do you know which prison?' I persisted, though what I thought to do with the information if I had it was not at all clear.

Silas shook his head. He gave me a cup of tea and found me an old address for Frank in Lambeth, saying it was the best he could do. Perhaps someone there would know how I might find him.

'You sure you're not up for the acting lark, miss?' he enquired. 'I think you'd be fine.'

It was a long walk to Lambeth but I had almost no money and the streets seemed easy after the miles I had trudged. Frank's room lay above a bedding and furnishing warehouse at 19 New Cut Street. Outside the shop, men in straw boaters discussed the war while women pushed past with their shopping baskets. Everyone was busy, too busy to notice me. Above my head men's shirts on hangers swung in the slight breeze and boots hung in racks on display. They might have fitted me but I could not even think such a thing. I needed to find Reggie, not pretend to be him.

Above the shop there seemed to be more people living than might reasonably fit into the warren of small rooms. A narrow staircase black with filth and smoke rose up from a small courtyard behind. Children were crying, women wailing, and the sound of temper hung in the air. The smell was terrible, a blend of effluence and bad food poorly cooked that cut the back of the throat. I climbed to the very top of the house, to the smallest room. There was a tiny window that had once let in light but it was so grey with grime that it might as well have been night outside. The grate was empty and cold and there was no furniture to speak of. On an old hearthrug lay a man smoking a strange glass pipe. At first I thought I had gone to the wrong room and that I had interrupted some aged gentleman about his pleasure, but as he turned to look at me I saw that it was Frank, or at least it had been Frank. I could not help but cry out.

He, who had been so beautiful, now had a rough scar which ran across his face. His eyes were strained and discoloured and his skin had become scurfy, with great patches peeling on his hands and face. A little light spilled on me from the hall and he looked up, squinting.

'Who is there?' he called and tried to get to his feet. It was clear he could not see me properly for, even dressed as I was in my women's clothes, he cried out, 'Reggie, have you come?'

He was so thin he could hardly stand and would have fallen had I not reached out to catch him. The smell was as bad as anything from the battlefield. He smelt of living death as he fell into my arms. His face was horribly pitted and scarred.

'It's me, Valentine,' I murmured. 'They said you were in prison.'

Frank's body was hunched as if in pain and he had to look up to see my face.

'Three months. I did three months,' he said. 'Lord Grey, he—'

'Did he get you out? My uncle?'

Frank put a hand out and touched my forehead.

'You have a scar too,' he muttered, before suddenly raising his voice and enquiring, 'So you think you're changed, do you?'

I was about to answer when he burbled on, '*"I'm afraid I am, sir," said Alice: "I can't remember things as I used – and I don't keep the same size for ten minutes together!" "Can't remember what things?" said the Caterpillar."*'

'Frank, sit. Let me get you some water.' I gently lowered him back to the carpet and went in search of water. In the rooms below a woman let me have a glass from her jug but she shook her head.

'No good that one up there,' she said. 'No good at all.'

To think that Frank, kind Frank, who was as beautiful as the Greek statues in the British Museum, who had taught me to ride a bicycle, led me to be kissed in a maze and to cry, 'Death to boredom!' was reduced to this.

When I returned, he was lying on his back, declaiming,

*'Weave a circle round him thrice,*
*And close your eyes with holy dread,*
*For he on honey-dew hath fed,*
*And drunk the milk of Paradise.'*

I held his head and tried to drip the water into his dry mouth.

'What are you saying, Frank?'

'Kubla Khan, Kubla Khan, a vision in a dream,' he replied.

I sat with him and cradled his head until he seemed more sensible.

'Frank, where is Reggie? Where is he?'

For a brief moment Frank roused himself and sat up. He looked at me as if he had not seen me at first. He began to shake and his lips trembled.

'Valentine,' he spoke with great effort, 'Lord Grey got me out but it was too late. Do you understand? I couldn't do anything. It was too late. They wouldn't let me help. Oh, Valentine, they have taken him. I could not stop them.'

'Taken him where?'

'Why, to the ... asylum. They have taken him. He is quite mad, they say.'

Tears ran down his dried and pitted face, a river in a desert. I could not quite follow what he had said. 'Why? What are you talking about? Who would do such a thing? Why?'

'Because he was mad. Mad to love me. Mad to let you go. Different worlds, you see, we didn't belong.'

'When did they take him? When?' I persisted.

Frank gave a great shudder. 'I don't know. I don't know anything any more.' He reached into his pocket and took out a small silver case.

'Here,' he said, thrusting it towards me, 'please take this. My mother . . . ' He stopped and stared into mid-air.

'My mother, she came to see me but I couldn't manage it. She left the case. Said she wished me well and my friend, she wished him well too, and now . . . now we are not well. We are quite mad instead.'

Suddenly he shook me off and something passed over his face, a look I did not understand. He staggered to his feet as if we had not had any conversation about Reggie. He seemed quite crazed, for next he waved his hand with the grandeur of the actor he once was and declared, 'I am late for the theatre but it is no matter for I no longer observe the motion of time.' With that he lay back down upon the floor and closed his eyes. He was making no sense and I didn't know what to do with him. I stood up to think. Above the blackened grate a small mantelpiece barely clung to the wall; on it was an empty candlestick and propped beside it a photograph. I knew the picture before I even picked it up. It was Frank and Reggie, looking so handsome and so happy together.

I turned to speak to Frank but there was a tread on the stair. A man stood in the doorway, a rough and ready fellow smelling of beer.

'Doing the girls as well now, are you, Frank?' he leered.

I put the photograph down and tried to appear calm.

'Who is this man, Frank?' Frank said nothing. 'Tell me,' I repeated.

Frank sighed and turned his head away. 'He is a man who has come for love,' he whispered. 'He'll be disappointed but I shall take his money just the same.'

I left with the name of the asylum and that was all. I returned to Inkerman House and sat smoking in the drawing room. The windows, ever shut tight, held the smoke in the room and for a brief moment I looked through it and saw Cooper running towards me. I heard the guns and smelt the acrid stench of burning flesh. I put the cigarette out and opened the window. It was autumn, a London autumn heading for winter, and the air was sharp. I breathed in deeply and it almost cut my lungs. I thought about bravery. I had not been brave but perhaps it was needed now.

The asylum lay in the town of Brookwood, south of London. At Waterloo Station I enquired about a ticket to Brookwood and the man looked at me as if he knew something about me.

'You for the asylum?'

'Me? No!' I said, embarrassed that he might have guessed my mission.

'Only you can have a discounted ticket if you get it stamped at the asylum before you return. Mind, it's third class. You all right with that, miss?'

I was all right. I who had slept standing up on a train across the veldt could manage third class. The conductor took my hand and helped me up. A man stood and tipped his hat. Here was my new role: a lady travelling to an asylum.

From the railway the hospital looked bizarrely like a picturesque Italian hilltop town. For all the world it might have been somewhere that a young man would visit on his Grand Tour. The tall chimneystacks and the secluded setting made the place seem most desirable. Avenues of tall trees led up to the main entrance, where a dairy farm, a gasworks and even its own fire brigade made the asylum more like a vast country estate than a place of incarceration.

I was shown into the office of the superintendent, a kindly man who ordered tea.

'Reginald Grey, indeed,' he intoned as a female member of staff saw to the cups. 'An honour, an honour, indeed. We tend,' he gave a slight cough, 'on the whole, to draw our patients from, shall we say, the poorer quarters. Paupers, you know, so Mr Grey ... well, a great honour.' The superintendent coughed again, as if the whole subject of why anyone might be enjoying a sojourn in his establishment was too indelicate for him to mention.

'Then why is he here?' I asked, looking at him directly.

If he was surprised at my plain speech the superintendent did not show it. I repeated the question.

'If your patients are mainly paupers, why is my cousin here?'

'Indeed, yes, ah well, uhm, discretion ... Miss ... '

'Grey.'

'Yes. Grey. We are some slight distance from the metropolis and I think your uncle felt, well, I've known him for many years. Always a great pleasure and he ... Mr Reginald's cousin, you say?' he continued. 'I must confess, if you will pardon me, that I was unaware the gentleman had a cousin.'

'I've been away,' I said evenly.

'Indeed.' There was a long pause as we sipped our drink. 'Somewhere stimulating, I trust?' he asked.

'Indeed,' I replied.

I am confident he did not wish me to see Reggie but I suspect he saw that I had no intention of departing until I had done so. My uncle did not possess anything as radical as a telephone and so, without any method of verifying what I had said, the superintendent decided, I think, to believe me.

The halls and rooms were clean, scrupulously clean, and not at all as spartan as I had imagined. There were bright colours, pictures on the walls, pot plants and crocheted tablecloths and chair covers which the superintendent assured me were the work of female patients. Male attendants in smart uniforms with peaked caps and females in starched white aprons and caps were bustling about – an army to keep those who had been incarcerated from fighting back.

'You are busy?' I asked as we walked, walked towards Reggie.

'Oh, my word, yes. We are full, as are the asylums at Caterham, Darenth and Leavesden which house almost six thousand patients.'

I felt the breath choke out of me as we approached Reggie's room, but I had been to war, I had faced the enemy and I could face this. How absurd to fear the dearest of men.

'How long do patients stay, in the main?' I asked casually.

The superintendent gave one of his slight coughs. 'We have many imbeciles and harmless lunatics who will no doubt be with us for the duration, but some recover. I am pleased to say that some recover. We do our best, Miss Grey, we do our very best.'

My steps echoed beneath me as we passed an old woman whose sole focus was on the net curtain she was making. She did not even look up as we passed.

'Do you have much trouble?' I continued, desperate to fill the silence.

The superintendent shook his head. 'No. It is my experience that the ... uhm ...' he coughed again, 'idiot is not as a rule irritable or wickedly disposed, unless under provocation. We treat them with kindness, Miss Grey, we give them work to do; something to occupy their minds. That seems to be the most effective treatment.'

Outside the tall windows, I could see men playing cricket on a lawn. Perhaps it was a good place; perhaps Reggie had just needed a break, a moment to himself. Now that I was here he could come home. I would look after him.

'What causes this malady?' I asked, determined to have the superintendent on my side. I needed him to like me. I needed him to give Reggie to me.

'In the main our population is drafted from the poorest in the land,' he explained. 'Idiocy, and idiocy combined with insanity are generally and sadly derived from want, intemperance, poverty, irregular living and, in an immense number of cases, habitual drunkenness in the parents. In fact, I think I may unhesitatingly state that the most prolific cause of idiocy among the poorer working classes is drunkenness in the parents.'

By now the superintendent was enjoying showing me his domain. We put our heads in at the door of one of the dormitories where perhaps thirty beds stood close together.

'It is warm, it is light, we give them wholesome food,' he continued, rather pleased with his tour.

'And my cousin?' I pressed. 'Which ward is he in?'

The superintendent looked down at his feet and coughed for some moments.

'Yes, Miss Grey. Your cousin, Mr Grey, is ... uhm ... in seclusion. It is most rare and most regrettable. We would prefer that he should remain in the dormitory but he is in general too ... uhm ... excitable. It was your uncle's request.'

We stopped in front of a door at the end of a corridor. An attendant seated on a chair outside stood to admit us.

'All well?' enquired the superintendent.

'Like a lamb,' replied the attendant.

The superintendent opened the door, a thick, heavy door.

The room was large and airy. It had a high ceiling and a single window allowed the sunlight to shine down in a great rectangle upon the floor. There was very little furniture – a narrow bed, a table and two chairs. At first I thought the place was empty until

I looked in one of the corners and there, curled up in a tight ball on the floor, was what was left of Reggie. My men: Uncle, Frank and now Reggie turned into rag dolls.

Gone were the brilliant colours of the dandy. Now he wore a shapeless suit of grey that appeared to have been borrowed from some other, much bigger man. His beard had been allowed to grow untrimmed and his hair was wild. His eyes stared at me as if I were part of the madness.

'Reggie!' I ran to him and fell upon his neck, hugging him to me and trying to get him to rise up off the floor. 'Reggie.' I kept repeating his name as if that might bring him to his senses. Far from being pleased to see me, Reggie stiffened and turned to hide his head entirely between his knees.

'Reggie, it's me, Valentine,' I pleaded as his hands locked tight about his legs.

'He does not speak,' explained the attendant. 'He has not spoken since he arrived.'

I looked up at the superintendent. 'I wish to speak to my cousin alone.'

He hesitated for a moment and then nodded. 'The ... uhm ... attendant will wait outside. I shall be in my office. Please ensure that I have an opportunity to bid you farewell when you depart.'

The two men closed the door behind me and I was alone with Reggie. I put my hand on his head to stroke his hair but he pulled away and began rocking back and forth. His distress was so apparent that I pulled back and moved to sit on one of the chairs. For a long while I sat in silence, not speaking at all.

'I was thinking about the bear,' I said finally, 'the one at the zoo who took Tuesdays off. Do you suppose he still does that?'

Reggie said nothing.

'I thought we might have cakes at Callard's soon.'

I carried on talking of nothing but inconsequential matters. Things that had made us smile – Rosherville, the fortune teller and the silly white girls being kissed by South African princes. The room had no clock and there was no sense of time. It was only when the attendant knocked to say it was time to leave that I realised quite how long I had been there.

The superintendent sent word to my uncle to tell him where I was and found me lodgings with a local woman. Each day I returned to Reggie. I sat and talked of life as if nothing had changed, as if we had neither of us been parted from the everyday concerns of Inkerman House. One morning he let me touch him and the next I combed his hair. The attendant helped me to get Reggie to his feet and gently placed him on one of the chairs. I pulled the other chair close to my cousin and sat down beside him. I took his hand and we sat together, allowing the sunlight from the window to warm us. We who had been through so much, who had so much to relate, sat in silence. My mind played over the past in slow motion and tears ran down my face.

I had been there a week perhaps when at last Reggie spoke.

'I thought I had killed you,' he whispered.

A great breath of relief flooded from me but I tried to stay calm. He was so easily upset and I did not want to lose him back into his silent abyss. I shook my head and tried to reply lightly.

'I would not die without telling you. Bad manners, remember?'

Reggie smiled. He recognised me.

That was all we could do that day but the next day he allowed the attendant to shave him. The man was kind and gentle. He brought hot water and towels. I watched each pass of the razor as it slowly revealed the boy I had known. When it was done, the man showed Reggie a mirror but he stared as if he did not know himself. Fresh clothes were brought and we had tea together. It was a step. I got him his favourite biscuits and persuaded him to eat. It was while I stirred sugar into his cup that Reggie began at last to speak. At first he was hesitant. His voice had become used to silence and it seemed deeper than I remembered. On that first day of speaking he said only that he didn't know his father would be at home. I couldn't make sense of it, but each day I returned and eventually, painfully slowly as Reggie came back to himself, he revealed his story.

'Father returned sooner than expected. It seemed he didn't like travelling. It didn't suit him. He'd never done it before. I don't know what he was thinking. I imagine he began to ... miss Mother ... although he wouldn't say so. There was no one home when he returned. You and I were gone. He sent for you to Aunt Jane but she wrote by return to say you had never been. That maid ...'

'Maisie?'

'Yes, Maisie. I don't think Father believed her at first. He tried to find me but then Frank got hurt and I brought him home. I would have been arrested but Father knew someone ... he always knows someone ... and it was all kept quiet. Frank was taken but I think Father was kind to him. Spoke to someone. I don't know, no one will tell me.' Suddenly Reggie brightened. 'Have you seen Frank? Is he all right?'

I lied. I looked him straight in the face and with my mother's acting running in my veins I said, 'I don't know where he is. I haven't seen him.'

Reggie held his head in his hands. 'I don't know why he doesn't come. I don't know why he doesn't come to get me.'

I reached out and stroked his head. 'Never mind that. I am here now. I have come for you and shall take you home.'

Reggie immediately stood up and began pacing. 'Oh, dear Valentine, don't you understand? They won't let you. I am to stay here. I am an imbecile, an idiot, and it's true, it's true. I cannot be cured. Father is in despair.'

'What does he tell people?'

Reggie stopped pacing and looked at me. 'Why, that I am still serving. That I am with the regiment. That I might die for the glory of the Empire.' Reggie looked out of the window. 'How fine that would be. How pleased it would make him.' For a moment he smiled at me. 'But you, my brave cousin, you did not die.'

'No.' I laughed and, thinking it might amuse him, I took from my bag the photographs Harry Hawkins had taken on the veldt when we all pretended to be dead. I had brought them to show Reggie. It was the last picture I had of Cooper and I wanted to tell him what had happened, but the first photograph that fell out on to the table was of myself lying dead.

'Look, how brave I am!' Reggie declared with glee, picking up the card and studying it closely. 'What would Colonel Talbot say to that?'

'Why Colonel Talbot?'

Reggie almost laughed. 'Why he was always proclaiming his duty to the Empire while actually spending the war here with a lieutenant from the Guards.'

'Colonel Talbot?'

'Oh yes, quite the man among mandrakes.'

Reggie looked once more at the photograph. It was well taken and although my uniformed body lay across a rocky outcrop my face was turned to the camera so that it could clearly be seen.

Reggie stared at it for a long while. 'So I am dead already,' he said at last.

I tried to laugh again. 'No, Reggie, you don't understand. It is pretend. Play-acting. It was a game for the fellow who took them. Look, here is Cooper pretending too.'

I had not looked at the pictures since my return. They were so life-like and Cooper ...

'So he is not dead either?' asked Reggie.

I did not know what to say. 'He was pretending ... ' I spoke slowly, not knowing how to tell the truth. 'He was pretending for the camera but we did ... we did lose him at Doornkop. I am so sorry.'

Reggie held the photo in his hand and then slowly put it down on the table.

'He was my friend. My friend since school. He did that for me. I should join him. Such fun to be had in heaven, I'm sure.' A look came into Reggie's eye that was almost the one he'd always had at the thought of an adventure. He picked up the picture card where I lay dead and held it up to me.

'I know!' He clapped his hands, as if it were a game. 'Show this to Father, Valentine,' he urged. 'Let him have it. Let him have it to show that I am dead.' Reggie struck a heroic pose and for a moment he was the boy of old who loved a lark. 'Reginald Grey lies buried in South Africa and can never return,' he declared, smiling.

'But, Reggie, you are not dead and neither am I.' I stood and shook the thought from my head. 'We shall make sense of this. You will come home with me. Perhaps we shall marry. The royals do it and the less well educated.'

Reggie gave a half-smile and shook his head.

'I shall speak to the superintendent and we shall have you released.' I headed for the door, utterly determined. As I reached out for the handle I distinctly heard him say, 'I love you,

Valentine.' But I don't know if he heard me when I replied, 'I love you too, Reggie.'

The next morning the superintendent was standing on the front steps when I returned from my lodgings. He looked pale and agitated.

'Miss Grey, Miss Grey,' he coughed and coughed, 'please come in, come in. A seat. Please take a seat. I have no way to dress this up. I have no way to say it except in the plainest of terms. Reginald Grey is dead.'

'Self-murder, I'm afraid,' said the attendant in dark tones as they showed me my beloved cousin laid upon his bed. He looked as though he was sleeping. He had died, as he had wished so long ago, in his bed. A butterfly who had lived a month of unbearable beauty.

Apparently he had seemed better after my visit, well enough to persuade the attendant that he might take some air in the garden. He had wandered under the trees, being so affable to everyone that he appeared quite well. He had asked to see the plants in the greenhouse and it was there that he had found a length of rope and secreted it into his coat pocket. The staff had placed a scarf around his neck to cover the mark from the noose. He looked quite theatrical. It was, I think – no, I'm certain – my fault. If I hadn't shown him the photograph, shown him a way out of the scandal and his father's grief ... I think he saw a chance for honour and he took it. Honour! What place did honour have any more? I realised a terrible thing – that if Reggie had gone to war as I had, he might not now be dead.

# Twenty-nine

I called for Harris and the rest of the staff as I came into the hall, throwing my hat and coat on to the table. I had made up my mind on the train back. I would not despair. I would not collapse. It was taking everything I had, but I knew that there was only one way to see out my glorious cousin, my Reggie. I swallowed the despair and tears and I put my thoughts to the side and marched on. I took charge like the soldier I had been trained to be, entirely certain of my battle orders. Mourning would come later.

'Harris, lights, turn on the lights. Tell Cook to make some tea, strong with sugar. Maisie, get me paper and pencil.'

I opened the library door and without asking permission moved to throw open the dark curtains that kept out the day. Sunlight streamed into the room and Uncle Charles shielded his eyes against the light.

'Valentine! What are you doing? Have you gone mad?'

Perhaps I had. Madness was in the air.

A telegram from the asylum sat on the table beside Uncle Charles; I had known it would precede me.

'No doubt, Uncle Charles, I'm quite mad. But it's all over now. We need to bury Reggie and we need to do it properly so I shall need your help. He deserves that we do it well.'

Uncle Charles began to sob quietly. His shoulders shook as waves of emotion hit a man who had spent his life avoiding them.

'What can we do, Valentine? My son, my son. What would Caroline think? I meant well. I was trying to help. The shame! The shame!'

'There will be no shame. Look at this.'

I knelt down in front of him and took the photograph of my play-acting death out of my bag. I held it for him to see and for a moment I think it didn't register.

'But, but—' he said, as his sobs slowed to a manageable pace.

'It's me, Uncle, pretending.'

'But it looks just like—'

'Just like Reggie, and so we shall tell everyone.'

And thus we set to work. The superintendent, not wishing his hospital to fall under the shadow of scandal, was more than willing to assist. I sent for a regimental uniform, knowing only too well the size of collar that would be needed. I arranged for an announcement in *The Times* about the death of Reginald Grey, only son of Lord Grey, from wounds sustained upon the battlefield at Doornkop, and with Reggie dressed in finest honours, I accompanied his body back to London. Throughout the following week I did not stop to think. I arranged to have the photograph of Reggie's glorious death published in the *Illustrated London News*. Reginald Grey had died honourably and everyone might mourn him – except me, I couldn't do that yet.

Uncle Charles spoke to someone and a service with an honour guard from the CIV was planned at St George's in Hanover Square. The funeral director remembered me from Aunt

Caroline's service and was more than helpful. He arranged for mourning cards to be printed, black and silver on white, embossed with the symbol of the City of London Volunteers, and these were sent out to all manner of society so that they might come to pay their respects.

*The Honourable Reginald Grey*
*lost in the service of his nation*
*from wounds inflicted at the*
*Battle of Doornkop, South Africa, aged twenty.*

I who had lost so many without ceremony now prepared everything possible for the celebration of death. The clocks were stopped, every mirror in the house was veiled and a laurel wreath tied with black ribbons was hung on the front door to inform passers-by that death had once more visited Inkerman House. The undertaker came with his book containing the particulars of funerals he might provide but there was no discussion. It was to be nothing but the best for Reggie: a gun carriage and four horses, many plumes of rich ostrich feathers.

'In white,' I said without hesitation.

'White?' repeated Uncle. 'Surely—'

'White,' I declared firmly. The undertaker gave a slight cough and wrote down 'white'. We had the best – a tufted mattress for him to lie on, covered in white velvet and ruffled with superfine cambric, and a linen pillow. His coffin was of lead with four pairs of best brass handles and grips, and bore an inscription plate reading *Private Reginald Grey*.

The undertaker closed his book and coughed again.

'And may I enquire,' he asked quietly, 'who will speak for the young man?'

This was something that had not occurred to me. 'Speak?' I said.

'From the regiment,' explained the funeral director. 'It is customary for someone who served alongside the deceased to speak of his heroism, battle honours, that sort of thing.'

This was impossible. There was no one except me and ... Ben White. It took me some time to find him. I made enquiries and spoke to many officers at the Honourable Artillery Company quarters. At last I heard that he was in a place of recuperation at the coast. I did not know if he was still blinded but I felt confident that even if his sight were returned he would not know me. Dressed as I now was, in my female clothes, I hardly recognised myself. I sought him out and one bright morning I found him on a terrace overlooking the sea. He sat quite still on a cast-iron bench and I thought he could not have noticed my arrival.

'Mr White?' I said quietly.

He smiled. 'Mr White, is it? What happened to just Ben?'

He reached up and put his hand gently on my face, feeling it with the lightest of touches.

'Ben,' I began. He smiled again and dropped his hands to mine.

'So you wear a skirt at last,' he said.

'What do you mean?' I replied, amazed.

'I can hear it. It rustles. But the hands are yours. I would know them anywhere. I remember a day on the boat when I took your hand in mine and—'

'And what? Only Cooper knew I was a woman,' I protested.

Ben shook his head. 'You could not have been anything but ... Your face, your hands, your eyes ... it was plain to me.'

I laughed at myself. 'And I thought I played my part so well.'

Ben smiled. 'You did, but the body does not lie. Even now I can see the line of your throat where no apple of Adam's will ever protrude.'

'Why did you not say anything?'

He shook his head. 'Which one of us knew the right thing to do about anything? What do they call you now? Not Reggie surely?'

I shook my head. 'No. My name is Valentine. Valentine Grey.'

'Valentine,' he repeated. 'Valentine.'

Ben's sight was slowly improving although the world still appeared in a haze. Perhaps not surprisingly, his wife had come to see him, but only to make him sign divorce papers and to tell him he couldn't see his son.

The doctors thought him well enough to attend Reggie's funeral and thus he arrived in full dress uniform at Inkerman House on the day of the service. He was still weak and the journey had tired him so he went to sit in Uncle's library. Guests were arriving and being shown into the drawing room, in which stood a large round table covered with refreshments. Above the mantelpiece hung a hastily completed portrait of Reggie in uniform. Eight members of the CIV – none of whom knew me and certainly not the real Reggie – stood toasting him with wine as they waited to act as pallbearers for his final journey. I was glad I would not have to dissemble with them.

Everything was in place. Uncle Charles stood holding his hat, ready to begin. He had lost weight and seemed half the man he once was. He reached for me.

'Valentine, I . . . I know that Caroline, Lady Grey—'

Maisie interrupted. 'A visitor, Miss Grey.'

I could not understand why she felt the need to inform me of another arrival. 'Show them into the drawing room,' I said.

'But they're not expected,' she insisted. 'I've got the list and they're not expected.'

'Well, who is it?' enquired Uncle.

'It's Lady Talbot, sir.'

Uncle mouthed to me, 'Trouble,' before turning to meet her. 'Good afternoon, Lady Talbot, what a pleasant surprise,' and giving a slight bow.

Ben entered the hall from the library. I noticed how handsome he looked, pale and thin, yet stronger than I remembered. He stood beside me.

Lady Talbot, oblivious of everything but her own urgency, pressed forward and looked at Uncle.

'Lord Grey, I hope you don't think me impertinent, but something odd has been going on here. No one can find any record of your son returning home.'

Uncle's face fell and for a moment I thought the game was up, that he wouldn't be able to go through with it. Before he could speak, I stepped between him and his adversary. I knew that Reggie wasn't the only one who hadn't gone to war.

'Lovely to see you, Lady Talbot,' I said, appearing to look behind her for someone. 'I see you've come alone. How is the colonel? Is he well? Is he in South Africa?'

I paused, waiting for her to register my words, before continuing with a smile. 'Oh no, he never did quite make it, did he? Too much – what shall we call it? – *charm* to be had at the bar of the Criterion, I believe.'

Lady Talbot paused. 'I don't know what you are talking about.'

But there was no doubt that Lady Talbot knew enough about her husband to grasp my meaning. I stood my ground and said no more.

'You wouldn't dare,' she blustered in a low hiss.

Ben moved towards Lady Talbot and took her arm.

'Is the front door this way?' he asked, indicating with a nod.

'Yes but—'

Despite his troubled vision Ben began to move Lady Talbot firmly towards the door.

'How very kind of you to come and see Reggie off in this way,' called Uncle as she departed.

He looked at me. 'How on earth did you know that, Valentine? About the colonel?'

'Reggie told me.'

Uncle nodded. 'How splendid! Reggie saved the day.'

And so it was to the sound of laughter that we headed to the funeral. Reggie would have loved it.

The hearse arrived as the first coach in the procession. It was black, with glass sides, but a huge canopy of white ostrich feathers covered the outside, making it look swanlike and almost cheerful. Inside lay the coffin covered with a white cloth and a blanket of white flowers. Six black horses pulled the hearse and they too had white ostrich-feather plumes on their heads. It was gloriously theatrical and I thought too how Frank would have loved it.

Men in mourning suits with crape bands around their top hats and women in black gowns with black veils and gloves filled the carriages that came behind. At walking pace we set off from Inkerman House to St George's. In smart unison, the men from the CIV carried the coffin in and laid it on a bier while all manner of men with silk hat-bands saw to the seating of the guests.

The mayor attended in all his City finery. I sat in the front pew, where one day a suffragette would leave her bomb in protest against women's silence. Now, I was a silent woman hidden by a veil. Ben, beloved Ben, rose to his feet and spoke about his comrade, Reginald Grey.

He spoke of our time together, of our fallen comrades, and I found myself crying at last for Reggie beneath my veil. When the bishop spoke of bravery and Empire as he committed Reggie's eternal soul to the soil I did not listen. Any belief I might have had in a God who watched over us had long ago blown away across the South African veldt.

A posthumous medal was granted. Lady Talbot kept her views to herself.

I had looked for Frank before the funeral but he was gone. His shabby room was now filled with other men going about business I did not understand. I never knew what happened to that glorious handsome man. Perhaps he sailed away in a marvellous double gondola, two canvas baskets one inside the other, suspended from a balloon flying high above us all. Perhaps he died a dramatic death with a hint of amusement for everyone left behind.

Reggie had gone in an interesting manner. There was plenty for his friends to discuss and, most pleasing of all, not long after his funeral Queen Victoria passed away and she too had white. Death to black.

# Thirty

Quietly, slowly, I began to run the house. I wore the clothes that had once confined me and for a while found comfort in the stays and laces which held me together. Perhaps I needed their strength, for alone in my room at night I would dread the dark hours when the horror still returned. Sleep frightened me and so I tried to stay awake. I did not lie in a bed but in a field hearing the thud of the pom-poms, the whine of the guns, the cries of someone felled by shrapnel. Was it Umfaan? A friend or someone I had never met? It didn't matter. Sharp flares of light filled my eyes and my ears hurt from the onslaught as I crawled through long grass, endlessly hearing the echo of a small duck quacking in the distance. Now I was in a maze and Reggie, who was supposed to watch me from a stepladder, was dead. If I slept at all I would awake sweating and calling out for Cooper. Exhausted by my nightly climbs up through scrubland towards the enemy, I was often tired out. There was not a single hour of the day when I felt at rest.

Ben had nowhere to go once his recuperation by the sea was

concluded, so it seemed natural that he should come to stay with us. Uncle liked him, though he was as far from the son he'd had in Reggie as I was from a soldier, but they were similar, contemplative souls and they began doing small things together – a walk in the park or a game of chess whose pieces Ben would touch before moving them.

We spent our days visiting doctors of every kind in search of sight for Ben. Slowly his eyes gained some little discernment of shade and light but never again would colour flood his mind. Uncle read to him and we each in our own way began to heal. I made small alterations to the house. We kept Reggie's bedroom as he'd left it – we weren't ready to make that change – but the curtains were always open in Uncle's study and the windows in the drawing room were opened each morning to let in the air. We discovered Maisie's true name was Ruth and so we called her that instead. I let her wear bloomers when she cleaned the stairs and sometimes she whistled as she worked. It was with such domestic matters that 1901 was upon us.

Ben and I did not talk about what we had gone through. I did not tell him about the camps, about Mrs Wolfaardt. I did nothing. I had closed that chapter of my life and could not bear to revisit it. I spent many hours focused on such trivial domestic matters as ensuring that the stairs were waxed, the silver polished and the food stores kept replete. I was the perfect woman and might have stayed that way had it not been for a small red tin and a visit from the Primrose League. I sometimes wonder if the dead can speak to us from beyond the grave.

I was tidying a drawer in my room when I came across the red tin entrusted to me by a dying boy in a field hospital. I sat on the bed and opened it. Inside the small container lay this boy's life – a photograph of a woman I took to be his mother, a letter from someone called Henry and a medal of St Christopher to keep him safe. On a scrap of paper a simple instruction was scribbled: 'If Found' the box should be returned to Seamus Duffy of Bethnal Green.

I was brought up short. I had made a promise to him and I had failed to keep it. I didn't do anything about it immediately but the tin preyed on my mind and I couldn't leave it alone. I was sitting in the drawing room once more going through its contents when I looked up and caught sight of myself in one of the mirrors positioned to reflect greenery into the room. Dressed in a gown that Aunt Caroline would have approved of, I was now able to draw back my hair into a bun. Even the scar across my forehead made me look like the sort of woman whose reputation needed protecting. Just the sort of woman who could not protect herself. I, who was free to do as she pleased, had begun to confine myself to the very room that had once held me captive.

I could not stay in the house a moment longer and, not stopping to get my hat or my coat, I almost ran out into the street. What was I doing? For a moment I stood stock-still upon the pavement, panicking, not knowing where to turn. How wonderful it had been that day when I had walked out for the first time without my hat. How splendid I had thought it to be free. Now I would have accepted any restrictions if only I could remain inside, to be safe in the drawing room with a rule for everything and the world at bay outside my window.

'You don't have your hat,' called Ruth from the front door. She came down the steps, bearing my bonnet.

'It's cold,' she said. 'You'll need your hat.' She was small and young. She reached up and fastened the hat to my head. I looked at her red hair and freckles and smiled.

I took the bus to Bethnal Green. Despite the reason for my journey it gave me great pleasure, until I found Seamus Duffy's home and it sobered my mood. It was down a narrow lane where two-storey houses stood back to back and side by side like exhausted soldiers on parade. The place was filthy and noise emanated from every property, each of which seemed full to overflowing. I had no house number and there were no names so I had to ask for Mrs Duffy the length of the row until at last I found her. She was doing her laundry and hanging it out in the street on a line. Inside the one room she possessed, an old woman lay asleep on the only bed. Children ran in and out as she went next door to fetch some tea to give me.

We sat and drank tea from mugs as I spoke of her boy.

'Was he brave?' she asked.

I had no idea. I did not know what that meant.

'Yes, of course,' I replied.

She took the tin and with great reverence placed it on a shelf beside a photograph of her boy in his uniform. As I was leaving she took my hand and held it for a moment.

'The thing I don't understand, miss, is what was he fighting for?'

A question to which I had no answer.

The next morning, Ruth appeared in the drawing room with word that a group of ladies had called and wished to see me. I had been sitting staring out of the window, wearing a dress that buttoned at the neck. It had been choking me, so in the quiet of the house I had undone the top buttons. Now I struggled to put them back in place as Ruth showed the women in. I recognised them from the Primrose League meetings. Most of them were on the committee and as I looked up at their familiar faces I continued to struggle with the buttons on my dress. The final fastening was obstinate and strained against the opening. I was aware of it as we sat and exchanged pleasantries. They were in the main of Aunt Caroline's age and each was schooled in the correct form of condolences, upon which we spent some time.

Once grief had been accorded proper respect, the chairwoman of our local group, a Lady Neild, moved on to other business.

'We were hoping, Miss Grey, that you might soon feel ready to return to the work of the league. We were always grateful for your aunt's energetic contributions.'

There was much murmuring about the league's invaluable work to society before Lady Neild dared to move towards the true reason for their visit. She cleared her throat before taking my hand and quietly beginning, 'The committee has been most concerned ...' Lady Neild's eyebrows rose ... 'You have been through a most trying time, Miss Grey. You are still so young and without the support of a husband, a man to guide you and ...'

'Well,' I innocently replied, 'I have my uncle and Mr White, who served with my cousin, Reginald.'

Lady Neild's lips tightened into a thin line. 'Indeed, there is Mr White, which brings us to a delicate matter. There has been some talk. Mr White is, I believe, a single gentleman. There is no other female of consequence in the house?'

I brightened. 'There is Ruth.'

'Ruth?'

'The maid.'

Lady Neild left a long silence before replying. 'Yes. We, the committee, have discussed this at much length, and, Miss Grey, we feel duty bound out of respect for your aunt ...'

'Such a tragedy,' murmured someone.

'... to point out to you that, truly, you cannot continue to live under the same roof as Mr White without a chaperone.'

I laughed so loud and with such force that the top button of my dress gave way and fell to the floor, bouncing towards Lady Neild. I watched it go and thought of another button, in a tent, which had fallen away from me. I thought of the woman I had been then and how faint I could make the entire committee if I told them some small truth of where I had been. The very idea made me smile again, and the ridiculous women watched as I began first to giggle and then to laugh. Soon I was laughing so much that tears streamed down my face and I was clutching my side, for once I had started I found it difficult to stop.

Ruth saw the ladies out and I stood to look out of the window and to watch them depart. Deliberately, I reached for a cigarette, put it in my mouth and lit it in full view of the street. It was with great satisfaction that I saw Lady Neild turn and see me.

As I stood there drawing the smoke into my lungs, I heard the door open behind me and half expected another deputation, but it was Ben.

'Valentine?'

'Yes, I'm here.'

'What did they want?'

'Nothing.'

Ben moved slowly towards me. The house had become familiar to him but he was still cautious. As he reached my side he touched my arm. 'My dear Valentine,' he said, 'it was not nothing.'

I pulled away and continued to smoke.

'What?' he asked again.

I gave a small laugh. 'They were concerned about my reputation.'

'Because of me?' he asked.

'Yes, because of you.'

Ben nodded and paused. 'So they should be,' he replied at last. Ben moved towards me and put his hand out to touch my cheek. Then he kissed me. Kissed me, just as the ladies had warned me that he might.

I pushed him away. 'Don't,' I cried.

Ben held my arms and would not let me go. 'I can't see you, Valentine, but I know what you feel.'

'You know nothing, Ben. You have no idea who I am.'

A week later a letter for Reginald Grey from South Africa dropped through the letterbox. I opened it with dread. It was Mrs van der Poel from the camp, writing to tell me of Mrs Wolfaardt's passing. I began to shake and then to cry and Ben tried to get me to sit but I could not, I was inconsolable. Why had I just been sitting at home since my return? I could hold nothing back any longer. With rage and pity for myself I blurted out everything. Through tears of anger and self-loathing I stood in front of Ben and I told him about the sergeant and the whisky, about Umfaan and Mrs Wolfaardt. I told him the truth. That I was ruined and could never be repaired and I had even broken my promise to a woman now dead.

When I was finally done he tried to reach for me.

'It was a war,' he said quietly.

I pushed him from me. I did not want excuses. I was ashamed of myself, of everything I had done and, more importantly, what I had not done since my return. I ran from him, from the house, and headed to the park. Not sure where I was going, nevertheless, I half ran as if I could not wait to get there. As I did so, I saw London anew. I felt shocked by the buses and the hansom cabs bustling about. It was impossible to imagine that everyone might simply go about their business while thousands of miles away war raged in their name.

That evening I stopped worrying about the servants and the meal and began concentrating on what Ben and Uncle Charles were saying to each other.

Ben had left me alone when I returned, windblown and exhausted. Now he sat at the table, earnest in his entreaties to my uncle about Kitchener's latest plans.

'I should do something,' I interrupted. 'What can I do? What can a woman do?'

Ben put down his knife and fork. I was startled to see how angry he was. 'Valentine – you saw what men did. They were ignorant and muddling, helpless and blundering. For God's sake, just get out there and make the world see that.'

I began to attend meetings at which speakers dared to condemn the war. I helped to organise them. Soon I was at Speakers' Corner handing out leaflets and before long I amazed myself by standing on a box speaking out against the violence.

'In your name,' I cried, 'Lord Kitchener has begun to carry out a policy in the Boer republics of unbelievable barbarism and gruesomeness which violates the most elementary principles of the international rules of war. Our men, our brave men, now move from valley to valley, lifting cattle and sheep, burning and looting, and turning out women and children to weep in despair beside the ruin of their once beautiful homesteads. This is not war against men, but against defenceless women and children.'

A few men in the crowd began to shout me down.

'Traitor! Traitor! Bloody traitor!'

'Pro-Boer! Kill 'er! Kill the bloody traitor!'

I carried on but the agitation was increasing.

'We must halt the pursuit of this disgraceful policy, this war against women and children. What would have been said by civilised mankind if Germany on her march on Paris had turned the whole country into a howling wilderness and concentrated the French women and children into camps where they died in the thousands? All civilised Europe would have rushed to their rescue. We cannot stand by and—'

Some men in the gathered throng decided that they could indeed not stand by. They surged forward to knock me from my box and within a moment a full-scale fight was under way. My hat was knocked from my head and when a fellow tapped me on the shoulder I turned and with every piece of instruction from George Sheridan echoing in my head I landed a punch square on his jaw. I looked down to see that the man I had just knocked flat was Ben White.

I don't know why but I seemed always destined to have the men in my life try to protect me. Perhaps they knew that I needed protecting from myself. Ben it seemed, half-blind Ben, and my dear uncle had been 'keeping an eye' on me. They had not stopped me from doing as I wished but they had been concerned.

Uncle Charles brought us home in his carriage and Ben's rather brilliantly coloured eye was soothed with a packet of ice. That night I found my uncle sitting on our stairs and I sat down beside him, taking his hand in mine.

'I have to do something, Uncle,' I said. 'I need to help my friends, my Boer friends who helped me, but I have no money.'

Uncle Charles sighed.

'What is it?' I asked, for I could see something else was troubling him.

'It must have been nice to be someone else for a while,' he said. 'To change your name and your clothes and to stride out into the world with no one knowing you.'

I nodded.

'When I left here to find my butterfly, my New Guinea butterfly, I thought I might do the same. I wanted an adventure, I wanted not to be Lord Grey, someone's husband, a dutiful son, but I was hopeless. I had been with your aunt so long I did not know how to manage things. I was confused and perhaps a little frightened, so I returned. Everything was in uproar when I got back. I should not have sent my boy to that … place but you have to understand, Valentine,' he turned to me with pleading in his eyes, 'he could have gone to prison. I could not have sent him to prison.'

'No,' I replied, 'not for love.'

'Love,' repeated my uncle as if the word were new to him. 'I did not understand. I'm afraid, my dear Valentine, that I have not been entirely honest with you. Your father's estate was settled some time ago. I had word and said nothing.'

I was bewildered. 'Why?'

Uncle smiled and stroked my hand. 'Because I did not want to lose you. I could not bear it but … ' He stood and I followed him into his study where he removed some papers from his desk. 'You are a wealthy woman, my dear. You may do as you please. You are so like your father,' he said. 'You have not just his smile but his soul. I see you must do this, that you have a mission and I will not persuade you otherwise but I will tell you this – you are not alone.'

We went back out into the hall and found Ben now sitting upon the stairs. We sat down and stayed for some time in silence. We knew there was work to do.

# Thirty-one

If I had thought the bicycle was an instrument of liberation for any woman, that was nothing compared to the freedom of an income. Having sat for so long, I now found myself full of almost unbearable energy.

Gone was the silent woman who had returned to England. Now I was bold. I did not hide away. I began to understand how the trail of a financial serpent snaked over the war from beginning to end. That all people like Cecil Rhodes wanted was to keep the gold mines in the hands of the owners. I found I had opinions on all manner of things about this imperial adventure paid for by the British taxpayer, fought for by British soldiers but benefiting only the millionaire elite who masqueraded as patriots. I quickly became just the sort of woman that my aunt Caroline had feared I might become.

We fought. We fought together, Uncle Charles, Ben and I. We marched, we spoke at meetings, shouting to the world about this 'gigantic and grievous blunder caused by crass male ignorance, helplessness and muddling'. Uncle spoke in the Lords and was called a liar, an enemy of the nation and worse, but nothing shook us from our purpose. News began to filter back that gave credence to our story. Women and children were dying in droves. A fourth of the entire Boer population was now held in camps. At one outside Bethulie, a place whose name one could scarcely credit meant 'Chosen by God', reports reached us of twelve hundred souls dying in one six-month period from pneumonia and measles and, of course, from hunger. The soil of South Africa was stained with the blood of children slain by England.

'What have we done?' sighed Uncle Charles.

'I have travelled to this land of sorrow,' I declared, standing on any stage that would have me. 'I have met officers whose success is defined in a weekly "bag" of killed, captured and wounded and now they are clearing the civilians, uprooting a whole nation. And those who survive are transported to empty tents where they will grope about in the dark, looking for their little bundles. Then they will sleep without any provision having been made for them and without anything to eat or to drink.'

One night at dinner, I asked my uncle, 'How do you think it will end?'

'End?' he repeated. 'I suspect history will tell of British victory but it will be victory without glory. Makes you ashamed of your own country.'

Ashamed to be British? What a thing to say yet my uncle, my patriotic uncle, said it. Both Ben and I, who had been prepared to die for our country, now sat silent. Ashamed to be British.

Later, I sat alone in the drawing room. I had been out speaking all day and was exhausted. There was a light knock on the door and Ben appeared. He smiled at me. We had not mentioned our kiss again but he sat down with an ease that would have horrified the Primrose ladies.

'I had news today,' he said quietly. 'Will you read it?'

I thought of Cooper reading Haddock's letter from home. I looked at the missive and smiled. 'It's from George. He's in Bloemfontein.'

'George? George Sheridan? How marvellous. Is he well?'

'He is fine. He and Jackson—'

'Jackson is alive?'

I grinned. 'Alive and kicking and teaching the Boer a thing or two about business.'

I paused.

'What?' asked Ben.

'He wants you to know about Pattenden,' I said at last. The very name sent a chill through me.

'Why?'

'He is unwell. Sheridan asks if you can help.'

'Unwell how?'

I read aloud. '*He is quite mad. No one knows what happened but they say he lost his mind at Dewetsdorp. That he began babbling and never again knew sense. He knows no one. Not even himself.*'

I put the letter down and added bitterly, 'I hope his mind survived long enough for him to have endured one moment at least when he knew what he had done.'

'We should help him,' said Ben quietly. When I did not reply, he waited and then went on. 'We came to fight, not behave like savages.'

I rubbed my eyes.

'You look tired,' said Ben.

'I thought you couldn't see properly.'

'I see you.'

Ben spoke with Uncle Charles and they arranged for Pattenden's transfer to an asylum in Surrey.

'I know a friendly superintendent,' said Uncle.

John Jackson made me smile. Ben contacted him about soap for the camp at Bloemfontein. He responded with his usual enthusiasm and arrived in the camp with boxes of the stuff. He and George Sheridan went into business together and ended their days men of great fortune, the soap kings bringing cleanliness and godliness to South Africa.

As for the war, a treaty was signed, people stopped fighting. In my lifetime South Africa had the independence they had sought all along but the blacks never got what they were promised and the whites lived to regret it. Now the history of the people once herded into places of misery has been blown away by the wind across the veldt. I wonder who climbs up the kopjes and looks out, imagining what it might have been like to fight for such a hill. To march up it, believing you carried with you the honour of Queen and country.

And the future? It was Ben who suggested the battle ahead. The night that the streets cheered for the end of the war we walked home together. I think perhaps I felt a little bereft without my cause to champion.

'What next, Ben? What shall I do?' I asked.

He took my arm and said, 'You are brave and you have proved yourself to be a gifted speaker. I do believe, Miss Grey, that you should run for Parliament.'

I laughed. 'Don't be silly. Women aren't even allowed to vote.'

'I'm pretty sure they weren't meant to serve in the war either.'

That evening as we sat at the dining table I looked at Uncle

Charles and noticed how much he had changed. He was no longer a pale, distant man. Instead he had the healthy look of a man who never sat indoors with the curtains closed against the light.

'Uncle,' I began hesitantly.

'Yes?'

'I've decided I want to stand for Parliament.'

'Indeed,' he replied.

'So I'm going to begin campaigning with the Suffrage Society.'

Uncle sipped at his soup. 'Anything else?'

Ben raised a quizzical eyebrow as he waited for my reply.

'Yes,' I said. 'I should like to learn to drive a motor car.'

Uncle nodded. 'Right,' he said, smiling slightly as he looked at me. 'That's quite a lot. Will it wait till after supper?'

# Acknowledgements

I have never been to war and can only imagine its horror. It would be impossible for me to write battle scenes without the assistance of contemporary writings and I am utterly indebted to the diaries and journals of men who served at the time, some of which are available online and some of which I sought out in the British Library. They included writings by:

Private John Jackson, 1st Battalion The Yorkshire Regiment: *An Experience of Twelve Months Active Service on the Veldt* (1899–1900), www.greenhowards.org.uk/dox/John%20Jackson.pdf

Cecil Thomas Wrigley Grimshaw, DSO, 2nd Battalion Dublin Fusiliers: *My Experiences of the Boer War (1899–1900)*, www.grimshaworigin.org/Webpages2/CecilGrimshaw.htm

Cyclist Fred James Percival Pickman, 13th Middlesex Rifle Volunteer Corps: Geoffrey Moore (ed.), *Pickman's Progress in the City Imperial Volunteers in South Africa, 1900: Based on the Diary of Cyclist Fred James Pickman (13th Middlesex Rifle Volunteer Corps)* (Huntingdon: G. Moore, n.d.)

Private J. W. Milne, 1st Service Company Volunteers, Gordon Highlanders: *Diary of No. 8080 Private J. W. Milne*, www.jwmilne.freeservers.com

Erskine Childers, *In the Ranks of the C. I. V.: A Narrative and Diary of Personal Experiences with the C. I. V. Battery (Honourable Battery Company) in South Africa* (London: Smith, Elder, 1900)

John Barclay Lloyd, *One Thousand Miles with the C. I. V.* (London: Methuen, 1901)

Guy H. Guillum Scott of the Inner Temple, Barrister-at-Law and Farrier Sergeant, CIV, and Geoffrey L. MacDonnell, *The Record of the Mounted Infantry of the City Imperial Volunteers* (London: E. & F. Spon, 1902)

William George Robert Mumford, *William Mumford's Diary* (1st January to 21st October 1900, including his period of service with the City Imperial Volunteers in South Africa during the Boer War), www.britishmedals.us/kevin/other/mumford.html

Major John Edward Pine-Coffin, DSO (ed. Susan Pine-Coffin), *One Man's Boer War 1900: The Diary of John Edward Pine-Coffin* (Bideford: Edward Gaskell, 1999)

Private William Fessey, DCM (ed. Heather Wilson), *Blue Bonnets, Boers and Biscuits: The Diary of Private William Fessey, DCM Serving in the King's Own Scottish Borderers during the Boer War* (London: H. Wilson, 1998)

Captain Frederick Sadleir Brereton, *With Rifle and Bayonet: A Story of the Boer War 1900*, www.gutenberg.org/ebooks/32918

And, most particularly, the contemporary war correspondent for the *Daily Mail*, George Warrington Steevens, who died of enteric fever on 15 January 1900. I have tried to blend the descriptions of their experience with my story and hope that I have not done them a disservice.

I am also grateful to Thomas Pakenham for his definitive book on the conflict, *The Boer War*; to Emily Hobhouse for her bravery and for writing about the concentration camps in *The Brunt of War*; *Cassell's Household Guide* for helping me run a Victorian house; and contemporary *Baedeker* guides for details about life in London at the time.

Apart from the voices from the past urging me to remind the world about this dreadful piece of history I have also had much contemporary help. There would be no book if it were not for my partner, Debbie, who travelled to South Africa with me in search of this neglected war and who inspires me to write at all; my friend Pip Broughton, always by my creative side; my truly splendid agent Gill Coleridge; the ever wonderful Vivien Redman with her eagle eye and kind words; and the astonishing Lennie Goodings, editor extraordinaire, who gently persuades me that there is always a little more to do. Without her neither Valentine nor Reggie would have found their voices.

# Additional Bibliography

## The War

Bennett, Will, *Absent-Minded Beggars: Yeomanry and Volunteers in the Boer War* (Barnsley: Leo Cooper, 1999)

Greenwall, Ryno, *Artists & Illustrators of the Anglo-Boer War* (Simon's Town: Fernwood Press, 1992)

Jackson, Tabitha, *The Boer War* (London: Channel 4, 1999)

Knight, Ian, *Boer Wars (2): 1898–1902* (Oxford: Osprey, 1997)

Lee, Emanoel, *To the Bitter End: A Photographic History of the Boer War 1899–1902* (Harmondsworth: Viking, 1985)

MacKenzie, John M. (ed.), *Imperialism and Popular Culture* (Manchester: Manchester University Press, 1986)

MacKenzie, John M., *Propaganda and Empire: The Manipulation of Public Opinion, 1880–1960* (Manchester: Manchester University Press, 1984)

McDonald, Ian, *The Boer War in Postcards* (Stroud: Alan Sutton, 1990)

Porter, Bernard, *The Absent-Minded Imperialists: Empire, Society and Culture in Britain* (Oxford: Oxford University Press, 2004)

Pretorius, Fransjohan, *Historical Dictionary of the Anglo-Boer War* (Lanham, MD: Scarecrow Press, 2009)

Reitz, Deneys, *Commando: A Boer Journal of the Boer War* (London: Faber & Faber, 1929)
Roberts, Brian, *Those Bloody Women: Three Heroines of the Boer War* (London: John Murray, 1991)
Wilson, Herbert Wrigley, *With the Flag to Pretoria: A History of the Boer War of 1899–1900*, 2 vols (London: Harmsworth Brothers, 1900–1)

## Victorian Life

*Baedeker's Guide: London and its Environs 1900* (Leipzig: Karl Baedeker, 1900)
Brandon, David, *London and the Victorian Railway* (Stroud: Amberley, 2010)
Chesney, Kellow, *The Victorian Underworld* (London: Maurice Temple Smith, 1970)
Cook, Matt, *London and the Culture of Homosexuality, 1885–1914* (Cambridge: Cambridge University Press, 2003)
Cox, Jane, *London's East End: Life and Traditions* (London: Weidenfeld & Nicolson, 1994)
Dowling, Linda C., *Hellenism and Homosexuality in Victorian Oxford* (Ithaca: Cornell University Press, 1994)
Georgano, Nick, *The London Taxi* (Princes Risborough: Shire, 1985)
Hill, Thomas E., *The Essential Handbook of Victorian Etiquette* (San Mateo: Bluewood, 1994)
Kift, Dagmar (trans. Roy Kift), *The Victorian Music Hall: Culture, Class and Conflict* (Cambridge: Cambridge University Press, 1996)
Kilgarriff, Michael, *Grace, Beauty and Banjos: Peculiar Lives and Strange Times of Music Hall and Variety Artistes* (London: Oberon, 1999)
Mitton, Lavinia, *The Victorian Hospital* (Princes Risborough: Shire, 2001)
Ramamurthy, Anandi, *Imperial Persuaders: Images of Africa and Asia in British Advertising* (Manchester: Manchester University Press, 2003)

Roberts, Robert, *Roberts' Guide for Butlers & Other Household Staff* (1827; Bedford, MA: Applewood, 1988)
Rutherford, Sarah, *The Victorian Asylum* (Oxford: Shire, 2008)
Thomson, John, *Victorian London Street Life in Historic Photographs* (New York: Dover, 1994)
Vicinus, Martha (ed.), *Suffer and Be Still: Women in the Victorian Age* (Bloomington: Indiana University Press, 1973)
Yorke, Trevor, *The Victorian House Explained* (Newbury: Countryside, 2005)

After graduating from Cambridge, Sandi Toksvig went into theatre as a writer and performer. Well known for her television and radio work as a presenter, writer and actor, she has written more than twenty books for children and adults. She also writes for theatre and television: her film *The Man*, starring Stephen Fry and Zoë Wanamaker, was broadcast on Sky Arts in May 2012, and her play *Bully Boy*, starring Anthony Andrews, opened the St James Theatre, London, autumn 2012. She is the new Chancellor of Portsmouth University. Sandi Toksvig lives in London and Kent.